Paris and the Parisians in 1835 by Frances Milton Trollope

Volume II of II

Frances Milton Trollope was born on March 10th, 1779 at Stapleton in Bristol.

The mother of the world famed Anthony Trollope, and his brother Thomas Adolphus Trollope, she was a late entrant to the ranks of authors being fifty when she embarked upon this new career, and even then more by necessity for income than by design.

Her first book, in 1832, Domestic Manners of the Americans, gained her immediate notice. Although it was a one sided view of the failings of Americans, it was also witty and acerbic.

But much of the attention she received was for her strong novels of social protest. Jonathan Jefferson Whitlaw, published in 1836, was the first anti-slavery novel, and was a great influence on the American writer Harriet Beecher Stowe and her more famous Uncle Tom's Cabin in 1852. Michael Armstrong: Factory Boy began publication in 1840 and was the first industrial novel to be published in Britain.

These were followed by three volumes of The Vicar of Wrexhill, which examined the corruption in the Church of England and evangelical circles.

However her greatest work is more often considered to be the Widow Barnaby trilogy (published between 1839–1843).

In later years Frances Milton Trollope continued to write novels and books on wide, varied and miscellaneous subjects, writing in all in excess of a quite incredible 100 volumes.

Frances Milton Trollope died on October 6th, 1863.

Index of Contents

LETTER XLIII.
Peculiar Air of Frenchwomen—Impossibility that an Englishwoman Should Not be Known for Such in Paris—Small Shops—Beautiful Flowers, and pretty arrangement of them—Native Grace—Disappearance of Rouge—Grey Hair—Every Article Dearer than in London—All Temptations to Smuggling Removed.
LETTER XLIV.
Exclusive Soirées—Soirée Doctrinaire—Duc de Broglie—Soirée Républicaine—Soirée Royaliste—PartieImpériale—Military Greatness—Dame de l'Empire.
LETTER XLV.
L'Abbé Lacordaire—Various Statements Respecting Him—Poetical Description of Notre Dame—The Prophecy of a Roman Catholic—Les Jeunes Gens de Paris—Their Omnipotence.
LETTER XLVI.
La Tour de Nesle.
LETTER XLVII.
Palais Royal—Variety of Characters—Party of English—Restaurant—Galerie d'Orléans—Number of Loungers—Convenient Abundance of Idle Men—Théâtre du Vaudeville.
LETTER XLVIII.

Literary Conversation—Modern Novelists—Vicomte d'Arlincourt—His Portrait—Châteaubriand—Bernardin de Saint Pierre—Shakspeare—Sir Walter Scott—French Familiarity with English Authors—Miss Mitford—Miss Landon—Parisian Passion for Novelty—Extent of General Information.
LETTER XLIX.

Trial by Jury—Power of the Jury in France—Comparative Insignificance of that Vested in the Judge—Virtual Abolition of Capital Punishments—Flemish Anecdote.
LETTER L.

English Pastry Cooks—French Horror of English Pastry—Unfortunate Experiment Upon a Muffin—The Citizen King.
LETTER LI.

Parisian Women—Rousseau's Failure in Attempting to Describe Them—Their Great Influence in Society—Their Grace in Conversation—Difficulty of Growing old—Do the Ladies of France or those of England Manage it Best?
LETTER LII.

La Sainte Chapelle—Palais de Justice—Traces of the Revolution of 1830—Unworthy Use Made of La Sainte Chapelle—Boileau—Ancient Records.
LETTER LIII.

French Ideas of England—Making Love—Precipitate Retreat of a Young Frenchman—Different Methods of Arranging Marriages—English Divorce—English Restaurans.
LETTER LIV.

Mixed Society—Influence of the English Clergy and their Families—Importance of their Station in Society.
LETTER LV.

Le Grand Opéra—Its Enormous Expense—Its Fashion—Its Acknowledged Dulness—'La Juive.'—Its Heavy Music—Its Exceeding Splendour—Beautiful Management of the Scenery—National Music.
LETTER LVI.

The Abbé Deguerry—His Eloquence—Excursion Across the Water—Library of Ste. Geneviève—Copy-book of the Dauphin—St. Etienne du Mont—Pantheon.
LETTER LVII.

Little Suppers—Great Dinners—Affectation of Gourmandise—Evil Effects of "dining out."—Evening Parties—Dinners in Private Under the Name of Luncheons—Late Hours.
LETTER LVIII.

Hôpital des Enfans Trouvés—Its Doubtful Advantages—Story of a Child Left There.
LETTER LIX.

Procès Monstre—Dislike of the Prisoners to the Ceremony of Trial—Société des Droits de l'Homme—Names Given to the Sections—Kitchen and Nursery Literature—Anecdote of Lagrange—Republican Law.
LETTER LX.

Memoirs of M. Châteaubriand—The Readings at L'Abbaye-aux-Bois—Account of These in the French Newspapers and Reviews—Morning at the Abbaye to Hear a Portion of these Memoirs—The Visit to Prague.
LETTER LXI.

Jardin des Plantes—Not Equal in Beauty to our Zoological Gardens—La Salpêtrière—Anecdote—Les Invalides—Difficulty of Finding English Colours There—The Dome.
LETTER LXII.

Expedition to Montmorency—Rendezvous in the Passage Delorme—St. Denis—Tomb Prepared for Napoleon—The Hermitage—Dîner sur l'Herbe.
LETTER LXIII.

George Sand. 8
LETTER LXIV.

"Angelo Tyran de Padoue."—Burlesque at the Théâtre du Vaudeville—Mademoiselle Mars—Madame Dorval—Epigram.
LETTER LXV.
Boulevard des Italiens—Tortoni's—Thunder Storm—Church of the Madeleine—Mrs. Butler's "Journal."
LETTER LXVI.
A Pleasant Party—Discussion Between an Englishman and a Frenchman—National Peculiarities.
LETTER LXVII.
Chamber of Deputies—Punishment of Journalists—Institute for the Encouragement of Industry—Men of Genius.
LETTER LXVIII.
Walk to the Marché des Innocens—Escape of a Canary Bird—A Street Orator—Burying Place of the Victims of July.
LETTER LXIX.
A Philosophical Spectator—Collection of Baron Sylvestre—Hôtel des Monnaies—Musée d'Artillerie.
LETTER LXX.
Concert in the Champs Elysées—Horticultural Exhibition—Forced Flowers—Republican Hats—Carlist Hats—Juste-Milieu Hats—Popular Funeral.
LETTER LXXI.
Minor French Novelists.
LETTER LXXII.
Breaking-up of the Paris Season—Soirée at MadameRécamier's—Recitation—Storm—Disappointment—Atonement—Farewell.
POSTSCRIPT
FRANCES MILTON TROLLOPE – A SHORT BIOGRAPHY
FRANCES MILTON TROLLOPE – A CONCISE BIBLIOGRAPHY

LETTER XLIII.

Peculiar Air of Frenchwomen—Impossibility that an Englishwoman Should Not Be Known for Such in Paris—Small Shops—Beautiful Flowers, and Pretty Arrangement of Them—Native Grace—Disappearance of Rouge—Grey Hair—Every Article Dearer than in London—All Temptations to Smuggling Removed.

Considering that it is a woman who writes to you, I think you will confess that you have no reason to complain of having been overwhelmed with the fashions of Paris: perhaps, on the contrary, you may feel rather disposed to grumble because all I have hitherto said on the fertile subject of dress has been almost wholly devoted to the historic and fanciful costume of the republicans. Personal appearance, and all that concerns it, is, however, a very important feature in the daily history of this showy city; and although in this respect it has been made the model of the whole world, it nevertheless contrives to retain for itself a general look, air, and effect, which it is quite in vain for any other people to attempt imitating. Go where you will, you see French fashions; but you must go to Paris to see how French people wear them.

The dome of the Invalides, the towers of Notre Dame, the column in the Place Vendôme, the windmills of Montmartre, do not come home to the mind as more essentially belonging to Paris, and Paris only, than does the aspect which caps, bonnets, frills, shawls, aprons, belts, buckles, gloves,—and above, though below, all things else—which shoes and stockings assume, when worn by Parisian women in the city of Paris.

It is in vain that all the women of the earth come crowding to this mart of elegance, each one with money in her sack sufficient to cover her from head to foot with all that is richest and best;—it is in vain that she calls to her aid all the tailleuses, coiffeuses, modistes, couturières, cordonniers, lingères, and friseurs in the town: all she gets for her pains is, when she has bought, and done, and put on all and everything they have prescribed, that, in the next shop she enters, she hears one grisette behind the counter mutter to another, "Voyez ce que désire cette dame anglaise;"—and that, poor dear lady! before she has spoken a single word to betray herself.

Neither is it only the natives who find us out so easily—that might perhaps be owing to some little inexplicable freemasonry among themselves; but the worst of all is, that we know one another in a moment. "There is an Englishman,"—"That is an Englishwoman," is felt at a glance, more rapidly than the tongue can speak it.

That manner, gait, and carriage,—that expression of movement, and, if I may so say, of limb, should be at once so remarkable and so impossible to imitate, is very singular. It has nothing to do with the national differences in eyes and complexion, for the effect is felt perhaps more strongly in following than in meeting a person; but it pervades every plait and every pin, every attitude and every gesture.

Could I explain to you what it is which produces this effect, I should go far towards removing the impossibility of imitating it: but as this is now, after twenty years of trial, pretty generally allowed to be impossible, you will not expect it of me. All I can do, is to tell you of such matters appertaining to dress as are open and intelligible to all, without attempting to dive into that very occult part of the subject, the effect of it.

In milliners' phrase, the ladies dress much less in Paris than in London. I have no idea that any Frenchwoman, after her morning dishabille is thrown aside, would make it a practice, during "the season," to change her dress completely four times in the course of the day, as I have known some ladies do in London. Nor do I believe that the most précieuses in such matters among them would deem it an insufferable breach of good manners to her family, did she sit down to dinner in the same apparel in which they had seen her three hours before it.

The only article of female luxury more generally indulged in here than with us, is that of cashmere shawls. One, at the very least, of these dainty wrappers makes a part of every young lady's trousseau, and is, I believe, exactly that part of the présent which, as Miss Edgeworth says, often makes a bride forget the future.

In other respects, what is necessary for the wardrobe of a French woman of fashion, is necessary also for that of an English one; only jewels and trinkets of all kinds are more frequently worn with us than with them. The dress that a young Englishwoman would wear at a dinner party, is very nearly the same as a Frenchwoman would wear at any ball but a fancy one; whereas the most elegant dinner costume in Paris is exactly the same as would be worn at the French Opera.

There are many extremely handsome "magasins de nouveautés" in every part of the town, wherein may be found all that the heart of woman can desire in the way of dress; and there are smart coiffeuses and modistes too, who know well how to fabricate and recommend every production of their fascinating art: but there is no Howell and James's wherein to assemble at a given point all the fine ladies of Paris; no reunions of tall footmen are to be seen lounging on benches outside the shops, and performing to the uninitiated the office of signs, by giving notice how many purchasers are at that moment engaged in cheapening the precious wares within. The shops in general are very much smaller than ours,—or when they stretch into great length, they have uniformly the appearance of warehouses. A much less quantity of goods of all kinds is displayed for purposes of show and decoration,—unless it be in china shops, or where or-molu ornaments, protected by glass covers, form the principal objects: here, or indeed wherever the articles sold can be exhibited without any danger of loss from injury, there is very considerable display; but, on the whole, there is much less appearance of large capital exhibited in the shops here than in London.

One great source of the gay and pretty appearance of the streets, is the number and elegant arrangement of the flowers exposed for sale. Along all the Boulevards, and in every brilliant Passage (with which latter ornamental invention Paris is now threaded in all directions), you need only shut your eyes in order to fancy yourself in a delicious flower-garden; and even on opening them again, if the delusion vanishes, you have something almost as pretty in its place.

Notwithstanding the multitudinous abominations of their streets—the prison-like locks on the doors of their salons, and the odious common stair which must be climbed ere one can get to them—there is an elegance of taste and love of the graceful about these people which is certainly to be found nowhere else. It is not confined to the spacious hotels of the rich and great, but may be traced through every order and class of society, down to the very lowest.

The manner in which an old barrow-woman will tie up her sous' worth of cherries for her urchin customers might give a lesson to the most skilful decorator of the supper-table. A bunch of wild violets, sold at a price that may come within reach of the worst-paid soubrette in Paris, is arranged with a grace that might make a duchess covet them; and I have seen the paltry stock-in-trade of a florist, whose only pavilion was a tree and the blue heavens, set off with such felicity in the mixture of colours, and the gradations of shape and form, as made me stand to gaze longer and more delightedly than I ever did before Flora's own palace in the King's Road.

After all, indeed, I believe that the mystical peculiarity of dress of which I have been speaking wholly arises from this innate and universal instinct of good taste. There is a fitness, a propriety, a sort of harmony in the various articles which constitute female attire, which may be traced as clearly amongst the cotton toques, with all their variety of brilliant tints, and the 'kerchief and apron to match, or rather to accord, as amongst the most elegant bonnets at the Tuileries. Their expressive phrase of approbation for a well-dressed woman, "faite à peindre," may often be applied with quite as much justice to the peasant as to the princess; for the same unconscious sensibility of taste will regulate them both.

It is this national feeling which renders their stage groups, their corps de ballet, and all the tableaux business of their theatres, so greatly superior to all others. On these occasions, a single blunder in colour, contrast, or position, destroys the whole harmony, and the whole charm with it: but you see the poor little girls hired to do angels and graces for a few sous a night, fall into the composition of the scene with an instinct as unerring, as that which leads a flight of wild geese to cleave the air in a well-adjusted triangular phalanx, instead of scattering themselves to every point of the compass; as, par example, our figurantes may be often seen to do, if not kept in order by the ballet-master as carefully as a huntsman whistles in his pack.

It is quite a relief to my eyes to find how completely rouge appears to be gone out of fashion here. I will not undertake to say that no bright eyes still look brighter from having a touch of red skilfully applied beneath them: but if this be done, it is so well done as to be invisible, excepting by its favourable effect; which is a prodigious improvement upon the fashion which I well remember here, of larding cheeks both young and old to a degree that was quite frightful.

Another improvement which I very greatly admire is, that the majority of old ladies have left off wearing artificial hair, and arrange their own grey locks with all the neatness and care possible. The effect of this upon their general appearance is extremely favourable: Nature always arranges things for us much better than we can do it for ourselves; and the effect of an old face surrounded by a maze of wanton curls, black, brown, or flaxen, is infinitely less agreeable than when it is seen with its own "sable silvered" about it.

I have heard it observed, and with great justice, that rouge was only advantageous to those who did not require it: and the same may be said with equal truth of false hair. Some of the towering pinnacles of shining jet that I have seen here, certainly have exceeded in quantity of hair the possible growth of any one head: but when this fabric surmounts a youthful face which seems to have a right to all the flowing honours that the friseur's art can contrive to arrange above it, there is nothing incongruous or disagreeable in the effect; though it is almost a pity, too, to mix anything approaching to deceptive art with the native glories of a young head. For which sentiment messieurs les fabricans of false hair will not thank me;—for having first interdicted the use of borrowed tresses to the old ladies, I now pronounce my disapproval of them for the young.

Au reste, all I can tell you farther respecting dress is, that our ladies must no longer expect to find bargains here in any article required for the wardrobe; on the contrary, everything of the kind is become greatly dearer than in London: and what is at least equally against making such purchases here is, that the fabrics of various kinds which we used to consider as superior to our own, particularly those of silks and gloves, are now, I think, decidedly inferior; and such as can be purchased at the same price as in England, if they can be found at all, are really too bad to use.

The only foreign bargains which I long to bring home with me are in porcelain: but this our custom-house tariff forbids, and very properly; as, without such protection, our Wedgewoods and Mortlakes would sell but few ornamental articles; for not only are their prices higher, but both their material and the fashioning of it are in my opinion extremely inferior. It is really very satisfactory to one's patriotic feelings to be able to say honestly, that excepting in these, and a few other ornamental superfluities, such as or-molu and alabaster clocks, etcætera, there is nothing that we need wish to smuggle into our own abounding land.

LETTER XLIV.

Exclusive Soirées—Soirée Doctrinaire—Duc de Broglie—Soirée Républicaine—Soirée Royaliste—Partie Impériale—Military Greatness—Dame de l'Empire.

Though the salons of Paris probably show at the present moment the most mixed society that can be found mingled together in the world, one occasionally finds oneself in the midst of a set evidently of one stamp, and indeed proclaiming itself to be so; for wherever this happens, the assembly is considered as peculiarly chosen and select, and as having all the dignity of exclusiveness.

The picture of Paris as it is, may perhaps be better caught at a glance at a party collected together without any reference to politics or principles of any kind; but I have been well pleased to find myself on three different occasions admitted to soirées of the exclusive kind.

At the first of these, I was told the names of most of the company by a kind friend who sat near me, and thus became aware that I had the honour of being in company with most of King Philippe's present ministry. Three or four of these gentlemen were introduced to me, and I had the advantage of seeing de près, during their hours of relaxation, the men who have perhaps at this moment as heavy a weight of responsibility upon their shoulders as any set of ministers ever sustained.

Nevertheless, nothing like gloom, preoccupation, or uneasiness, appeared to pervade them; and yet that chiefest subject of anxiety, the Procès Monstre, was by no means banished from their discourse. Their manner of treating it, however, was certainly not such as to make one believe that they were at all likely to sink under their load, or that they felt in any degree embarrassed or distressed by it.

Some of the extravagances of les accusés were discussed gaily enough, and the general tone was that of men who knew perfectly well what they were about, and who found more to laugh at than to fear in the opposition and abuse they encountered. This light spirit however, which to me seemed fair enough in the hours of recreation, had better not be displayed on graver occasions, as it naturally produces exasperation on the part of the prisoners, which, however little dangerous it may be to the state, is nevertheless a feeling which should not be unnecessarily excited. In that amusing paper or magazine—I know not which may be its title—called the "Chronique de Paris," I read some days ago a letter describing one of the séances of the Chamber of Peers on this procès, in which the gaiety manifested by M. de Broglie is thus censured:—

"J'ai fait moi-même partie de ce public privilégié que les accusés ne reconnaissent pas comme un vrai public, et j'ai pu assister jeudi à cette dramatique audience où la voix tonnante d'un accusé lisant une protestation, a couvert la voix du ministère public. J'étais du nombre de ceux qui ont eu la fièvre de cette scène, et je n'ai pu comprendre, au milieu de l'agitation générale, qu'un homme aussi bien élevé que M. de Broglie (je ne dis pas qu'un ministre) trouvât seul qu'il y avait là sujet de rire en lorgnant ce vrai Romain, comparable à ces tribuns qui, dans les derniers temps de la république, faisaient trembler les patriciens sur leurs chaises curules."

"Ce vrai Romain," however, rather deserved to be scourged than laughed at; for never did any criminal when brought to the bar of his country insult its laws and its rulers more grossly than the prisoner Beaune on this occasion. If indeed the accounts which reach us by the daily papers are not exaggerated, the outrageous conduct of the accused furnishes at every sitting sufficient cause for anger and indignation, however unworthy it may be of inspiring anything approaching to a feeling of alarm: and the calm, dignified, and temperate manner in which the Chamber of Peers has hitherto conducted itself may serve, I think, as an example to many other legislative assemblies.

The ministers of Louis-Philippe are very fortunate that the mode of trial decided on by them in this troublesome business is likely to be carried through by the upper house in a manner so little open to reasonable animadversion. The duty, and a most harassing one it is, has been laid upon them, as many think, illegally; but the task has been imposed by an authority which it is their duty to respect, and they have entered upon it in a spirit that does them honour.

The second exclusive party to which I was fortunate enough to be admitted, was in all respects quite the reverse of the first. The fair mistress of the mansion herself assured me that there was not a single doctrinaire present.

Here, too, the eternal subject of the Procès Monstre was discussed, but in a very different tone, and with feelings as completely as possible in opposition to those which dictated the lively and triumphant sort of persiflage to which I had before listened. Nevertheless, the conversation was anything but triste, as the party was in truth particularly agreeable; but, amidst flashes of wit, sinister sounds that foreboded future revolutions grumbled every now and then like distant thunder. Then there was shrugging of shoulders, and shaking of heads, and angry taps upon the snuff-box;

and from time to time, amid the prattle of pretty women, and the well-turned gentillesses of those they prattled to, might be heard such phrases as, "Tout n'est pas encore fini".... "Nous verrons ... nous verrons".... "S'ils sont arbitraires!" ... and the like.

The third set was as distinct as may be from the two former. This reunion was in the quartier St. Germain; and, if the feeling which I know many would call prejudice does not deceive me, the tone of first-rate good society was greatly more conspicuous here than at either of the others. By all the most brilliant personages who adorned the other two soirées which I have described, I strongly suspect that the most distinguished of this third would be classed as rococo; but they were composed of the real stuff that constitutes the true patrician, for all that. Many indeed were quite of the old régime, and many others their noble high-minded descendants: but whether they were old or young,—whether remarkable for having played a distinguished part in the scenes that have been, or for sustaining the chivalric principles of their race, by quietly withdrawing from the scenes that are,—in either case they had that air of inveterate superiority which I believe nothing on earth but gentle blood can give.

There is a fourth class still, consisting of the dignitaries of the Empire, which, if they ever assemble in distinct committee, I have yet to become acquainted with. But I suspect that this is not the case: one may perhaps meet them more certainly in some houses than in others; but, unless it be around the dome of the Invalides, I do not believe that they are to be found anywhere as a class apart.

Nothing, however, can be less difficult than to trace them: they are as easily discerned as a boiled lobster among a panier full of such as are newly caught.

That amusing little vaudeville called, I think, "La Dame de l'Empire," or some such title, contains the best portrait of a whole clique, under the features of an individual character, of any comedy I know.

None of the stormy billows which have rolled over France during the last forty years have thrown up a race so strongly marked as those produced by the military era of the Empire. The influence of the enormous power which was then in action has assuredly in some directions left most noble vestiges. Wherever science was at work, this power propelled it forward; and ages yet unborn may bless for this the fostering patronage of Napoleon: some midnight of devastation and barbarism must fall upon the world before what he has done of this kind can be obliterated.

But the same period, while it brought forth from obscurity talent and enterprise which without its influence would never have been greeted by the light of day, brought forward at the same time legions of men and women to whom this light and their advanced position in society are by no means advantageous in the eyes of a passing looker-on.

I have heard that it requires three generations to make a gentleman. Those created by Napoleon have not yet fairly reached a second; and, with all respect for talent, industry, and valour be it spoken, the necessity of this slow process very frequently forces itself upon one's conviction at Paris.

It is probable that the great refinement of the post-imperial aristocracy of France may be one reason why the deficiencies of those now often found mixed up with them is so remarkable. It would be difficult to imagine a contrast in manner more striking than that of a lady who would be a fair specimen of the old Bourbon noblesse, and a bouncing maréchale of Imperial creation. It seems as if every particle of the whole material of which each is formed gave evidence of the different birth of the spirit that dwells within. The sound of the voice is a contrast; the glance of the eye is a contrast; the smile is a contrast; the step is a contrast. Were every feature of a dame de l'Empire and a femme noble formed precisely in the same mould, I am quite sure that the two would look no more alike than Queen Constance and Nell Gwyn.

Nor is there at all less difference in the two races of gentlemen. I speak not of the men of science or of art; their rank is of another kind: but there are still left here and there specimens of decorated greatness which look as if they must have been dragged out of the guard-room by main force; huge moustached militaires, who look at every slight rebuff as if they were ready to exclaim, "Sacré nom de D—! je suis un héros, moi! Vive l'Empereur!"

A good deal is sneeringly said respecting the parvenus fashionables of the present day: but station, and place, and court favour, must at any rate give something of reality to the importance of those whom the last movement has brought to the top; and this is vastly less offensive than the empty, vulgar, camp-like reminiscences of Imperial patronage which are occasionally brought forward by those who may thank their sabre for having cut a path for them into the salons of Paris. The really great men of the Empire—and there are certainly many of them—have taken care to have other claims to distinction attached to their names than that of having been dragged out of heaven knows what profound obscurity by Napoleon: I may say of such, in the words of the soldier in Macbeth—

"If I say sooth, I must report they were
As cannon overcharged with double cracks."

As for the elderly ladies, who, from simple little bourgeoises demoiselles, were in those belligerent days sabred and trumpeted into maréchales and duchesses, I must think that they make infinitely worse figures in a drawing-room, than those who, younger in years and newer in dignity, have all their blushing honours fresh upon them. Besides, in point of fact, the having one Bourbon prince instead of another upon the throne, though greatly to be lamented from the manner in which it was accomplished, can hardly be expected to produce so violent a convulsion among the aristocracy of France, as must of necessity have ensued from the reign of a soldier of fortune, though the mightiest that ever bore arms.

Many of the noblest races of France still remain wedded to the soil that has been for ages native to their name. Towards these it is believed that King Louis-Philippe has no very repulsive feelings; and should no farther changes come upon the country—no more immortal days arise to push all men from their stools, it is probable that the number of these will not diminish in the court circles.

Meanwhile, the haut-ton born during the last revolution must of course have an undisputed entrée everywhere; and if by any external marks they are particularly brought forward to observation, it is only, I think, by a toilet among the ladies more costly and less simple than that of their high-born neighbours; and among the gentlemen, by a general air of prosperity and satisfaction, with an expression of eye sometimes a little triumphant, often a little patronizing, and always a little busy.

It was a duchess, and no less, who decidedly gave me the most perfect idea of an Imperial parvenue that I have ever seen off the stage. When a lady of this class attains so very elevated a rank, the perils of her false position multiply around her. A quiet bourgeoise turned into a noble lady of the third or fourth degree is likely enough to look a little awkward; but if she has the least tact in the world, she may remain tranquil and sans ridicule under the honourable shelter of those above her. But when she becomes a duchess, the chances are terribly against her: "Madame la Duchesse" must be conspicuous; and if in addition to mauvais ton she should par malheur be a bel esprit, adding the pretension of literature to that of station, it is likely that she will be very remarkable indeed.

My parvenu duchess is very remarkable indeed. She steps out like a corporal carrying a message: her voice is the first, the last, and almost the only thing heard in the salon that she honours with her presence,—except it chance, indeed, that she lower her tone occasionally to favour with a whisper some gallant décoré, military, scientific or artistic, of the same standing as herself; and moreover, she promenades her eyes over the company as if she had a right to bring them all to roll-call.

Notwithstanding all this, the lady is certainly a person of talent; and had she happily remained in the station in which both herself and her husband were born, she might not perhaps have thought it necessary to speak quite so loud, and her bons mots would have produced infinitely greater effect. But she is so thoroughly out of place in the grade to which she has been unkindly elevated, that it seems as if Napoleon had decided on her fate in a humour as spiteful as that of Monsieur Jourdain, when he said—

"Votre fille sera marquise, en dépit de tout le monde: et si vous me mettez en colère, je la ferai duchesse."

LETTER XLV.

L'Abbé Lacordaire—Various Statements Respecting Him—Poetical Description of Notre Dame—The Prophecy of a Roman Catholic—Les Jeunes Gens de Paris—Their Omnipotence.

The great reputation of another preacher induced us on Sunday to endure two hours more of tedious waiting before the mass which preceded the sermon began. It is only thus that a chair can be hoped for when the Abbé Lacordaire mounts the pulpit of Notre Dame. The penalty is really heavy; but having heard this celebrated person described as one who "appeared sent by Heaven to restore France to Christianity"—as "a hypocrite that set Tartuffe immeasurably in the background"—as "a man whose talent surpassed that of any preacher since Bossuet"—and as "a charlatan who ought to harangue from a tub, instead of from the chaire de Notre Dame de Paris,"—I determined upon at least seeing and hearing him, however little I might be able to decide on which of the two sides of the prodigious chasm that yawned between his friends and enemies the truth was most likely to be found. There were, however, several circumstances which lessened the tedium of this long interval: I might go farther, and confess that this period was by no means the least profitable portion of the four hours which we passed in the church.

On entering, we found the whole of the enormous nave railed in, as it had been on Easter Sunday for the concert (for so in truth should that performance be called); but upon applying at the entrance to this enclosure, we were told that no ladies could be admitted to that part of the church—but that the side aisles were fully furnished with chairs, and afforded excellent places.

This arrangement astonished me in many ways:—first, as being so perfectly un-national; for go where you will in France, you find the best places reserved for the women,—at least, this was the first instance in which I ever found it otherwise. Next, it astonished me, because at every church I had entered, the congregations, though always crowded, had been composed of at least twelve women to one man. When, therefore, I looked over the barrier upon the close-packed, well-adjusted rows of seats prepared to receive fifteen hundred persons, I thought that unless all the priests in Paris came in person to do honour to their eloquent confrère, it was very unlikely that this uncivil arrangement should be found necessary. There was no time, however, to waste in conjecture; the crowd already came rushing in at every door, and we hastened to secure the best places that the side aisles afforded. We obtained seats between the pillars immediately opposite to the pulpit, and felt well enough contented, having little doubt that a voice which had made itself heard so well must have power to reach even to the side aisles of Notre Dame.

The first consolation which I found for my long waiting, after placing myself in that attitude of little ease which the straight-backed chair allowed, was from the recollection that the interval was to be passed within the venerable walls of Notre Dame. It is a glorious old church, and though not comparable in any way to Westminster Abbey, or to Antwerp, or Strasburg, or Cologne, or indeed to many others which I might name, has enough to occupy the eye very satisfactorily for a considerable time. The three elegant rose-windows, throwing in their coloured light from north, west, and south, are of themselves a very pretty study for half an hour or so; and besides, they brought back, notwithstanding their miniature diameter of forty feet, the remembrance of the magnificent circular western window of Strasburg—the recollection of which was almost enough to while away another long interval. Then I employed myself, not very successfully, in labouring to recollect the quaint old verses which I had fallen upon a few days before, giving the dimensions of the church, and which I will herewith transcribe for your use and amusement, in case you should ever find yourself sitting as I was, bolt upright, as we elegantly express ourselves when describing this ecclesiastical-Parisian attitude, while waiting the advent of the Abbé Lacordaire.

"Si tu veux savoir comme est ample
De Notre Dame le grand temple,
Il y a, dans oeuvre, pour le seur,
Dix et sept toises de hauteur,
Sur la largeur de vingt-quatre,
Et soixante-cinq, sans rebattre,
A de long; aux tours haut montées
Trente-quatre sont comptées;
Le tout fondé sur pilotis—
Aussi vrai que je te le dis."

While repeating this poetical description, you have only to remember that une toise is the same as a fathom,—that is to say, six feet; and then, as you turn your head in all directions to look about you, you will have the satisfaction of knowing exactly how far you can see in each.

I had another source of amusement, and by no means a trifling one, in watching the influx of company. The whole building soon contained as many human beings as could be crammed into it; and the seats, which we thought, as we took them, were very so-so places indeed, became accomodations for which to be most heartily thankful. Not a pillar but supported the backs of as many men as could stand round it; and not a jutting ornament, the balustrade of a side altar, or any other "point of 'vantage," but looked as if a swarm of bees were beginning to hang upon it.

But the sight which drew my attention most was that displayed by the exclusive central aisle. When told that it was reserved for gentlemen, I imagined of course that I should see it filled by a collection of staid-looking, middle-aged, Catholic citizens, who were drawn together from all parts of the town, and perhaps the country too, for the purpose of hearing the celebrated preacher: but, to my great astonishment, instead of this I saw pouring in by dozens at a time, gay, gallant, smart-looking young men, such indeed as I had rarely seen in Paris on any other religious occasion. Amongst these was a sprinkling of older men; but the great majority were decidedly under thirty. The meaning of this phenomenon I could by no means understand; but while I was tormenting myself to discover some method of obtaining information respecting it, accident brought relief to my curiosity in the shape of a communicative neighbour.

In no place in the world is it so easy, I believe, to enter into conversation with strangers as in Paris. There is a courteous inclination to welcome every attempt at doing so which pervades all ranks, and any one who wishes it may easily find or make opportunities of hearing the opinions of all classes. The present time, too, is peculiarly favourable for this; a careless freedom in uttering opinions of all kinds being, I think, the most remarkable feature in the manners of Paris at the present day.

I have heard that it is difficult to get a tame, flat, short, matter-of-fact answer from a genuine Irishman;—from a genuine Frenchman it is impossible: let his reply to a question which seeks information contain as little of it as the dry Anglicism "I don't know," it is never given without a tone or a turn of phrase that not only relieves its inanity, but leaves you with the agreeable persuasion that the speaker would be more satisfactory if he could, and moreover that he would be extremely happy to reply to any further questions you may wish to ask, either on the same, or any other subject whatever.

It was in consequence of my moving my chair an inch and a half to accommodate the long limbs of a grey-headed neighbour, that he was induced to follow his "Milles pardons, madame!" with an observation on the inconvenience endured on the present occasion by the appropriation of all the best places to the gentlemen. It was quite contrary, he added, to the usual spirit of Parisian arrangements; and yet, in fact, it was the only means of preventing the ladies suffering from the tremendous rush of jeunes gens who constantly came to hear the Abbé Lacordaire.

"I never saw so large a proportion of young men in any congregation," said I, hoping he might explain the mystery to me. What I heard, however, rather startled than enlightened me.

"The Catholic religion was never so likely to be spread over the whole earth as it is at present," he replied. "The kingdom of Ireland will speedily become fully reconciled to the see of Rome. Le Sieur O'Connell desires to be canonized. Nothing, in truth, remains for that portion of your country to do, but to follow the example we set during our famous Three Days, and place a prince of its own choosing upon the throne."

I am persuaded that he thought we were Irish Roman Catholics: our sitting with such exemplary patience to wait for the preaching of this new apostle was not, I suppose, to be otherwise accounted for. I said nothing to undeceive him, but wishing to bring him back to speak of the congregation before us, I replied,

"Paris at least, if we may judge from the vast crowd collected here, is more religious than she has been of late years."

"France," replied he with energy, "as you may see by looking at this throng, is no longer the France of 1823, when her priests sang canticles to the tune of "Ça ira." France is happily become most deeply and sincerely Catholic. Her priests are once more her orators, her magnates, her highest dignitaries. She may yet give cardinals to Rome—and Rome may again give a minister to France."

I knew not what to answer: my silence did not seem to please him, and I believe he began to suspect he had mistaken the party altogether, for after sitting for a few minutes quite silent, he rose from the place into which he had pushed himself with considerable difficulty, and making his way through the crowd behind us, disappeared; but I saw him again, before we left the church, standing on the steps of the pulpit.

The chair he left was instantly occupied by another gentleman, who had before found standing-room near it. He had probably remarked our sociable propensities, for he immediately began talking to us.

"Did you ever see anything like the fashion which this man has obtained?" said he. "Look at those jeunes gens, madame! ... might one not fancy oneself at a première représentation?"

"Those must be greatly mistaken," I replied, "who assert that the young men of Paris are not among her fidèles."

"Do you consider their appearing here a proof that they are religious?" inquired my neighbour with a smile.

"Certainly I do, sir," I replied: "how can I interpret it otherwise?"

"Perhaps not—perhaps to a stranger it must have this appearance; but to a man who knows Paris...." He smiled again very expressively, and, after a short pause, added—"Depend upon it, that if a man of equal talent and eloquence with this Abbé Lacordaire were to deliver a weekly discourse in favour of atheism, these very identical young men would be present to hear him."

"Once they might," said I, "from curiosity: but that they should follow him, as I understand they do, month after month, if what he uttered were at variance with their opinions, seems almost inconceivable."

"And yet it is very certainly the fact," he replied: "whoever can contrive to obtain the reputation of talent at Paris, let the nature of it be of what kind it may, is quite sure that les jeunes gens will resort to hear and see him. They believe themselves of indefeasible right the sole arbitrators of intellectual reputation; and let the direction in which it is shown be as foreign as may be to their own pursuits, they come as a matter of prescriptive right to put their seal upon the aspirant's claim, or to refuse it."

"Then, at least, they acknowledge that the Abbé's words have power, or they would not grant their suffrage to him."

"They assuredly acknowledge that his words have eloquence; but if by power, you mean power of conviction, or conversion, I do assure you that they acknowledge nothing like it. Not only do I believe that these young men are themselves sceptics, but I do not imagine that there is one in ten of them who has the least faith in the Abbé's own orthodoxy."

"But what right have they to doubt it?... Surely he would hardly be permitted to preach at Notre Dame, where the archbishop himself sits in judgment on him, were he otherwise than orthodox?"

"I was at school with him," he replied: "he was a fine sharp-witted boy, and gave very early demonstrations of a mind not particularly given either to credulity, or subservience to any doctrines that he found puzzling."

"I should say that this was the greatest proof of his present sincerity. He doubted as a boy—but as a man he believes."

"That is not the way the story goes," said he. "But hark! there is the bell: the mass is about to commence."

He was right: the organ pealed, the fine chant of the voices was heard above it, and in a few minutes we saw the archbishop and his splendid train escorting the Host to its ark upon the altar.

During the interval between the conclusion of the mass and the arrival of the Abbé Lacordaire in the pulpit, my sceptical neighbour again addressed me.

"Are you prepared to be very much enchanted by what you are going to hear?" said he.

"I hardly know what to expect," I replied: "I think my idea of the preacher was higher when I came here, than since I have heard you speak of him."

"You will find that he has a prodigious flow of words, much vehement gesticulation, and a very impassioned manner. This is quite sufficient to establish his reputation for eloquence among les jeunes gens."

"But I presume you do not yourself subscribe to the sentence pronounced by these young critics?"

"Yes, I do,—as far, at least, as to acknowledge that this man has not attained his reputation without having displayed great ability. But though all the talent of Paris has long consented to receive its crown of laurels from the hands of her young men, it would be hardly reasonable to expect that their judgment should be as profound as their power is great."

"Your obedience to this beardless synod is certainly very extraordinary," said I: "I cannot understand it."

"I suppose not," said he, laughing; "it is quite a Paris fashion; but we all seem contented that it should be so. If a new play appears, its fate must be decided by les jeunes gens; if a picture is exhibited, its rank amidst the works of modern art can only be settled by them: does a dancer, a singer, an actor, or a preacher appear—a new member in the tribune, or a new prince upon the throne,—it is still les jeunes gens who must pass judgment on them all; and this judgment is quoted with a degree of deference utterly inconceivable to a stranger."

"Chut! ... chut!" ... was at this moment uttered by more than one voice near us: "le voilà!" I glanced my eye towards the pulpit, but it was still empty; and on looking round me, I perceived that all eyes were turned in the direction of a small door in the north aisle, almost immediately behind us. "Il est entré là!" said a young woman near us, in a tone that seemed to indicate a feeling deeper than respect, and, in truth, not far removed from adoration. Her eyes were still earnestly fixed upon the door, and continued to be so, as well as those of many others, till it reopened and a slight young man in the dress of a priest prepared for the chaire appeared at it. A verger made way for him through the crowd, which, thick and closely wedged as it was, fell back on each side of him, as he proceeded to the pulpit, with much more docility than I ever saw produced by the clearing a passage through the intervention of a troop of horse.

Silence the most profound accompanied his progress; I never witnessed more striking demonstrations of respect: and yet it is said that three-fourths of Paris believe this man to be a hypocrite.

As soon as he had reached the pulpit, and while preparing himself by silent prayer for the duty he was about to perform, a movement became perceptible at the upper part of the choir; and presently the archbishop and his splendid retinue of clergy were seen moving in a body towards that part of the nave which is immediately in front of the preacher. On arriving at the space reserved for them, each noiselessly dropped into his allotted seat according to his place and dignity, while the whole congregation respectfully stood to watch the ceremony, and seemed to

"Admirer un si bel ordre, et reconnaître l'église."

It is easier to describe to you everything which preceded the sermon, than the sermon itself. This was such a rush of words, such a burst and pouring out of passionate declamation, that even before I had heard enough to judge of the matter, I felt disposed to prejudge the preacher, and to suspect that his discourse would have more of the flourish and furbelow of human rhetoric than of the simplicity of divine truth in it.

His violent action, too, disgusted me exceedingly. The rapid and incessant movement of his hands, sometimes of one, sometimes of both, more resembled that of the wings of a humming-bird than anything else I can remember: but the hum proceeded from the admiring congregation. At every pause he made, and like the claptraps of a bad actor, they were frequent, and evidently faits exprès: a little gentle laudatory murmur ran through the crowd.

I remember reading somewhere of a priest nobly born, and so anxious to keep his flock in their proper place, that they might not come "between the wind and his nobility," that his constant address to them when preaching was, "Canaille Chrétienne!" This was bad—very bad, certainly; but I protest, I doubt if the Abbé Lacordaire's manner of addressing his congregation as "Messieurs" was much less unlike the fitting tone of a Christian pastor. This mundane apostrophe was continually repeated throughout the whole discourse, and, I dare say, had its share in producing the disagreeable effect I experienced from his eloquence. I cannot remember having ever heard a preacher I less liked, reverenced, and admired, than this new Parisian saint. He made very pointed allusions to the reviving state of the Roman Catholic Church in Ireland, and anathematized pretty cordially all such as should oppose it.

In describing the two hours' prologue to the mass, I forgot to mention that many young men—not in the reserved places of the centre aisle, but sitting near us, beguiled the tedious interval by reading. Some of the volumes they held had the appearance of novels from a circulating library, and others were evidently collections of songs, probably less spiritual than spirituels.

The whole exhibition certainly showed me a new page in the history of Paris as it is, and I therefore do not regret the four hours it cost me: but once is enough—I certainly will never go to hear the Abbé Lacordaire again.

LETTER XLVI.

La Tour de Nesle.

It is, I believe, nearly two years ago since the very extraordinary drama called "La Tour de Nesle" was sent me to read, as a specimen of the outrageous school of dramatic extravagance which had taken possession of all the theatres in Paris; but I certainly did not expect that it would keep its place as a favourite spectacle with the people of this great and enlightened capital long enough for me to see it, at this distance of time, still played before a very crowded audience.

That this is a national disgrace, is most certain: but the fault is less attributable to the want of good taste, than to the lamentable blunder which permits every species of vice and abomination to be enacted before the eyes of the people, without any restraint or check whatever, under the notion that they are thereby permitted to enjoy a desirable privilege and a noble freedom. Yet in this same country it is illegal to sell a deleterious drug! There is no logic in this.

It is however an undeniable fact, as I think I have before stated, that the best class of Parisian society protest against this disgusting license, and avoid—upon principle loudly proclaimed and avowed—either reading or seeing acted these detestable compositions. Thus, though the crowded audiences constantly assembled whenever they are brought forward prove but too clearly that such persons form but a small minority, their opinion is nevertheless sufficient, or ought to be so, to save the country from the disgrace of admitting that such things are good.

We seem to pique ourselves greatly on the superiority of our taste in these matters; but let us pique ourselves rather on our theatrical censorship. Should the clamours and shoutings of misrule lead to the abolition of this salutary restraint, the consequences would, I fear, be such as very soon to rob us of our present privilege of abusing our neighbours on this point.

While things do remain as they are, however, we may, I think, smile a little at such a judgment as Monsieur de Saintfoix passes upon our theatrical compositions, when comparing them to those of France.

"Les actions de nos tragédies," says he, "sont pathétiques et terribles; celles des tragédies angloises sont atroces. On y met sous les yeux du spectateur les objets les plus horribles; un mari qui discourt avec sa femme, qui la caresse et l'étrangle."

Might one not think that the writer of this passage had just arrived from witnessing the famous scene in the "Monomane," only he had mistaken it for English? But he goes on—

"Une fille toute sanglante...." (Triboulet's daughter Blanche, for instance.)—"Après l'avoir violée...."

He then proceeds to reason upon the subject, and justly enough, I think—only we should read England for France, and France for England.

"Il n'est pas douteux que les arts agréables ne réussissent chez un peuple qu'autant qu'ils en prennent le génie, et qu'un auteur dramatique ne sauroit espérer de plaire si les objets et les images qu'il présente ne sont pas analogues au caractère, au naturel, et au goût de la nation: on pourroit donc conclure de la différence des deux théâtres, que l'âme d'un ANGLAIS est sombre, féroce, sanguinaire; et que celle d'un FRANÇAIS est vive, impatiente, emportée, mais généreuse même dans sa haine; idolatrant l'honneur"—(just like Buridan in this same drama of the Tour de Nesle—this popular production of la Jeune France—la France régénérée)—"idolatrant l'honneur, et ne cessant jamais de l'apercevoir, malgré le trouble et toute la violence des passions."

Though it is impossible to read this passage without a smile, at a time when it is so easy for the English to turn the tables against this patriotic author, one must sigh too, while reflecting on the lamentable change which has taken place in the moral feeling of revolutionised France since the period at which it was written.

What would Saintfoix say to the notion that Victor Hugo had "heaved the ground from beneath the feet of Corneille and Racine"? The question, however, is answered by a short sentence in his "Essais Historiques," where he thus expresses himself:—

"Je croirois que la décadence de notre nation seroit prochaine, si les hommes de quarante ans n'y regardoient pas CORNEILLE comme le plus grand génie qui ait jamais été."

If the spirit of the historian were to revisit the earth, and float over the heads of a party of Parisian critics while pronouncing sentence on his favourite author, he might probably return to the shades unharmed, for he would only hear "Rococo! Rococo! Rococo!" uttered as by acclamation; and unskilled to comprehend the new-born eloquence, he would doubtless interpret it as a refrain to express in one pithy word all reverence, admiration, and delight.

But to return to "La Tour de Nesle." The story is taken from a passage in Brantôme's history "des Femmes Galantes," where he says, "qu'une reine de France"—whom however he does not name, but who is said to have been Marguérite de Bourgogne, wife of Louis Dix—"se tenoit là (à la Tour de Nesle) d'ordinaire, laquelle fesant le guet aux passans, et ceux qui lui revenoient et agréoient le plus, de quelque sorte de gens que ce fussent, les fesoit appeler et venir à soy, et après ... les fesoit précipiter du haut de la tour en bas, en l'eau, et les fesoit noyer. Je ne veux pas," he continues, "assurer que cela soit vrai, mais le vulgaire, au moins la plupart de Paris, l'affirme, et n'y a si commun qu'en lui montrant la tour seulement, et en l'interrogeant, que de lui-même ne le die."

This story one might imagine was horrible and disgusting enough; but MM. Gaillardet et — (it is thus the authors announce themselves) thought otherwise, and accordingly they have introduced her majesty's sisters, the ladies Jeanne and Blanche of Burgundy, who were both likewise married to sons of Philippe-le-Bel, the brothers of Louis Dix, to share her nocturnal orgies. These "imaginative and powerful" scenic historians also, according to the fashion of the day among the theatrical writers of France, add incest to increase the interest of the drama.

This is enough, and too much, as to the plot; and for the execution of it by the authors, I can only say that it is about equal in literary merit to the translations of an Italian opera handed about at the Haymarket. It is in prose—and, to my judgment, very vulgar prose; yet it is not only constantly acted, but I am assured that the sale of it has been prodigiously great, and still continues to be so.

That a fearful and even hateful story, dressed up in all the attractive charm of majestic poetry, and redeemed in some sort by the noble sentiments of the personages brought into the scenes of which it might be the foundation—that a drama so formed might captivate the imagination even while it revolted the feelings, is very possible, very natural, and nowise disgraceful either to the poet, or to those whom his talent may lead captive. The classic tragedies which long served as models to France abound in fables of this description. Alfieri, too, has made use of such, following with a poet's wing the steady onward flight of remorseless destiny, yet still sublime in pathos and in dignity, though appalling in horror. In like manner, the great French dramatists have triumphed by the power of their genius, both over the disgust inspired by these awful classic mysteries, and the unbending strictness of the laws which their antique models enforced for their composition.

If we may herein deem the taste to have been faulty, the grace, the majesty, the unswerving dignity of the tragic march throughout the whole action—the lofty sentiments, the bursts of noble passion, and the fine drapery of stately verse in which the whole was clothed, must nevertheless raise our admiration to a degree that may perhaps almost compete with what we feel for the enchanting wildness and unshackled nature of our native dramas.

But what can we think of those who, having ransacked the pages of history to discover whatever was most revolting to the human soul, should sit down to arrange it in action, detailed at full length, with every hateful circumstance exaggerated and brought out to view for the purpose of tickling the curiosity of his countrymen and countrywomen, and by that means beguiling them into the contemplation of scenes that Virtue would turn from with loathing, and before which Innocence must perish as she gazes? No gleam of goodness throughout the whole for the heart to cling to,—no thought of remorseful penitence,—no spark of noble feeling; nothing but vice,—low, grovelling, brutal vice,—from the moment the curtain rises to display the obscene spectacle, to that which sees it fall between the fictitious infamy on one side, and the real impurity left on the other!

As I looked on upon the hideous scene, and remembered the classic horrors of the Greek tragedians, and of the mighty imitators who have followed them, I could not help thinking that the performance of MM. Gaillardet et — was exceedingly like that of a monkey mimicking the operations of a man. He gets hold of the same tools, but turns the edges the wrong way; and instead of raising a majestic fabric in honour of human genius, he rolls the materials in mud, begrimes his own paws in the slimy cement, and then claws hold of every unwary passenger who comes within his reach, and bespatters him with the rubbish he has brought together. Such monkeys should be chained, or they will do much mischief.

It is hardly possible that such dramas as the "Tour de Nesle" can be composed with the intention of producing a great tragic effect; which is surely the only reason which can justify bringing sin and misery before the eyes of an audience. There is in almost every human heart a strange love for scenes of terror and of woe. We love to have our sympathies awakened—our deepest feelings roused; we love to study in the magic mirror of the scene what we ourselves might feel did such awful visitations come upon us; and there is an unspeakable interest inspired by looking on, and fancying that were it so with us, we might so act, so feel, so suffer, and so die. But is there in any land a wretch so lost, so vile, as to be capable of feeling sympathy with any sentiment or thought expressed throughout the whole progress of this "Tour de Nesle"? God forbid!

I have heard of poets who have written under the inspiration of brandy and laudanum—the exhalations from which are certainly not likely to form themselves into images of distinctness or beauty; but the inspiration that dictated the "Tour de Nesle" must have been something viler still, though not less powerful. It must, I think, have been the cruel calculation of how many dirty francs might be expressed from the pockets of the idle, by a spectacle new from its depth of atrocity, and attractive from its newness.

But, setting aside for a moment the sin and the scandal of producing on a public stage such a being as the woman to whom MM. Gaillardet et — have chosen to give the name of Marguérite de Bourgogne, it is an object of some curiosity to examine the literary merits of a piece which, both on the stage and in the study, has been received by so many thousands—perhaps millions—of individuals belonging to "la grande nation" as a work deserving their patronage and support—or at least as deserving their attention and attendance for years; years, too, of hourly progressive intellect—years during which the march of mind has outdone all former marches of human intelligence—years during which Young France has been labouring to throw off her ancient coat of worn-out rococoism, and to clothe herself in new-fledged brightness. During these years she has laid on one shelf her once-venerated Corneille,—on another, her almost worshipped Racine. Molière is named but as a fine antique; and Voltaire himself, spite of his strong claims upon their revolutionary affections, can hardly be forgiven for having said of the two whom Victor Hugo is declared to have overthrown, that "Ces hommes enseignèrent à la nation, à penser, à sentir, à s'exprimer; leurs auditeurs, instruits par eux seuls, devinrent enfin des juges sévères pour eux mêmes qui les avaient éclairés." Let any one whose reason is not totally overthrown by the fever and delirium of innovation read the "Tour de Nesle," and find out if he can any single scene, speech, or phrase deserving the suffrage which Paris has accorded to it. Has the dialogue either dignity, spirit, or truth of nature to recommend it? Is there a single sentiment throughout the five acts with which an honest man can accord? Is there even an approach to grace or beauty in the tableaux? or skill in the arrangement of the scenes? or keeping of character among the demoniacal dramatis personæ which MM. Gaillardet et — have brought together? or, in short, any one merit to recommend it—except only its superlative defiance of common decency and common sense?

If there be any left among the men of France; I speak not now of her boys, the spoilt grandchildren of the old revolution;—but if there be any left among her men, as I in truth believe there are, who deprecate this eclipse of her literary glory, is it not sad that they should be forced to permit its toleration, for fear they should be sent to Ham for interfering with the liberty of the press?

It is impossible to witness the representation of one of these infamous pieces without perceiving, as you glance your eye around the house, who are its patrons and supporters. At no great distance from us, when we saw the "Tour de Nesle," were three young men who had all of them a most thoroughly "jeunes gens" and republican cast of countenance, and tournure of person and dress. They tossed their heads and snuffed the theatrical air of "la Jeune France," as if they felt that they were, or ought to be, her masters: and it is a positive fact that nothing pre-eminently absurd or offensive was done or said upon the stage, which this trio did not mark with particular admiration and applause.

There was, however, such a saucy look of determination to do what they knew was absurd, that I gave them credit for being aware of the nonsense of what they applauded, from the very fact that they did applaud it.

It is easy enough sometimes to discover "le vrai au travers du ridicule;" and these silly boys were not, I am persuaded, such utter blockheads as they endeavoured to appear. It is a bad and mischievous tone, however; and the affecting a vice where you have it not, is quite as detestable a sort of hypocrisy as any other.

Some thousand years hence perhaps, if any curious collectors of rare copies should contrive among them to preserve specimens of the French dramas of the present day, it may happen that while the times that are gone shall continue to be classed as the Iron, the Golden, the Dark, and the Augustan ages, this day of ours may become familiar in all men's mouths as the Diabolic age,—unless, indeed, some charitable critic shall step forward in our defence, and bestow upon it the gentler appellation of "the Idiot era."

LETTER XLVII.

Palais Royal—Variety of Characters—Party of English—Restaurant—Galerie d'Orléans—Number of Loungers—Convenient Abundance of Idle Men—Théâtre du Vaudeville.

Though, as a lady, you may fancy yourself quite beyond the possibility of ever feeling any interest in the Palais Royal, its restaurans, its trinket-shops, ribbon-shops, toy-shops &c. &c. &c. and all the world of misery, mischief, and good cheer which rises étage after étage above them; I must nevertheless indulge in a little gossip respecting it, because few things in Paris—I might, I believe, say nothing—can show an aspect so completely un-English in all ways as this singular region. The palace itself is stately and imposing, though not externally in the very best taste. Corneille, however, says of it,—

"L'univers entier ne peut voir rien d'égal

Au superbe dehors du Palais Cardinal,"

as it was called from having been built and inhabited by the Cardinal de Richelieu. But it is the use made of the space which was originally the Cardinal's garden, which gives the place its present interest.

All the world—men, women and children, gentle and simple, rich and poor,—in short, I suppose every living soul that enters Paris, is taken to look at the Palais Royal. But though many strangers linger there, alas! all too long, there are many others who, according to my notions, do not linger there long enough. The quickest eye cannot catch at one glance, though that glance be in activity during a tour made round the whole enclosure, all the national characteristic, picturesque, and comic groups which float about there incessantly through at least twenty hours of the twenty-four. I know that the Palais Royal is a study which, in its higher walks and profoundest depths, it would be equally difficult, dangerous, and disagreeable to pursue: but with these altitudes and profundities I have nothing to do; there are abundance of objects to be seen there, calculated and intended to meet the eyes of all men, and women too, which may furnish matter for observation, without either diving or climbing in pursuit of knowledge that, after all, would be better lost than found.

But one should have the talent of Hogarth to describe the different groups, with all their varied little episodes of peculiarity, which render the Palais Royal so amusing. These groups are, to be sure, made up only of Parisians, and of the wanderers who visit la belle ville in order to see and be seen in every part of it; yet it is in vain that you would seek elsewhere the same odd selection of human beings that are to be found sans faute in every corner of the Palais Royal.

How it happens I know not, but so it is, that almost every person you meet here furnishes food for speculation. If it be an elegant well-appointed man of fashion, the fancy instantly tracks him to a salon de jeu; and if you are very good-natured, your heart will ache to think how much misery he is likely to carry home with him. If it be a low, skulking, semi-genteel moustache, with large, dark, deep-set eyes rolling about to see whom he can devour, you are as certain that he too is making for a salon, as that a man with a rod and line on his shoulder is going to fish. That pretty soubrette, with her neat heels and smart silk apron, who has evidently a few francs tied up in the corner of the handkerchief which she holds in her hand—do we not know that she is peering through the window of every trinket-shop to see where she can descry the most tempting gold ear-rings, for the purchase of which a quarter's wages are about to be dis-kerchiefed?

We must not overlook, and indeed it would not be easy to do so, that well-defined domestic party of our country-folks who have just turned into the superb Galerie d'Orléans. Father, mother, and daughters—how easy to guess their thoughts, and almost their words! The portly father declares that it would make a capital Exchange: he has not yet seen La Bourse. He looks up to its noble height—then steps forward a pace or two, and measures with his eye the space on all sides—then stops, and perhaps says to the stately lady on his arm, (whose eyes meanwhile are wandering amidst shawls, gloves, Cologne bottles, and Sèvres china, first on one side and then on the other,)—"This is not badly built; it is light and lofty—and the width is very considerable for so slight-looking a roof; but what is it compared to Waterloo-bridge!"

Two pretty girls, with bright cheeks, dove-like eyes, and "tresses like the morn," falling in un-numbered ringlets, so as almost to hide their curious yet timid glances, precede the parent pair; but, with pretty well-taught caution, pause when they pause, and step on when they step on. But they can hardly look at anything; for do they not know, though their downcast eyes can hardly be said to see it, that those youths with coal-black hair, favoris and imperials, are spying at them with their lorgnettes?

Here too, as at the Tuileries, are little pavilions to supply the insatiable thirst for politics; and here, too, we could distinguish the melancholy champion of the elder branch of the Bourbons, who is at least sure to find the consolation of his faithful "Quotidienne," and the sympathy of "La France." The sour republican stalks up, as usual, to seize upon the "Réformateur;" while the comfortable doctrinaire comes forth from the Café Véry, ruminating on the "Journal des Débats," and the chances of his bargains at Tortoni's or La Bourse.

It was in a walk taken round three sides of the square that we marked the figures I have mentioned, and many more too numerous to record, on a day that we had fixed upon to gratify our curiosity by dining—not at Véry's, or any other far-famed artist's, but tout bonnement at a restaurant of quarante sous par tête. Having made our tour, we mounted au second at numéro—I forget what, but it was where we had been especially recommended to make this coup d'essai. The scene we entered upon, as we followed a long string of persons who preceded us, was as amusing as it was new to us all.

I will not say that I should like to dine three days in the week at the Palais Royal for quarante sous par tête; but I will say, that I should have been very sorry not to have done it once, and moreover, that I heartily hope I may do it again.

The dinner was extremely good, and as varied as our fancy chose to make it, each person having privilege to select three or four plats from a carte that it would take a day to read deliberately. But the dinner was certainly to us the least important part of the business. The novelty of the spectacle, the number of strange-looking people, and the perfect amenity and good-breeding which seemed to reign among them all, made us look about us with a degree of interest and curiosity that almost caused the whole party to forget the ostensible cause of their visit.

There were many English, chiefly gentlemen, and several Germans with their wives and daughters; but the majority of the company was French; and from sundry little circumstances respecting taking the places reserved for them, and different words of intelligence between themselves and the waiters, it was evident that many among them were not chance visitors, but in the daily habit of dining there. What a singular mode of existence is this, and how utterly inconceivable to English feelings!... Yet habit, and perhaps prejudice, apart, it is not difficult to perceive that it has its advantages. In the first place, there is no management in the world, not even that of Mrs. Primrose herself, which could enable a man to dine at home, for the sum of two francs, with the same degree of luxury as to what he eats, that he does at one of these restaurans. Five hundred persons are calculated upon as the daily average of company expected; and forty pounds of ready money in Paris, with the skilful aid of French cooks, will furnish forth a dinner for this number, and leave some profit besides. Add to which, the sale of wine is, I believe, considerable. Some part of the receipts, however, must be withdrawn as interest upon the capital employed. The quantity of plate is very abundant, not only in the apparently unlimited supply of forks and spoons, but in furnishing the multitude of grim-looking silver bowls in which the potage is served.

On the whole, however, I can better understand the possibility of five hundred dinners being furnished daily for two francs each, by one of these innumerable establishments, than I can the marvel of five hundred people being daily found by each of these to eat them. Hundreds of these houses exist in Paris, and all of them are constantly furnished with guests. But this manner of living, so unnatural to us, seems not only natural, but needful to them. They do it all so well—so pleasantly! Imagine for a moment the sort of tone and style such a dining-room would take in London. I do not mean, if limited to the same price, but set it greatly beyond the proportion: let us imagine an establishment where males and females should dine at five shillings a-head—what din, what unsocial, yet vehement clattering, would inevitably ensue!—not to mention the utter improbability that such a place, really and bonâ fide open to the public, should continue a reputable resort for ladies for a week after its doors were open.

But here, everything was as perfectly respectable and well arranged as if each little table had been placed with its separate party in a private room at Mivart's. It is but fair, therefore, that while we hug ourselves, as we are all apt to do, on the refinement which renders the exclusive privacy of our own dining-rooms necessary to our feelings of comfort, we should allow that equal refinement, though of another kind, must exist among those who, when thrown thus promiscuously together, still retain and manifest towards each other the same deference and good-breeding which we require of those whom we admit to our private circle.

At this restaurant, as everywhere else in Paris, we found it easy enough to class our gens. I feel quite sure that we had around us many of the employés du gouvernement actuel—several anciens militaires of Napoleon's—some specimens of the race distinguished by Louis Dix-huit and Charles Dix—and even, if I do not greatly mistake, a few relics of the Convention, and of the unfortunate monarch who was its victim.

But during this hour of rest and enjoyment all differences seem forgotten; and however discordant may be their feelings, two Frenchmen cannot be seated near each other at table, without exchanging numberless civilities, and at last entering into conversation, so well sustained and so animated, that instead of taking them for strangers who had never met before, we, in our stately shyness, would be ready to pronounce that they must be familiar friends.

Whether it be this causant, social temper which makes them prefer thus living in public, or that thus living in public makes them social, I cannot determine to my own satisfaction; but the one is not more remarkable and more totally unlike our own manners than the other, and I really think that no one who has not dined thus in Paris can have any idea how very wide, in some directions, the line of demarcation is between the two countries.

I have on former occasions dined with a party at places of much higher price, where the object was to observe what a very good dinner a very good cook could produce in Paris. But this experiment offered nothing to our observation at all approaching in interest and nationality to the dinner of quarante sous.

In the first place, you are much more likely to meet English than French society at these costly repasts; and in the second, if you do encounter at them a genuine native gourmet of la Grande Nation, he will, upon this occasion, be only doing like ourselves,—that is to say, giving himself un repas exquis, instead of regaling himself at home with his family—

"Sur un lièvre flanqué de deux poulets étiques."

But at the humble restaurant of two francs, you have again a new page of Paris existence to study,—and one which, while it will probably increase your English relish for your English home, will show you no unprofitable picture of the amiable social qualities of France. I think that if we could find a people composed in equal proportions of the two natures, they would be as near to social perfection as it is possible to imagine.

The French are almost too amiable to every one they chance to sit near. The lively smile, the kind empressement, the ready causerie, would be more flattering did we not know that it was all equally at the service of the whole world. Whereas we are more than equally wrong in the other extreme;

having the air of suspecting that every human being who happens to be thrown into contact with us, before we know his birth, parentage, and education, is something very dangerous, and to be guarded against with all possible care and precaution. Query—Do not the Germans furnish something very like this juste milieu?

Having concluded our unexpensive repast with the prescribed tasse de café noir, we again sallied forth to take the tour of the Palais Royal, in order to occupy the time till the opening of the Théâtre du Vaudeville, with which, as we were so very close to it, we determined to finish the evening.

We returned, as we came, through the noble Galerie d'Orléans, which was now crowded with the assembled loungers of all the numerous restaurans. It is a gay and animated scene at any time of the day; but at this particular hour, just before the theatres open, and just after the gay people have all refreshed their animal spirits, Paris itself seems typified by the aspect of the lively, laughing, idle throng assembled there.

One reason, I believe, why Paris is so much more amusing to a looker-on than London, is, that it contains so many more people, in proportion to its population, who have nothing in the world to do but to divert themselves and others. There are so many more idle men here, who are contented to live on incomes that with us would be considered as hardly sufficient to supply a lodging; small rentiers, who prefer being masters of their own time and amusing themselves with a little, to working very hard and being very much ennuyés with a great deal of money. I am not quite sure that this plan answers well when youth is past—at least for the individuals themselves: it is probable, I think, that as the strength, and health, and spirits fade away, something of quieter and more substantial comfort must often be wished for, when perhaps it is too late to obtain it; but for others—for all those who form the circle round which the idle man of pleasure skims thus lightly, he is a never-failing resource. What would become of all the parties for amusement which take place morning, noon, and night in Paris, if this race were extinct? Whether they are married or single, they are equally eligible, equally necessary, equally welcome wherever pleasure makes the business of the hour. With us, it is only a small and highly-privileged class who can permit themselves to go wherever and whenever pleasure beckons; but in France, no lady arranging a fête, let it be of what kind it may, has need to think twice and thrice before she can answer the important but tormenting question of—"But what men can we get?"

The Vaudeville was very full, but we contrived to get a good box au second, from whence we saw, greatly to our delectation and amusement, three pretty little pieces,—"Les Gants Jaunes," "Le Premier Amour," and "Elle est Folle;" which last was of the larmoyante school, and much less to my taste than the lively nonsense of the two former; yet it was admirably well played too. But I always go to a vaudeville with the intention of laughing; and if this purpose fail, I am disappointed.

Literary Conversation—Modern Novelists—Vicomte d'Arlincourt—His Portrait—Châteaubriand—Bernardin de Saint Pierre—Shakspeare—Sir Walter Scott—French Familiarity with English Authors—Miss Mitford—Miss Landon—Parisian Passion for Novelty—Extent of General Information.

We were last night at a small party where there was neither dancing, music, cards, nor—(wonderful to say!) politics to amuse or occupy us: nevertheless, it was one of the most agreeable soirées at which I have been present in Paris. The conversation was completely on literary subjects, but totally without the pretension of a literary society. In fact, it was purely the effect of accident; and it was just as likely that we might have passed the evening in talking of pictures, or music, or rocks and rivers, as of books. But Fate decreed that so it should be; and the consequence was, that we had the pleasure of hearing three Frenchmen and two Frenchwomen talk for three hours of the literature of their country. I do not mean to assert that no other person spoke—but the frais de la conversation were certainly furnished by the five natives.

One of the gentlemen, and that too the oldest man in company, was more tolerant towards the present race of French novel-writers than any person of his age and class that I have yet conversed with; but nevertheless, his approval went no farther than to declare that he thought the present mode of following human nature with a microscope into all the recesses to which passion, and even vice, could lead it, was calculated to make a better novelist than the fashion which preceded it, of looking at all things through a magnifying medium, and of straining and striving, in consequence, to make that appear great, which was by its nature essentially the reverse.

The Vicomte d'Arlincourt was the author he named to establish the truth of his proposition: he would not admit him to be an exaggeration of the school which has passed away, but only the perfection of it.

"I remember," said he, "to have seen at the Louvre, many years ago, a full-length portrait of this gentleman, which I thought at the time was as perfect a symbol of what is called in France le style romantique, as it was well possible to conceive. He was standing erect on the rocky point of a precipice, with eye inspired, and tablets in his hand: a foaming torrent rolled its tortured waters at his feet, whilst he, calm and sublime, looked not 'comme une jeune beauté qu'on arrache au sommeil,' but very like a young incroyable snatched from a fashionable salon to meditate upon the wild majesty of nature, with all the inspiring adjuncts of tempest, wildness, and solitude. He appeared dressed in an elegant black coat and waistcoat, black silk stockings, and dancing pumps. It would be lost labour," he continued, "should I attempt to give you a more just idea of his style of writing than the composition of this portrait conveys. It is in vain that M. le Vicomte places himself amidst rocks and cataracts—he is still M. le Vicomte; and his silk stockings and dancing pumps will remain visible, spite of all the froth and foam he labours to raise around him."

"It was not D'Arlincourt, however," said M. de C—, "who has either the honour or dishonour of having invented this style romantique—but a much greater man: it was Châteaubriand who first broke through all that was left of classic restraint, and permitted his imagination to run wild among everything in heaven and earth."

"You cannot, however, accuse him of running this wild race with his imagination en habit bourgeois," said the third gentleman: "his style is extravagant, but never ludicrous; Châteaubriand really has, what D'Arlincourt affected to have, a poetical and abounding fancy, and a fecundity of imagery which has often betrayed him into bad taste from its very richness; but there is nothing strained, forced, and unnatural in his eloquence,—for eloquence it is, though a soberer imagination and a severer judgment might have kept it within more reasonable bounds. After all that can be said against his taste, Châteaubriand is a great man, and his name will live among the literati of France; but God forbid that any true prophet should predict the same of his imitators!"

"And God forbid that any true prophet should predict the same of the school that has succeeded them!" said Madame V— a delightful old woman, who wears her own grey hair, and does not waltz. "I have sometimes laughed and sometimes yawned over the productions of the école D'Arlincourt," she added; "but I invariably turn with disgust and indignation from those of the domestic style which has succeeded to it."

"Invariably?" ... said the old gentleman interrogatively.

"Yes, invariably; because, if I see any symptom of talent, I lament it, and feel alarmed for the possible mischief which may ensue. I can never wish to see high mental power, which is the last and best gift of Heaven, perverted so shamelessly."

"Come, come, dear lady," replied the advocate of what Goethe impressively calls 'la littérature du désespoir,' you must not overthrow the whole fabric because some portion of it is faulty. The object of our tale-writers at present is, beyond all doubt, to paint men as they are: if they succeed, their labours cannot fail of being interesting—and I should think they might be very useful too."

"Fadaise que tout cela!" exclaimed the old lady eagerly. "Before men can paint human nature profitably, they must see it as it really is, my good friend—and not as it appears to these misérables in their baraques and greniers. We have nothing to do with such scenes as they paint; and they have nothing to do (God help them!) with literary labours. Have you got Bernardin de Saint Pierre, ma chère?" said she, addressing the lady of the house. The little volume was immediately handed to her from a chiffonnière that stood behind us. "Now this," she continued, having found the passage she sought,—"this is what I conceive to be the legitimate object of literature;" and she read aloud the following passage:—

"Les lettres sont un secours du Ciel. Ce sont des rayons de cette sagesse qui gouverne l'univers, que l'homme, inspiré par un art céleste, a appris à fixer sur la terre.... Elles calment les passions; elles répriment les vices; elles excitent les vertus par les exemples augustes des gens de bien qu'elles célèbrent, et dont elles nous présentent les images toujours honorées."

"Eh bien! a-t-il raison, ce Bernardin?" said she, laying aside her spectacles and looking round upon us. Every one admired the passage. "Is this the use your French romancers make of letters?" she continued, looking triumphantly at their advocate.

"Not exactly," he replied, laughing,—"or at least not always: but I could show you passages in Michel Raymond...."

"Bah!" exclaimed the old lady, interrupting him; "I will have nothing to do with his passages. I think it is Chamfort who says, that "un sot qui a un moment d'esprit, étonne et scandalise comme des chevaux de fiacre au galop." I don't like such unexpected jerks of sublimity—they startle more than they please me."

The conversation then rambled on to Shakspeare, and to the mischief—such was the word—to the mischief his example, and the passionate admiration expressed for his writings, had done to the classic purity of French literature. This phrase, however, was not only cavilled at, but in true French style was laughed to death by the rest of the party. The word "classic" was declared too rococo for use, and Shakspeare loudly proclaimed to be only defective as a model because too mighty to imitate.

I have, however, some faint misgivings as to the perfect sincerity of this verdict,—and this chiefly because there was but one Frenchman present who affected to know anything about him excepting through the medium of translation. Now, notwithstanding that the talent shown by M. Ducis in the translation of some passages is very considerable, we all know that Shakspeare may be very nearly as fairly judged from the Italian "Otello" as the "French Hamlet." The party were however quite sincere, I am sure, in the feeling they expressed of reverence for the unequalled bard, founded upon the rank he held in the estimation of his countrymen; this being, as the clear-headed old lady observed, the only sure criterion, for foreigners, of the station which he ought to hold among the poets of the earth.

Then followed some keen enough observations—applicable to any one but Shakspeare—of the danger there might be, that in mixing tragedy and comedy together, farce might unfortunately be the result; or, if the "fusion," as it has been called, of tragedy and comedy into one were very skilfully performed, the sublime and prodigious monster called melodrame might be hoped for, as the happiest product that could be expected.

It being thus civilly settled that our Shakspeare might be as wild as he chose, but that it would be advisable for other people to take care how they attempted to follow him, the party next fell into a review, more individual and particular than I was well able to follow, or than I can now repeat, of many writers of verses and of novels that, I was fain to confess, I had never heard of before. One or two of the novel-writers were declared to be very successful imitators of the style and manner of Sir Walter Scott: and when this was stated, I was, to say the truth, by no means sorry to plead total and entire ignorance of their name and productions; for, having, as I fear, manifested a little national warmth on the subject of Shakspeare, I should have been sorry to start off in another tirade concerning Sir Walter Scott, which I might have found it difficult to avoid, had I known exactly what it was which they ventured to compare to him.

I do not quite understand how it happens that the Parisians are so much better acquainted with the generality of our light literature, than we are with the generality of theirs. This is the more unaccountable, from the fact so universally known, that for one French person who reads English, there are at least ten English who read French. It is, however, impossible to deny that such is the fact. I am sure I have heard the names of two or three dozen authors, since I have been here, of whose existence, or of that of their works, neither I, nor any of my literary friends, I believe, have had the least knowledge; and yet we have considered ourselves quite au courant du jour in such matters, having never missed any opportunity of reading every French book that came in our way, and moreover of sedulously consulting the Foreign Quarterly. In canvassing this difference between us, one of the party suggested that it might perhaps arise from the fact that no work which was popular in England ever escaped being reprinted on the Continent,—that is to say, either at Paris or Brussels. Though this is done solely as a sort of piratical speculation, for the purpose of inducing all the travelling English to purchase new books for four francs here, instead of giving thirty shillings for them at home, it is nevertheless a natural consequence of this manoeuvre, that the names of English books are familiarly known here even before they have been translated.

Many of our lady authors have the honour apparently of being almost as well known at Paris as at home. I had the pleasure of hearing Miss Mitford spoken of with enthusiasm; and one lady told me, that, judging her from her works, she would rather become acquainted with her than with any author living.

Miss Landon is also well known and much admired. Madame Tastu told me she had translated many of her compositions, and thought very highly of them. In short, English literature and English literati are at present very hospitably treated in France.

I was last night asked innumerable questions about many books, and many people, whose renommée I was surprised to find had crossed the Channel; and having communicated pretty nearly all the information I possessed upon the subject, I began to question in my turn, and heard abundance of anecdotes and criticisms, many of them given with all the sparkling keenness of French satire.

Many of les petits ridicules that we are accustomed to hear quizzed at home seem to exist in the same manner, and spite of the same light chastisement, here. The manner, for example, of making a very little wit and wisdom go a great way, by means of short lines and long stops, does not appear to be in any degree peculiar to our island. As a specimen of this, a quotation from a new romance by Madame Girardin (ci-devant Mademoiselle Delphine Gay) was shown me in a newspaper. I will copy it for you as it was printed, and I think you will allow that our neighbours at least equal us in this ingenious department of literary composition.

"Pensez-vous Qu'Arthur voulût revoir Mademoiselle de Sommery?"

"NON: Au lieu de l'aimer, Il la détestait!"

"OUI, Il la détestait!"

I think our passion for novelty is pretty strong; but if the information which I received last night respecting the same imperious besoin here was not exaggerated by the playful spirit of the party who were amusing themselves by describing its influence, we are patient and tame in our endurance of old "by-gones," in comparison to the Parisians. They have, indeed, a saying which in few words paints this craving for novelty, as strongly as I could do, did I torment my memory to repeat to you every word said by my lively friends last night:

"Il nous faut du nouveau, n'en fût-il plus au monde."

It is delightful to us to get hold of a new book or a new song—a new preacher or a new fiddler: it is delightful to us, but to the Parisians it is indispensable. To meet in society and have nothing new for the causette, would be worse than remaining at home.

"This fond desire, this longing after" fresh materials for the tongue to work upon, is at least as old as the days of Molière. It was this which made Madelon address herself with such energy to Mascarille, assuring him that she should be "obligée de la dernière obligation" if he would but report to her daily "les choses qu'il faut savoir de nécessité, et qui sont de l'essence d'un bel esprit;" for, as she truly observes, "C'est là ce qui vous fait valoir dans les compagnies, et si l'on ignore ces choses, je ne donnerais pas un clou de tout l'esprit qu'on peut avoir;"—while her cousin Cathos gives her testimony to the same truth by this impressive declaration: "Pour moi, j'aurais toutes les hontes du monde s'il fallait qu'on vînt à me demander si j'aurais vu quelque chose de nouveau que je n'aurais pas vu."

I know not how it is that people who appear to pass so few hours of every day out of sight contrive to know so well everything that has been written and everything that has been done in all parts of the world. No one ever appears ignorant on any subject. Is this tact? Or is it knowledge,—real, genuine, substantial information respecting all things? I suspect that it is not wholly either the one or the other; and that many circumstances contribute both to the general diffusion of information, as well as to the rapid manner of receiving and the brilliant style of displaying it.

This at least is certain, that whatever they do know is made the very most of; and though some may suspect that so great display of general information indicates rather extent than depth of knowledge, none, I think, can refuse to acknowledge that the manner in which a Frenchman communicates what he has acquired is particularly amiable, graceful, and unpedantic.

Trial by Jury—Power of the Jury in France—Comparative Insignificance of that Vested in the Judge—Virtual Abolition of Capital Punishments—Flemish Anecdote.

Do not be terrified, my dear friend, and fancy that I am going to exchange my idle, ambling pace, and my babil de femme, to join the march of intellect, and indite wisdom. I have no such ambition in my thoughts; and yet I must retail to you part of a conversation with which I have just been favoured by an extremely intelligent friend, on the very manly subject of.... Not political economy;—be tranquil on that point; the same drowsy dread falls upon me when those two portentous words sound in my ears with which they seem to have inspired Coleridge;—not political economy, but trial by jury.

M. V—, the gentleman in question, gave me credit, I believe, for considerably more savoir than I really possess, as to the actual and precise manner in which this important constitutional right works in England. My ignorance, however, though it prevented my giving much information, did not prevent my receiving it; and I repeat our conversation for the purpose of telling you in what a very singular manner, according to his account, it appears to work in France.

I must, however, premise that my friend is a stanch Henri-Quintist; which, though I am sure that in his case it would not produce any exaggeration in the statement of facts, may nevertheless be fairly presumed to influence his feelings, and consequently his manner of stating them.

The circumstance which gave rise to this grave discussion was a recent judgment passed here upon a very atrocious case of murder. I am not particularly fond of hanging; nevertheless, I was startled at hearing that this savage and most ferocious slayer of men was condemned to imprisonment and travail forcé, instead of death.

"It is very rarely that any one now suffers the extreme penalty of the law in this country," said M. V—, in reply to my remark on this sentence.

"Is it since your last revolution," said I, "that the punishment of death has been commuted for that of imprisonment and labour?"

"No such commutation has taken place as an act of the legislature," he replied: "it rests solely with the jury whether a murderer be guillotined, or only imprisoned."

I fancied that I misunderstood him, and repeated his words,—"With the jury?"

"Oui, madame—absolument."

This statement appeared to me so singular, that I still supposed I must be blundering, and that the words le jury in France did not mean the same thing as the word jury in England.

In this, as it subsequently appeared, I was not much mistaken. Notwithstanding, my informer, who was not only a very intelligent person, but a lawyer to boot, continued to assure me that trial by jury was exactly the same in both countries as to principle, though not as to effect.

"But," said I, "our juries have nothing to do with the sentence passed on the criminal: their business is to examine into the evidence brought forward by the witnesses to prove the guilt of the prisoner, and according to the impression which this leaves on their minds, they pronounce him 'guilty,' or 'not guilty;' and here their duty ends."

"Yes, yes—I understand that perfectly," replied M. V—; "and it is precisely the same thing with us;—only, it is not in the nature of a Frenchman to pronounce a mere dry, short, unspeculating verdict of 'guilty,' or 'not guilty,' without exercising the powers of his intellect upon the shades of culpability which attach to the acts of each delinquent."

This impossibility of giving a verdict without exercising the power of intellect reminded me of an assize story on record in Cornwall, respecting the sentence pronounced by a jury upon a case in which it was very satisfactorily proved that a man had murdered his wife, but where it also appeared from the evidence that the unhappy woman had not conducted herself remarkably well. The jury retired to consult, and upon re-entering their box the foreman addressed the court in these words: "Guilty—but sarved her right, my lord." It was in vain that the learned judge desired them to amend their verdict, as containing matter wholly irrelevant to the duty they had to perform; the intellect of the jurymen was, upon this occasion, in a state of too great activity to permit their returning any other answer than the identical "Guilty—but sarved her right." I could hardly restrain a smile as this anecdote recurred to me; but my friend was too much in earnest in his explanation for me to interrupt him by an ill-timed jest, and he continued—

"This frame of mind, which is certainly essentially French, is one cause, and perhaps the most inveterate one, which makes it impossible that the trial by jury should ever become the same safe and simple process with us that it is in England."

"And in what manner does this activity of intellect interfere to impede the course of justice?" said I.

"Thus," he replied. "Let us suppose the facts of the case proved to the entire satisfaction of the jury: they make up their minds among themselves to pronounce a verdict of 'guilty;' but their business is by no means finished,—they have still to decide how this verdict shall be delivered to the judge—whether with or without the declaration that there are circumstances calculated to extenuate the crime."

"Oh yes! I understand you now," I replied. "You mean, that when there are extenuating circumstances, the jury assume the privilege of recommending the criminal to mercy. Our juries do this likewise."

"But not with the same authority," said he, smiling. "With us, the fate of the culprit is wholly in the power of the jury; for not only do they decide upon the question of guilty or not guilty, but, by the use of this word extenuating, they can remit by their sole will and pleasure the capital part of the punishment, let the crime be of what nature it may. No judge in this country dare sentence a criminal to capital punishment where the verdict against him has been qualified by this extenuating clause."

"It should seem then," said I, "that the duty of judge, which is attended with such awful responsibilities with us, is here little more than the performance of an official ceremony?"

"It is very nearly such, I assure you."

"And your jurymen, according to a phrase of contempt common among us, are in fact judge and jury both?"

"Beyond all contradiction they are so," he replied: "and I conceive that criminal justice is at this time more loosely administered in France than in any other civilised country in the world. In fact, our artisans have become, since the revolution of 1830, not only judge and jury, but legislators also. Different crimes have different punishments assigned to them by our penal code; but it rarely, or I might say never, occurs in our days that the punishment inflicted has any reference to that which is assigned by the law. That guilt may vary even when the deed done does not, is certain; and it is just and righteous therefore that a judge, learned in the law of the land, and chosen by high authority from among his fellows as a man of wisdom and integrity,—it is quite just and righteous that such a one should have the power—and a tremendous power it is—of modifying the extent of the penalty according to his view of the individual case. The charge too of an English judge is considered to be of immense importance to the result of every trial. All this is as it should be; but we have departed most widely from the model we have professed to follow. With us the judge has no such power—at least not practically: with us a set of chance-met artisans, ignorant alike of the law of the land and of the philosophy of punishment, have this tremendous power vested in them. It matters not how clearly the crime has been proved, and still less what penalty the law has adjudged to it; the punishment inflicted is whatever it may please the jury to decide, and none other."

"And what is the effect which this strangely assumed power has produced on your administration of justice?" said I.

"The virtual abolition of capital punishment," was the reply. "When a jury," continued M. V—, "delivers a verdict to the judge of 'Guilty, but with extenuating circumstances,' the judge dare not condemn the criminal to death, though the law of the land assign that punishment to his offence, and though his own mind is convinced, by all which has come out upon the trial, that instead of extenuating circumstances, the commission of the crime has been attended with every possible aggravation of atrocity. Such is the practical effect of the revolution of 1830 on the administration of criminal justice."

"Does public opinion sanction this strange abuse of the functions of jurymen?" said I.

"Public opinion cannot sanction it," he replied, "any more than it could sanction the committal of the crime itself. The one act is, in fact, as lawless as the other; but the populace have conceived the idea that capital punishment is an undue exercise of power, and therefore our rulers fear to exercise it."

This is a strange statement, is it not? The gentleman who made it is, I am sure, too much a man of honour and integrity to falsify facts; but it may perhaps be necessary to allow something for the colouring of party feeling. Whatever the present government does, or permits to be done, contrary to the system established during the period of the restoration, is naturally offensive to the feelings of the legitimatists, and repugnant to their judgments; yet, in this case, the relaxation of necessary power must so inevitably lead to evil, that we must, I think, expect to see the reins gathered up, and the command resumed by the proper functionaries, as soon as the new government feels itself seated with sufficient firmness to permit the needful exertion of strength to be put forth with safety.

It is certain that M. V— supported his statement by reciting so many strong cases in which the most fearful crimes, substantiated by the most unbroken chain of evidence, have been reported by the jury to the judge as having "extenuating circumstances" attached to them, that it is impossible, while things remain as they are, not to feel that such a mode of administering justice must make the habit of perjury as familiar to their jurymen as that of taking their oaths.

This conversation brought to my recollection some strange stories which I had heard in Belgium apropos of the trial by jury there. If those stories were correct, they are about as far from comprehending, or at least from acting upon, our noble, equitable, and well-tried institution there, as they appear to be here—but from causes apparently exactly the reverse. There, I am told, it often happens that the jury can neither read nor write; and that when they are placed in their box, they are, as might be expected, quite ignorant of the nature of the duty they are to perform, and often so greatly embarrassed by it, that they are ready and willing—nay, thankful—to pronounce as their verdict whatever is dictated to them.

I heard an anecdote of one man—and a thorough honest Fleming he was—who having been duly empannelled, entered the jury-box, and having listened attentively to a trial that was before the court, declared, when called upon for his verdict, that he had not understood a single word from the beginning to the end of it. The court endeavoured to explain the leading points of the question; but still the worthy burgher persisted in declaring that the business was not in his line, and that he could not comprehend it sufficiently to give any opinion at all. The attempt at explanation was repeated, but in vain; and at length the conscientious Fleming paid the fine demanded for the non-performance of the duty, and was permitted to retire.

In France, on the contrary, it appears that human intellect has gone on so fast and so far, that no dozen of men can be found simple-minded enough to say 'yes' or 'no' to a question asked, without insisting that they must legislate upon it.

In this case, at least, England shows a beautiful specimen of the juste milieu.

English Pastry Cook's—French Horror of English Pastry—Unfortunate Experiment Upon a Muffin—The Citizen King.

We have been on a regular shopping tour this morning; which was finished by our going into an English pastry-cook's to eat buns. While thus engaged, we amused ourselves by watching the proceedings of a French party who entered also for the purpose of making a morning goûter upon cakes.

They had all of them more or less the air of having fallen upon a terra incognita, showing many indications of surprise at sight of the ultra-marine compositions which appeared before them;—but there was a young man of the party who, it was evident, had made up his mind to quiz without measure all the foreign dainties that the shop afforded, evidently considering their introduction as a very unjustifiable interference with the native manufacture.

"Est-il possible!" said he, with an air of grave and almost indignant astonishment, as he watched a lady of his party preparing to eat an English bun,—"Est-il possible that you can prefer these strange-looking comestibles à la pâtisserie française?"

"Mais goûtez-en," said the lady, presenting a specimen of the same kind as that she was herself eating: "ils sont excellens."

"No, no! it is enough to look at them!" said her cavalier, almost shuddering. "There is no lightness, no elegance, no grace in any single gâteau here."

"Mais goûtez quelque chose," reiterated the lady.

"Vous le voulez absolument!" exclaimed the young man; "quelle tyrannie! ... and what a proof of obedience I am about to give you!... Voyons donc!" he continued, approaching a plate on which were piled some truly English muffins—which, as you know, are of a somewhat mysterious manufacture, and about as palatable if eaten untoasted as a slice from a leathern glove. To this gâteau, as he supposed it to be, the unfortunate connoisseur in pâtisserie approached, exclaiming with rather a theatrical air, "Voilà donc ce que je vais faire pour vos beaux yeux!"

As he spoke, he took up one of the pale, tough things, and, to our extreme amusement, attempted to eat it. Any one might be excused for making a few grimaces on such an occasion,—and a Frenchman's privilege in this line is well known: but this hardy experimentalist outdid this privilege;—he was in a perfect agony, and his spittings and reproachings were so vehement, that friends, strangers, boutiquier, and all, even down to a little befloured urchin who entered at the moment with a tray of patties, burst into uncontrollable laughter, which the unfortunate, to do him justice, bore with extreme good humour, only making his fair countrywoman promise that she would never insist upon his eating English confectionary again.

Had this scene continued a minute longer, I should have missed seeing what I should have been sorry not to have seen, for I certainly could not have left the pastry-cook's shop while the young Frenchman's sufferings lasted. Happily, however, we reached the Boulevard des Italiens in time to see King Louis-Philippe, en simple bourgeois, passing on foot just before Les Bains Chinois, but on the opposite side of the way.

Excepting a small tri-coloured cockade in his hat, he had nothing whatever in his dress to distinguish him from any other gentleman. He is a well-looking, portly, middle-aged man, with something of dignity in his step which, notwithstanding the unpretending citizen-like style of his promenade, would have drawn attention, and betrayed him as somebody out of the common way, even without the plain-speaking cocarde tricolore. There were two gentlemen a few paces behind him, as he passed us, who, I think, stepped up nearer to him afterwards; but there were no other individuals near who could have been in attendance upon him. I observed that he was recognised by many, and some few hats were taken off, particularly by two or three Englishmen who met him; but his appearance excited little emotion. I was amused, however, at the nonchalant air with which a young man at some distance, in full Robespierrian costume, used his lorgnon to peruse the person of the monarch as long as he remained in sight.

The last king I saw in the streets of Paris was Charles the Tenth returning from a visit to one of his suburban palaces, escorted and accompanied in kingly state and style. The contrast in the men and in the mode was striking, and calculated to awaken lively recollections of all the events which had occurred to both of them since the last time that I turned my head to look after a sovereign of France.

My fancy flew to Prague, and to the three generations of French monarchs stationed there almost as peaceably as if they had taken up their quarters at St. Denis!

How like a series of conjurer's tricks is their history! Think of this Charles the Tenth in the flower of his youth and comeliness—the gallant, gay, and dissolute Comte d'Artois; recall the noble range of windows belonging to his apartments at Versailles, and imagine him there radiant in youth and joy— the thoughtless, thriftless cadet of his royal race—the brother and the guest of the good king who appeared to reign over a willing people, by every human right, as well as right divine! Louis Seize was king of France; but the gay Comte d'Artois reigned sovereign of all the pleasures of Versailles. What joyous fêtes! ... what brilliant jubilees!... Meanwhile

"Malignant Fate sat by and smiled."

Had he then been told that he should live to be crowned king of France, and live thus many years afterwards, would he not have thought that a most brilliant destiny was predicted to him?

Few men, perhaps, have suffered so much from the ceaseless changes of human events as Charles the Tenth of France. First, in the person of his eldest brother, dethroned and foully murdered; then in his own exile, and that of another royal brother; and again, when Fortune seemed to smile upon his race, and the crown of France was not only placed upon that brother's head, but appeared fixed in assured succession on his own princely sons, one of those sons was murdered: and lastly, having reached the throne himself, and seen this lost son reviving in his hopeful offspring, comes another stroke of Fate, unexpected, unprepared for, overwhelming, which hurls him from his throne, and drives him and his royal race once more to exile and to civil death.... Has he seen the last of the political earthquakes which have so shaken his existence? or has his restless star to rise again? Those who wish most kindly to him cannot wish for this.

But when I turned my thoughts from the dethroned and banished king to him who stepped on in unguarded but fearless security before me, and thought too on the vagaries of his destiny, I really felt as if this earth and all the people on it were little better than so many children's toys, changing their style and title to serve the sport of an hour.

It seemed to me at that moment as if all men were classed in their due order only to be thrown into greater confusion—knocked down but to be set up again, and so eternally dashed from side to side, so powerless in themselves, so wholly governed by accidents, that I shrunk, humbled, from the contemplation of human helplessness, and turned from gazing on a monarch to meditate on the insignificance of man. How vain are all the efforts he can make to shape the course of his own existence! There is, in truth, nothing but trusting to surer wisdom, and to surer power, which can enable any of us, from the highest to the lowest, to pass on with tranquil nerves through a world subject to such terrible convulsions.

LETTER LI.

Parisian Women—Rousseau's Failure in Attempting to Describe Them—Their Great Influence in Society—Their Grace in Conversation—Difficulty of Growing Old—Do the Ladies of France or Those of England manage it best?

There is perhaps no subject connected with Paris which might give occasion to such curious and inexhaustible observation as the character, position, and influence of its women. But the theme, though copious and full of interest, is not without its difficulties; and it is no small proof of this, that Rousseau, who rarely touched on any subject without persuading his reader that he was fully master of it, has nevertheless almost wholly failed on this. In one of the letters of "La Nouvelle Héloïse," he sketches the characters of a few very commonplace ladies, whom he abuses unmercifully for their bad taste in dress, and concludes his abortive attempt at making us acquainted with the ladies of Paris by acknowledging that they have some goodness of heart.

This is but a meagre description of this powerful portion of the human race, and I can hardly imagine a volume that I should read with greater pleasure than one which should fully supply all its deficiencies. Do not imagine, however, that I mean to undertake the task. I am even less capable of it than the sublime misanthrope himself; for though I am of opinion that it should be an unimpassioned spectator, and not a lover, who should attempt to paint all the delicate little atoms of exquisite mosaic-work which constitute une Parisienne, I think it should not be a woman.

All I can do for you on this subject is to recount the observations I have been myself led to make in the passing glances I have now the opportunity of giving them, supported by what I have chanced to hear from better authority than my own: but I am aware that I can do little more than excite your wish to become better acquainted with them than it is in my power to make you.

It is impossible to be admitted into French society without immediately perceiving that the women play a very distinguished part in it. So, assuredly, do the women of England in their own: yet I cannot but think that, setting aside all cases of individual exception, the women of France have more power and more important influence than the women of England.

I am aware that this is a very bold proposition, and that you may feel inclined to call me to account for it. But be I right or wrong in this judgment, it is at least sincere, and herein lies its chief value; for I am by no means sure that I shall be able to explain very satisfactorily the grounds on which it is formed.

France has been called "the paradise of women;" and if consideration and deference be sufficient to constitute a paradise, I think it may be called so justly. I will not, however, allow that Frenchmen make better husbands than Englishmen; but I suspect they make politer husbands—

"Je ne sais pas, pour moi, si chacun me ressemble,
Mais j'entends là-dessous un million de mots:"

and, all pleasantry apart, I am of opinion that this more observant tone or style, or whatever it may be termed, is very far from superficial—at least in its effects. I should be greatly surprised to hear from good authority that a French gentleman had ever been heard to speak rudely to his wife.

Rousseau says, when he means to be what he himself calls "souverainement impertinent," that "il est convenu qu'un homme ne refusera rien à aucune femme, fût-ce même la sienne." But it is not only in refusing her nothing that a French husband shows the superiority which I attribute to him; I know many English husbands who are equally indulgent; but, if I mistake not, the general consideration enjoyed by Frenchwomen has its origin not in the conjugal indulgence they enjoy, but in the domestic respect universally shown them. What foundation there may be for the idea which prevails amongst us, that there is less strictness of morality among married women in France than in England, I will not attempt to decide; but, judging from the testimonies of respect shown them by fathers, husbands, brothers, and sons, I cannot but believe that, spite of travellers' tales, innuendoes, and all the authority of les contes moraux to boot, there must be much of genuine virtue where there is so much genuine esteem.

In a recent work on France, to which I have before alluded, a comparison is instituted between the conversational powers of the sex in England and in France; and such a picture is drawn of the frivolous inanity of the author's fair countrywomen, as, were the work considered as one of much authority in France, must leave the impression with our neighbours that the ladies of England are tant soit peu Agnès.

Now this judgment is, I think, as little founded in truth as that of the traveller who accused us all of being brandy-drinkers. It is indeed impossible to say what effect might have been produced upon the ladies from whom this description was drawn, by the awful consciousness that they were conversing with a person of overwhelming ability. There is such a thing as being "blasted by excess of light;" but where this unpleasant accident does not occur, I believe that those who converse with educated Englishwomen will find them capable of being as intellectual companions as any in the world.

Our countrywomen however, particularly the younger part of them, labour under a great disadvantage. The majority of them I believe to be as well, or perhaps better informed than the majority of Frenchwomen; but, unfortunately, it frequently happens that they are terrified at the idea of appearing too much so: the terror of being called learned is in general much more powerful than that of being classed as ignorant.

Happily for France, there is no blue badge, no stigma of any kind attached to the female possessors of talent and information. Every Frenchwoman brings forward with equal readiness and grace all she knows, all she thinks, and all she feels on every subject that may be started; whereas with us, the dread of imputed blueism weighs down many a bright spirit, and sallies of wit and fancy are withheld from the fear of betraying either the reading or the genius with which many a fair girl is endued who would rather be thought an idiot than a BLUE.

This is, however, a very idle fear; and that it is so, a slight glance upon society would show, if prejudice did not interfere to blind us. It is possible that here and there a sneer or a shrug may follow this opprobrious epithet of "blue;" but as the sneer and the shrug always come from those whose suffrage is of the least importance in society, their coming at all can hardly be a sufficient reason for putting on a masquerade habit of ignorance and frivolity.

It is from this cause, if I mistake not, that the conversation of the Parisian women takes a higher tone than that to which English females venture to soar. Even politics, that fearful quicksand which engulfs so many of our social hours, dividing our drawing-rooms into a committee of men and a coterie of women,—even politics may be handled by them without danger; for they fearlessly mix with that untoward subject so much lively persiflage, so much acuteness, and such unerring tact, that many a knotty point which may have made puzzled legislators yawn in the Chamber, has been played with in the salon till it became as intelligible as the light of wit could make it.

No one who is familiar with that delightful portion of French literature contained in their letters and memoirs, which paint the manners and the minds of those they treat of with more truth of graphic effect than any other biography in the world,—no one acquainted with the aspect of society as it is painted there, but must be aware that the character of Frenchmen has undergone a great and important change during the last century. It has become perhaps less brilliant, but at the same time less frivolous; and if we are obliged to confess that no star remains above the horizon of the same magnitude as those which composed the constellation that blazed during the age of Louis Quatorze and his successor, we must allow also that it would be difficult to find a minister of state who should now write to his friend as the Cardinal de Retz did to Boisrobert,—"Je me sauve à la nage dans ma chambre, au milieu des parfums."

If, however, these same minute records can be wholly trusted, I should say that no proportionate change has taken place among the women. I often fancy I can trace the same "genre d'esprit" amongst them with which Madame du Deffand has made us so well acquainted. Fashions must change—and their fashions have changed, not merely in dress perhaps, but in some things which appear to go deeper into character, or at least into manners; but the essentials are all the same. A petite maîtresse is a petite maîtresse still; and female wit—female French wit—continues to be the same dazzling, playful, and powerful thing that it ever was. I really do not believe that if Madame de Sévigné herself were permitted to revisit the scene of her earthly brightness, and to find herself in the midst of a Paris soirée to-morrow, that she would find any difficulty in joining the conversation of those she would find there, in the same tone and style that she enjoyed so keenly in days of yore with Madame de la Fayette, Mademoiselle Scuderie, or any other sister sparkler of that glorious via lactea—provided indeed that she did not talk politics,—on that subject she might not perhaps be well understood.

Ladies still write romances, and still write verses. They write memoirs too, and are moreover quite as keen critics as ever they were; and if they had not left off giving petits soupers, where they doomed the poets of the day to oblivion or immortality according to their will, I should say, that in no good gifts either of nature or of art had they degenerated from their admired great-grandmothers.

It can hardly, I think, be accounted a change in their character, that where they used to converse respecting a new comedy of Molière, they now discuss the project of a new law about to be passed in the Chamber. The reason for this is obvious: there is no longer a Molière, but there is a Chamber; there are no longer any new comedies greatly worth talking about, but there are abundance of new laws instead.

In short, though the subjects are changed, they are canvassed in the same spirit; and however much the marquis may be merged in the doctrinaire, the ladies at least have not left off being light, bright, witty, and gay, in order to become advocates for the "positif," in opposition to the "idéal." They still keep faithful to their vocation of charming; and I trust they may contrive so far to combat this growing passion for the "positif" in their countrymen, as to prevent their turning every salon—as they have already turned the Boulevards before Tortoni's—into a little Bourse.

I was so much struck by the truth and elegance of "a thought" apropos to this subject, which I found the other day in turning over the leaves of a French lady's album, that I transcribed it:—

"Proscrire les arts agréables, et ne vouloir que ceux qui sont absolument utiles, c'est blâmer la Nature, qui produit les fleurs, les roses, les jasmins, comme elle produit des fruits."

This sentiment, however, simple and natural as it is, appears in some danger of being lost sight of while the mind is kept upon such a forced march as it is at present: but the unnatural oblivion cannot fall upon France while her women remain what they are. The graces of life will never be sacrificed by them to the pretended pursuit of science; nor will a purblind examination of political economy be ever accepted in Paris as a beautiful specimen of light reading, and a first-rate effort of female genius.

Yet nowhere are the higher efforts of the female mind more honoured than in France. The memory of Madame de Staël seems enshrined in every woman's heart, and the glory she has brought to her country appears to shed its beams upon every female in it. I have heard, too, the name of Mrs. Somerville pronounced with admiration and reverence by many who confessed themselves unable to appreciate, or at least to follow, the efforts of her extraordinary mind.

In speaking of the women of Paris, however, I must not confine myself to the higher classes only; for, as we all know but too well, "les dames de la Halle," or, as they are more familiarly styled, "les poissardes," have made themselves important personages in the history of Paris. It is not, however, to the hideous part which they took in the revolution of Ninety-three that I would allude; the doing so would be equally disagreeable and unnecessary, for the deeds of Alexander are hardly better known than their infernal acts;—it is rather to the singular sort of respect paid to them in less stormy times that I would call your attention, because we have nothing analogous to it with us. Upon all great public occasions, such as the accession of a king, his restoration, or the like, these women are permitted to approach the throne by a deputation, and kings and queens have accepted their bouquets and listened to their harangues. The newspapers in recording these ceremonious visitings never name these poissardes by any lesser title than "les dames de la Halle;" a phrase which could only be rendered into English by "the ladies of Billingsgate."

These ladies have, too, a literature of their own, and have found troubadours among the beaux-esprits of France to chronicle their bons-mots and give immortality to their adventures in that singular species of composition known by the name of "Chansons Grivoises."

When Napoleon returned from Elba, they paid their compliments to him at the Tuileries, and sang "La Carmagnole" in chorus. One hundred days after, they repeated the ceremony of a visit to the palace; but this time the compliment was addressed to Louis Dix-huit, and the refrain of the song with which they favoured him was the famous calembourg so much in fashion at the time—

"Rendez-nous notre père de Gand."

Not only do these "dames" put themselves forward upon all political occasions, but, if report say true, they have, parfois, spite of their revolutionary ferocity, taken upon themselves to act as conservators of public morals. When Madame la Comtesse de N— and her friend Madame T— appeared in the garden of the Tuileries with less drapery than they thought decency demanded, les dames de la Halle armed themselves with whips, and repairing in a body to the promenade, actually flogged the audacious beauties till they reached the shelter of their homes.

The influence and authority of these women among the men of their own rank is said to be very great; and that through all the connexions of life, as long as his mother lives, whatever be her rank, a Frenchman repays her early care by affection, deference, and even by obedience. "Consolez ma pauvre mère!" has been reported in a thousand instances to have been the last words of French soldiers on the field of battle; and whenever an aged female is found seated in the chimney-corner, it is to her footstool that all coaxing petitions, whether for great or small matters, are always carried.

I heard it gravely disputed the other day, whether the old ladies of England or the old ladies of France have the most bonheur en partage amongst them. Every one seemed to agree that it was a very difficult thing for a pretty woman to grow old in any country—that it was terrible to "devenir chenille après avoir été papillon;" and that the only effectual way of avoiding this shocking transition was, while still a few years on the handsome side of forty, to abandon in good earnest all pretensions to beauty, and claiming fame and name by the perennial charm of wit alone, to bid defiance to time and wrinkles.

This is certainly the best parachute to which a drooping beauty can trust herself on either side of the Channel: but for one who can avail herself of it, there are a thousand who must submit to sink into eternal oblivion without it; and the question still remains, which nation best understands the art of submitting to this downfall gracefully.

There are but two ways of rationally setting about it. The one is, to jump over the Rubicon at once at sight of the first grey hair, and so establish yourself betimes on a sofa, with all the comforts of footstool and elbow-room; the other is, to make a desperate resolution never to grow old at all. Nous autres Anglaises generally understand how to do the first with a respectable degree of resignation; and the French, by means of some invaluable secret which they wisely keep to themselves, are enabled to approach very nearly to equal success in the other.

LETTER LII.

La Sainte Chapelle—Palais de Justice—Traces of the Revolution of 1830—Unworthy use made of La Sainte Chapelle—Boileau—Ancient Records.

A week or two ago we made a vain and unprofitable expedition into the City for the purpose of seeing "La Sainte Chapelle;" sainte to all good Catholics from its having been built by Louis Neuf (St. Louis) expressly for the purpose of receiving all the ultra-extra-super-holy relics purchased by St. Louis from Baldwin Emperor of Constantinople, and almost equally sainte to us heretics from having been the scene of Boileau's poem.

Great was our disappointment at being assured, by several flitting officials to whom we addressed ourselves in and about Le Palais de Justice, that admission was not to be obtained—that workmen were employed upon it, and I know not what besides; all, however, tending to prove that a long, lingering look at its beautiful exterior was all we had to hope for.

In proportion to this disappointment was the pleasure with which I received an offer from a new acquaintance to conduct us over the Palais de Justice, and into the sacred precints of La Sainte Chapelle, which in fact makes a part of it. My accidental introduction to M. J—, who has not only shown us this, but many other things which we should probably never have seen but for his kindness, has been one of the most agreeable circumstances which have occurred to me in Paris. I have seldom met a man so "rempli de toutes sortes d'intelligences" as is this new Parisian acquaintance; and certainly never received from any stranger so much amiable attention, shown in so profitable a manner. I really believe he has a passe-partout for everything that is most interesting and least easy of access in Paris; and as he holds a high judicial situation, the Palais de Justice was of course open to him even to its remotest recesses: and of all the sight-seeing mornings I remember to have passed, the one which showed me this interesting edifice, with the commentary of our deeply-informed and most agreeable companion, was decidedly one of the most pleasant. There is but one drawback to the pleasure of having met such a man—and this is the fear that in losing sight of Paris we may lose sight of him also.

The Palais de Justice is from its extent alone a very noble building; but its high antiquity, and its connexion with so many points and periods of history, render it one of the most interesting buildings imaginable. We entered all the courts, some of which appeared to be in full activity. They are in general large and handsome. The portrait of Napoleon was replaced in one of them during the Three Days, and there it still remains: the old chancellor d'Auguesseau hangs opposite to him, being one of the few pictures permitted to retain their places. The vacant spaces, and in some instances the traces of violence with which others have been removed, indicate plainly enough that this venerable edifice was not held very sacred by the patriots of 1830.

The capricious fury of the sovereign people during this reign of confusion, if not of terror, has left vestiges in almost every part of the building. The very interesting bas relief which I remember on the pedestal of the fine statue of Malesherbes, the intrepid defender of Louis Seize, has been torn away; and the brute masonry which it has left displayed, is as striking and appropriate a memento of the spoilers, as the graphic group they displaced was of the scene it represented. M. J— told me the sculpture was not destroyed, and would probably be replaced. I heartily hope, for the honour of Frenchmen, that this may happen: but if it should not, I trust that, for the sake of historic effect, the statue and its mutilated pedestal will remain as they are—both the one and the other mark an epoch in the history of France.

But it was in the obscurer parts of the building that I found the most interest. In order to take a short cut to some point to which our kind guide wished to lead us, we were twisted through one of the old—the very old towers of this venerable structure. It had been, I think they said, the kitchen of St. Louis himself; and the walls, as seen by the enormous thickness pierced for the windows, are substantial enough to endure another six hundred years at least.

In one of the numerous rooms which we entered, we saw an extremely curious old picture, seized in the time of Louis Quinze from the Jesuits, as containing proof of their treasonable disrespect for kings: and certainly there is not wanting evidence of the fact; very speaking portraits of Henry the Third and Henry the Fourth are to be found most unequivocally on their way to the infernal regions. The whole performance is one of the most interesting specimens of Jesuitical ingenuity extant.

Having fully indulged our curiosity in the palace, we proceeded to the chapel. It is exquisitely beautiful, and so perfect in its delicate proportions, that the eye is satisfied, and dwells with full contentment on the whole for many minutes before the judgment is at leisure to examine and criticise the different parts of it. But even when this first effect is over, the perfect elegance of this diminutive structure still rests upon the mind, producing a degree of admiration which seems disproportioned to its tiny dimensions.

It was built for a shrine in which to preserve relics; and Pierre de Montreuil, its able architect, appears to have sought rather to render it worthy by its richness and its grace to become the casket for those holy treasures, than to give it the dignity of a church. That beautiful miniature cathedral, St. George's Chapel at Windsor, is an enormous edifice compared to this; but less light, less lofty in its proportions—in short, less enchanting in its general effect, than the lovely bijou of St. Louis.

Of all the cruel profanations I have ever witnessed, that of turning this exquisite chef-d'oeuvre into a chest for old records is the most unpardonable: as if Paris could not furnish four walls and a roof for this purpose, without converting this precious châsse to it! It is indeed a pitiful economy; and were I the Archbishop of Paris, I would besiege the Tuileries with petitions that these hideous presses might be removed; and if it might not be restored to the use of the church, that we might at least say of it—

— "la Sainte ChapelleConservait du vieux tems l'oisiveté fidèle."

This would at least be better than seeing it converted into a cupboard of ease to the overflowing records of the Palais de Justice. The length of this pretty reliquaire exactly equals its height, which is divided by a gallery into a lower and upper church, resembling in some degree as to its arrangement the much older structure at Aix-la-Chapelle,—the high minster there being represented by the Sainte Couronne here.

As we stood in the midst of the floor of the church, M. J— pointed to a certain spot—

"Et bientôt LE LUTRIN se fait voir à nos yeux."

He placed me to stand where that offensive mass of timber stood of yore; and I could not help thinking that if the poor chantre hated the sight of it as much as I did that of the ignoble cases containing the old parchments, he was exceedingly right in doing his utmost to make it disappear.

Boileau lies buried here. The spot must have been chosen in consequence of the connexion he had established in the minds of all men between himself and its holy precincts. But it was surely the most lively and light-hearted connexion that ever was hallowed by so solemn a result. One might fairly steal or parody Vanburgh's epitaph for him—

"Rise graceful o'er him, roof! for he
Raised many a graceful verse to thee."

The preservation of the beautiful painted glass of the windows through the two revolutions which (both of them) were so busy in labours of metamorphosis and destruction in the immediate neighbourhood, not to mention all the ordinary chances against the safety of so frail a treasure during so many years, is little short of miraculous; and, considering the extraordinary sanctity of the place, it is probably so interpreted by les fidèles.

A remarkable proof of the reverence in which this little shrine was held, in consequence, I presume, of the relics it contained, may be found in the dignified style of its establishment. Kings and popes seem to have felt a holy rivalry as to which should most distinguish it by gifts and privileges. The wealth of its functionaries appears greatly to have exceeded the bounds of Christian moderation; and their pride of place was sustained, notwithstanding the petitesse of their dominions, by titles and prerogatives such as no chapelains ever had before. The chief dignitary of the establishment had the title of archichapelain; and, in 1379, Pope Clement VII. permitted him to wear a mitre, and to pronounce his benediction on the people when they were assembled during any of the processions which took place within the enclosure of the palace. Not only, indeed, did this arch-chaplain take the title of prelate, but in some public acts he is styled "Le Pape de la Sainte Chapelle." In return for all these riches and honours, four out of the seven priests attached to the establishment were obliged to pass the night in the chapel, for the purpose of watching the relics. Nevertheless, it appears that, in the year 1575, a portion of the vraie croix was stolen in the night between the 19th and 20th of May. The thief, however, was strongly suspected to be no less a personage than King Henry III. himself; who, being sorely distressed for money, and knowing from old experience that a traffic in relics was a right royal traffic, bethought him of a means of extracting a little Venetian gold from this true cross, by leaving it in pawn with the Republic of Venice. At any rate, this much-esteemed fragment disappeared from the Sainte Chapelle, and a piece of the holy rood was left en gage with the Venetians by Henry III.

I have transcribed, for your satisfaction, the list I find in Dulaure of the most sacred of the articles for the reception of which this chapel was erected:—

Du sang de Notre Seigneur Jésus-Christ.

Les drapeaux dont Notre Sauveur fut enveloppé en sonenfance.

Du sang qui miraculeusement a distillé d'une image de Notre Seigneur, ayant été frappé d'un infidèle.

La chaîne et lien de fer, en manière d'anneau, dont Notre Seigneur fut lié.

La sainte touaille, ou nappe, en un tableau.

Du lait de la Vierge.

Une partie du suaire dont il fut enseveli.

La verge de Moïse.

Les chefs des Saints Blaise, Clément, et Simon.

Is it not wonderful that the Emperor of Constantinople could consent to part with such precious treasures for the lucre of gain? I should like to know what has become of them all.

As late as the year 1770, the annual ceremony of turning out devils on Good Friday, from persons pretending to be possessed, was performed in this chapel. The form prescribed was very simple, and always found to answer perfectly. As soon as it was understood that all the demoniacs were assembled, le grand chantre appeared, carrying a cross, which, spite of King Henry's supercherie, was declared to enclose in its inmost recesses a morsel of the vraie croix, and in an instant all the contortions and convulsions ceased, and the possessed became perfectly calm and tranquil, and relieved from every species of inconvenience.

Having seen all that this lovely chapel had to show, and particularly examined the spot where the battle of the books took place, the passe-partout of M. J— caused a mysterious-looking little door in the Sainte Couronne to open for us; and, after a little climbing, we found ourselves just under the roof of the Palais de Justice. The enormous space of the grande salle below is here divided into three galleries, each having its entire length, and one-third of its width. The manner in which these galleries are constructed is extremely curious and ingenious, and well deserves a careful examination. I certainly never found myself in a spot of greater interest than this. The enormous collection of records which fill these galleries, arranged as they are in the most exquisite order, is one of the most marvellous spectacles I ever beheld.

Amidst the archives of so many centuries, any document that may be wished for, however remote or however minute, is brought forward in an instant, with as little difficulty as Dr. Dibdin would find in putting his hand upon the best-known treasure in Lord Spencer's library.

Our kind friend obtained for us the sight of the volume containing all the original documents respecting the trial of poor Joan of Arc, that most ill-used of heroines. Vice never braved danger and met death with such steady, unwavering courage as she displayed. We saw, too, the fatal warrant which legalised the savage murder of this brave and innocent fanatic.

Several other death-warrants of distinguished persons were also shown to us, some of them of great antiquity; but no royal hand had signed them. This painful duty is performed in France by one of the superior law-officers of the crown, but never by the hand of majesty.

Another curious trial that was opened for our satisfaction, was that of the wretched Marquise de Brinvilliers, the famous empoisonneuse, who not only destroyed father, brother, husband, at the instigation of her lover, but appears to have used her power of compounding fatal drugs upon many other occasions. The murderous atrocities of this woman seem to surpass everything on record, except those of Marguérite de Bourgogne, the inconceivable heroine of the "Tour de Nesle."

I was amused by an anecdote which M. J— told me of an Englishman to whom he, some years ago, showed these same curious papers—among which is the receipt used by Madame de Brinvilliers for the composition of the poison whose effects plunged Paris in terror.

"Will you do me the favour to let me copy this receipt?" said the Englishman.

"I think that my privilege does not reach quite so far as that," was the discreet reply; and but for this, our countryman's love for chemical science might by this time have spread the knowledge of the precious secret over the whole earth.

LETTER LIII.

French Ideas of England—Making Love—Precipitate Retreat of a Young Frenchman—Different Methods of Arranging Marriages—English Divorce—English Restaurans.

It now and then happens, by a lucky chance, that one finds oneself full gallop in a conversation the most perfectly unreserved, without having had the slightest idea or intention, when it began, of either giving or receiving confidence.

This occurred to me a few days ago, while making a morning visit to a lady whom I had never seen but twice before, and then had not exchanged a dozen words with her. But, upon this occasion, we found ourselves very nearly tête-à-tête, and got, I know not how, into a most unrestrained discussion upon the peculiarities of our respective countries.

Madame B— has never been in England, but she assured me that her curiosity to visit our country is quite as strong as the passion for investigation which drew Robinson Crusoe from his home to visit the...."

"Savages," said I, finishing the sentence for her.

"No! no! no!... To visit all that is most curious in the world."

This phrase, "most curious," seemed to me of doubtful meaning, and so I told her; asking whether it referred to the museums, or the natives.

She seemed doubtful for a moment whether she should be frank or otherwise; and then, with so pretty and playful a manner as must, I think, have disarmed the angry nationality of the most thin-skinned patriot alive, she answered—

"Well then—the natives."

"But we take such good care," I replied, "that you should not want specimens of the race to examine and make experiments upon, that it would hardly be worth your while to cross the Channel for the sake of seeing the natives. We import ourselves in such prodigious quantities, that I can hardly conceive you should have any curiosity left about us."

"On the contrary," she replied, "my curiosity is only the more piquée: I have seen so many delightful English persons here, that I die to see them at home, in the midst of all those singular customs, which they cannot bring with them, and which we only know by the imperfect accounts of travellers."

This sounded, I thought, very much as if she were talking of the good people of Mongo Creek, or Karakoo Bay; but being at least as curious to know what her notions were concerning the English in their remote homes, and in the midst of all their "singular customs," as she could be to become better acquainted with them, I did my best to make her tell me all she had heard about us.

"I will tell you," she said, "what I want to see beyond everything else: I want to see the mode of making love tout-à-fait à l'Anglaise. You know that you are all so polite as to put on our fashions here in every respect; but a cousin of mine, who was some years ago attached to our Embassy at London, has described the style of managing love affairs as so ... so romantic, that it perfectly enchanted me, and I would give the world to see how it was done (comment cela se fait)."

"Pray tell me how he described it," said I, "and I promise faithfully to tell you if the picture be correct."

"Oh, that is so kind!... Well then," she continued, colouring a little, from the idea, as I suppose, that she was going to say something terribly atrocious, "I will tell you exactly what happened to him. He had a letter of introduction to a gentleman of great estate—a member of the chamber of your parliament, who was living with his family at his chateau in one of the provinces, where my cousin forwarded the letter to him. A most polite reply was immediately returned, containing a pressing invitation to my cousin to come to the chateau without delay, and pass a month with them for the hunting season. Nothing could be more agreeable than this invitation, for it offered the best possible opportunity of studying the manners of the country. Every one can cross from Calais to Dover, and spend half their year's income in walking or driving through the long wide streets of London for six weeks; but there are very few, you know, who obtain an entrée to the chateaux of the noblesse. In short, my cousin was enchanted, and set off immediately. He arrived just in time to arrange his toilet before dinner; and when he entered the salon, he was perfectly dazzled by the exceeding beauty of the three daughters of his host, who were all décolletées, and full-dressed, he says, exactly as if they were going to some very elegant bal paré. There was no other company, and he felt a little startled at being received in such a ceremonious style.

The young ladies all performed on the piano-forte and harp, and my cousin, who is very musical, was in raptures. Had not his admiration been too equally drawn to each, he assures me that before the end of that evening he must inevitably have been the conquest of one. The next morning, the whole family met again at breakfast: the young ladies were as charming as ever, but still he felt in doubt as to which he admired most. Whilst he was exerting himself to be as agreeable as he could, and talking to them all with the timid respect with which demoiselles are always addressed by Frenchmen, the father of the family startled and certainly almost alarmed my cousin by suddenly saying,—"We cannot hunt to-day, mon ami, for I have business which will keep me at home; but you shall ride into the woods with Elizabeth: she will show you my pheasants. Get ready, Elizabeth, to attend Monsieur...!"

Madame B— stopped short, and looked at me as if expecting that I should make some observation.

"Well?" said I.

"Well!" she repeated, laughing; "then you really find nothing extraordinary in this proceeding— nothing out of the common way?"

"In what respect?" said I: "what is it that you suppose was out of the common way?"

"That question," said she, clasping her hands in an ecstasy at having made the discovery—"That question puts me more au fait than anything else you could say to me. It is the strongest possible proof that what happened to my cousin was in truth nothing more than what is of every-day occurrence in England."

"What did happen to him?"

"Have I not told you?... The father of the young ladies whom he so greatly admired, selected one of them and desired my cousin to attend her on an excursion into the woods. My dear madame ... national manners vary so strangely.... I beseech you not to suppose that I imagine that everything may not be exceedingly well arranged notwithstanding. My cousin is a very distinguished young man—excellent character—good name—and will have his father's estate ... only the manner is so different...."

"Did your cousin accompany the young lady?" said I.

"No, he did not—he returned to London immediately."

This was said so gravely—so more than gravely—with an air of so much more meaning than she thought it civil to express, that my gravity and politeness gave way together, and I laughed most heartily.

My amiable companion, however, did not take it amiss—she only laughed with me; and when we had recovered our gravity, she said, "So you find my cousin very ridiculous for throwing up the party?—un peu timide, peut-être?"

"Oh no!" I replied—"only a little hasty."

"Hasty!... Mais que voulez-vous? You do not seem to comprehend his embarrassment."

"Perhaps not fully; but I assure you his embarrassment would have ceased altogether, had he trusted himself with the young lady and her attendant groom: I doubt not that she would have led the way through one of our beautiful pheasant preserves, which are exceedingly well worth seeing; but most certainly she would have been greatly astonished, and much embarrassed in her turn, had your cousin taken it into his head to make love to her."

"You are in earnest?" said she, looking in my face with an air of great interest.

"Indeed I am," I replied; "I am very seriously in earnest; and though I know not the persons of whom we have been speaking, I can venture to assure you positively, that it was only because no gentleman so well recommended as your cousin could be suspected of abusing the confidence reposed in him, that this English father permitted him to accompany the young lady in her morning ride."

"C'est donc un trait sublime!" she exclaimed: "what noble confidence—what confiding honour! It is enough to remind one of the paladins of old."

"I suspect you are quizzing our confiding simplicity," said I; "but, at any rate, do not suspect me of quizzing you—for I have told you nothing more than a very simple and certain fact."

"I doubt it not the least in the world," she replied; "but you are indeed, as I observed at first, superiorly romantic." She appeared to meditate for a moment, and then added, "Mais dites moi un peu ... is not this a little inconsistent with the stories we read in the 'novels of fashionable life' respecting the manner in which husbands are acquired for the young ladies of England?... You refuse yourselves, you know, the privilege of disposing of your daughters in marriage according to the mutual interests of the parties; and therefore, as young ladies must be married, it follows that some other means must be resorted to by the parents. All Frenchmen know this, and they may perhaps for that reason be sometimes too easily induced to imagine that it is intended to lead them into marriage by captivating their senses. This is so natural an inference, that you really must forgive it."

"I forgive it perfectly," I replied; "but as we have agreed not to mystify each other, it would not be fair to leave you in the belief that it is the custom, in order to 'acquire' husbands for the young ladies, that they should be sent on love-making expeditions into the woods with the premier venu. But what you have said enables me to understand a passage which I was reading the other day in a French story, and which puzzled me most exceedingly. It was on the subject of a young girl who had been forsaken by her lover; and some one, reproaching him for his conduct, uses, I think, these words: 'Après l'avoir compromise autant qu'il est possible de compromettre une jeune miss—ce qui n'est pas une chose absolument facile dans la bienheureuse Albion....' This puzzled me more than I can express; because the fact is, that we consider the compromising the reputation of a young lady as so tremendous a thing, that excepting in novels, where neither national manners nor natural probabilities are permitted to check the necessary accumulation of misery on the head of a heroine, it NEVER occurs; and this, not because nothing can compromise her, but because nothing that can compromise her is ever permitted, or, I might almost say, ever attempted. Among the lower orders, indeed, stories of seduction are but too frequent; but our present examination of national manners refers only to the middle and higher classes of society."

Madame B— listened to me with the most earnest attention; and after I had ceased speaking, she remained silent, as if meditating on what she had heard. At length she said, in a tone of much more seriousness than she had yet used,—"I am quite sure that every word you say is parfaitement exact—your manner persuades me that you are speaking neither with exaggeration nor in jest: cependant ... I cannot conceal from you my astonishment at your statement. The received opinion among us is, that private and concealed infidelities among married women are probably less frequent in England than in France—because it seems to be essentially dans vos moeurs de faire un grand scandale whenever such a circumstance occurs; and this, with the penalties annexed to it, undoubtedly acts as a prevention. But, on the other hand, it is universally considered as a fact, that you are as lenient to the indiscretions of unmarried ladies, as severe to those of the married ones. Tell me—is there not some truth in this idea?"

"Not the least in the world, I do assure you. On the contrary, I am persuaded that in no country is there any race of women from whom such undeviating purity and propriety of conduct is demanded as from the unmarried women of England. Slander cannot attach to them, because it is as well known as that a Jew is not qualified to sit in parliament, that a single woman suspected of indiscretion immediately dies a civil death—she sinks out of society, and is no more heard of; and it is therefore that I have ventured to say, that a compromised reputation among the unmarried ladies of England NEVER occurs."

"Nous nous sommes singulièrement trompés sur tout cela donc, nous autres," said Madame B— . "But the single ladies no longer young?" she continued;—"forgive me ... but is it really supposed that they pass their entire lives without any indiscretion at all?"

This question was asked in a tone of such utter incredulity as to the possibility of a reply in the affirmative, that I again lost my gravity, and laughed heartily; but, after a moment, I assured her very seriously that such was most undoubtedly the case.

The naïve manner in which she exclaimed in reply, "Est-il possible!" might have made the fortune of a young actress. There was, however, no acting in the case; Madame B— was most perfectly unaffected in her expression of surprise, and assured me that it would be shared by all

Frenchwomen who should be so fortunate as to find occasion, like herself, to receive such information from indisputable authority. "Quant aux hommes," she added, laughing, "je doute fort si vous en trouverez de si croyans."

We pursued our conversation much farther; but were I to repeat the whole, you would only find it contained many repetitions of the same fact—namely, that a very strong persuasion exists in France, among those who are not personally well acquainted with English manners, that the mode in which marriages are arranged, rather by the young people themselves than by their relatives, produces an effect upon the conduct of our unmarried females which is not only as far as possible from the truth, but so preposterously so, as never to have entered into any English head to imagine.

So few opportunities for anything approaching to intimacy between French and English women arise, that it is not very easy for us to find out exactly what their real opinion is concerning us. Nothing in Madame B—'s manner could lead me to suspect that any feeling of reprobation or contempt mixed itself with her belief respecting the extraordinary license which she supposed was accorded to unmarried woman. Nothing could be more indulgent than her tone of commentary on our national peculiarities, as she called them. The only theme which elicited an expression of harshness from her was the manner in which divorces were obtained and paid for: "Se faire payer pour une aventure semblable! ... publier un scandale si ridicule, si offensant pour son amour-propre—si fortement contre les bonnes moeurs, pour en recevoir de l'argent, was," she said, "perfectly incomprehensible in a nation de si braves gens que les Anglais."

I did my best to defend our mode of proceeding in such cases upon the principles of justice and morality; but French prejudices on this point are too inveterate to be shaken by any eloquence of mine. We parted, however, the best friends in the world, and mutually grateful for the information we had received.

This conversation only furnished one, among several instances, in which I have been astonished to discover the many popular errors which are still current in France respecting England. Can we fairly doubt that, in many cases where we consider ourselves as perfectly well-informed, we may be quite as much in the dark respecting them? It is certain that the habit so general among us of flying over to Paris for a week or two every now and then, must have made a great number of individuals acquainted with the external aspect of France between Calais and Paris, and also with all the most conspicuous objects of the capital itself—its churches and its theatres, its little river and its great coffee-houses: but it is an extremely small proportion of these flying travellers who ever enter into any society beyond what they may encounter in public; and to all such, France can be very little better known than England is to those who content themselves with perusing the descriptions we give of ourselves in our novels and newspapers.

Of the small advance made towards obtaining information by such visits as these, I have had many opportunities of judging for myself, both among English and French, but never more satisfactorily than at a dinner-party at the house of an old widow lady, who certainly understands our language perfectly, and appears to me to read more English books, and to be more interested about their authors, than almost any one I ever met with. She has never crossed the Channel, however, and has rather an overweening degree of respect for such of her countrymen as have enjoyed the privilege of looking at us face to face on our own soil.

The day I dined with her, one of these travelled gentlemen was led up and presented to me as a person well acquainted with my country. His name was placed on the cover next to the one destined for me at table, and it was evidently intended that we should derive our principal amusement from the conversation of each other. As I never saw him before or since, as I never expect to see him again, and as I do not even remember his name, I think I am guilty of no breach of confidence by repeating to you a few of the ideas upon England which he had acquired on his travels.

His first remark after we were placed at table was,—"You do not, I think, use table-napkins in England;—do you not find them rather embarrassing?" The next was,—"I observed during my stay in England that it is not the custom to eat soup: I hope, however, that you do not find it disagreeable to your palate?"... "You have, I think, no national cuisine?" was the third observation; and upon this singularity in our manners he was eloquent. "Yet, after all," said he consolingly, "France is in fact the only country which has one: Spain is too oily—Italy too spicy. We have sent artists into Germany; but this cannot be said to constitute une cuisine nationale. Pour dire vrai, however, the rosbif of England is hardly more scientific than the sun-dried meat of the Tartars. A Frenchman would be starved in England did he not light upon one of the imported artists,—and, happily for travellers, this is no longer difficult."

"Did you dine much in private society?" said I.

"No, I did not: my time was too constantly occupied to permit my doing so."

"We have some very good hotels, however, in London."

"But no tables d'hôte!" he replied with a shrug. "I did very well, nevertheless; for I never permitted myself to venture anywhere for the purpose of dining excepting to your celebrated Leicester-square. It is the most fashionable part of London, I believe; or, at least, the only fashionable restaurans are to be found there."

I ventured very gently to hint that there were other parts of London more à-la-mode, and many hotels which had the reputation of a better cuisine than any which could be found in Leicester-square; but the observation appeared to displease the traveller, and the belle harmonie which it was intended should subsist between us was evidently shaken thereby, for I heard him say in a half-whisper to the person who sat on the other side of him, and who had been attentively listening to our discourse,—"Pas exact...."

LETTER LIV.

Mixed Society—Influence of the English Clergy and their Families—Importance of their Station in Society.

Though I am still of opinion that French society, properly so called,—that is to say, the society of the educated ladies and gentlemen of France,—is the most graceful, animated, and fascinating in the world; I think, nevertheless, that it is not as perfect as it might be, were a little more exclusiveness permitted in the formation of it.

No one can be really well acquainted with good society in this country without being convinced that there are both men and women to be found in it who to the best graces add the best virtues of social life; but it is equally impossible to deny, that admirable as are some individuals of the circle, they all exercise a degree of toleration to persons less estimable, which, when some well-authenticated anecdotes are made known to us, is, to say the least of it, very startling to the feelings of those who are not to this easy manner either born or bred.

To look into the hearts of all who form either a Parisian or a London lady's visiting list, in order to discover of what stuff each individual be made, would not perhaps be very wise, and is luckily quite impossible. Nothing at all approaching to such a scrutiny can be reasonably wished or expected from those who open their doors for the reception of company; but where society is perfectly well ordered, no one of either sex, I think, whose outward and visible conduct has brought upon them the eyes of all and the reprobation of the good, should be admitted.

That such are admitted much more freely in France than in England, cannot be denied; and though there are many who conscientiously keep aloof from such intercourse, and more who mark plainly enough that there is a distance in spirit even where there is vicinity of person, still I think it is greatly to be regretted that such a leven of disunion should ever be suffered to insinuate itself into meetings which would be so infinitely more agreeable as well as more respectable without it.

One reason, I doubt not, why there is less exclusiveness and severity of selection in the forming a circle here is, that there are no individuals, or rather no class of individuals, in the wide circle which constitutes what is called en grand the society of Paris, who could step forward with propriety and say, "This may not be."

With us, happily, the case is as yet different. The clergy of England, their matronly wives and highly-educated daughters, form a distinct caste, to which there is nothing that answers in the whole range of continental Europe. In this caste, however, are mingled a portion of every other; yet it has a dignity and aristocracy of its own: and in this aristocracy are blended the high blood of the noble, the learning which has in many instances sufficed to raise to a level with it the obscure and needy, and the piety which has given station above either to those whose unspotted lives have marked them out as pre-eminent in the holy profession they have chosen.

While such men as these mingle freely in society, as they constantly do in England, and bring with them the females who form their families, there is little danger that notorious vice should choose to obtrude itself.

It will hardly be denied, I believe, that many a frail fair one, who would boldly push her way among ermine and coronets where the mitre was not, would shrink from parading her doubtful honours where it was: and it is equally certain, that many a thoughtless, easy, careless giver of fine parties has been prevented from filling up her constellation of beauties because "It is impossible to have Lady This, or Mrs. That, when the bishop and his family are expected."

Nor is this wholesome influence confined to the higher ranks alone;—the rector of the parish—nay, even his young curate, with a smooth cheek and almost unrazored chin, will in humbler circles produce the same effect. In short, wherever an English clergyman or an English clergyman's family appears, there decency is in presence, and the canker of known and tolerated vice is not.

Whenever we find ourselves weary of this restraint, and anxious to mix (unshackled by the silent rebuke of such a presence) with whatever may be most attractive to the eye or amusing to the spirit, let the stamp of vice be as notorious upon it as it may, whenever we reach this state, it will be the right and proper time to pass the Irish Church Bill.

These meditations have been thrust upon me by the reply I received in answer to a question which I addressed to a lady of my acquaintance at a party the other evening.

"Who is that very elegant-looking woman?" said I.

"It is Madame de C—," was the reply. "Have you never met her before? She is very much in society; one sees her everywhere."

I replied, that I had seen her once or twice before, but had never learned her name; adding, that it was not only her name I was anxious to learn, but something about her. She looked like a personage, a heroine, a sybil: in short, it was one of those heads and busts that one seems to have the same right to stare at, as at a fine picture or statue; they appear a part of the decorations, only they excite a little more interest and curiosity.

"Can you not tell me something of her character?" said I: "I never saw so picturesque a figure; I could fancy that the spirit of Titian had presided at her toilet."

"It was only the spirit of coquetry, I suspect," answered my friend with a smile. "But if you are so anxious to know her, I can give you her character and history in very few words:—she is rich, high-born, intellectual, political, and unchaste."

I do not think I started; I should be shocked to believe myself so unfit for a salon as to testify surprise thus openly at anything; but my friend looked at me and laughed.

"You are astonished at seeing her here? But I have told you that you may expect to meet her everywhere; except, indeed, chez moi, and at a few exceedingly rococo houses besides."

As the lady I was talking to happened to be an Englishwoman, though for many years a resident in Paris, I ventured to hint the surprise I felt that a person known to be what she described Madame de C— should be so universally received in good society.

"It is very true," she replied: "it is surprising, and more so to me perhaps than to you, because I know thoroughly well the irreproachable character and genuine worth of many who receive her. I consider this," she continued, "as one of the most singular traits in Parisian society. If, as many travellers have most falsely insinuated, the women of Paris were generally corrupt and licentious, there would be nothing extraordinary in it: but it is not so. Where neither the husband, the relatives, the servants, nor any one else, has any wish or intention of discovering or exposing the frailty of a wife, it is certainly impossible to say that it may not often exist without being either known or suspected: but with this, general society cannot interfere; and those whose temper or habits of mind lead them to suspect evil wherever it is possible that it may be concealed, may often lose the pleasure of friendship founded on esteem, solely because it is possible that some hidden faults may render their neighbour unworthy of it. That such tempers are not often to be found in France, is certainly no proof of the depravity of national manners; but where notorious irregularity of conduct has brought a woman fairly before the bar of public opinion, it does appear to me very extraordinary that such a person as our hostess, and very many others equally irreproachable, should receive her."

"I presume," said I, "that Madame de C— is not the only person towards whom this remarkable species of tolerance is exercised?"

"Certainly not. There are many others whose liaisons are as well known as hers, who are also admitted into the best society. But observe—I know no instance where such are permitted to enter within the narrower circle of intimate domestic friendship. No one in Paris seems to think that they have any right to examine into the private history of all the élégantes who fill its salons; but I believe they take as good care to know the friends whom they admit to the intimacy of their private hours as we do. There, however, this species of decorum ends; and they would no more turn back from entering a room where they saw Madame de C— , than a London lady would drive away from the opera because she saw the carriage of Lady — at the door."

"There is no parallel, however, between the cases," said I.

"No, certainly," she replied; "but it is not the less certain that the Parisians appear to think otherwise."

Now it appears evident to me, that all this arises much less from general licentiousness of morals than from general easiness of temper. SANS SOUCI is the darling device of the whole nation: and how can this be adhered to, if they set about the very arduous task of driving out of society all those who do not deserve to be in it? But while feeling sincerely persuaded, as I really do, that this difference in the degree of moral toleration practised by the two countries does not arise from any depravity in the French character, I cannot but think that our mode of proceeding in this respect is infinitely better. It is more conducive, not only to virtue, but to agreeable and unrestrained intercourse; and for this reason, if for no other, it is deeply our interest to uphold with all possible reverence and dignity that class whose presence is of itself sufficient to guarantee at least the reputation of propriety, in every circle in which they appear.

Though not very german to Paris and the Parisians, which I promised should make the subjects of my letters as long as I remained among them, I cannot help observing how utterly this most important influence would be destroyed in the higher circles—which will ever form the model of those below them—if the riches, rank, and worldly honours of this class are wrested from them. It is indeed very certain that a clergyman, whether bishop, priest, or deacon, may perform the duty of a minister in the desk, at the altar, or in the pulpit, though he has to walk home afterwards to an humble dwelling and an humble meal: he may perform this duty well, and to the entire satisfaction of the rich and great, though his poverty may prevent him from ever taking his place among them; but he may not—he can not, while such is the station allotted him, produce that effect on society, and exert that influence on the morals of the people, which he would do were his temporal place and power such as to exalt him in the eyes even of the most worldly.

Amidst all the varieties of cant to which it is the destiny of the present age to listen, there is none which I endure with so little patience as that which preaches the "humility of the church." Were there the shadow of reason or logic in the arguments for the degradation of the clergy drawn from the Scriptures, they must go the length of showing that, in order to follow the example of the great Master, they must all belong to the class of carpenters and fishermen. Could we imagine another revelation of the Divinity accorded to man, it would be natural enough to conceive that the rich gift of direct inspiration should be again given to those who had neither learning, knowledge, pride, nor power of any kind, to combat or resist, to explain or to weaken, the communication which it was their duty simply to record and spread abroad. But the eternal word of God once delivered, does it follow that those who are carefully instructed in all the various learning which can assist in giving strength and authority to the propagation of it should alone, of all the sons of men, be for ever doomed to the lower walks of social life in order to imitate the humility of the Saviour of the world?

I know not if there be more nonsense or blasphemy in this. The taking the office of preaching his own blessed will to man was an act of humility in God; but the taking upon themselves to instruct their fellow-men in the law thus solemnly left us, is a great assumption of dignity in men,—and where the offices it imposes are well performed, it becomes one of the first duties of the believers in the doctrine they have made it their calling to expound, to honour them with such honour as mortals can understand and value. If any one be found who does not perform the duties of this high calling in the best manner which his ability enables him to do, let him be degraded as he deserves;

but while he holds it, let him not be denied the dignity of state and station to which all his fellow-citizens in their different walks aspire, in order forsooth to keep him humble! Humble indeed—yea, humbled to the dust, will our long-venerated church and its insulted ministers be, if its destiny and their fortune be left at the mercy of those who have lately undertaken to legislate for them. I often feel a sort of vapourish, vague uncertainty of disbelief, as I read the records of what has been passing in the House of Commons on this subject. I cannot realise it, as the Americans say, that the majority of the English parliament should consent to be led blind-fold upon such a point as this, by a set of low-born, ignorant, bullying papists. I hope, when I return to England, I shall awake and find that it is not so.

And now forgive me for this long digression: I will write to you to-morrow upon something as essentially French as possible, to make up for it.

Le Grand Opéra—Its Enormous Expense—Its Fashion—Its Acknowledged Dulness—'La Juive'—Its Heavy Music—Its Exceeding Splendour—Beautiful Management of the Scenery—National Music.

Can I better keep the promise I gave you yesterday than by writing you a letter of and concerning le grand opéra? Is there anything in the world so perfectly French as this? Something like their pretty opéra comique may exist elsewhere; we have our comic opera, and Italy has her buffa; the opéra Italien, too, may be rather more than rivalled at the Haymarket: but where out of Paris are we to look for anything like the Académie Royale de Musique? ... le grand opéra? ... l'opéra par excellence?—I may safely answer, nowhere.

It is an institution of which the expenses are so enormous, that though it is more constantly and fully attended perhaps than any other theatre in the world, it could not be sustained without the aid of funds supplied by the government. The extraordinary partiality for this theatre seems to have existed among the higher classes, without any intermission from change of fashion, occasional inferiority of the performances, or any other cause, from the time of Louis Quatorze to the present. That immortal monarch, whose whim was power, and whose word was law, granted a patent privilege to this establishment in favour of the musical Abbé Perrin, but speedily revoked it, to bestow one more ample still on Lulli. In this latter act, it is ordained that "tous gentilshommes et demoiselles puissent chanter aux dites pièces et représentations de notre dite Académie Royale sans que pour ça ils soient censés déroger au dit titre de noblesse et à leurs priviléges."

This was a droll device to exalt this pet plaything of the fashionable world above all others. Voltaire fell into the mode like the rest of the fine folks, and thus expressed his sensibility to its attractions:—

"Il faut se rendre à ce palais magique,Où les beaux vers, la danse, la musique,L'art de charmer les yeux par les couleurs,L'art plus heureux de séduire les coeurs,De cent plaisirs font un plaisir unique."

But the most incomprehensible part of the business is, that with all this enthusiasm, which certainly rather goes on increasing than diminishing, every one declares that he is ennuyé à la mort at le grand opéra.

I do not mean that their being ennuyés is incomprehensible—Heaven knows that I understand that perfectly: but why, when this is avowed, they should continue to persecute themselves by going there two or three times in every week, I cannot comprehend.

If attendance at the opera were here, as it is with us, a sort of criterion of the love of music and other fine arts, it would be much less difficult to understand: but this is far from being the case, as both the Italian and the comic operas have more perfect orchestras. The style and manner of singing, too, are what no genuine lover of music could ever be brought to tolerate. When the remembrance of a German or Italian opera comes across one while listening to the dry, heavy recitative of the Academy, it produces a feeling of impatience difficult to conceive by those who have never experienced it.

If, however, instead of being taken in by the name of opera, and expecting the musical treat which that name seems to promise, we go to this magnificent theatre for the purpose of seeing the most superb and the best-fancied decorations in the world, we shall at least not be disappointed, though before the end of the entertainment we may probably become heartily weary of gazing at and admiring the dazzling pageant. I told you just now what Voltaire said of the opera, either when he was particularly enchanted by some reigning star—the adorable Sophie Arnould perhaps—or else when he chose to be particularly à-la-mode: but he seems more soberly in earnest, I think, when he says afterwards, "L'opéra n'est qu'un rendezvous publique, où l'on s'assemble à certains jours, sans trop savoir pourquoi: c'est une maison où tout le monde va, quoiqu'on pense mal du maître, et qu'il soit assez ennuyeux."

That little phrase, "où tout le monde va," contains, I suspect after all, the only true solution of the mystery. "Man is a gregarious animal," say the philosophers; and it is therefore only in conformity to this well-known law of his nature that hes and shes flock by thousands to be pent up together, in defiance of most triste musique and a stifling atmosphere, within the walls of this beautiful puppet-show.

That it is beautiful, I am at this moment particularly willing to avouch, as we have just been regaling ourselves, or rather our eyes, with as gorgeous a spectacle there as it ever entered into the heart of a carpenter to étaler on the stage of a theatre. This splendid show is known by the name of "La Juive;" but it should rather have been called "Le Cardinal," for a personage of no less dignity is decidedly its hero. M. Halévy is the composer, and M. Scribe the author of the "paroles."

M. Scribe stands so high as a dramatic composer, that I suppose he may sport a little with his fame without running much risk of doing it an injury: but as the Académie Royale has the right of drawing upon the Treasury for its necessities, it is to be hoped that the author of "Bertrand et Raton" is well paid for lending his name to the pegs on which ermine and velvet, feathers and flowers, cardinals' hats and emperors' mantles, are hung up to view for the amusement of all who may be curious in such matters. I suspect, however, that the composition of this piece did not cost the poet many sleepless nights: perhaps he remembered that excellent axiom of the Barbier de Seville,—"Ce qui ne vaut pas la peine d'être dit, on le chante;" and under this sentence I think such verses as the following, which strongly remind one of the famous Lilliputian ode in the Bath Guide, may fairly enough be condemned to music.

"Fille chèrePrès d'un père Viens mourir;
Et pardonne
Quand il donne
La couronne
Du martyr!
Plus de plainte—Vaine crainte
Est éteinte
En mon coeur; Saint délire!

Dieu m'inspire,
Et j'expire Vainqueur."

Unhappily, however, the music is at least as worthless as the rhymes. There is one passage, nevertheless, that is singularly impressive and beautiful. This is the chorus at the opening of the second act, where a party of Jews assembled to eat the passover chant a grace in these words:—

"Oh! Dieu de nos pères!Toi qui nous éclaires,
Parmi nous descends!"   &c. &c. &c.

This is very fine, but perhaps it approaches rather too closely to the "Dieu d'Israël" in Méhul's opera of "Joseph" to be greatly vaunted on the score of originality.

Yet, with all these "points of 'vantage" at which it may be hostilely attacked, "La Juive" draws thousands to gaze at its splendour every time it is performed. Twice we attempted to get in without having secured places, and were told on both occasions that there was not even standing-room for gentlemen.

Among its attractions are two which are alike new to me as belonging to an opera: one is the performance of the "Te Deum laudamus," and the other the entrance of Franconi's troop of horse.

But, after all, it was clear enough that, whatever may have been the original object of this institution, with its nursery academies of music and dancing, its royal patronage and legalised extravagance, its present glory rests almost wholly on the talents of the Taglioni family, and with the sundry MM. décorateurs who have imagined and arranged the getting up this extraordinary specimen of scenic magnificence, as well as the many others of the same kind which have preceded it.

I have seen many very fine shows of the kind in London, but certainly never anything that could at all be compared with this. Individual scenes—as, for instance, that of the masqued ball in "Gustavus"— may equal, by the effect of the first coup-d'oeil, any scene in "La Juive"; but it is the extraordinary propriety and perfection of all the accessaries which make this part of the performance worthy of a critical study from the beginning to the end of it. I remember reading in some history of Paris, that it was the fashion to be so précieuse as to the correctness of the costumes of the French opera, that the manager could not venture to bring out "Les Trois Sultanes" without sending to Constantinople to obtain the dresses. A very considerable portion of the same spirit has evidently been at work to render the appearance of a large detachment of the court of Rome and the whole court of the Emperor Sigismund comme il faut upon the scene.

But, with all a woman's weakness at my heart in favour of velvet, satin, gold tissue, and ermine, I cannot but confess that these things, important as they are, appear but secondary aids in the magical scenic effects of "La Juive." The arrangement and management of the scenery were to me perfectly new. The coulisses have vanished, side scenes are no more,—and, what is more important still, these admirable mechanists have found the way of throwing across the stage those accidental masses of shadow by aid of which Nature produces her most brilliant effects; so that, instead of the aching eyes having to gaze upon a blaze of reflected light, relieved only by an occasional dip of the foot-lights and a sudden paling of gas in order to enact night, they are now enchanted and beguiled by exactly such a mixture of light and shade as an able painter would give to a picture.

How this is effected, Heaven knows! There are, I am very sure, more things at present above, about, and underneath the opera stage, than are dreamed of in any philosophy, excepting that of a Parisian carpenter. In the first scene of the "Juive," a very noble-looking church rears its sombre front exactly in the centre of the stage, throwing as fine, rich, deep a shadow on one side of it as Notre Dame herself could do. In another scene, half the stage appears to be sunk below the level of the eye, and is totally lost sight of, a low parapet wall marking the boundary of the seeming river.

Our box was excellently situated, and by no means distant from the stage; yet we often found it impossible to determine at what point, in different directions, the boards ended and the scenery began. The arrangement of the groups too, not merely in combinations of grace and beauty, but in such bold, easy, and picturesque variety, that one might fancy Murillo had made the sketches for them, was another source of wonder and admiration; and had all these pretty sights been shown us in the course of two acts instead of five, I am sure we should have gone home quite delighted and in the highest possible good-humour. But five acts of raree-show is too much; and accordingly we yawned, and talked of Grétry, Méhul, Nicolo, and I know not whom beside;—in short, became as splenetic and pedantic as possible.

We indulged ourselves occasionally in this unamiable mood by communicating our feelings to each other, in a whisper however which could not go beyond our own box, and with the less restraint because we felt sure that the one stranger gentleman who shared it with us could not understand our language. But herein we egregiously deceived ourselves: though in appearance he was Français jusqu'aux ongles, we soon found out that he could speak English as well as any of us; and, with much real politeness, he had the good-nature to let us know this before we had uttered anything too profoundly John Bullish to be forgiven.

Fortunately, too, it appeared that our judgments accorded as well as if we had all been born in the same parish. He lamented the decadence of music in this, which ought to be its especial theatre; but spoke with enthusiasm of the Théâtre Italien, and its great superiority in science over every other in Paris. This theatre, to my great vexation, is now closed; but I well remember that such too was my judgment of it some seven years ago.

The English and the French are generally classed together as having neither one nor the other any really national music of their own. We have both of us, however, some sweet and perfectly original airs, which will endure as long as the modulations of sound are permitted to enchant our mortal ears. Nevertheless, I am not going to appeal against a sentence too often repeated not to be universally received as truth. But, notwithstanding this absence of any distinct school of national music, it is impossible to doubt that the people of both countries are fondly attached to the science. More sacrifices are made by both to obtain good music than the happy German and Italian people would ever dream of making. Nor would it, I think, be fair to argue, from the present style of the performances at the Académie, that the love of music is on the decline here. The unbounded expense bestowed upon decorations, and the pomp and splendour of effect which results from it, are quite enough to attract and dazzle the eyes of a more "thinking people" than the Parisians; and the unprecedented perfection to which the mechanists have brought the delusion of still-life seems to permit a relaxation in the efforts of the manager to obtain attraction from other sources.

But this will not last. The French people really love music, and will have it. It is more than probable that the musical branch of this academic establishment will soon revive; and if in doing so it preserve its present superiority of decoration, it will again become an amusement of unrivalled attraction.

I believe the French themselves generally consider us as having less claim to the reputation of musical amateurship than themselves; but, with much respect for their judgment on such subjects, I differ from them wholly in this. When has France ever shown, either in her capital or out of it, such a glorious burst of musical enthusiasm as produced the festivals of Westminster Abbey and of York?

It was not for the sake of encouraging an English school of music, certainly, that these extraordinary efforts were made. They were not native strains which rang along the vaulted roofs; but it was English taste, and English feeling, which recently, as well as in days of yore, conceived and executed a scheme of harmony more perfect and sublime than I can remember to have heard of elsewhere.

I doubt, too, if in any country a musical institution can be pointed out in purer taste than that of our ancient music concert. The style and manner of this are wholly national, though the compositions performed there are but partially so; and I think no one who truly and deeply loves the science but must feel that there is a character in it which, considering the estimation in which it has for so many years been held, may fairly redeem the whole nation from any deficiency in musical taste.

There is one branch of the "gay science," if I may so call it, which I always expect to find in France, but respecting which I have hitherto been always disappointed: this is in the humble class of itinerant musicians. In Germany they abound; and it not seldom happens that their strains arrest the feet and enchant the ear of the most fastidious. But whenever, in France, I have encountered an ambulant troubadour, I confess I have felt no inclination to linger on my way to listen to him. I do not, however, mean to claim much honour for ourselves on the score of our travelling minstrels. If we fail to pause in listening to those of France, we seldom fail to run whenever our ears are overtaken by our own. Yet still we give strong proof of our love of music, in the more than ordinary strains which may be occasionally heard before every coffee-house in London, when the noise and racket of the morning has given place to the hours of enjoyment. I have heard that the bands of wind instruments which nightly parade through the streets of London receive donations which, taken on an average throughout the year, would be sufficient to support a theatre. This can only proceed from a genuine propensity to being "moved by concord of sweet sounds;" for no fashion, as is the case at our costly operas, leads to it. On the contrary, it is most decidedly mauvais ton to be caught listening to this unexclusive harmony; yet it is encouraged in a degree that clearly indicates the popular feeling.

Have I then proved to your satisfaction, as completely as I undoubtedly have to my own, that if without a national music, at least we are not without a national taste for it?

LETTER LVI.

The Abbé Deguerry—His Eloquence—Excursion Across the Water—Library of Ste. Geneviève—Copy-book of the Dauphin—St. Etienne du Mont—Pantheon.

The finest sermon I have heard since I have been in Paris—and, I am almost inclined to think, the finest I ever heard anywhere—was preached yesterday by the Abbé Deguerry at St. Roch. It was a discourse calculated to benefit all Christian souls of every sect and denomination whatever—had no shade of doctrinal allusion in it of any kind, and was just such a sermon as one could wish every soi-disant infidel might be forced to listen to while the eyes of a Christian congregation were fixed upon him. It would do one good to see such a being cower and shrink, in the midst of his impotent and petulant arrogance, to feel how a "plain word could put him down."

The Abbé Deguerry is a young man, apparently under thirty; but nature seems to have put him at once in possession of a talent which generally requires long years to bring to perfection. He is eloquent in the very best manner; for it is an eloquence intended rather to benefit the hearer than to do honour to the mere human talent of the orator. Beautifully as his periods flowed, I felt certain, as I listened to him, that their harmonious rhythm was the result of no study, but purely the effect, unconsciously displayed, of a fine ear and an almost unbounded command of language. He had studied his matter,—he had studied and deeply weighed his arguments; but, for his style, it was the free gift of Heaven.

Extempore preaching has always appeared to me to be a fearfully presumptuous exercise. Thoughts well digested, expressions carefully chosen, and arguments conscientiously examined, are no more than every congregation has a right to expect from one who addresses them with all the authority of place on subjects of most high importance; and rare indeed is the talent which can produce this without cautious and deliberate study. But in listening to the Abbé Deguerry, I perceived it was possible that a great and peculiar talent, joined to early and constant practice, might enable a man to address his fellow-creatures without presumption even though he had not written his sermon;— yet it is probable that I should be more correct were I to say, without reading it to his congregation, for it is hardly possible to believe that such a composition was actually and altogether extempore.

His argument, which was to show the helpless insufficiency of man without the assistance of revelation and religious faith, was never lost sight of for an instant. There was no weak wordiness, no repetition, no hacknied ornaments of rhetoric; but it was the voice of truth, speaking in that language of universal eloquence which all nations and all creeds must feel; and it flowed on with unbroken clearness, beauty, and power, to the end.

Having recently quitted Flanders, where everything connected with the Roman Catholic worship is sustained in a style of stately magnificence which plainly speaks its Spanish origin, I am continually surprised by the comparatively simple vestments and absence of ostentatious display in the churches of Paris. At the metropolitan church of Notre Dame, indeed, nothing was wanting to render its archiepiscopal dignity conspicuous; but everywhere else, there was a great deal less of pomp and circumstance than I expected. But nowhere is the relaxation of clerical dignity in the clergy of Paris so remarkable as in the appearance of the young priests whom we occasionally meet in the streets. The flowing curls, the simple round hat, the pantaloons, and in some cases the boots also, give them the appearance of a race of men as unlike as possible to their stiff and primitive predecessors. Yet they all look flourishing, and well pleased with themselves and the world about them: but little of mortification or abstinence can be traced on their countenances; and if they do fast for some portion of every week, they may certainly say with Father Philip, that "what they take prospers with them marvellously."

We have this morning made an excursion to the other side of the water, which always seems like setting out upon a journey; and yet I know not why it should be so, for as the river is not very wide, the bridges are not very long; but so it is, that for some reason or other, if it were not for the magnetic Abbaye-aux-Bois, we should very rarely find ourselves on the left bank of the Seine.

On this occasion, our object was to visit the famous old library of Ste. Geneviève, on the invitation of a gentleman who is one of the librarians. Nothing can be more interesting than an expedition of this sort, with an intelligent and obliging cicisbeo, who knows everything concerning the objects displayed before you, and is kindly willing to communicate as much of his savoir as the time may allow, or as may be necessary to make the different objects examined come forth from that venerable but incomprehensible accumulation of treasures, which form the mass of all the libraries and museums in the world, and which, be he as innocent of curiosity as an angel, every stranger is bound over to visit, under penalty, when honestly reciting his adventures, of hearing exclamations from all the friends he left at home, of—"What! ... did you not see that?... Then you have seen nothing!"

I would certainly never expose myself to this cutting reproach, could I always secure as agreeable a companion as the one who tempted us to mount to the elevated repository which contains the hundred thousand volumes of the royal library of Ste. Geneviève. Were I a student there, I should grumble prodigiously at the long and steep ascent to this temple of all sorts of learning: but once reached, the tranquil stillness, and the perfect seclusion from the eternal hum of the great city that surrounds it, are very delightful, and might, I think, act as a sedative upon the most restive and truant imagination that ever beset a student.

I was sorry to hear that symptoms of decay in the timbers of the venerable roof make it probable that this fine old room must be given up, and the large collection it has so long sheltered be conveyed elsewhere. The apartment is in the form of a cross, with a dome at the point of intersection, painted by the elder Restout. Though low, and in fact occupying only the roof of the college, formerly the Abbaye of Sainte Geneviève, there is something singularly graceful and pleasing to the eye in this extensive chamber, its ornaments and general arrangement;—something monastic, yet not gloomy; with an air of learned ease, and comfortable exclusion of all annoyance, that is very enviable.

The library appears to be kept up in excellent style, and in a manner to give full effect to its liberal regulations, which permit the use of every volume in the collection to all the earth. The wandering scholar at distance from his own learned cell, and the idle reader for mere amusement, may alike indulge their bookish propensities here, with exactly the same facilities that are accorded to the students of the college. The librarians or their deputies are ready to deliver to them any work they ask for, with the light and reasonable condition annexed that the reader shall accompany the person who is to find the volume or volumes required, and assist in conveying them to the spot which he has selected for his place of study.

The long table which stretches from the centre under the doom, across the transepts of the cross, was crowded with young men when we were there, who really seemed most perfectly in earnest in their occupation—gazing on the volumes before them "with earnest looks intent," even while a large party swept past them to examine a curious model of Rome placed at the extremity of one of the transepts. A rigorous silence, however, is enjoined in this portion of the apartments; so that even the ladies were obliged to postpone their questions and remarks till they had passed out of it.

After looking at splendid editions, rare copies, and so forth, our friend led us to some small rooms, fitted up with cases for the especial protection under lock and key of the manuscripts of the collection. Having admired the spotless vellum of some, and the fair penmanship of others, a thin morocco-bound volume was put into my hands, which looked like a young lady's collection of manuscript waltzes. This was the copy-book of the Dauphin, father of the much-regretted Duke de Bourgogne, and grandfather of Louis Quinze.

The characters were evidently written with great care. Each page contained a moral axiom, and all of them more or less especially applicable to a royal pupil. There was one of these which I thought might be particularly useful to all such at the present day: it was entitled, in large letters—

SE MOQUEUR DE LIBELLES

—the superfluous U being erased by a dash of the master's pen. Then followed, in extremely clear and firm characters, these lines:—

Si de vos actions la satyre réjoue,
Feignez adroitement de ne la pas ouïr:

Qui relève une injure, il semble qu'il l'avoue;
Qui la scait mépriser, la fait évanouir.

L LOUIS LOUIS LOUIS LOUIS

In one of these smaller rooms hangs the portrait of a negress in the dress of a nun. It has every appearance of being a very old painting, and our friend M. C— told us that a legend had been ever attached to it, importing that it was the portrait of a daughter of Mary Queen of Scots, born before she left France for Scotland. What could have originated such a very disagreeable piece of scandal, it is difficult to imagine; but I can testify that all the internal evidence connected with it is strong against its truth, for no human countenance can well be conceived which would show less family likeness to our lovely and unfortunate northern queen than does that of this grim sister.

From the library of Ste. Geneviève, we went under the same kind escort to look at the barbaric but graceful vagaries of St. Etienne du Mont. The galleries suspended as if by magic between the pillars of the choir, and the spiral staircases leading to them, out of all order as they are, must nevertheless be acknowledged as among the lightest and most fairy-like constructions in the world. This singular church, capricious in its architecture both within and without, is in some parts of great antiquity, and was originally built as a chapel of ease to the old church of Ste. Geneviève, which stood close beside it, and of which the lofty old tower still remains, making part of the college buildings. As a proof of the entire dependance of this pretty little church upon its mother edifice, it was not permitted to have any separate door of its own, the only access to it being through the great church. This subsidiary chapel, now dignified into a parish church, has at different periods been enlarged and beautified, and has again and again petitioned for leave from its superior to have a door of its own; but again and again it was refused, and it was not till the beginning of the sixteenth century that this modest request was at length granted. The great Pascal lies buried in this church.

I was very anxious to give my children a sight of the interior of that beautiful but versatile building called, when I first saw it, the Pantheon—when I last saw it, Ste. Geneviève, and which is now again known to all the world, or at least to that part of it which has been fortunate enough to visit Paris since the immortal days, as the Pantheon.

We could not, however, obtain an entrance to it; and it is very likely that before we shall again find ourselves on its simple and severe, but very graceful threshold, it will have again changed its vocation, and be restored to the use of the Christian church—Ainsi soit-il!

LETTER LVII.

Little Suppers—Great Dinners—Affectation of Gourmandise—Evil Effects of "dining out"—Evening Parties—Dinners in Private Under the Name of Luncheons—Late Hours.

How I mourn for the departed petits soupers of Paris!... and how far are her pompous dinners from being able to atone for their loss! For those people, and I am afraid there are many of them, who really and literally live to eat, I know that the word "dinner" is the signal and symbol of earth's best, and, perhaps, only bliss. For them the steaming vapour, the tedious long array, the slow and solemn progress of a dîner de quatre services, offers nothing but joy and gladness; but what is it to those who only eat to live?

I know no case in which injustice and tyranny are so often practised as at the dinner-table. Perhaps twenty people sit down to dinner, of whom sixteen would give the world to eat just no more than they like and have done with it: but it is known to the Amphitryon that there are four heavy persons present whose souls hover over his ragoûts like harpies over the feast of Phinæus, and they must not be disturbed, or revilings instead of admiration will repay the outlay and the turmoil of the banquet.

A tedious, dull play, followed by a long, noisy, and gunpowder-scented pantomime, upon the last scene of which your party is determined to see the curtain fall; a heavy sermon of an hour long, your pew being exactly in front of the preacher; a morning visit from a lady who sends her carriage to fetch her boys from school at Wimbleton, and comes to entertain you with friendly talk about her servants till it comes back;—each of these is hard to bear and difficult to escape; but which of them can compare in suffering to a full-blown, stiff, stately dinner of three hours long, where the talk is of food, and the only relief from this talk is to eat it?... How can you get away? How is it possible to find or invent any device that can save you from enduring to the end? With cheeks burning from steam and vexation, can you plead a sudden faintness? Still less can you dare to tell the real truth, and confess that you are dying of disgust and ennui. The match is so unfair between the different parties at such a meeting as this—the victims so utterly helpless!... And, after all, there is no occasion for it. In London there are the clubs and the Clarendon; in Paris are Périgord's and Véry's, and a score beside, any one of whom could furnish a more perfect dinner than can be found at any private mansion whatever, where sufferings are often inflicted on the wretched lookers-on very nearly approaching to those necessary for the production of the foie gras.

Think not, however, that I am inclined in the least degree to affect indifference or dislike to an elegant, well-spread table: on the contrary, I am disposed to believe that the hours when mortals meet together, all equally disposed to enjoy themselves by refreshing the spirits, recruiting the strength, and inspiring the wit, with the cates and the cups most pleasing to the palate of each, may be reckoned, without any degradation to human pride, among the happiest hours of life. But this no more resembles the endless crammings of a repas de quatre services, than a work in four volumes on political economy to an epigram in four lines upon the author of it.

In fact, to give you a valuable hint upon the subject, I am persuaded that some of the most distinguished gourmets of the age have plunged themselves and their disciples into a most lamentable error in this matter. They have overdone the thing altogether. Their object is to excite the appetite as much as possible, in order to satisfy it as largely as possible; and this end is utterly defeated by the means used. But I will not dwell on this; neither you nor I are very particularly interested in the success either of the French or English eaters by profession; we will leave them to study their own business and manage it as well as they can.

For the more philosophical enjoyers of the goods the gods provide I feel more interest, and I really lament the weakness which leads so many of them to follow a fashion which must be so contrary to all their ideas of real enjoyment; but, unhappily, it is daily becoming more necessary for every man who sits down at a fashionable table to begin talking like a cook. They surely mistake the thing altogether. This is not the most effectual way of proving the keenness of their gourmandise.

In nine cases out of ten, I believe this inordinate passion for good eating is pure affectation; and I suspect that many a man, especially many a young man, both in Paris and London, would often be glad to eat a reasonably good dinner, and then change the air, instead of sitting hour after hour, while dishes are brought to his elbow till his head aches in shaking it as a negative to the offer of them, were it not that it would be so dreadfully bourgeois to confess it.

If, however, on the other hand, an incessant and pertinacious "diner-out" should take up the business in good earnest, and console himself for the long sessions he endures by really eating on from soup to ice, what a heavy penalty does he speedily pay for it! I have lived long enough to watch more than one svelte, graceful, elegant young man, the glory of the drawing-room, the pride of the Park, the hero of Almack's, growing every year rounder and redder; the clear, well-opened eye becoming dull and leaden—the brilliant white teeth looking "not what they were, but quite the reverse," till the noble-looking, animated being, that one half the world was ready to love, and the other to envy, sank down into a heavy, clumsy, middle-aged gentleman, before half his youth was fairly past; and this solely for the satisfaction of continuing to eat every day for some hours after he had ceased to be hungry.

It is really a pity that every one beginning this career does not set the balance of what he will gain and what he will lose by it fairly before him. If this were done, we should probably have much fewer theoretical cooks and practical crammers, but many more lively, animated table-companions, who might oftener be witty themselves, and less often the cause of wit in others.

The fashion for assembling large parties, instead of selecting small ones, is on all occasions a grievous injury to social enjoyment. It began perhaps in vanity: fine ladies wished to show the world that they had "a dear five hundred friends" ready to come at their call. But as everybody complains of it as a bore, from Whitechapel to Belgrave-square, and from the Faubourg St. Antoine to the Faubourg du Roule, vanity would now be likely enough to put a general stop to it, were it not that a most disagreeable species of economy prevents it. "A large party kills such a prodigious number of birds," as I once heard a friend of mine say, when pleading to her husband for permission to overflow her dinner-table first, and then her drawing-rooms, "that it is the most extravagant thing in the world to have a small one." Now this is terrible, because it is true: but, at least, those blest with wealth might enjoy the extreme luxury of having just as many people about them as they liked, and no more; and if they would but be so very obliging as to set the fashion, we all know that it would speedily be followed in some mode or other by all ranks, till it would be considered as positively mauvais ton to have twice as many people in your house as you have chairs for them to sit on.

The pleasantest evening parties remaining in Paris, now that such delightful little committees as Molière brings together after the performance of "L'Ecole des Femmes" can meet no more, are those assembled by an announcement made by Madame une Telle to a somewhat select circle, that she shall be at home on a certain evening in every week, fortnight, or month, throughout the season. This done, nothing farther is necessary; and on these evenings a party moderately large drop in without ceremony, and depart without restraint. No preparation is made beyond a few additional lights; and the albums and portfolios in one room, with perhaps a harp or pianoforte in another, give aid, if aid be wanted, to the conversation going on in both. Ices, eau sucrée, syrup of fruits, and gaufres are brought round, and the party rarely remain together after midnight.

This is very easy and agreeable,—incomparably better, no doubt, than more crowded and more formal assemblées. Nevertheless, I am so profoundly rococo as to regret heartily the passing away of the petits soupers, which used to be the favourite scene of enjoyment, and the chosen arena for the exhibition of wit, for all the beaux esprits, male and female, of Paris.

I was told last spring, in London, that at present it was the parvenus only who had incomes unscathed by the stormy times; and that, consequently, it was rather elegant than otherwise to chanter misère upon all occasions. I moreover heard a distinguished confectioner, when in conversation with a lady on the subject of a ball-supper, declare that "orders were so slack, that he had countermanded a set of new ornaments which he had bespoken from Paris."

Such being the case, what an excellent opportunity is the present for a little remuement in the style of giving entertainments! Poverty and the clubs render fine dinners at once dangerous, difficult, and unnecessary; but does it follow that men and women are no more to meet round a banqueting table? "Because we are virtuous, shall there be no more cakes and ale?"

I have often dreamed, that were I a great lady, with houses and lands, and money at will, I would see if I could not break through the tyrannous yoke of fashion, often so confessedly galling to the patient wearers of it, and, in the place of heavy, endless dinners, which often make bankrupt the spirit and the purse, endeavour to bring into vogue that prettiest of all inventions for social enjoyment—a real supper-table: not a long board, whereat aching limbs and languid eyes may yawningly wait to receive from the hand of Mr. Gunter what must cost the giver more, and profit the receiver less, than any imaginable entertainment of the kind I propose, and which might be spread by an establishment as simply monté as that of any gentleman in London.

Then think of the luxury of sitting down at a table neither steaming with ragoûts, nor having dyspepsia hid under every cover; where neither malignant gout stands by, nor servants swarm and listen to every idle word; where you may renew the memory of the sweet strains you have just listened to at the opera, instead of sitting upon thorns while you know that your favourite overture is in the very act of being played! All should be cool and refreshing, nectarine and ambrosial,— uncrowded, easy, intimate, and as witty as Englishmen and Englishwomen could contrive to make it!

Till this experiment has been fairly made and declared to fail, I will never allow that the conversational powers of the women of England have been fully proved and found wanting. The wit of Mercury might be weighed to earth by the endurance of three long, pompous courses; and would it not require spirits lighter and brighter than those of a Peri to sustain a woman gaily through the solemn ceremonies of a fine dinner?

In truth, the whole arrangement appears to me strangely defective and ill-contrived. Let English ladies be sworn to obey the laws of fashion as faithfully as they will, they cannot live till eight o'clock in the evening without some refreshment more substantial than the first morning meal. In honest truth and plain English, they all dine in the most unequivocal manner at two or three o'clock; nay, many of those who meet their hungry brethren at dinner-parties have taken coffee or tea before they arrive there. Then what a distasteful, tedious farce does the fine dinner become!

Now just utter a "Passe! passe!" and, by a little imaginative legerdemain, turn from this needless dinner to such a petit souper as Madame de Maintenon gave of yore. Let Fancy paint the contrast; and let her take the gayest colours she can find, she cannot make it too striking. You must, however, rouse your courage, and strengthen your nerves, that they may not quail before this fearful word— SUPPER. In truth, the sort of shudder I have seen pass over the countenances of some fashionable men when it is pronounced may have been natural and unaffected enough; for who that has been eating in despite of nature from eight to eleven can find anything appétissant in this word "supper" uttered at twelve.

But if we could persuade Messieurs nos Maîtres, instead of injuring their health by the long fast which now precedes their dinner, during which they walk, talk, ride, drive, read, play billiards, yawn—nay, even sleep, to while away the time, and to accumulate, as it were, an appetite of inordinate dimensions;—if, instead of this, they would for one season try the experiment of dining at five o'clock, and condescend afterwards to permit themselves to be agreeable in the drawing-room, they would find their wit sparkle brighter than the champagne at their supper-tables, and moreover their mirrors would pay them the prettiest compliments in the world before they had tried the change for a fortnight.

But, alas! all this is very idle speculation; for I am not a great lady, and have no power whatever to turn dull dinners into gay suppers, let me wish it as much as I may.

Hôpital des Enfans Trouvés—Its Doubtful Advantages—Story of a Child Left There.

Like diligent sight-seers, as we are, we have been to visit the hospital for les Enfans Trouvés. I had myself gone over every part of the establishment several years before, but to the rest of my party it was new—and certainly there is enough of strangeness in the spectacle to repay a drive to the Rue d'Enfer. Our kind friend and physician, Dr. Mojon, who by the way is one of the most amiable men and most skilful physicians in Paris, was the person who introduced us; and his acquaintance with the visiting physician, who attended us round the rooms, enabled us to obtain much interesting information. But, alas! it seems as if every question asked on this subject could only elicit a painful answer. The charity itself, noble as it is in extent, and admirable for the excellent order which reigns throughout every department of it, is, I fear, but a very doubtful good. If it tend, as it doubtless must do, to prevent the unnatural crime of infanticide, it leads directly to one hardly less hateful in the perpetration, and perhaps more cruel in its result,—namely, that of abandoning the creature whom nature, unless very fearfully distorted, renders dearer than life. Nor is it the least melancholy part of the speculation to know that one fourth of the innocent creatures, who are deposited at the average rate of above twenty each day, die within the first year of their lives. But this, after all, perhaps is no very just cause of lamentation: one of the sisters of charity who attend at the hospital told me, in reply to an inquiry respecting the education of these immortal but unvalued beings, that the charity extended not its cares beyond preserving their animal life and health—that no education whatever was provided for them, and that, unless some lucky and most rare accident occurred to change their destiny, they generally grew up in very nearly the same state as the animals bred upon the farms which received them.

Peasants come on fixed days—two or three times a week, I believe—to receive the children who appear likely to live, as nurslings; and they convey them into the country, sometimes to a great distance from Paris, partly for the sake of a consideration in money which they receive, but chiefly for the value of their labour.

It is a singular fact, that during the years which immediately followed the revolution, the number of children deposited at the hospital was greatly diminished; but, among those deposited, the proportion of deaths was still more greatly increased. In 1797, for instance, 3,716 children were received, 3,108 of whom died.

I have lately heard a story, of which a child received at this hospital is in some sort the heroine; and as I thought it sufficiently interesting to insert in my note-book, I am tempted to transcribe it for you. The circumstances occurred during the period which immediately followed the first revolution; but the events were merely domestic, and took no colour from the times.

M. le Comte de G— was a nobleman of quiet and retired habits, whom delicate health had early induced to quit the service, the court, and the town. He resided wholly at a paternal chateau in Normandy, where his forefathers had resided before him too usefully and too unostentatiously to have suffered from the devastating effects of the revolution. The neighbours, instead of violating their property, had protected it; and in the year 1799, when my story begins, the count with his wife and one little daughter were as quietly inhabiting the mansion his ancestors had inhabited before him, as if it stood on English soil.

It happened, during that year, that the wife of a peasant on his estate, who had twice before made a journey to Paris, to take a nursling from among the enfans trouvés, again lost a new-born baby, and again determined upon supplying its place from the hospital. It seemed that the poor woman was either a bad nurse or a most unlucky one; for not only had she lost three of her own, but her two foster-children also.

Of this excursion, however, she prophesied a better result; for the sister of charity, when she placed in her arms the baby now consigned to her care, assured her it was the loveliest and most promising child she had seen deposited during ten years of constant attendance among the enfans trouvés. Nor were her hopes disappointed: the little Alexa (for such was the name pinned on her dress) was at five years old so beautiful, so attractive, so touching, with her large blue eyes and dark chesnut curls, that she was known and talked of for a league round Pont St. Jacques. M. and Madame de G—, with their little girl, never passed the cottage without entering to look at and caress the lovely child.

Isabeau de G— was just three years older than the little foundling; but a most close alliance subsisted between them. The young heiress, with all the pride of a juvenile senior, delighted in nothing so much as in extending her patronage and protection to the pretty Alexa; and the forsaken child gave her in return the prémices of her warm heart's fondness.

No Sunday evening ever passed throughout the summer without seeing all the village assembled under an enormous lime-tree, that grew upon a sort of platform in front of the primitive old mansion, with a pepper-box at each corner, dignified with the title of Château Tourelles.

The circular bench which surrounded this giant tree afforded a resting-place for the old folks;—the young ones danced on the green before them—and the children rolled on the grass, and made garlands of butter-cups, and rosaries of daisies, to their hearts' content. On these occasions it was of custom immemorial that M. le Comte and Madame la Comtesse, with as many offspring as they were blessed withal, should walk down the strait pebbled walk which led from the chateau to the tree exactly as the clock struck four, there to remain for thirty minutes and no longer, smiling, nodding, and now and then gossiping a little, to all the poor bodies who chose to approach them.

Of late years, Mademoiselle Isabeau had established a custom which shortened the time of her personal appearance before the eyes of her future tenants to somewhat less than one-sixth of the allotted time; for five minutes never elapsed after the little lady reached the tree, before she contrived to slip her tiny hand out of her mother's, and pounce upon the little Alexa, who, on her side, had long learned to turn her beautiful eyes towards the chateau the moment she reached the ground, nor removed them till they found Isabeau's bright face to rest upon instead. As soon as she had got possession of her pet, the young lady, who had not perhaps altogether escaped spoiling, ran off with her, without asking leave of any, and enjoyed, either in the aristocratic retirement of her own nursery, or her own play-room or her own garden, the love, admiration, and docile obedience of her little favourite.

But if this made a fête for Isabeau, it was something dearer still to Alexa. It was during these Sabbath hours that the poor child learned to be aware that she knew a great many more wonderful things than either Père Gautier or Mère Françoise. She learned to read—she learned to speak as good French as Isabeau or her Parisian governess; she learned to love nothing so well as the books, and the pianoforte, and the pictures, and the flowers of her pretty patroness; and, unhappily, she learned also to dislike nothing so much as the dirty cottage and cross voice of Père Gautier, who, to say truth, did little else but scold the poor forsaken thing through every meal of the week, and all day long on a Sunday.

Things went on thus without a shadow of turning till Alexa attained her tenth, and Isabeau her thirteenth year. At this time the summer Sunday evenings began to be often tarnished by the tears of the foundling as she opened her heart to her friend concerning the sufferings she endured at home. Père Gautier scolded more than ever, and Mère Françoise expected her to do the work of a woman;—in short, every day that passed made her more completely, utterly, hopelessly wretched; and at last she threw her arms round the neck of Isabeau, and told her so, adding, in a voice choked with sobs, "that she wished ... that she wished ... she could die!"

They were sitting together on a small couch in the young heiress's play-room when this passionate avowal was made. The young lady disengaged herself from the arms of the weeping child, and sat for a few moments in deep meditation. "Sit still in this place, Alexa," she said at length, "till I return to you;" and having thus spoken, with an air of unusual gravity she left the room.

Alexa was so accustomed to show implicit obedience to whatever her friend commanded, that she never thought of quitting the place where she was left, though she saw the sun set behind the hills through a window opposite to her, and then watched the bright horizontal beams fading into twilight, and twilight vanishing in darkness. It was strange, she thought, for her to be at the chateau at night; but Mademoiselle Isabeau had bade her sit there, and it must be right. Weary with watching, however, she first dropped her head upon the arm of the sofa, then drew her little feet up to it, and at last fell fast asleep. How long she lay there my story does not tell; but when she awoke, it was suddenly and with a violent start, for she heard the voice of Madame de G— and felt the blaze of many lights upon her eyes. In another instant, however, they were sheltered from the painful light in the bosom of her friend.

Isabeau, her eyes sparkling with even more than their usual brightness, her colour raised, and out of breath with haste and eagerness, pressed her fondly to her heart, and covered her curls with kisses; then, having recovered the power of speaking, she exclaimed, "Look up, my dear Alexa! You are to be my own sister for evermore: papa and mamma have said it. Cross Père Gautier has consented to give you up; and Mère Françoise is to have little Annette Morneau to live with her."

How this had all been arranged it is needless to repeat, though the eager supplication of the daughter and the generous concessions of the parents made a very pretty scene as I heard it described; but I must not make my story too long. To avoid this, I will now slide over six years, and bring you to a fine morning in the year 1811, when Isabeau and Alexa, on returning from a ramble in the village, found Madame de G— with an open letter in her hand, and an air of unusual excitement in her manner.

"Isabeau, my dear child," she said, "your father's oldest friend, the Vicomte de C—, is returned from Spain. They are come to pass a month at V—; and this letter is to beg your father and me to bring you to them immediately, for they were in the house when you were born, my child, and they love you as if you were their own. Your father is gone to give orders about horses for to-morrow. Alexa dear, what will you do without us?"

"Cannot Alexa go too, mamma?" said Isabeau.

"Not this time, my dear: they speak of having their chateau filled with guests."

"Oh, dearest Isabeau! do not stand to talk about me; you know I do not love strangers: let me help you to get everything ready."

The party set off the next morning, and Alexa, for the first time since she became an inhabitant of Château Tourelles, was left without Isabeau, and with no other companion than their stiff governess; but she rallied her courage, and awaited their return with all the philosophy she could muster.

Time and the hour wear through the longest fortnight, and at the end of this term the trio returned again. The meeting of the two friends was almost rapturous: Monsieur and Madame had the air of being parfaitement contents, and all things seemed to go on as usual. Important changes, however, had been decided on during this visit. The Vicomte de C. had one son. He is the hero of my story, so believe him at once to be a most charming personage in all ways—and in fact he was so. A marriage between him and Isabeau had been proposed by his father, and cordially agreed to by hers; but it was decided between them that the young people should see something more of each other before this arrangement was announced to them, for both parents felt that the character of their children deserved and demanded rather more deference to their inclinations that was generally thought necessary in family compacts of this nature.

The fortnight had passed amidst much gaiety: every evening brought waltzing and music; Isabeau sang à ravir; but as there were three married ladies at the chateau who proclaimed themselves to be unwearying waltzers, young Jules, who was constrained to do the honours of his father's house, had never found an opportunity to dance with Isabeau excepting for the last waltz, on the last evening; and then there never were seen two young people waltzing together with more awkward restraint.

Madame de G—, however, fancied that he had listened to Isabeau's songs with pleasure, and moreover observed to Monsieur son Mari that it was impossible he should not think her beautiful.

Madame was quite right—Jules did think her daughter beautiful: he thought, too, that her voice was that of a syren, and that it would be easy for him to listen to her till he forgot everything else in the world.

I would not be so abrupt had I more room; but as it is necessary to hasten over the ground, I must tell you at once that Isabeau, on her side, was much in the same situation. But as a young lady should never give her heart anywhere till she is asked, and in France not before her husband has politely expressed his wish to be loved as he leads her to her carriage from the altar, Isabeau took especial good care that nobody should find out the indiscretion her feelings had committed, and having not only a mind of considerable power, but also great confidence and some pride in her own strength, she felt little fear but that she should be able both to conceal and conquer a passion so every way unauthorised.

Now it unfortunately happened that Jules de C. was, unlike the generality of his countrymen, extremely romantic;—but he had passed seven years in Spain, which may in some degree excuse it. His education, too, had been almost wholly domestic: he knew little of life except from books, and he had learned to dread, as the most direful misfortune that could befall him, the becoming enamoured of, and perhaps marrying, a woman who loved him not.

Soon after the departure of Isabeau and her parents, the vicomte hinted to his son that he thought politeness required a return of the visit of the de G— family; and as both himself and his lady were un peu incommodés by some malady, real or supposititious, he conceived that it would be right that he, Jules, should present himself at Château Tourelles to make their excuses. The heart of Jules gave a prodigious leap; but it was not wholly a sensation of pleasure: he felt afraid of Isabeau,—he was afraid of loving her,—he remembered the cold and calm expression of countenance with which she received his farewell—his trembling farewell—at the door of the carriage. Yet still he accepted the commission; and in ten days after the return of the de G— family, Jules de C. presented himself before them. His reception by the comte and his lady was just what may be imagined,—all kindness and cordiality of welcome. That of Isabeau was constrained and cold. She turned a little pale, but then she blushed again; and the shy Jules saw nothing but the beauty of the blush—was conscious only of the ceremonious curtsy, and the cold "Bonjour, Monsieur Jules." As for Alexa, her only feeling was that of extreme surprise. How could it be that Isabeau had seen a person so very graceful, handsome and elegant, and yet never say one word to her about him!... Isabeau must be blind, insensible, unfeeling, not to appreciate better such a being as that. Such was the effect produced by the appearance of Jules on the mind of Alexa,—the beautiful, the enthusiastic, the impassioned Alexa. From that moment a most cruel game of cross purposes began to be played at Château Tourelles. Alexa commenced by reproaching Isabeau for her coldness, and ended by confessing that she heartily wished herself as cold. Jules ceased not to adore Isabeau, but every day strengthened his conviction that she could never love him; and Isabeau, while every passing hour showed more to love in Jules, only drew from thence more reasons for combating and conquering the flame that inwardly consumed her.

There could not be a greater contrast between two girls, both good, than there was both in person and mind between these two young friends. Isabeau was the prettiest little brunette in France—et c'est beaucoup dire: Alexa was, perhaps, the loveliest blonde in the world. Isabeau, with strong feelings, had a command over herself that never failed: in a good cause, she could have perished at the stake without a groan. Alexa could feel, perhaps, almost as strongly as her friend; but to combat those feelings was beyond her power: she might have died to show her love, but not to conceal it; and had some fearful doom awaited her, she would not have lived to endure it.

Such being the character and position of the parties, you will easily perceive the result. Jules soon perceived the passion with which he had inspired the young and beautiful Alexa, and his heart, wounded by the uniform reserve of Isabeau, repaid her with a warmth of gratitude, which though not love, was easily mistaken for it by both the innocent rivals. Poor Jules saw that it was, and already felt his honour engaged to ratify hopes which he had never intended to raise. Repeatedly he determined to leave the chateau, and never to see either of its lovely inmates more; but whenever he hinted at such an intention, M. and Madame de G— opposed it in such a manner that it seemed impossible to persevere in it. They, good souls, were perfectly satisfied with the aspect of affairs: Isabeau was perhaps a little pale, but lovelier than ever; and the eyes of Jules were so often fixed upon her, that there could be no doubt as to his feelings. They were very right,—yet, alas! they were very wrong too: but the situation of Alexa put her so completely out of all question of marriage with a gentleman d'une haute naissance, that they never even remembered that she too was constantly with Jules.

About three weeks had passed in this mischief-working manner, when Isabeau, who clearly saw traces of suffering on the handsome face of poor Jules, believing firmly that it arose from the probable difficulty of obtaining his high-born father's consent to his marriage with a foundling, determined to put every imaginable means in requisition to assist him.

Alexa had upon her breast a mark, evidently produced by gunpowder. Her nurse, and everybody else who had seen it, declared it to be perfectly shapeless, and probably a failure from the awkwardness of some one who had intended to impress a cipher there; but Isabeau had a hundred times examined it, and as often declared it to be a coronet. Hitherto this notion had only been a source of mirth to both of them, but now it became a theme of incessant and most anxious meditation to Isabeau. She remembered to have heard that when a child is deposited at the Foundling Hospital of

Paris, everything, whether clothes or token, which is left with it, is preserved and registered, with the name and the date of the reception, in order, if reclamation be made within a certain time, that all assistance possible shall be given for the identification. What space this "certain time" included Isabeau knew not, but she fancied that it could not be less than twenty years; and with this persuasion she determined to set about an inquiry that might at least lead to the knowledge either that some particular tokens had been left with Alexa, or that there were none.

With this sort of feverish dream working in her head, Isabeau rose almost before daylight one morning, and escaping the observation of every one, let herself out by the door of a salon which opened on the terrace, and hastened to the abode of Mère Françoise. It was some time before she could make the old woman understand her object; but when she did, she declared herself ready to do all and everything Mademoiselle desired for her "dear baby," as she persisted to call the tall, the graceful, the beautiful Alexa.

As Isabeau had a good deal of trouble to make her plans and projects clearly understood to Mère Françoise, it will be better not to relate particularly what passed between them: suffice it to say, that by dint of much repetition and a tolerably heavy purse, Françoise at last agreed to set off for Paris on the following morning, "without telling a living soul what for." Such were the conditions enforced; which were the more easily adhered to, because cross Père Gautier had grumbled himself into his grave some years before.

On reaching the hospital, Françoise made her demand, "de la part d'une grande dame," for any token which they possessed relative to a baby taken ... &c. &c. &c. The first answer she received was, that the time of limitation for such inquiries had long expired; and she was on the point of leaving the bureau, all hope of intelligence abandoned, when an old sister of charity who chanced to be there for some message from the superior, and who had listened to her inquiries and all the particulars thus rehearsed, stopped her by saying, that it was odd enough two great ladies should send to the hospital with inquiries for the same child. "But, however," she added, "it can't much matter now to either of them, for the baby died before it was a twelvemonth old."

"Died!" screamed Françoise: "why, I saw her but four days ago, and a more beautiful creature the sun never shone upon."

An explanation ensued, not very clear in all its parts, for there had evidently been some blunder; but it plainly appeared, that within a year after the child was sent to nurse, inquiries had been made at the hospital for a baby bearing the singular name of Alexa, and stating that various articles were left with her expressly to ensure the power of recognition. An address to a peasant in the country had been given to the persons who had made these inquiries, and application was immediately made to her: but she stated that the baby she had received from the hospital at the time named had died three months after she took it; but what name she had received with it she could not remember, as she called it Marie, after the baby she had lost. It was evident from this statement that a mistake had been made between the two women, who had each taken a female foundling into the country on the same day.

It was more easy, however, to hit the blunder than to repair it. Communication was immediately held with some of the chefs of the establishment; who having put in action every imaginable contrivance to discover any traces which might remain of the persons who had before inquired for the babe named Alexa, at length got hold of a man who had often acted as commissionnaire to the establishment, and who said he remembered about that time to have taken letters from the hospital to a fine hôtel near the Elysée Bourbon.

This man was immediately conveyed to the Elysée Bourbon, and without hesitation pointed out the mansion to which he had been sent. It was inhabited by an English gentleman blessed with a family of twelve children, and who assured the gentleman entrusted with the inquiry that he had not only never deposited any of his children at the Enfans Trouvés, but that he could not give them the slightest assistance in discovering whether any of his predecessors in that mansion had done so. Discouraged, but not chilled in the ardour of his pursuit, the worthy gentleman proceeded to the proprietor of the hôtel: he had recently purchased it; from him he repaired to the person from whom he had bought it. He was only an agent; but at last, by means of indefatigable exertion during three days, he discovered that the individual who must have inhabited the hôtel when these messages were stated to have been sent thither from the Enfans Trouvés was a Russian nobleman of high rank, who, it was believed, was now residing at St. Petersburg. His name and title, however, were both remembered; and these, with a document stating all that was known of the transaction, were delivered to Mère Françoise, who, hardly knowing if she had succeeded or failed in her mission, returned to her young employer within ten days of the time she left her.

Isabeau, generously as her noble heart beat at learning what she could not but consider as a favourable report of her embassy, did feel nevertheless something like a pang when she remembered to what this success would lead. But she mastered it, and, with all the energy of her character, instantly set to work to pursue her enterprise to the end. It was certainly a relief to her when Jules, after passing a month of utter misery in the society of the woman he adored, took his leave. The old people were still perfectly satisfied: it was not the young man's business, they said, to break through the reserve which his parents had enjoined, and a few days would doubtless bring letters from them which would finally settle the business.

Alexa saw him depart with an aching heart; but she believed that he was returning home only to ask his father's consent to their union. Isabeau fed her hopes, for she too believed that the young man's heart was given to Alexa. During this time Isabeau concealed her hope of discovering the parents of the foundling from all. Day after day wore away, and brought no tidings from Jules. The hope of Alexa gave way before this cruel silence. The circumstances of her birth, which rankled at her heart more deeply than even her friend imagined, now came before her in a more dreadful shape than ever. Sin, shame, and misery seemed to her the only dot she had to bring in marriage, and her mind brooded over this terrible idea till it overpowered every other; her love seemed to sink before it, and, after a sleepless night of wretched meditation, she determined never to bring disgrace upon a husband—she heroically determined never to marry.

As she was opening her heart on this sad subject to Isabeau, and repeating to her with great solemnity the resolution she had taken, a courier covered with dust galloped up to the door of the chateau. Isabeau instantly suspected the truth, but could only say as she kissed the fair forehead of the foundling, "Look up, my Alexa!... You shall be happy at least."

Before any explanation of these words could even be asked for, a splendid travelling equipage stopped at the door, and, according to the rule in all such cases, a beautiful lady descended from it, handed out by a gentleman of princely rank: in brief, for I cannot tell you one half his titles and honours, or one quarter of the circumstances which had led to the leaving their only child at the Hôpital des Enfans Trouvés, Alexa was proved to be the sole and most lawful idol and heiress of this noble pair. The wonder and joy, and all that, you must guess: but poor Isabeau!... O! that all this happiness could but have fallen upon them before she had seen Jules de C—!

On the following morning, while Alexa, seated between her parents, was telling them all she owed to Isabeau, the door of the apartment opened and the young Jules entered. This was the moment at which the happy girl felt the value of all she had gained with the most full and perfect consciousness of felicity. Her bitter humiliation was changed to triumph; but Jules saw it not—he heard not the pompous titles of her father as she proudly rehearsed them, but, in a voice choking with emotion, he stammered out—"Où donc est Isabeau?"

Alexa was too happy, too gloriously happy, to heed his want of politeness, but gaily exclaiming, "Pardon, maman!" she left the room to seek for her friend.

Jules was indeed come on no trifling errand. His father, having waited in vain for some expression of his feelings respecting the charming bride he intended for him, at last informed him of his engagement, for the purpose of discovering whether the young man were actually made of ice or no. On this point he was speedily satisfied; for the intelligence robbed the timid lover of all control over his feelings, and the father had the great pleasure of perceiving that his son was as distractedly in love as he could possibly desire. As to his doubts and his fears, the experienced vicomte laughed them to scorn. "Only let her see you as you look now, Jules," said the proud father, "and she will not disobey her parents, I will answer for it. Go to her, my son, and set your heart at ease at once."

With a courage almost as desperate as that which leads a man firm and erect to the scaffold, Jules determined to follow this advice, and arrived at Château Tourelles without having once thought of poor Alexa and her tell-tale eyes by the way;—nay, even when he saw her before him, his only sensation was that of impatient agony that the moment which was to decide upon his destiny was still delayed.

As Alexa opened the door to seek her friend, she appeared, and they returned together. At the unexpected sight of Jules, Isabeau lost her self-possession, and sank nearly fainting on a chair. In an instant he was at her feet. "Isabeau!" he exclaimed, in a voice at once solemn and impassioned— "Isabeau! I adore you—speak my fate in one word!—Isabeau! can you love me?"

The noble strangers had already left the room. They perceived that there was some knotty point to be explained upon which their presence could throw no light. They would have led their daughter with them, but she lingered. "One moment ... and I will follow you," she said. Then turning to her almost fainting friend, she exclaimed, "You love him, Isabeau!—and it is I who have divided you!"... She seized a hand of each, and joining them together, bent her head upon them and kissed them both. "God for ever bless you, perfect friend!... I am still too happy!... Believe me, Jules,—believe me, Isabeau,—I am happy—oh! too happy!" The arms that were thrown round them both, relaxed as she uttered these words, and she fell to the ground.

Alexa never spoke again. She breathed faintly for a few hours, and then expired,—the victim of intense feelings, too long and too severely tried.

This story, almost verbally as I have repeated it to you, was told me by a lady who assured me that she knew all the leading facts to be true; though she confessed that she was obliged to pass rather slightly over some of the details, from not remembering them perfectly. If the catastrophe be indeed true, I think it may be doubted whether the poor Alexa died from sorrow or from joy.

LETTER LIX.

Procès Monstre—Dislike of the Prisoners to the Ceremony of Trial—Société des Droits de l'Homme—Names Given to the Sections—Kitchen and Nursery Literature—Anecdote of Lagrange—Republican Law.

It is a long time since I have permitted a word to escape me about the trial of trials; but do not therefore imagine that we are as free from it and its daily echo as I have kindly suffered you to be.

It really appears to me, after all, that this monster trial is only monstrous because the prisoners do not like to be tried. There may perhaps have been some few legal incongruities in the manner of proceeding, arising very naturally from the difficulty of ascertaining exactly what the law is, in a country so often subjected to revolution as this has been. I own I have not yet made out completely to my own satisfaction, whether these gentry were accused in the first instance of high treason, or whether the whole proceedings rest upon an indictment for a breach of the peace. It is however clear enough, Heaven knows, both from evidence and from their own avowals, that if they were not arraigned for high treason, many of them were unquestionably guilty of it; and as they have all repeatedly proclaimed that it was their wish to stand or fall together, I confess that I see nothing very monstrous in treating them all as traitors.

It is only within these few last hours that I have been made to understand what object these simultaneous risings in April 1834 had in view. The document which has been now put into my hands appeared, I believe, in all the papers; but it was to me, at least, one of the thousand things that the eye glances over without taking the trouble of communicating to the mind what it finds. I will not take it for granted, however, that you are as ignorant or unobservant as myself, and therefore I shall not recite to you the evidence I have been just reading to prove that the union calling itself "La Société des Droits de l'Homme" was in fact the mainspring of the whole enterprise; but in case the expressive titles given by the central committee of this association to its different sections should have escaped you, I will transcribe them here,—or rather a part of them, for they are numerous enough to exhaust your patience, and mine too, were I to give them all. Among them, I find as pet and endearing names for their separate bands of employés the following: Section Marat, Section Robespierre, Section Quatre-vingt-treize, Section des Jacobins; Section de Guerre aux Châteaux—Abolition de la Propriété—Mort aux Tyrans—Des Piques—Canon d'Alarme—Tocsin—Barricade St. Méri,—and one which when it was given was only prophetic—Section de l'Insurrection de Lyon. These speak pretty plainly what sort of REFORM these men were preparing for France; and the trying those belonging to them who were taken with arms in their hands in open rebellion against the existing government, as traitors, cannot very justly, I think, be stigmatised as an act of tyranny, or in any other sense as a monstrous act.

The most monstrous part of the business is their conceiving (as the most conspicuous among them declare they do) that their refusing to plead, or, as they are pleased to call it, "refusing to take any part in the proceedings," was, or ought to be, reason sufficient for immediately stopping all such proceedings against them. These persons have been caught, with arms in their hands, in the very fact of enticing their fellow-citizens into overt acts of rebellion; but because they do not choose to answer when they are called upon, the court ordained to try them are stigmatised as monsters and assassins for not dismissing them untried!

If this is to succeed, we shall find the fashion obtain vogue amongst us, more rapidly than any of Madame Leroy's. Where is the murderer arraigned for his life who would not choose to make essay of so easy a method of escaping from the necessity of answering for his crime?

The trick is well imagined, and the degree of grave attention with which its availability is canvassed— out of doors at least—furnishes an excellent specimen of the confusion of intellect likely to ensue from confusion of laws amidst a population greatly given to the study of politics.

Never was there a finer opportunity for revolution and anarchy to take a lesson than the present. It is, I think, impossible for a mere looker-on, unbiassed by party or personal feelings of any kind, to deny that the government of Louis-Philippe is acting at this trying juncture with consummate courage, wisdom, and justice: but it is equally impossible not to perceive what revolution and revolt have done towards turning lawful power into tyranny. This is and ever must be inevitable wherever there is a hope existing that the government which follows the convulsion shall be permanent.

Fresh convulsions may arise—renewed tumult, destruction of property and risk of life may ensue; but at last it must happen that some strong hand shall seize the helm, and keep the reeling vessel to her stays, without heeding whether the grasp he has got of her be taken in conformity to received tactics or not.

Hardly a day passes that I do not hear of some proof of increased vigour on the part of the present government of France; and though I, for one, am certainly very far from approving the public acts which have given the present dynasty its power, I cannot but admire the strength and ability with which it is sustained.

The example, however, can avail but little to the legitimate monarchs who still occupy the thrones their forefathers occupied before them. No legitimate sovereign, possessing no power beyond what long-established law and precedent have given him, could dare show equal boldness. A king chosen in a rebellion is alone capable of governing rebels: and happy is it for the hot-headed jeunes gens of France that they have chanced to hit upon a prince who is neither a parvenu nor a mere soldier! The first would have had no lingering kindness at all for the still-remembered glories of the land; and the last, instead of trying them by the Chamber of Peers, would have had them up by fifties to a drum-head court martial, and probably have ordered the most troublesome among them to be picked off by their comrades, as an exercise at sharp-shooting, and as a useful example of military promptitude and decision.

The present government has indeed many things in its favour. The absence of every species of weakness and pusillanimity in the advisers of the crown is one; and the outrageous conduct of its enemies is another.

It is easy to perceive in the journals, and indeed in all the periodical publications which have been hitherto considered as belonging to the opposition, a gradual giving way before the overwhelming force of expediency. Conciliatory words come dropping in to the steady centre from côté droit and from côté gauche; and the louder the factious rebels roar around them, the firmer does the phalanx in which rests all the real strength of the country knit itself together.

The people of France are fully awakened to the feeling which Sheridan so strongly expresses when he says, that "the altar of liberty has been begrimed at once with blood and mire," and they are disposed to look towards other altars for their protection.

All the world are sick of politics in England; and all the world are sick of politics in France. It is the same in Spain, the same in Italy, the same in Germany, the same in Russia. The quiet and peaceably-disposed are wearied, worried, tormented, and almost stunned, by the ceaseless jarring produced by the confusion into which bad men have contrived to throw all the elements of social life. Chaos seems come again—a moral chaos, far worse for the poor animal called man than any that a comet's tail could lash the earth into. I assure you I often feel the most unfeigned longing to be out of reach of every sight and sound which must perforce mix up questions of government with all my womanly meditations on lesser things; but the necessity de parler politique seems like an evil spirit that follows whithersoever you go.

I often think, that among all the revolutions and rumours of revolutions which have troubled the earth, there is not one so remarkable as that produced on conversation within the last thirty years. I speak not, however, only of that important branch of it—"the polite conversation of sensible women," but of all the talk from garret to cellar throughout the world. Go where you will, it is the same; every living soul seems persuaded that it is his or her particular business to assist in arranging the political condition of Europe.

A friend of mine entered her nursery not long ago, and spied among her baby-linen a number of the Westminster Quarterly Review.

"What is this, Betty?" said she.

"It is only a book, ma'am, that John lent me to read," answered the maid.

"Upon my word, Betty," replied her mistress, "I think you would be much better employed in nursing the child than in reading books which you cannot understand."

"It does not hinder me from nursing the child at all," rejoined the enlightened young woman, "for I read as the baby lies in my lap; and as for understanding it, I don't fear about that, for John says it is no more than what it is the duty of everybody to understand."

So political we are, and political we must be—for John says so.

Wherefore I will tell you a little anecdote apropos of the Procès Monstre. An English friend of mine was in the Court of Peers the other day, when the prisoner Lagrange became so noisy and troublesome that it was found necessary to remove him. He had begun to utter in a loud voice, which was evidently intended to overpower the proceedings of the court, a pompous and inflammatory harangue, accompanied with much vehement action. His fellow-prisoners listened, and gazed at him with the most unequivocal marks of wondering admiration, while the court vainly endeavoured to procure order and silence.

"Remove the prisoner Lagrange!" was at last spoken by the president—and the guards proceeded to obey. The orator struggled violently, continuing, however, all the time to pour forth his rhapsody.

"Yes!" he cried,—"yes, my countrymen! we are here as a sacrifice. Behold our bosoms, tyrants! ... plunge your assassin daggers in our breasts! we are your victims ... ay, doom us all to death, we are ready—five hundred French bosoms are ready to...."

Here he came to a dead stop: his struggles, too, suddenly ceased.... He had dropped his cap,—the cap which not only performed the honourable office of sheltering the exterior of his patriotic head, but of bearing within its crown the written product of that head's inspired eloquence! It was in vain that he eagerly looked for it beneath the feet of his guards; the cap had been already kicked by the crowd far beyond his reach, and the bereaved orator permitted himself to be led away as quiet as a lamb.

The gentleman who related this circumstance to me added, that he looked into several papers the following day, expecting to see it mentioned; but he could not find it, and expressed his surprise to a friend who had accompanied him into court, and who had also seen and enjoyed the jest, that so laughable a circumstance had not been noticed.

"That would not do at all, I assure you," replied his friend, who was a Frenchman, and understood the politics of the free press perfectly; "there is hardly one of them who would not be afraid of making a joke of anything respecting les prévenus d'Avril."

Before I take my final leave of these precious prévenus, I must give you an extract from a curious volume lent me by my kind friend M. J—, containing a table of the law reports inserted in the Bulletin of the Laws of the Republic. I have found among them ordinances more tyrannical than ever despot passed for the purpose of depriving of all civil rights his fellow-men; but the one I am about to give you is certainly peculiarly applicable to the question of allowing prisoners to choose their counsel from among persons not belonging to the bar,—a question which has been setting all the hot heads of Paris in a flame.

"Loi concernant le Tribunal Révolutionnaire du 22Prairial, l'an deuxième de la République Française une etindivisible.

"La loi donne pour défenseurs aux patriotes calomniés, (theword 'accused' was too harsh to use in the case of thesebloody patriots,)—La loi donne pour défenseurs auxpatriotes calomniés, des jurés patriotes. Elle n'en accordepoint aux conspirateurs."

What would the LIBERALS of Europe have said of King Louis-Philippe, had he acted upon this republican principle? If he had, he might perhaps have said fairly enough—

"Cæsar does never wrong but with just cause,"

for they have chosen to take their defence into their own hands; but how the pure patriots of l'an deuxième would explain the principle on which they acted, it would require a republican to tell.

Memoirs of M. de Châteaubriand—The Readings at L'Abbaye-aux-Bois—Account of These in the French Newspapers and Reviews—Morning at the Abbaye to Hear a Portion of These Memoirs—The Visit to Prague.

In several visits which we have lately made to the ever-delightful Abbaye-aux-Bois, the question has been started, as to the possibility or impossibility of my being permitted to be present there "aux lectures des Mémoires de M. de Châteaubriand."

The apartment of my agreeable friend and countrywoman, Miss Clarke, also in this same charming Abbaye, was the scene of more than one of these anxious consultations. Against my wishes—for I really was hardly presumptuous enough to have hopes—was the fact that these lectures, so closely private, yet so publicly talked of and envied, were for the present over—nay, even that the gentleman who had been the reader was not in Paris. But what cannot zealous kindness effect? Madame Récamier took my cause in hand, and ... in a word, a day was appointed for me and my daughters to enjoy this greatly-desired indulgence.

Before telling you the result of this appointment, I must give you some particulars respecting these Memoirs, not so much apropos of myself and my flattering introduction to them, as from being more interesting in the way of Paris literary intelligence than anything I have met with.

The existence of these Memoirs is of course well known in England; but the circumstance of their having been read chez Madame Récamier, to a very select number of the noble author's friends, is perhaps not so—at least, not generally; and the extraordinary degree of sensation which this produced in the literary world of Paris was what I am quite sure you can have no idea of. This is the more remarkable from the well-known politics of M. de Châteaubriand not being those of the day. The circumstances connected with the reading of these Memoirs, and the effect produced on the public by the peep got at them through those who were present, have been brought together into a very interesting volume, containing articles from most of the literary periodicals of France, each one giving to its readers the best account it had been able to obtain of these "lectures de l'Abbaye." Among the articles thus brought together, are morceaux from the pens of every political party in France; but there is not one of them that does not render cordial—I might say, fervent homage to the high reputation, both literary and political, of the Vicomte de Châteaubriand.

There is a general preface to this volume, from the pen of M. Nisard, full of enthusiasm for the subject, and giving an animated and animating account of all the circumstances attending the readings, and of the different publications respecting them which followed.

It appears that the most earnest entreaties have been very generally addressed to M. de Châteaubriand to induce him to publish these Memoirs during his lifetime, but hitherto without effect. There is something in his reasonings on the subject equally touching and true: nevertheless, it is impossible not to lament that one cannot wish for a work so every way full of interest, without wishing at the same time that one of the most amiable men in the world should be removed out of it. All those who are admitted to his circle must, I am very sure, most heartily wish never to see any more of his Memoirs than what he may be pleased himself to show them: but he has found out a way to make the world at large look for his death as for a most agreeable event. Notwithstanding all his reasonings, I think he is wrong. Those who have seen the whole, or nearly the whole of this work, declare it to be both the most important and the most able that he has composed; and embracing as it does the most interesting epoch of the world's history, and coming from the hand of one who has played so varied and distinguished a part in it, we can hardly doubt that it is so.

Of all the different articles which compose the volume entitled "Lectures des Mémoires de M. de Châteaubriand," the most interesting perhaps (always excepting some fragments from the Memoirs themselves) are the preface of M. Nisard, and an extract from the Revue du Midi, from the pen of M. de Lavergne. I must indulge you with some short extracts from both. M. Nisard says—

"Depuis de longues années, M. de Châteaubriand travaille à ses Mémoires, avec le dessein de ne les laisser publier qu'après sa mort. Au plus fort des affaires, quand il était ministre, ambassadeur, il oubliait les petites et les grandes tracasseries en écrivant quelques pages de ce livre de prédilection."... "C'est le livre que M. de Châteaubriand aura le plus aimé, et, chose étrange! c'est le livre en qui M. de Châteaubriand ne veut pas être glorifié de son vivant."

He then goes on to speak of the manner in which the readings commenced ... and then says,—"Cette lecture fut un triomphe; ceux qui avaient été de la fête nous la racontèrent, à nous qui n'en étions pas, et qui déplorions que le salon de Madame Récamier, cette femme qui s'est fait une gloire de bonté et de grâce, ne fut pas grand comme la plaine de Sunium. La presse littéraire alla demander à l'illustre écrivain quelques lignes, qu'elle encadra dans de chaudes apologies: il y eut un moment où toute la littérature ne fut que l'annonce et la bonne nouvelle d'un ouvrage inédit."

M. Nisard, as he says, "n'était pas de la fête;" but he was admitted to a privilege perhaps more desirable still—namely, that of reading some portion of this precious MS. in the deep repose of the author's own study. He gives a very animated picture of this visit.

"... J'osai demander à M. de Châteaubriand la grace de me recevoir quelques heures chez lui, et là, pendant qu'il écrirait ou dicterait, de m'abandonner son porte-feuille et de me laisser m'y plonger à discretion ... il y consentit. Au jour fixe, j'allai Rue d'Enfer: le coeur me battait; je suis encore assez jeune pour sentir des mouvemens intérieurs à l'approche d'une telle joie. M. de Châteaubriand fit demander son manuscrit. Il y en a trois grands porte-feuilles: ceux-là, nul ne les lui disputera; ni les révolutions, ni les caprices de roi, ne les lui peuvent donner ni reprendre.

"Il eut la bonté de me lire les sommaires des chapitres—Lequel choisir, lequel préférer? ... je ne l'arrêtais pas dans la lecture, je ne disais rien ... enfin il en vint au voyage à Prague. Une grosse et sotte interjection me trahit; du fruit défendu c'était la partie la plus défendue. Je demandai donc le voyage à Prague. M. de Châteaubriand sourit, et me tendait le manuscrit.... Je mets quelque vanité à rappeler ces détails, bien que je tienne à ce qu'on sache bien que j'ai été encore plus heureux que vain d'une telle faveur; mais c'est peut-être le meilleur prix que j'ai reçu encore de quelques habitudes de dignité littéraire, et à ce titre il doit m'être pardonné de m'en enorgueillir.

"Quand j'eus le précieux manuscrit, je m'accoudai sur la table, et me mis a la lecture avec une avidité recueillie.... Quelquefois, à la fin des chapitres, regardant par-dessus mes feuilles l'illustre écrivain appliqué à son minutieux travail de révision, effaçant, puis, après quelque incertitude, écrivant avec lenteur une phrase en surcharge, et l'effaçant à moitié écrite, je voyais l'imagination et le sens aux prises. Quand, après mes deux heures de délices, amusé, instruit, intéressé, transporté, ayant passé du rire aux larmes, et des larmes au rire, ayant vu tour à tour, dans sa plus grande naïveté de sentimens, le poète, le diplomate, le voyageur, le pèlerin, le philosophe, je me suis jeté sur la main de M. de Châteaubriand, et lui ai bredouillé quelques paroles de gratitude tendre et profonde: ni lui ni moi n'étions gênés, je vous jure;—moi, parce que je donnais cours à un sentiment vrai; lui, parce qu'à ce moment-là il voulait bien mesurer la valeur de mes louanges sur leur sincérité."

This is, I think, very well conté; and as I have myself been de la fête, and heard read precisely this same admirable morceau, the Voyage à Prague, I can venture to say that the feeling expressed is in no degree exaggerated.

"Que puis-je dire maintenant de ces Mémoires?" ... he continues. "Sur le voyage à Prague ma plume est gênée; je ne me crois pas le droit de trahir le secret de M. de Châteaubriand—mais qui est-ce qui l'ayant suivi dans tous les actes de sa glorieuse vie, ne devine pas d'avance, sauf les détails secrets, et les milles beautés de rédaction, quelle peut être la pensée de cette partie des Mémoires! Qui ne sait à merveille qu'on y trouvera la vérité pour tout le monde, douce pour ceux qui ont beaucoup perdu et beaucoup souffert, dure pour les médiocrités importantes, qui se disputent les ministères et les ambassades auprès d'une royauté qui ne peut plus même donner de croix d'honneur? Qui est-ce qui ne s'attend à des lamentations sublimes sur des infortunes inouïes, à des attendrissemens de coeur sur toutes les misères de l'exil; sur le délabrement des palais où gîtent les royautés déchues; sur ces longs corridors éclairés par un quinquet à chaque bout, comme un corps de garde, ou un cloître; sur ces salles des gardes sans gardes; sur ces antichambres sans sièges pour s'asseoir; sur ces serviteurs rares, dont un seul fait l'étiquette qui autrefois en occupait dix; sur les malheurs toujours plus grands que les malheureux, qu'on plaint de loin pour ceux qui les souffrent, et de près pour soi-même?... Et puis après la politique vient la poésie; après les leçons sévères, les descriptions riantes, les observations de voyage, fines, piquantes, comme si le voyageur n'avait pas causé la veille avec un vieux roi d'un royaume perdu...."

I have given you this passage because it describes better than I could do myself the admirable narrative which I had the pleasure of hearing. M. Nisard says much more about it, and with equal truth; but I will only add his concluding words—"Voilà le voyage à Prague.... J'y ai été remué au plus profond et au meilleur de mon coeur par les choses touchantes, et j'ai pleuré sur la légitimité tombée, quoique n'ayant jamais compris cet ordre d'idées, et y étant resté, toute ma jeunesse, non seulement étranger, mais hostile."

I have transcribed this last observation for the purpose of proving to you that the admiration inspired by this work of M. de Châteaubriand's is not the result of party feeling, but in complete defiance of it.

In the "Revue de Paris" for March 1834 is an extremely interesting article from M. Janin, who was present, I presume, at the readings, and who must have been permitted, I think, now and then to peep over the shoulder of the reader, with a pencil in his hand, for he gives many short but brilliant passages from different parts of the work. This gentlemen states, upon what authority he does not say, that English speculators have already purchased the work at the enormous price of 25,000 francs for each volume. It already consists of twelve volumes, which makes the purchase amount to £12,000 sterling,—a very large sum, even if the acquisition could be made immediately available; but as we must hope that many years may elapse before it becomes so, it appears hardly credible that this statement should be correct.

Whenever these Memoirs are published, however, there can be no doubt of the eagerness with which they will be read. M. Janin remarks, that "M. de Châteaubriand, en ne croyant écrire que ses mémoires, aura écrit en effet l'histoire de son siècle;" and adds, "D'où l'on peut prédire, que si jamais une époque n'a été plus inabordable pour un historien, jamais aussi une époque n'aura eu une histoire plus complète et plus admirablement écrite que la nôtre. Songez donc, que pendant que M. de Châteaubriand fait ses mémoires, M. de Talleyrand écrit aussi ses mémoires. M. de Châteaubriand et M. de Talleyrand attelés l'un et l'autre à la même époque!—l'un qui en représente le sens poétique et royaliste, l'autre qui en est l'expression politique et utilitaire: l'un l'héritier de Bossuet, le conservateur du principe religieux; l'autre l'héritier de Voltaire, et qui ne s'est jamais prosterné que devant le doute, cette grande certitude de l'histoire: l'un enthousiaste, l'autre ironique; l'un éloquent partout, l'autre éloquent dans son fauteuil, au coin de son feu: l'un homme de génie, et qui le prouve; l'autre qui a bien voulu laisser croire qu'il était un homme d'esprit: celui-ci plein de l'amour de l'humanité, celui-là moins égoïste qu'on ne le croit; celui-ci bon, celui-là moins méchant qu'il ne veut le paraître: celui-ci allant par sauts et par bonds, impétueux comme un tonnerre, ou comme une phrase de l'Ecriture; celui-là qui boite, et qui arrive toujours le premier: celui-ci qui se montre toujours quand l'autre se cache, qui parle quand l'autre se tait; l'autre qui arrive toujours quand il faut arriver, qu'on ne voit guère, qu'on n'entend guère, qui est partout, qui voit tout, qui sait presque tout: l'un qui a des partisans, des enthousiastes, des admirateurs; l'autre qui n'a que des flatteurs, des parens, et des valets: l'un aimé, adoré, chanté; l'autre à peine redouté: l'un toujours jeune, l'autre toujours vieux; l'un toujours battu, l'autre toujours vainqueur; l'un victime des causes perdues, l'autre héros des causes gagnées; l'un qui mourra on ne sait où, l'autre qui mourra prince, et dans sa maison, avec un archevêque à son chevet; l'un grand écrivain à coup sûr, l'autre qui est un grand écrivain sans qu'on s'en doute; l'un qui a écrit ses mémoires pour les lire à ses amis, l'autre qui a écrit ses mémoires pour les cacher à ses amis; l'un qui ne les publie pas par caprice, l'autre qui ne les publie pas, parce qu'ils ne seront terminés que huit jours après sa mort; l'un qui a vu de haut et de loin, l'autre qui a vu d'en bas et de près: l'un qui a été le premier gentilhomme de l'histoire contemporaine, qui l'a vue en habit et toute parée; l'autre qui en a été le valet de chambre, et qui en sait toutes les plaies cachées;—l'un qu'on appelle Châteaubriand, l'autre qu'on appelle le Prince de Bénévent. Tels sont les deux hommes que le dix-neuvième siècle désigne à l'avance comme ses deux juges les plus redoutables, comme ses deux appréciateurs les plus dangereux, comme les deux historiens opposés, sur lesquels la postérité le jugera."

This parallel, though rather long perhaps, is very clever, and, à ce qu'on dit, very just.

Though my extracts from this very interesting but not widely-circulated volume have already run to a greater length than I intended, I cannot close it without giving you a small portion of M. de Lavergne's animated recital of the scene at the old Abbaye-aux-Bois;—an Abbaye, by the way, still partly inhabited by a society of nuns, and whose garden is sacred to them alone, though a portion of the large building which overlooks it is the property of Madame Récamier.

"A une des extrémités de Paris on trouve un monument d'une architecture simple et sévère. La cour d'entrée est fermée par une grille, et sur cette grille s'élève une croix. La paix monastique règne dans les cours, dans les escaliers, dans les corridors; mais sous les saintes voûtes de ce lieu se cachent aussi d'élégans réduits qui s'ouvrent par intervalle aux bruits du monde. Cette habitation se nomme l'Abbaye-aux-Bois,—nom pittoresque d'où s'exhale je ne sais quel parfum d'ombre et de mystère, comme si le couvent et la forêt y confondaient leurs paisibles harmonies. Or, dans un des angles de cet édifice il y a un salon que je veux décrire, moi aussi, car il reparaît bien souvent dans mes rêves. Vous connaissez le tableau de Corinne de Gérard: Corinne est assise au Cap Misène, sur un rocher, sa belle tête levée vers le ciel, son beau bras tombant vers la terre, avec sa lyre détendue; le chant vient de finir, mais l'inspiration illumine encore ses regards divins.... Ce tableau couvre tout un des murs du salon, en face la cheminée avec une glace, des girandoles, et des fleurs.... Des deux autres murs, l'un est percé de deux fenêtres qui laissent voir les tranquilles jardins de l'Abbaye, l'autre disparaît presque tout entier sous des rayons chargés de livres. Des meubles élégans sont épars çà et là, avec un gracieux désordre. Dans un des coins, la porte qui s'entr'ouvre, et dans l'autre une harpe qui attend.

"Je vivrais des milliers d'années que je n'oublierais jamais rien de ce que j'ai vu là.... D'autres ont rapporté des courses de leur jeunesse le souvenir d'un site grandiose, ou d'une ruine monumentale; moi, je n'ai vu ni la Grèce ... etc: ... mais il m'a été ouvert ce salon de l'Europe et du siècle, où l'air est en quelque sorte chargé de gloire et de génie.... Là respire encore l'âme enthousiaste de Madame de Staël; là reparaît, à l'imagination qui l'évoque, la figure mélancolique et pâle de Benjamin Constant; là retentit la parole vibrante et libre du grand Foy. Tous ces illustres morts viennent faire cortège à celle qui fut leur amie; car cet appartement est celui d'une femme célèbre dont on a déjà deviné le nom. Malgré cette pudeur de renommée qui la fait ainsi se cacher dans le silence, Madame Récamier appartient à l'histoire; c'est désormais un de ces beaux noms de femme qui brillent dans la couronne des grandes époques ainsi que des perles sur un bandeau. Révélée au monde par sa beauté, elle l'a charmé peut-être plus encore par les graces de son esprit et de son coeur. Mêlée par de hautes amitiés aux plus grands événemens de l'époque, elle en a traversé les vicissitudes sans en connaître les souillures, et, dans sa vie toute d'idéal, le malheur même et l'exil n'ont été pour elle que des charmes de plus. A la voir aujourd'hui si harmonieuse et si sereine, on dirait que les orages de la vie n'ont jamais approché de ses jours; à la voir si simple et si bienveillante, on dirait que sa célébrité n'est qu'un songe, et que les plus superbes fronts de la France moderne n'ont jamais fléchi devant elle. Aimée des poètes, des grands, et du Ciel, c'est à-la-fois Laure, Eléonore et Béatrix, dont Pétrarque, Tasse et le Dante ont immortalisé les noms.

"Un jour de Février dernier il y avait dans le salon de Madame Récamier une réunion convoquée pour une lecture. L'assemblée était bien peu nombreuse, et il n'est pas d'homme si haut placé par le rang ou par le génie qui n'eût été fier de s'y trouver. A côté d'un Montmorency, d'un

Larochefoucauld, et d'un Noailles, représentans de la vieille noblesse française, s'asseyaient leurs égaux par la noblesse du talent, cet autre hasard de la naissance; Saint-Beuve et Quinet, Gerbet et Dubois, Lenormand et Ampère: vous y étiez aussi, Ballanche!...

"Il parut enfin celui dont le nom avait réuni un tel auditoire, et toutes les têtes s'inclinèrent.... Son front avait toute la dignité des cheveux gris, mais ses yeux vifs brillaient de jeunesse. Il portait à la main, comme un pèlerin ou un soldat, un paquet enveloppé dans un mouchoir de soie. Cette simplicité me parut merveilleuse dans un pareil sujet; car ce noble vieillard, c'était l'auteur des Martyrs, du Génie du Christianisme, de René—ce paquet du pèlerin, c'étaient les Mémoires de M. de Châteaubriand.... Mais quelle douloureuse émotion dans les premiers mots—'Mémoires d'Outre-tombe!... Préface testamentaire!'...

"Continuez, Châteaubriand, à filer en paix votre suaire. Aussi bien, il n'y a de calme aujourd'hui que le dernier sommeil, il n'y a de stable que la mort!... Vieux serviteur de la vieille monarchie! vous n'avez pas visité sans tressaillir ces sombres galeries du Hradschin, où se promènent trois larves royales, avec une ombre de couronne sur le front. Vous avez baigné de vos pleurs les mains de ce vieillard qui emporte avec lui toute une société, et la tête de cet enfant dont les graces n'ont pu fléchir l'inexorable destinée qui s'attache aux races antiques.... Filez votre suaire de soie et d'or, Châteaubriand, et enveloppez-vous dans votre gloire; il n'est pas de progrès qui vous puisse ravir votre immortalité."

I think that by this time you must be fully aware, my dear friend, that this intellectual fête to which we were invited at the Abbaye-aux-Bois was a grace and a favour of which we have very good reason to be proud. I certainly never remember to have been more gratified in every way than I was on this occasion. The thing itself, and the flattering kindness which permitted me to enjoy it, were equally the source of pleasure. I may say with all truth, like M. de Lavergne, "Je vivrais des milliers d'années que je ne l'oublierais jamais."

The choice of the morceau, too, touched me not a little: "du fruit défendu, cette partie la plus défendue" was most assuredly what I should have eagerly chosen had choice been offered. M. de Châteaubriand's journey to Prague furnishes as interesting an historical scene as can well be imagined; and I do not believe that any author that ever lived, Jean-Jacques and Sir Walter not excepted, could have recounted it better—with more true feeling or more finished grace: simple and unaffected to perfection in its style, yet glowing with all the fervour of a poetical imagination, and all the tenderness of a most feeling heart. It is a gallery of living portraits that he brings before the eye as if by magic. There is no minute painting, however: the powerful, the painfully powerful effect of the groups he describes, is produced by the bold and unerring touch of a master. I fancied I saw the royal race before me, each one individual and distinct; and I could have said, as one does in seeing a clever portrait, "That is a likeness, I'll be sworn for it." Many passages made a profound impression on my fancy and on my memory; and I think I could give a better account of some of the scenes described than I should feel justified in doing as long as the noble author chooses to keep them from the public eye. There were touches which made us weep abundantly; and then he changed the key, and gave us the prettiest, the most gracious, the most smiling picture of the young princess and her brother, that it was possible for pen to trace. She must be a fair and glorious creature, and one that in days of yore might have been likely enough to have seen her colours floating on the helm of all the doughtiest knights in Christendom. But chivalry is not the fashion of the day;—there is nothing positif, as the phrase goes, to be gained by it;—and I doubt if "its ineffectual fire" burn very brightly at the present time in any living heart, save that of M. de Châteaubriand himself.

The party assembled at Madame Récamier's on this occasion did not, I think, exceed seventeen, including Madame Récamier and M. de Châteaubriand. Most of these had been present at the former readings. The Duchesses de Larochefoucauld and Noailles, and one or two other noble ladies, were among them. I felt it was a proof that genius is of no party, when I saw a granddaughter of General Lafayette enter among us. She is married to a gentleman who is said to be of the extreme côté gauche; but I remarked that they both listened with as much deep interest to all the touching details of this mournful visit as the rest of us. Who, indeed, could help it?—This lady sat between me and Madame Récamier on one sofa; M. Ampère the reader, and M. de Châteaubriand himself, on another, immediately at right angles with it,—so that I had the pleasure of watching one of the most expressive countenances I ever looked at, while this beautiful specimen of his head and his heart was displayed to us. On the other side of me was a gentleman whom I was extremely happy to meet—the celebrated Gérard; and before the reading commenced, I had the pleasure of conversing with him: he is one of those whose aspect and whose words do not disappoint the expectations which high reputation always gives birth to. There was no formal circle;—the ladies approached themselves a little towards THE sofa which was placed at the feet of Corinne, and the gentlemen stationed themselves in groups behind them. The sun shone delicately into the room through the white silk curtains—delicious flowers scented the air—the quiet gardens of the Abbaye, stretched to a sufficient distance beneath the windows to guard us from every Parisian sound—and, in short, the whole thing was perfect. Can you wonder that I was delighted? or that I have thought the occurrence worth dwelling upon with some degree of lingering fondness?

The effect this delightful morning has had on us is, I assure you, by no means singular: it would be easy to fill a volume with the testimonies of delight and gratitude which have been offered from various quarters in return for this gratification. Madame Tastu, whom I have heard called the Mrs. Hemans of France, was present at one or more of the readings, and has returned thanks in some very pretty lines, which conclude thus fervently:—

"Ma têteS'incline pour saisir jusques aux moindres sons,
Et mon genou se ploie à demi, quand je prête,
Enchantée et muette,   L'oreille à vos leçons!"

Apropos of tributary verses on this subject, I am tempted to conclude my unmercifully long epistle by giving you some lines which have as yet, I believe, been scarcely seen by any one but the person to whom they are addressed. They are from the pen of the H. G. who so beautifully translated the twelve first cantos of the "Frithiof Saga," which was so favourably received in England last spring.

H. G. is an Englishwoman, but from the age of two to seventeen she resided in the United States of America. Did I not tell you this, you would be at a loss to understand her allusion to the distant dwelling of her youth.

This address, as you will perceive, is not as an acknowledgment for having been admitted to the Abbaye, but an earnest prayer that she may be so; and I heartily hope it will prove successful.

TO M. LE VICOMTE DE CHATEAUBRIAND.

In that distant region, the land of the West,
Where my childhood and youth glided rapidly by,
Ah! why was my bosom with sorrow oppress'd?
Why trembled the tear-drop so oft in mine eye?

No! 'twas not that pleasures they told me alone

Were found in the courts where proud monarchs reside;
My knee could not bend at the foot of a throne,
My heart could not hallow an emperor's pride.

But, oh! 'twas the thought that bright genius there dwelt,
And breathed on a few holy spirits its flame,
That awaken'd the grief which in childhood I felt,
When, Europe! I mutter'd thy magical name.

And now that as pilgrim I visit thy shore,
I ask not where kings hold their pompous array;
But I fain would behold, and all humbly adore,
The wreath which thy brows, Châteaubriand! display.

My voice may well falter—unknown is my name,
But say, must my accents prove therefore in vain?
Beyond the Atlantic we boast of thy fame,
And repeat that thy footstep has traversed our plain.

Great bard!—then reject not the prayer that I speak With trembling emotion, and offer thee now;In thy eloquent page, oh! permit me to seek The joys and the sorrows that genius may know.

H. G.

LETTER LXI.

Jardin des Plantes—Not Equal in Beauty to our Zoological Gardens—La Salpêtrière—Anecdote—Les Invalides—Difficulty of Finding English Colours There—The Dome.

Another long morning on the other side of the water has given us abundant amusement, and sent us home in a very good humour with the expedition, because, after very mature and equitable consideration, we were enabled honestly to decide that our Zoological Gardens are in few points inferior, in many equal, and in some greatly superior, to the long and deservedly celebrated Jardin des Plantes.

If considered as a museum and nursery for botanists, we certainly cannot presume to compare our comparatively new institution to that of Paris; but, zoologically speaking, it is every way superior. The collection of animals, both birds and beasts, is, I think, better, and certainly in finer condition. I confess that I envy them their beautiful giraffe; but what else have they which we cannot equal? Then as to our superiority, look at the comparative degree of beauty of the two enclosures. "O England!" as I once heard a linen-draper exclaim in the midst of his shop, intending in his march of mind to quote Byron—

"O England! with all thy faults, I can't help loving thee still."

And I am quite of the linen-draper's mind: I cannot help loving those smooth-shaven lawns, those untrimmed flowing shrubs, those meandering walks, now seen, now lost amidst a cool green labyrinth of shade, which are so truly English. You have all this at the Zoological Gardens—we have none of it in the Jardin des Plantes; and, therefore, I like the Zoological Gardens best.

We must not say a word, my friend, about the lectures, or the free admission to them—that is not our forte; and if the bourgeoisie go on much longer as they do at present, becoming greater and more powerful with every passing day, and learning to know, as their mercantile neighbours have long known, that it is quite necessary both governments and individuals should turn all things to profit;—

"Car dans le siècle où nous sommes,
On ne donne rien pour rien;"—

if this happens, as I strongly suspect it will, then we shall have no more lectures gratis even in Paris.

From the Jardin des Plantes, we visited that very magnificent hospital, La Salpêtrière. I will spare you, however, all the fine things that might be said about it, and only give you a little anecdote which occurred while we stood looking into the open court where the imbecile and the mad are permitted to take their exercise. By the way, without at all presuming to doubt that there may be reasons which the managers of this establishment conceive to be satisfactory, why these wretched objects, in different stages of their dreadful calamity, should be thus for ever placed before each other's eyes, I cannot but observe, that the effect upon the spectator is painful beyond anything I ever witnessed.

With my usual love for the terrible, I remained immovable for above twenty minutes, watching the manner in which they appeared to notice each other. If fancy did not cheat me, those who were least wildly deranged looked with a sort of triumph and the consciousness of superiority on those who were most so: some looked on the mad movements of the others and laughed distractedly;—in short, the scene is terribly full of horror.

But to return to my anecdote. A stout girl, who looked more imbecile than mad, was playing tricks, that a woman who appeared to have some authority among them endeavoured to stop. The girl evidently understood her, but with a sort of dogged obstinacy persevered, till the nurse, or matron, or whatever she was, took hold of her arm, and endeavoured to lead her into the house. Upon this the girl resisted; and it was not without some degree of violence that she was at last conquered and led away.

"What dreadful cruelty!" exclaimed a woman who like ourselves was indulging her curiosity by watching the patients. An old crone, a very aged and decrepid pensioner of the establishment, was passing by on her crutches as she spoke. She stopped in her hobbling walk, and addressing the stranger in the gentle voice of quiet good sense, and in a tone which made me fancy she had seen better days, said—"Dreadful cruelty, good woman?... She is preventing her from doing what ought not to be done. If you had the charge of her, you would think it your duty to do the same, and then it would be right. But 'dreadful cruelty!' is easily said, and sounds good-hearted; and those who know not what it is to govern, generally think it is a sin and a shame to use authority in any way." And so saying, the old woman hobbled on, leaving me convinced that La Salpêtrière did not give its shelter to fools only.

From this hospital we took a very long drive to another, going almost from the extremest east to the extremest west of Paris. The Invalides was now our object; and its pleasant, easy, comfortable aspect offered a very agreeable contrast to the scene we had left. We had become taciturn and melancholy at La Salpêtrière; but this interesting and noble edifice revived our spirits completely. Two of the party had never been there before, and the others were eloquent in pointing out all that their former visits had shown them. No place can be better calculated to stimulate conversation;

there is so much to be said about our own Greenwich and Queen Elizabeth, versus Louis le Grand and the Invalides. Then we had the statue of a greater than he—even of Napoleon—upon which to gaze and moralise. Some veteran had climbed up to it, despite a wooden leg, or a single arm perhaps, and crowned the still-honoured head with a fresh wreath of bays.

While we stood looking at this, the courteous bow and promising countenance of a fine old man arrested the whole party, and he was questioned and chatted to, till he became the hero of his own tale, and we soon knew exactly where he had received his first wound, what were his most glorious campaigns, and, above all, who was the general best deserving the blessing of an old soldier.

Those who in listening to such chronicles in France expect to hear any other name than that of Napoleon will be disappointed. We may talk of his terrible conscriptions, of poisonings at Jena or forsakings at Moscow, as we will; the simple fact which answers all is, that he was adored by his soldiers when he was with them, and that his memory is cherished with a tender enthusiasm to which history records no parallel. The mere tone of voice in which the name of "NAPOLEON!" or the title of "L'EMPEREUR!" is uttered by his veterans, is of itself enough to prove what he was to them. They stand taller by an inch when he is named, and throw forward the chest, and snuff the air, like an old war-horse that hears the sound of a trumpet.

But still, with all these interesting speculations to amuse us, we did not forget what must ever be the primary object of a stranger's visit to the Invalides—the interior of the dome. But this is only to be seen at particular hours; and we were too late for the early, and too early for the late, opening of the doors for this purpose. Four o'clock was the hour we had to wait for—as yet it was but three. We were invited into the hall and into the kitchen; we were admitted, too, into sundry little enclosures, appropriated to some happy individuals favoured for their skill in garden craft, who, turning their muskets into hoes and spades, enjoy their honourable leisure ten times more than their idle brethren. In three out of four of these miniature domains we found plaister Napoleons of a foot high stuck into a box-tree or a rose-bush: one of these, too, had a wreath of newly-gathered leaves twisted round the cocked-hat, and all three were placed and displayed with as much attention to dignity and effect as the finest statues in the Tuileries.

If the spirit of Napoleon is permitted to hover about Paris, to indulge itself in gathering the scattered laurels of his posthumous fame, it is not to the lofty chambers of the Tuileries that it should betake itself;—nor would it be greatly soothed by listening to the peaceful counsels of his once warlike maréchals. No—if his ghost be well inspired, it will just glide swiftly through the gallery of the Louvre, to compare it with his earthly recollections; balance itself for a moment over the statue of the Place Vendôme, and abide, for the rest of the time allotted for this mundane visit, among his faithful invalids. There only would he meet a welcome that would please him. The whole nation, it is true, dearly love to talk of his greatness; but there is little now left in common between them and their sometime emperor.

France with a charter, and France without, differs not by many degrees so widely as France military, and France bourgeoise and boursière. Under Napoleon she was the type of successful war; under Louis-Philippe, she will, I think—if the republicans will let her alone—become that of prosperous peace: a sword and a feather might be the emblem of the one—a loom and a long purse of the other.

But still it was not four o'clock. We were next invited to enter the chapel; and we did so, determined to await the appointed hour reposing ourselves on the very comfortable benches provided for the veterans to whose use it is appropriated.

Here, stretched and lounging at our ease, we challenged each other to discover English colours among the multitude of conquered banners which hung suspended above our heads. It is hardly possible that some such should not be there; yet it is a positive fact, that not all our familiar acquaintance with the colours we sought could enable us to discover them. There is indeed one torn and battered relic, that it is just possible might have been hacked and sawed from the desperately firm grasp of an Englishman; but the morsel of rag left is so small, that it was in fact more from the lack of testimony than the presence of it that we at length came to the conclusion that this relic of a stick might once have made part of an English standard.

Not in any degree out of humour at our disappointment in this search after our national banner, we followed the guide who summoned us at last to the dome, chatting and laughing as cheerily and as noisily as if we had not been exhausting our spirits for the last four hours by sight-seeing. But what fatigue could not achieve, was the next moment produced by wonder, admiration, and delight. Never did muter silence fall upon a talking group, than the sight of this matchless chapel brought on us. Speech is certainly not the first or most natural resource that the spirit resorts to, when thus roused, yet chastened—enchanted, yet subdued.

I have not yet been to Rome, and know not how I shall feel if ever I find myself under the dome of St. Peter's. There, I conceive that it is a sense of vastness which seizes on the mind; here it is wholly a feeling of beauty, harmony, and grace. I know nothing like it anywhere: the Pantheon (ci-devant Ste. Geneviève), with all its nobleness and majesty, is heavy, and almost clumsy, when compared to it. Though possessing no religious solemnity whatever, and in this respect inferior beyond the reach of comparison to the choir of Cologne, or King's College Chapel at Cambridge, it nevertheless produces a stronger effect upon the senses than either of them. This is owing, I suspect, to the circumstance of there being no mixture of objects: the golden tabernacle seems to complete rather than destroy its unity. If I could give myself a fête, it should be, to be placed within the pure, bright, lofty loveliness of this marble sanctuary, while a full and finished orchestra performed the chefs-d'oeuvre of Handel or Mozart in the church.

LETTER LXII.

Expedition to Montmorency—Rendezvous in the Passage Delorme—St. Denis—Tomb Prepared for Napoleon—The Hermitage—Dîner sur l'herbe.

It is more than a fortnight ago, I think, that we engaged ourselves with a very agreeable party of twenty persons to take a long drive out of Paris and indulge ourselves with a very gay "dîner sur l'herbe." But it is no easy matter to find a day on which twenty people shall all be ready and willing to leave Paris. However, a steadfast will can conquer most things. The whole twenty were quite determined that they would go to Montmorency, and to Montmorency at last we have been. The day was really one of great enjoyment, but yet it did not pass without disasters. One of these which occurred at the moment of starting very nearly overthrew the whole scheme. The place of general rendezvous for us and our hampers was the Galerie Delorme, and thither one of the party who had undertaken that branch of the business had ordered the carriages to come. At ten o'clock precisely, the first detachment of the party was deposited with their belongings at the southern extremity of the gallery; another and another followed till the muster-roll was complete. Baskets were piled on baskets; and the passers-by read our history in these, and in our anxious eyes, which ceased not to turn with ever-increasing anxiety the way the carriages should come.

What a supplice!... Every minute, every second, brought the rolling of wheels to our ears, but only to mock us: the wheels rolled on—no carriages came for us, and we remained in statu quo to look at each other and our baskets.

Then came forth, as always happens on great and trying occasions, the inward character of each. The sturdy and firm-minded set themselves down on the packages, determined to abide the eyes of all rather than shrink from their intent. The timid and more frail of purpose gently whispered proposals that we should all go home again; while others, yet listening to

"Hope's enchanting measure,
Which still promised coming pleasure,"

smiled, and looked forth from the gallery, and smiled again—though still no carriage came.

It was, as I suspect, these young hopes and smiles which saved us from final disappointment: for the young men belonging to the cortége, suddenly rousing themselves from their state of listless watching, declared with one voice and one spirit, that les demoiselles should not be disappointed; and exchanging consignes which were to regulate the number and species of vehicles each was to seek—and find, too, on peril of his reputation,—they darted forth from the gallery, leaving us with renewed spirits and courage to bear all the curious glances bestowed upon us.

Our half-dozen aides-de-camp returned triumphantly in a few minutes, each one in his delta or his citadine; and the Galerie Delorme was soon left far behind us.

It is lucky for you that we had not to make a "voyage par mer" and "retour par terre," or my story might be as long—if resembling it in no other way—as the immortal expedition to St. Cloud. I shall not make a volume of it; but I must tell you that we halted at St. Denis.

The church is beautiful—a perfect bijou of true Gothic architecture—light, lofty, elegant; and we saw it, too, in a manner peculiarly advantageous, for it had neither organ, altar, nor screen to distract the eye from the great and simple beauty of the original design. The repairs going on here are of a right royal character—on a noble scale and in excellent taste. Several monuments restored from the collection made under the Empire aux Petits Augustins are now again the glory of St. Denis; and some of them have still much remaining which may entitle them to rank as very pure and perfect specimens of highly-antiquated monumental sculpture. But the chiselled treasures of a thousand years' standing cannot be made to travel about like the scenery of strolling players, in conformity to the will and whim of the successive actors who play the part of king, without great injury. In some instances the original nooks in this venerable mausoleum of royal bones have again received the effigies originally carved to repose within them; but the regal image has rarely been replaced without showing itself in some degree way-worn. In other cases, the monumental portrait, venerable and almost hallowed by its high antiquity, is made to recline on a whitened sepulchre as bright as Parisian masonry can make it.

Having fully examined the church and its medley of old and new treasures, we called a council as to the possibility of finding time for descending to the crypts: but most of the party agreeing in opinion that we ought not to lose the opportunity of visiting what a wit amongst us happily enough designated "le Palais Royal de la Mort," we ordered the iron gates to be unbarred for us, and proceeded with some solemnity of feeling into the pompous tomb. And here the unfortunate result of that bold spirit of change which holds nothing sacred is still more disagreeably obvious than in the church. All the royal monuments of France that could be collected are assembled in this magnificent vault, but with such incongruity of dates belonging to different parts of the same structure, as almost wholly to destroy the imposing effect of this gorgeous grave.

But if the spectator would seek farther than his eye can carry him, and inquire where the mortal relics of each sculptured monarch lie, the answer he will receive must make him believe that the royal dust of France has been scattered to the four winds of heaven. Nothing I have heard has sounded more strangely to me than the naïveté with which our guide informed us that, among all this multitude of regal tombs, there was not one which contained a single vestige of the mortal remains of those they commemorate.

For the love of good taste and consistency, these guardians of the royal sepulchre of France should be taught a more poetical lesson. It is inconceivable how, as he spoke, the solemn memorials of the illustrious dead, near which my foot had passed cautiously and my voice been mute, seemed suddenly converted into something little more sacred than the show furnishing of a stone-mason's shop. The bathos was perfect.

I could not but remember with a feeling of national pride the contrast to this presented by Westminster Abbey and St. George's Chapel. The monuments of these two royal fanes form a series as interesting in the history of art as of our royal line, and no painful consciousness of desecration mixes itself with the solemn reverence with which we contemplate the honoured tombs.

The most interesting object in the crypts of St. Denis, and which comes upon the moral feeling with a force increased rather than diminished by the incongruities which surround it, is the door of the vault prepared by Napoleon for himself. It is inscribed,

ICI REPOSENTLES DÉPOUILLES MORTELLESDE

This inscription still remains, as well as the massive brazen gates with their triple locks, which were designed to close the tomb. These rich portals are not suspended on hinges, but rest against a wall of solid masonry, over which the above inscription is seen. The imperial vault thus chosen by the living despot as the sanctuary for bones which it was our fortune to dispose of elsewhere is greatly distinguished by its situation, being exactly under the high altar, and in the centre of the crypts, which follow the beautiful curve of the Lady Chapel above. It now contains the bodies of Louis Dix-huit and the Duc de Berri, and is completely bricked up.

In another vault, at one end of the circular crypts, and perfectly excluded from the light of day, but made visible by a single feeble lamp, are two coffins enclosing the remains of the two last defunct princes of the blood royal; but I forget their names. When I inquired of our conductor why these two coffins were thus exposed to view, he replied, with the air of a person giving information respecting what was as unchangeable as the laws of the Medes and Persians, "C'est toujours ainsi;" adding, "When another royal corpse is interred, the one of these two which was the first deposited will be removed, to be placed beneath its monument; but two must ever remain thus."

"Always" and "ever" are words which can seldom be used discreetly without some reservation; but respecting anything connected with the political state of France, I should think they had better never be used at all.

We returned to the carriages and pursued our pretty drive. The latter part of the route is very beautiful, and we all walked up one long steep hill, as much, or more perhaps, to enjoy the glorious view, and the fresh delicious air, as to assist the horses.

Arrived at the famous Cheval Blanc at Montmorency, (a sign painted, as the tradition says, by no less a hand than that of Gérard, who, in a youthful pilgrimage with his friend Isabey to this region consecrated to romance, found himself with no other means of defraying their bill than by painting a sign for his host,) we quitted our wearied and wearisome citadines, and began to seek, amidst the multitude of horses and donkeys which stood saddled and bridled around the door of the inn, for twenty well-conditioned beasts, besides a sumpter-mule or two, to carry us and our provender to the forest.

And, oh! the tumult and the din that accompanied this selection! Multitudes of old women and ragamuffin boys assailed us on all sides—"Tenez, madame; voilà mon âne! y a-t-il une autre bête comme la mienne?..." "Non, non, non, belles dames! Ne le croyez pas; c'est la mienne qu'il vous faut..." "Et vous, monsieur—c'est un cheval qui vous manque, n'est-ce pas? en voilà un superbe...."

The multitude of hoarse old voices, and shrill young ones, joined to our own noisy mirth, produced a din that brought out half the population of Montmorency to stare at us: but at length we were mounted—and, what was of infinitely more consequence, and infinitely more difficulty also, our hampers and baskets were mounted too.

But before we could think of the greenwood tree, and the gay repast to be spread under it, we had a pilgrimage to make to the shrine which has given the region all its fame. Hitherto we had thought only of its beauty,—who does not know the lovely scenery of Montmorency?—even without the name of Rousseau to give a fanciful interest to every path around it, there is enough in its hills and dales, its forest and its fields, to cheer the spirits and enchant the eye.

A day stolen from the dissipation, the dust, and the noise of a great city, is always delightful; but when it is enjoyed in the very fullest green perfection of the last days of May, when every new-born leaf and blossom is fully expanded to the delicious breeze, and not one yet fallen before it, the enjoyment is perfect. It is like seeing a new piece while the dresses and decorations are all fresh; and never can the mind be in a state to taste with less of pain, and more of pleasure, the thoughts suggested by such a scene as the Hermitage. I have, however, no intention of indulging myself in a burst of tender feeling over the melancholy memory of Rousseau, or of enthusiastic gratitude at the recollection of Grétry, though both are strongly brought before the mind's eye by the various memorials of each so carefully treasured in the little parlour in which they passed so many hours: yet it is impossible to look at the little rude table on which the first and greatest of these gifted men scribbled the "Héloïse," or on the broken and untuneable keys of the spinette with which the eloquent visionary so often soothed his sadness and solitude, without some feeling tant soit peu approaching to the sentimental.

Before the window of this small gloomy room, which opens upon the garden, is a rose-tree planted by the hand of Rousseau, which has furnished, as they told us, cuttings enough to produce a forest of roses. The house is as dark and dull as may be; but the garden is pretty, and there is something of fanciful in its arrangement which makes me think it must be as he left it.

The records of Grétry would have produced more effect if seen elsewhere,—at least I thought so;—yet the sweet notes of "O Richard! O mon roi!" seemed to be sounding in my ears, too, as I looked at his old spectacles, and several other little domestic relics that were inscribed with his name. But the "Rêveries du Promeneur Solitaire" are worth all the notes that Grétry ever wrote.

A marble column stands in a shady corner of the garden, bearing an inscription which states that her highness the Duchesse de Berri had visited the Hermitage, and taken "le coeur de Grétry" under her august protection, which had been unjustly claimed by the Liégeois from his native France. What this means, or where her highness found the great composer's heart, I could not learn.

We took the objects of our expedition in most judicious order, fasting and fatigue being decidedly favourable to melancholy; but, even with these aids, I cannot say that I discovered much propensity to the tender vein in the generality of our party. Sentiment is so completely out of fashion, that it would require a bold spirit to confess before twenty gay souls that you felt any touch of it. There was one young Italian, however, of the party whom I missed from the time we entered the precincts of the Hermitage; nor did I see him till some time after we were all mounted again, and in full chase for the well-known chesnut-trees which have thrown their shadow over so many al-fresco repasts. When he again joined us, he had a rose in his button-hole: I felt quite certain that it was plucked from the tree the sad philosopher had planted, and that he, at least, had done homage to his shade, whoever else had failed to do so.

Whatever was felt at the Hermitage, however, was now left behind us, and a less larmoyante party never entered the Forest of Montmorency. When we reached the spot on which we had fixed by anticipation for our salle-à-manger, we descended from our various montures, which were immediately unsaddled and permitted to refresh themselves, tied together in very picturesque groups, while all the party set to work with that indescribable air of contented confusion and happy disorder which can only be found at a pic-nic. I have heard a great many very sensible remarks, and some of them really very hard to answer, upon the extreme absurdity of leaving every accommodation which is considered needful for the comfort of a Christian-like dinner, for the sole purpose of devouring this needful repast without one of them. What can be said in defence of such an act?... Nothing,—except perhaps that, for some unaccountable reason or other, no dinner throughout the year, however sumptuously served or delicately furnished, ever does appear to produce one half so much light-hearted enjoyment as the cold repast round which the guests crouch like so many gipsies, with the turf for their table and a tree for their canopy. It is very strange—but it is very true; and as long as men and women continue to experience this singular accession of good spirits and good humour from circumstances which might be reasonably expected to destroy both, nothing better can be done than to let them go on performing the same extraordinary feat as long as the fancy lasts.

And so we sat upon the grass, caring little for what the wise might say of us, for an hour and a half at the very least. Our attendant old women and boys, seated at convenient distance, were eating as heartily and laughing as merrily as ourselves; whilst our beasts, seen through the openings of the thicket in which they were stabled, and their whimsical housings piled up together at the foot of an old thorn at its entrance, completed the composition of our gipsy festival.

At length the signal was given to rise, and the obedient troop were on their feet in an instant. The horses and the asses were saddled forthwith: each one seized his and her own and mounted. A council was then called as to whither we should go. Sundry forest paths stretched away so invitingly in different directions, that it was difficult to decide which we should prefer. "Let us all meet two hours hence at the Cheval Blanc," said some one of brighter wit than all the rest: whereupon we all set off, fancy-led, by twos and by threes, to put this interval of freedom and fresh air to the best account possible.

I was strongly tempted to set off directly for Eaubonne. Though I confess that Jean-Jacques' descriptions (tant vantées!) of some of the scenes which occurred there between himself and his good friend Madame d'Houdetot, in which she rewards his tender passion by constant assurances of her own tender passion for Saint-Lambert, have always appeared to me the very reverse of the sublime and beautiful; yet still the place must be redolent of the man whose "Rêveries" have made its whole region classic ground: and go where I will, I always love to bring the genius of the place as near to me as possible. But my wishes were effectually checked by the old lady whose donkey carried me.

"Oh! dame—il ne faut pas aller par là ... ce n'est pas là le beau point de vue; laissez-moi faire ... et vous verrez...."

And then she enumerated so many charming points of forest scenery that ought to be visited by "tout le monde," that I and my companions decided it would be our best course to permit the laisser faire she asked for; and accordingly we set off in the direction she chose. We had no cause to regret it, for she knew her business well, and, in truth, led us as beautiful a circuit as it was well possible to imagine. If I did not invoke Rousseau in his bosquet d'Eaubonne, or beside the "cascade dont," as he says, "je lui avais donné l'idée, et qu'elle avait fait exécuter,"—(Rousseau had never seen Niagara, or he would not have talked of his Sophie's having executed his idea of a cascade;)—though we did not seek him there, we certainly met him, at every step of our beautiful forest path, in the flowers and mosses whose study formed his best recreation at Montmorency. "Herboriser" is a word which, I think, with all possible respect for that modern strength of intellect that has fixed its stigma upon sentiment, Rousseau has in some sort consecrated. There is something so natural, so genuine, so delightfully true, in his expressions, when he describes the pleasure this occupation has given him, contrasted as it is with his sour and querulous philosophy, and still more perhaps with the eloquent but unrighteous bursts of ill-directed passion, that its impression on my mind is incomparably greater than any he has produced by other topics.

"Brillantes fleurs, émail des prés!" ... is an exclamation a thousand times more touching, coming from the poor solitary J.J. at sixty-five, than any of the most passionate exclamations which he makes St. Preux utter; and for this reason the woods of Montmorency are more interesting from their connexion with him than any spot the neighbourhood of Vévay could offer.

The view from the Rendezvous de Chasse is glorious. While pausing to enjoy it, our old woman began talking politics to us. She told us that she had lost two sons, who both died fighting beside "notre grand Empereur," who was certainly "le plus grand homme de la terre; cependant, it was a great comfort for poor people to have bread for onze sous—and that was what King Louis-Philippe had done for them."

After our halt, we turned our heads again towards the town, and were peacefully pursuing our deliciously cool ride under the trees, when a holla! from behind stopped us. It proceeded from one of the boys of our cortége, who, mounted upon a horse that one of the party had used, was galloping and hollaing after us with all his might. The information he brought was extremely disagreeable: one of the gentlemen had been thrown from his horse and taken up for dead; and he had been sent, as he said, to collect the party together, to know what was to be done. The gentleman who was with our detachment immediately accompanied the boy to the spot; but as the unfortunate sufferer was quite a stranger to me, and was already surrounded by many of the party, I and my companion decided upon returning to Montmorency, there to await at Le Cheval Blanc the appearance of the rest. A medical man, we found, had been already sent for. When at length the whole party, with the exception of this unfortunate young man and a friend who remained with him, were assembled, we found, upon comparing notes together, that no less than four of our party had been unhorsed or undonkeyed in the course of the day; but happily three of these were accidents followed by no alarming results. The fourth was much more serious; but the report from the Montmorency surgeon, which we received before we left the town, assured us that no ultimate danger was to be apprehended.

One circumstance attending this disagreeable contre-tems was very fortunate. The accident took place at the gates of a chateau, the owners of which, though only returned a few hours before from a tour in Italy, received the sufferer and his friend with the greatest kindness and hospitality. Thus, though only eighteen of us returned to Paris to recount the day's adventures, we had at least the consolation of having a very interesting, and luckily not fatal, episode to narrate, in which a castle and most courteous knights and dames bore a part, while the wounded cavalier on whom their generous cares were bestowed had not only given signs of life, but had been pronounced, to the great joy of all the company, quite out of danger either of life or limb.

So ended our day at Montmorency, which, spite of our manifold disasters, was declared upon the whole to have been one of very great enjoyment.

LETTER LXIII.

George Sand.

I have more than once mentioned to you my observations on the reception given in Paris to that terrible school of composition which derives its power from displaying, with strength that exaggerates the vices of our nature, all that is worst and vilest in the human heart. I have repeatedly dwelt upon the subject, because it is one which I have so often heard treated unfairly, or at least ignorantly, in England; and a love of truth and justice has therefore led me to assure you, with reiterated protestations, that neither these mischief-doing works nor their authors meet at all a better reception in Paris than they would in London.

It is this same love of truth and justice which prompts me to separate from the pack one whom nature never intended should belong to it. The lady who writes under the signature of George Sand cannot be set aside by the sternest guardian of public morals without a sigh. With great—perhaps, at the present moment, with unequalled power of writing, Madame de D— perpetually gives indications of a heart and mind which seem to prove that it was intended her place should be in a very different set from that with which she has chosen to mingle.

It is impossible that she should write as she has done without possessing some of the finest qualities of human nature; but she is and has been tossed about in that whirlpool of unsettled principles, deformed taste and exaggerated feeling, in which the distempered spirits of the day delight to bathe and disport themselves, and she has been stained and bruised therein. Yet she has nothing in common with their depraved feelings and distorted strength; and there is so much of the divine spirit of real genius within her, that it seems as if she could not sink in the vortex that has engulfed her companions. She floats and rises still; and would she make one bold effort to free herself from this slough, she might yet become one of the brightest ornaments of the age.

Not her own country only, but all the world have claims on her; for genius is of no nation, but speaks in a language that can be heard and understood by all. And is it possible that such a mind as hers can be insensible to the glory of enchanting the best and purest spirits in the world?... Can she prefer the paltry plaudits of the obscure herd who scorn at decency, to the universal hymn of love and praise which she must hear rising from the whole earth to do honour to the holy muse of Walter Scott?

The powers of this lady are of so high an order as in fact to withdraw her totally, though seemingly against her will, from all literary companionship or competition with the multitude of little authors whose moral theories appear of the same colour as her own; and in the tribute of admiration which justice compels me to pay her, my memory dwells only on such passages as none but herself could write, and which happily all the world may read.

It is sad, indeed, to be forced to read almost by stealth volumes which contain such passages, and to turn in silence from the lecture with one's heart glowing with admiration of thoughts that one might so proudly quote and boast of as coming from the pen of a woman! But, alas! her volumes are closed to the young and innocent, and one may not dare to name her among those to whom the memory clings with gratitude as the giver of high mental enjoyment.

One strong proof that the native and genuine bent of her genius would carry her far above and quite out of sight of the whole décousu school is, that, with all her magical grace of expression, she is always less herself, less original, a thousand times less animated and inspired, when she sets herself to paint scenes of unchaste love, and of unnatural and hard indifference to decorum, than when she throws the reins upon the neck of her own Pegasus, and starts away into the bright region of unsoiled thoughts and purely intellectual meditation.

I should be sorry to quote the titles of any books which ought never to have been written, and which had better not be read, even though there should be buried in them precious gems of thought and expression which produce the effect of a ray of sunshine that has entered by a crevice into a dark chamber; but there are some morsels by George Sand which stand apart from the rest, and which may be cited without mischief. "La Revue des Deux Mondes" has more than once done good service to the public by putting forth in its trustworthy pages some of her shorter works. Amongst these is a little story called "André," which if not quite faultless, may yet be fairly quoted to prove of what its author might be capable. The character of Geneviève, the heroine of this simple, natural little tale, is evidence enough that George Sand knows what is good. Yet even here what a strange perversity of purpose and of judgment peeps out! She makes this Geneviève, whose character is conceived in a spirit of purity and delicacy that is really angelic,—she makes this sweet and exquisitely innocent creature fall into indiscretion with her lover before she marries him, though the doing so neither affects the story nor changes the catastrophe in the slightest degree. It is an impropriety à pure perte, and is in fact such a deplorable incongruity in the character of Geneviève—so perfectly gratuitous and unnecessary, and so utterly out of keeping with the rest of the picture, that it really looks as if Madame D— might not publish a volume that was not timbré with the stamp of her clique. It would not, I suppose, pass current among them without it.

This story of "André" is still before me; and though it is quite impossible that I should be able to give you any idea of it by extracts, I will transcribe a few lines to show you the tone of thought in which its author loves to indulge.

Speaking of the universal power or influence of poetry, which certainly, like M. Jourdain's prose, often exists in the mind sans qu'on en sache rien, she says,—

"Les idées poétiques peuvent s'ajuster à la taille de tous les hommes. L'un porte sa poésie sur son front, un autre dans son coeur; celui-ci la cherche dans une promenade lente et silencieuse au sein des plaines, celui-là la poursuit au galop de son cheval à travers les ravins; un troisième l'arrose sur sa fenêtre, dans un pot de tulipes. Au lieu de demander où elle est, ne devrait-on pas demander où n'est-elle pas? Si ce n'était qu'une langue, elle pourrait se perdre; mais c'est une essence qui se compose de deux choses, la beauté répandue dans la nature extérieure, et le sentiment départi à toute l'intelligence ordinaire."

Again she shows the real tone of her mind when, speaking of a future state, she says,—

"Qui sait si, dans un nouveau code de morale, un nouveau catéchisme religieux, le dégoût et la tristesse ne seront pas flétris comme des vices, tandis que l'amour, l'espoir, et l'admiration seront récompensés comme des vertus?"

This is a beautiful idea of the duties belonging to a happier state of existence; nay, I think that if we were only as good as we easily might be here, even this life would become rather an act of thanksgiving than what it too often is—a record of sighs.

I know not where I should look in order to find thoughts more true, or fanciful ideas more beautifully expressed, than I have met with in this same story, where the occupations and reveries of its heroine are described. Geneviève is by profession a maker of artificial flowers, and the minute study necessary to enable her to imitate skilfully her lovely models has led her to an intimate acquaintance with them, the pleasures of which are described, and her love and admiration of them dwelt upon, in a strain that I am quite persuaded none other but George Sand could utter. It is evident, indeed, throughout all her writings, that the works of nature are the idols she worships. In the "Lettres d'un Voyageur,"—which I trust are only begun, for it is here that the author is perfect, unrivalled, and irreproachable,—she gives a thousand proofs of a heart and imagination which can only be truly at home when far from "the rank city." In writing to a friend in Paris, whom she addresses as a person devoted to the cares and the honours of public life, she says,—"Quand tu vois passer un pauvre oiseau, tu envies son essor, et tu regrettes les cieux." Then she exclaims, "Que ne puis-je t'emmener avec moi sur l'aile des vents inconstans, te faire respirer le grand air des solitudes et t'apprendre le secret des poètes et des Bohémiens!" She has learned that secret, and the use she makes of it places her, in my estimation, wondrously above most of the descriptive poets that France has ever boasted. Yet her descriptions, exquisite as they sometimes are, enchant me less perhaps than the occasional shooting, if I may so express it, of a bold new thought into the regions of philosophy and metaphysics; but it is done so lightly, so playfully, that it should seem she was only jesting when she appears to aim thus wildly at objects so much beyond a woman's ken. "Tous les trônes de la terre ne valent pas pour moi une petite fleur au bord d'un lac des Alpes," she says; and then starts off with this strange query: "Une grande question serait celle de savoir si la Providence a plus d'amour et de respect pour notre charpente osseuse, que pour les pétales embaumés de ses jasmins."

She professes herself (of course) to be a republican; but only says of it, "De toutes les causes dont je ne me soucie pas, c'est la plus belle;" and then adds, quite in her own vein, "Du moins, les mots de patrie et de liberté sont harmonieux—tandis que ceux de légitimité et d'obéissance sont grossiers, mal-sonnans, et faits pour des oreilles de gendarmes."... "Aduler une bûche couronnée," is, she declares, "renoncer à sa dignité d'homme, et se faire académicien."

However, she quizzes her political friend for being "le martyr des nobles ambitions;" adding, "Gouvernez-moi bien tous ces vilains idiots ... je vais chanter au soleil sur une branche, pendant ce tems-là."

In another place, she says that she is "bonne à rien qu'à causer avec l'écho, à regarder lever la lune, et à composer des chants mélancoliques ou moqueurs pour les étudians poètes et les écoliers amoureux."

As a specimen of what this writer's powers of description are, I will give you a few lines from a little story called "Mattéa,"—a story, by the way, that is beautiful, one hardly knows why,—just to show you how she can treat a theme worn threadbare before she was born. Is there, in truth, any picture much less new than that of a gondola, with a guitar in it, gliding along the canals of Venice? But see what she makes of it.

"La guitare est un instrument qui n'a son existence véritable qu'à Venise, la ville silencieuse et sonore. Quand une gondole rase ce fleuve d'encre phosphorescente, où chaque coup de rame enfonce un éclair, tandis qu'une grêle de petites notes légères, nettes, et folâtres, bondit et rebondit sur les cordes que parcourt une main invisible, on voudrait arrêter et saisir cette mélodie faible mais distincte qui agace l'oreille des passans, et qui fuit le long des grandes ombres des palais, comme pour appeler les belles aux fenêtres, et passer en leur disant—Ce n'est pas pour vous la sérénade; et vous ne saurez ni d'où elle vient, ni où elle va."

Could Rousseau himself have chosen apter words? Do they not seem an echo to the sound she describes?

The private history of an author ought never to mix itself with a judgment of his works. Of that of George Sand I know but little; but divining it from the only source that the public has any right to examine,—namely, her writings,—I should be disposed to believe that her story is the old one of affection either ill requited, or in some way or other unfortunate; and there is justice in quoting the passages which seem to indicate this, because they are written in a spirit that, let the circumstances be what they will, must do her honour.

In the "Lettres d'un Voyageur" already mentioned, the supposed writer of them is clearly identified with George Sand by this passage:—"Meure le petit George quand Dieu voudra, le monde n'en ira pas plus mal pour avoir ignoré sa façon de penser. Que veux-tu que je te dise? Il faut que je te parle encore de moi, et rien n'est plus insipide qu'une individualité qui n'a pas encore trouvé le mot de sa destinée. Je n'ai aucun intérêt à formuler une opinion quelconque. Quelques personnes qui lisent mes livres ont le tort de croire que ma conduite est une profession de foi, et le choix des sujets de mes historiettes une sorte de plaidoyer contre certaines lois: bien loin de là, je reconnais que ma vie est pleine de fautes, et je croirais commettre une lâcheté si je me battais les flancs pour trouver un système d'idées qui en autorisât l'exemple."

After this, it is impossible to read, without being touched by it, this sublime phrase used in speaking of one who would retire into the deep solitudes of nature from struggling with the world:—

"Les astres éternels auront toujours raison, et l'homme, quelque grand qu'il soit parmi les hommes, sera toujours saisi d'épouvante quand il voudra interroger ce qui est au-dessus de lui. O silence effrayant, réponse éloquente et terrible de l'éternité!"

In another place, speaking with less lightness of tone than is generally mixed throughout these charming letters with the gravest speculations, George Sand says:—

"J'ai mal vécu, j'ai mal usé des biens qui me sont échus, j'ai négligé les oeuvres de charité; j'ai vécu dans la mollesse, dans l'ennui, dans les larmes vaines, dans les folles amours, dans les vains plaisirs. Je me suis prosterné devant des idoles de chair et de sang, et j'ai laissé leur souffle enivrant effacer les sentences austères que la sagesse des livres avait écrites sur mon front dans ma jeunesse.... J'avais été honnête autrefois, sais-tu bien cela, Everard? C'est de notoriété bourgeoise dans notre pays; mais il y avait peu de mérite,—j'étais jeune, et les funestes amours n'étaient pas éclos dans mon sein. Ils ont étouffé bien des qualités; mais je sais qu'il en est auxquelles je n'ai pas fait la plus légère tache au milieu des plus grands revers de ma vie, et qu'aucune des autres n'est perdu pour moi sans retour."

I could go on very long quoting with pleasure from these pages; but I cannot, I think, conclude better than with this passage. Who is there but must wish that all the great and good qualities of this gifted woman (for she must have both) should break forth from whatever cloud sorrow or misfortune of any kind may have thrown over her, and that the rest of her days may pass in the tranquil developement of her extraordinary talents, and in such a display of them to the public as shall leave its admiration unmixed?

"Angelo Tyran de Padoue"—Burlesque at the Théâtre du Vaudeville—Mademoiselle Mars—Madame Dorval—Epigram.

We have seen and enjoyed many very pretty, very gay little pieces at most of the theatres since we have been here; but we never till our last visit to the Théâtre Français enjoyed that uncontrollable movement of merriment which, setting all lady-like nonchalance at defiance, obliged us to yield ourselves up to hearty, genuine laughter; in which, however, we had the consolation of seeing many of those around us join.

And what was the piece, can you guess, which produced this effect upon us?... It was "Angelo!" It was the "Tyran de Padoue"—pas doux du tout, as the wits of the parterre aver. But, in truth, I ought not to assent to this verdict, for never tyrant was so doux to me and mine as this, and never was a very long play so heartily laughed at to the end.

But must I write to you in sober earnest about this comic tragedy? I suppose I must; for, except the Procès Monstre, nothing has been more talked of in Paris than this new birth of M. Hugo. The cause for this excitement was not that a new play from this sufficiently well-known hand was about to be put upon the scene, but a circumstance which has made me angry and all Paris curious. This tragedy, as you shall see presently, has two heroines who run neck and neck through every act, leaving it quite in doubt which ought to come in prima donna. Mademoiselle Mars was to play the part of one—but who could venture to stand thus close beside her in the other part?—nobody at the Français, as it should seem: and so, wonderful to tell, and almost impossible to believe, a lady, a certain Madame Dorval, well known as a heroine of the Porte St. Martin, I believe, was enlisted into the corps of the Français to run a tilt with—Mars.

This extraordinary arrangement was talked of, and asserted, and contradicted, and believed, and disbelieved, till the noise of it filled all Paris. You will hardly wonder, then, that the appearance of this drama has created much sensation, or that the desire to see it should extend beyond the circle of M. Hugo's young admirers.

I have been told, that as soon as this arrangement was publicly made known, the application for boxes became very numerous. The author was permitted to examine the list of all those who had applied, and no boxes were positively promised till he had done so. Before the night for the first representation was finally fixed, a large party of friends and admirers assembled at the poet's house, and, amongst them, expunged from this list the names of all such persons as were either known or suspected to be hostile to him or his school. Whatever deficiencies this exclusive system produced in the box-book were supplied by his particular partisans. The result on this first night was a brilliant success.

"L'auteur de Cromwell," says the Revue des Deux Mondes, "a proclamé d'une voix dictatoriale la fusion de la comédie et de la tragédie dans le drame." It is for this reason, perhaps, that M. Hugo has made his last tragedy so irresistibly comic. The dagger and the bowl bring on the catastrophe,—

therefore, sans contredire, it is a tragedy: but his playful spirit has arranged the incidents and constructed the dialogue,—therefore, sans faute, it is a comedy.

In one of his exquisite prefaces, M. Hugo says, that he would not have any audience quit the theatre without carrying with them "quelque moralité austère et profonde;" and I will now make it my task to point out to you how well he has redeemed this promise in the present instance. In order to shake off all the old-fashioned trammels which might encumber his genius, M. Hugo has composed his "Angelo" in prose,—prose such as old women love—(wicked old women I mean,)—lengthy, mystical, gossiping, and mischievous. I will give you some extracts; and to save the trouble of describing the different characters, I will endeavour so to select these extracts that they shall do it for me. Angelo Tyran de Padoue thus speaks of himself:—

"Oui ... je suis le podesta que Venise met sur Padoue.... Et savez-vous ce que c'est que Venise?... C'est le conseil des dix. Oh! le conseil des dix!... Souvent la nuit je me dresse sur mon séant, j'écoute, et j'entends des pas dans mon mur.... Oui, c'est ainsi, Tyran de Padoue, esclave de Venise. Je suis bien surveillé, allez. Oh! le conseil des dix!"

This gentleman has a young, beautiful, and particularly estimable wife, by name Catarina Bragadini, (which part is enacted on the boards of the Théâtre Français by Madame Dorval, from the Théâtre de la Porte St. Martin,) but unfortunately he hates her violently. He could not, however, as he philosophically observes himself, avoid doing so, and he shall again speak for himself to explain this.

"ANGELO.

"La haine c'est dans notre sang. Il faut toujours qu'un Malipieri haïsse quelqu'un. Moi, c'est cette femme que je hais. Je ne vaux pas mieux qu'elle, c'est possible—mais il faut qu'elle meure. C'est une nécessité—une résolution prise."

This necessity for hating does not, however, prevent the Podesta from falling very violently in love with a strolling actress called La Tisbe (personated by Mademoiselle Mars). The Tisbe also is a very remarkably virtuous, amiable, and high-minded woman, who listens to the addresses of the Tyrant pas doux, but hates him as cordially as he hates his lady-wife, bestowing all her tenderness and private caresses upon a travelling gentleman, who is a prince in disguise, but whom she passes off upon the Tyrant for her brother. La Tisbe, too, shall give you her own account of herself.

"LA TISBE (addressing Angelo).

"Vous savez qui je suis? ... rien, une fille du peuple, une comédienne.... Eh bien! si peu que je suis, j'ai eu une mère. Savez-vous ce que c'est que d'avoir une mère? En avez-vous eu une, vous?... Eh bien! j'avais une mère, moi."

This appears to be a species of refinement upon the old saying, "It is a wise child that knows its own father." The charming Tisbe evidently piques herself upon her sagacity in being quite certain that she had a mother;—but she has not yet finished her story.

"C'était une pauvre femme sans mari qui chantait des chansons dans les places publiques." (The "delicate" Esmeralda again.) "Un jour, un sénateur passa. Il regarde, il entendit," (she must have been singing the Ça ira of 1549,) "et dit au capitaine qui le suivait—A la potence cette femme! Ma mère fut saisie sur-le-champ—elle ne dit rien ... a quoi bon? ... m'embrassa avec une grosse larme, prit son crucifix et se laissa garrotter. Je le vois encore ce crucifix en cuivre poli, mon nom Tisbe écrit en bas.... Mais il y avait avec le sénateur une jeune fille.... Elle se jeta aux pieds du sénateur et obtint la grace de ma mère.... Quand ma mère fut déliée, elle prit son crucifix, ma mère, et le donna à la belle enfant, en lui disant, Madame, gardez ce crucifix—il vous portera bonheur."

Imagine Mademoiselle Mars uttering this trash!... Oh, it was grievous! And if I do not greatly mistake, she admired her part quite as little as I did, though she exerted all her power to make it endurable,—and there were passages, certainly, in which she succeeded in making one forget everything but herself, her voice, and her action.

But to proceed. On this crucifix de cuivre poli, inscribed with the name of Tisbe, hangs all the little plot. Catarina Bragadini, the wife of the Tyrant, and the most ill-used and meritorious of ladies, is introduced to us in the third scene of the second day (new style—acts are out of fashion,) lamenting to her confidential femme de chambre the intolerable long absence of her lover. The maid listens, as in duty bound, with the most respectful sympathy, and then tells her that another of her waiting-maids for whom she had inquired was at prayers. Whereupon we have a morsel of naïveté that is impayable.

"CATARINA.

"Laisse-la prier—Hélas! ... moi, cela ne me fait rien de prier!"

This, I suspect, is what is called "the natural vein," in which consists the peculiar merit of this new style of writing. After this charming burst of natural feeling, the Podesta's virtuous lady goes on with her lament.

"CATARINA.

"Il y a cinq semaines—cinq semaines éternelles que je ne l'ai vu!... Je suis enfermée, gardée, en prison. Je le voyais une heure de tems en tems: cette heure si étroite, et si vite fermée, c'était le seul soupirail[1] par où entrait un peu d'air et de soleil dans ma vie. Maintenant tout est muré.... Oh Rodolpho!... Dafné, nous avons passé, lui et moi, de bien douces heures!... Est-ce que c'est coupable tout ce que je dis là de lui? Non, n'est-ce pas?"

Now you must know, that this Signor Rodolpho plays the part of gallant to both these ladies, and, though intended by the author for another of his estimable personages, is certainly, by his own showing, as great a rascal as can well be imagined. He loves only the wife, and not the mistress of Angelo; and though he permits her par complaisance to be his mistress too, he addresses her upon one occasion, when she is giving way to a fit of immoderate fondness, with great sincerity.

"RODOLPHO.

"Prenez garde, Tisbe, ma famille est une famille fatale. Il y a sur nous une prédiction, une destinée qui s'accomplit presque inévitablement de père en fils. Nous tuons qui nous aime."

From this passage, and one before quoted, it should seem, I think, that notwithstanding all the innovations of M. Hugo, he has still a lingering reverence for the immutable power of destiny which overhangs the classic drama. How otherwise can he explain these two mystic sentences?—"Ma famille est une famille fatale. Il y a sur nous une destinée qui s'accomplit de père en fils." And this other: "La haine c'est dans notre sang: il faut toujours qu'un Malipieri haïsse quelqu'un."

The only other character of importance is a very mysterious one called Homodei; and I think I may best describe him in the words of the excellent burlesque which has already been brought out upon this "Angelo" at the Vaudeville. There they make one of the dramatis personæ, when describing this very incomprehensible Homodei, say of him,—

"C'est le plus grand dormeur de France et de Navarre."

In effect, he far out-sleeps the dozing sentinels in the "Critic;" for he goes on scene after scene sleeping apparently as sound as a top, till all on a sudden he starts up wide awake, and gives us to understand that he too is exceedingly in love with Madame la Podesta, but that he has been rejected. He therefore determines to do her as much mischief as possible, observing that "Un Sbire (for such is his humble rank) qui aime est bien petit—un Sbire qui se venge est bien grand."

This great but rejected Sbire, however, is not contented with avenging himself on Catarina for her scorn, but is pushed, by his destiny, I presume, to set the whole company together by the ears.

He first brings Rodolpho into the bed-room of Catarina, then brings the jealous Tisbe there to look at them, and finally contrives that the Tyrant himself should find out his wife's little innocent love affair—for innocent she declares it is.

Fortunately, during this unaccountable reunion in the chamber of Madame, la Tisbe discovers that her mother the ballad-singer's crucifix is in the possession of her rival Catarina; whereupon she not only decides upon resigning her claim upon the heart of Signor Rodolpho in her favour, but determines upon saving her life from the fury of her jealous husband, who has communicated to the Tisbe, as we have seen above, his intention of killing his wife, because "il faut toujours qu'un Malipieri haïsse quelqu'un."

Fortunately, again, it happens that the Tisbe has communicated to her lover the Tyrant, in a former conversation, the remarkable fact that another lover still had once upon a time made her a present of two phials—one black, the other white—one containing poison, the other a narcotic. After he has discovered Catarina's innocent weakness for Rodolpho, he informs the Tisbe that the time is come for him to kill his lady, and that he intends to do it by cutting her head off privately. The Tisbe tells him that this is a bad plan, and that poison would do much better.

"ANGELO.

"Oui! Le poison vaudrait mieux. Mais il faudrait un poison rapide, et, vous ne me croirez pas, je n'en ai pas ici.

"LA TISBE.

"J'en ai, moi.

"ANGELO.

"Où?

"LA TISBE.

"Chez moi.

"ANGELO.

"Quel poison?

"LA TISBE.

"Le poison Malispine, vous savez: cette boîte que m'a envoyée le primicier de Saint Marc."

After this satisfactory explanation, Angelo accepts her offer, and she trots away home and brings him the phial containing the narcotic.

The absurdity of the scene that takes place when Angelo and the Tisbe are endeavouring to persuade Catarina to consent to be killed is such, that nothing but transcribing the whole can give you an idea of it: but it is too long for this. Believe me, we were not the only part of the audience that laughed at this scene à gorge déployée.

Angelo begins by asking if she is ready.

"CATARINA.

"Prête à quoi?

"ANGELO.

"A mourir.

"CATARINA.

"... Mourir! Non, je ne suis pas prête. Je ne suis pas prête. Je ne suis pas prête du tout, monsieur!

"ANGELO.

"Combien de temps vous faut-il pour vous préparer?

"CATARINA.

"Oh! je ne sais pas—beaucoup de temps!"

Angelo tells her she shall have an hour, and then leaves her alone: upon which she draws aside a curtain and discovers a block and an axe. She is naturally exceedingly shocked at this spectacle; her soliloquy is sublime!

"CATARINA (replacing the curtain).

"Derrière moi! c'est derrière moi. Ah! vous voyez bien que ce n'est pas un rêve, et que c'est bien réel ce qui passe ici, puisque voilà des choses là derrière le rideau!"

Corneille! Racine! Voltaire!—This is tragedy,—tragedy played on the stage of the Théâtre Français— tragedy which it has been declared in the face of day shall "lift the ground from under you!" Such is the march of mind!

After this glorious soliloquy, her lover Rodolpho pays Catarina a visit—again in her bed-room, in her guarded palace, surrounded by spies and sentinels. How he gets there, it is impossible to guess: but in the burlesque at the Vaudeville they make this matter much clearer;—for there these unaccountable entrées are managed at one time by the falling down of a wall; at another, by the lover's rising through the floor like a ghost; and at another, by his coming flying down on a wire from an opening in the ceiling like a Cupid.

The lovers have a long talk; but she does not tell him a word about the killing, for fear it should bring him into mischief,—though where he got in, it might be easy enough for her to get out. However, she says nothing about "les choses" behind the curtain, but gives him a kiss, and sends him away in high glee.

No sooner does he disappear, than Angelo and the Tisbe enter, and a conversation ensues between the three on the manner of the doomed lady's death that none but M. Victor Hugo could have written. He would represent nature, and he makes a high-born princess, pleading for her life to a sovereign who is her husband, speak thus: "Parlons simplement. Tenez ... vous êtes infâme ... et puis, comme vous mentez toujours, vous ne me croirez pas. Tenez, vraiment je vous méprise: vous m'avez épousée pour mon argent...."

Then she makes a speech to the Tisbe in the same exquisite tone of nature; with now and then a phrase or expression which is quite beyond even the fun of the Vaudeville to travestie; as for instance—"Je suis toujours restée honnête—vous me comprenez, vous—mais je ne puis dire cela à mon mari. Les hommes ne veulent jamais nous croire, vous savez; cependant nous leur disons quelquefois des choses bien vraies...."

At last the Tyrant gets out of patience.

"ANGELO.

"C'en est trop! Catarina Bragadina, le crime fait, veut un châtiment; la fosse ouverte, veut un cercueil; le mari outragé, veut une femme morte. Tu perds toutes les paroles qui sortent de ta bouche (montrant le poison).

"Voulez vous, madame?

"CATARINA.

"Non!

"ANGELO.

"Non?... J'en reviens à ma première idée alors. Les épées! les épées! Troilo! qu'on aille me chercher.... J'y vais!"

Now we all know that his première idée was not to stab her with one or more swords, but to cut her head off on a block—and that les choses are all hid ready for it behind the curtain. But this "J'y vais" is part of the machinery of the fable; for if the Tyrant did not go away, the Tisbe could have found no opportunity of giving her rival a hint that the poison was not so dangerous as she believed. So when Angelo returns, the Tisbe tells him that "elle se résigne au poison."

Catarina drinks the potion, falls into a trance, and is buried. (Victor Hugo is always original, they say.) The Tisbe digs her up again, and lays her upon a bed in her own house, carefully drawing the curtains round her. Then comes the great catastrophe. The lover of the two ladies uses his privilege, and enters the Tisbe's apartment, determined to fulfil his destiny and murder her, because she loves him—as written in the book of fate—and also because she has poisoned his other and his favourite love Catarina. The Signor Rodolpho knows that she brought the phial, because one of the maids told him so: this is another instance of the ingenious and skilful machinery of the fable. Rodolpho tells the poor woman what he is come for; adding, "Vous avez un quart d'heure pour vous préparer à la mort, madame!"

There is something in this which shows that M. Hugo, notwithstanding he has some odd décousu notions, is aware of the respect which ought to be paid to married ladies, beyond what is due to those who are not so. When the Podesta announced the same intention to his wife, he says—"Vous avez devant vous une heure, madame." At the Vaudeville, however, they give another turn to this variation in the time allowed under circumstances so similar: they say—

"Catarina eut une heure au moins de son mari:Le tems depuis tantôt est donc bien renchéri."

The unfortunate Tisbe, on receiving this communication from her dear Rodolpho, exclaims—"Ah! vous me tuez! Ah! c'est la première idée qui vous vient?"

Some farther conversation takes place between them. On one occasion he says—like a prince as he is—"Mentez un peu, voyons!"—and then he assures her that he never cared a farthing for her, repeating very often, because, as he says, it is her supplice to hear it, that he never loved anybody but Catarina. During the whole scene she ceases not, however, to reiterate her passionate protestations of love to him, and at last the dialogue ends by Rodolpho's stabbing her to the heart.

I never beheld anything on the stage so utterly disgusting as this scene. That Mademoiselle Mars felt weighed down by the part, I am quite certain;—it was like watching the painful efforts of a beautiful racer pushed beyond its power—distressed, yet showing its noble nature to the last. But even her exquisite acting made the matter worse: to hear the voice of Mars uttering expressions of love, while the ruffian she addresses grows more murderous as she grows more tender, produced an effect at once so hateful and so absurd, that one knows not whether to laugh or storm at it. But, what was the most terrible of all, was to see Mars exerting her matchless powers to draw forth tears, and then to look round the house and see that she was rewarded by—a smile!

After Tisbe is stabbed, Catarina of course comes to life; and the whole farce concludes by the dying Tisbe's telling the lovers that she had ordered horses for them; adding tenderly, "Elle est déliée—(how?)—morte pour le podesta, vivante pour toi. Trouves-tu cela bien arrangé ainsi?" Then Rodolpho says to Catarina, "Par qui as-tu été sauvée?"

"LA TISBE (in reply).

"Par moi, pour toi!"

M. Hugo, in a note at the end of the piece, apologises for not concluding with these words—"Par moi, pour toi," which he seems to think particularly effective: nevertheless, for some reason which he does not very clearly explain, he concludes thus;—

"LA TISBE.

"Madame, permettez-moi de lui dire encore une fois, Mon Rodolpho. Adieu, mon Rodolpho! partez vite à présent. Je meurs. Vivez. Je te bénis!"

It is impossible in thus running through the piece to give you any adequate idea of the loose, weak, trumpery style in which it is written. It really seems as if the author were determined to try how low he might go before the boys and grisettes who form the chorus of his admirers shall find out that he is quizzing them. One peculiarity in the plot of "this fine tragedy" is, that the hero Angelo never appears, nor is even alluded to, after the scene in which he commissions la Tisbe to administer the poison to Madame. His sudden disappearance is thus commented upon at the Vaudeville. The Tyrant there makes his appearance after it is all over, exclaiming—

"Je veux en être, moi ... l'on osera peut-êtreFinir un mélodrame en absence du traître?Suis-je un hors-d'oeuvre, un inutile article,Une cinquième roue ajoutée au tricycle?"

In the preface to this immortal performance there is this passage:—

"Dans l'état où sont aujourd'hui toutes ces questions profondes qui touchent aux racines même de la société, il semblait depuis long-tems à l'auteur de ce drame qu'il pourrait y avoir utilité et grandeur" (utilité et grandeur!) "à développer sur le théâtre quelque chose de pareil à l'idée que voici...."

And then follows what he calls his idea: but this preface must be read from beginning to end, if you wish to see what sort of stuff it is that humbug and impudence can induce the noisiest part of a population to pronounce "fine!" But you must hear one sentence more of this precious preface, for fear "the work" may not fall into your hands.

"Le drame, comme l'auteur de cet ouvrage le voudrait faire, doit donner à la foule une philosophie; aux idées, une formule; à la poésie, des muscles, du sang, et de la vie; à ceux qui pense, une explication désintéressée; aux âmes altérées un breuvage, aux plaies secrètes un baume—à chacun un conseil, à tous une loi." (!!!!)

He concludes thus:—

"Au siècle où nous vivons, l'horizon de l'art est bien élargi. Autrefois le poète disait, le public; aujourd'hui le poète dit, le peuple."

Is it possible to conceive affected sublimity and genuine nonsense carried farther than this? Let us not, however, sit down with the belief that the capital of France is quite in the condition he describes;—let us not receive it quite as gospel that the raptures, the sympathy of this "foule sympathique et éclairée," that he talks of, in his preface to "Angelo," as coming nightly to the theatre to do him honour, exists—or at least that it exists beyond the very narrow limits of his own clique. The men of France do not sympathise with Victor Hugo, whatever the boys may do. He has made himself a name, it is true,—but it is not a good one; and in forming an estimate of the present state of literature in France, we shall greatly err if we assume as a fact that Hugo is an admired writer.

I would not be unjustly severe on any one; but here is a gentleman who in early life showed considerable ability;—he produced some light pieces in verse, which are said to be written with good moral feeling, and in a perfectly pure and correct literary taste. We have therefore a right to say that M. Hugo turned his talents thus against his fellow-creatures, not from ignorance—not from simple folly—but upon calculation. For is it possible to believe that any man who has once shown by his writings a good moral feeling and a correct taste, can expose to the public eye such pieces as "Lucrèce Borgia," "Le Roi s'amuse," "Angelo," and the rest—in good faith, believing the doing so to be, as he says, "une tâche sainte?" Is this possible?... and if it be not, what follows?... Why, that the author is making a job of corrupting human hearts and human intellects. He has found out that the mind of man, particularly in youth, eagerly seeks excitement of any kind: he knows that human beings will go to see their fellows hanged or guillotined by way of an amusement, and on this knowledge he speculates.

But as the question relates to France, we have not hitherto treated it fairly. I am persuaded that had our stage no censorship, and were dramas such as those of Dumas and Victor Hugo to be produced, they would fill the theatres at least as much as they do here. Their very absurdity—the horror—nay, even the disgust they inspire, is quite enough to produce this effect; but it would be unwise to argue thence that such trash had become the prevailing taste of the people.

That the speculation, as such, has been successful, I have no doubt. This play, for instance, has been very generally talked of, and many have gone to see it, not only on its own account, but in order to behold the novel spectacle of Mademoiselle Mars en lutte with an actress from La Porte St. Martin. As for Madame Dorval, I imagine she must be a very effective melodramatic performer when seen in her proper place; but, however it may have flattered her vanity, I do not think it can have added to her fame to bring her into this dangerous competition. As an actress, she is, I think, to Mademoiselle Mars much what Victor Hugo is to Racine,—and perhaps we shall hear that she has "heaved the ground from under her."

Among various stories floating about on the subject of the new play and its author, I heard one which came from a gentleman who has long been in habits of intimacy with M. Hugo. He went, as in duty bound, to see the tragedy, and had immediately afterwards to face his friend. The embarrassment of the situation required to be met by presence of mind and a coup de main: he showed himself, however, equal to the exigency; he spoke not a word, but rushing towards the author, threw his arms round him, and held him long in a close and silent embrace.

Another pleasantry on the same subject reached me in the shape of four verses, which are certainly droll enough; but I suspect that they must have been written in honour, not of "Angelo," but of some one of the tragedies in verse—"Le Roi s'amuse," perhaps, for they mimic the harmony of some of the lines to be found there admirably.

"Où, ô Hugo! huchera-t-on ton nom?Justice encore rendu, que ne t'a-t-on?Quand donc au corps qu'académique on nomme,Grimperas-tu de roc en roc, rare homme?"

And now farewell to Victor Hugo! I promise to trouble you with him no more; but the consequence which has been given to his name in England, has induced me to speak thus fully of the estimation in which I find him held in France.

"RARE HOMME!"

FOOTNOTE: [1] Vent-hole.

LETTER LXV.

Boulevard des Italiens—Tortoni's—Thunder Storm—Church of the Madeleine—Mrs. Butler's "Journal."

All the world has been complaining of the tremendous heat of the weather here. The thermometer stands at.... I forget what, for the scale is not my scale; but I know that the sun has been shining without mercy during the last week, and that all the world declare that they are baked. Of all the cities of the earth to be baked in, surely Paris is the best. I have been reading that beautiful story of George Sand's about nothing at all, called "Lavinia," and chose for my study the deepest shade of the Tuileries Garden. If we could but have sat there all day, we should have felt no inconvenience from the sun, but, on the contrary, only have watched him from hour to hour caressing the flowers, and trying in vain to find entrance for one of his beams into the delightful covert we had chosen: but there were people to be seen, and engagements to be kept; and so here we are at home again, looking forward to a large party for the evening!

The Boulevard as we came along was prettier than ever;—stands of delicious flowers tempting one at every step—a rose, and a bud, and two bits of mignonette, and a sprig of myrtle, for five sous; but all arranged so elegantly, that the little bouquet was worth a dozen tied up less tastefully. I never saw so many sitters in a morning; the people seemed as if they were reposing from necessity—as if they sat because they could walk no farther. As we passed Tortoni's, we were amused by a group, consisting of a very pretty woman and a very pretty man, who were seated on two chairs close together, and flirting apparently very much to their own satisfaction; while the third figure in the group, a little Savoyard, who had probably begun by asking charity, seemed spell-bound, with his eyes fixed on the elegant pair as if studying a scene for the gaie science, of which, as he carried a mandoline, I presume he was a disciple. We were equally entertained by the pertinacious staring of the little minstrel, and the utter indifference to it manifested by the objects of his admiration.

A few steps farther, our eyes were again arrested by an exquisite, who had taken off his hat, and was deliberately combing his coal-black curls as he walked. In a brother beau, I doubt not he would have condemned such a degree of laisser-aller; but in himself, it only served to relever the beauty of his forehead and the general grace of his movements. I was glad that no fountain or limpid lake opened beneath his feet,—the fate of Narcissus would have been inevitable.

Last night we had intended to make a farewell visit to the Feydeau,—Feydeau no longer, however,—to the Opéra Comique, I should say. But fortunately we had not secured a box, and therefore enjoyed the privilege of changing our minds,—a privilege ever dear, but in such weather as this inestimable. Instead of going to the theatre, we remained at home till it began to grow dark and cool—cooler at least by some degrees, but still most heavily sultry. We then sallied forth to eat ices at Tortoni's. All Paris seemed to be assembled upon the Boulevard to breathe: it was like a very crowded night at Vauxhall, and hundreds of chairs seemed to have sprung up from the ground to meet the exigences of the moment, for double rows of sitters occupied each side of the pavement.

Frenchwomen are so very lovely in their evening walking-dress, that I would rather see them thus than when full-dressed at parties. A drawing-room full of elegantly-dressed women, all looking prepared for a bal paré, is no unusual sight for English eyes; but truth obliges me to confess that it would be in vain at any imaginable evening promenade in London to look for such a spectacle as the Italian Boulevard showed us last night. It is the strangest thing in the world that it should be so—for it is certain that neither the bonnets, nor the pretty faces they shelter, are in any way inferior in England to any that can be seen elsewhere; but Frenchwomen have more the habit and the knack of looking elegantly-dressed without being full-dressed. It is impossible to enter into detail in order to explain this—nothing less skilful than a milliner could do this; and I think that even the most skilful of the profession would not find it easy: I can only state the fact, that the general effect of an evening promenade in Paris is more elegant than it is in London.

We were fortunate enough to secure the places of a large party that were leaving a window in the upper room at Tortoni's as we entered it: and here again is a scene as totally un-English as that of a restaurant in the Palais Royal. Both the rooms above, as well as those below, were quite full of gay company, each party sitting round their own little marble table, with the large carafe of ice—for so it may well be called, for it only melts as you want it—the very sight of which, even if you venture not to drain a draught from the slowly yielding mass, creates a feeling of delicious coldness. Then the incessant entrées of party-coloured pyramids, with their accompaniment of gaufres,—the brilliant light within, the humming crowd without,—the refreshing coolness of the delicate regale, and the light gaiety which all the world seem to share at this pleasant hour of perfect idleness,—all are incontestably French, and, more incontestably still, not English.

While we were still at our window, amused by all within and all without, we were started by some sharp flashes of lightning which began to break through a heavy cloud of most portentous blackness that I had been for some time admiring, as forming a beautiful contrast to the blaze of light on the Boulevard. No rain was as yet falling, and I proposed to my party a walk towards the Madeleine, which I thought would give us some fine effects of light and darkness on such a night as this. The proposal was eagerly accepted, and we wandered on till we left the crowd and the gas behind us. We walked to the end of the Rue Royale, and then turned round slowly and gradually to approach the church. The effect was infinitely finer than anything I had anticipated: the moon was only a few days past the full; and even when hid behind the heavy clouds that were gathering together as it seemed from all parts of the sky, gave light enough for us dimly, yet distinctly, to discern the vast and beautiful proportions of the magnificent portico. It looked like the pale spectre of a Grecian temple. With one accord we all paused at the point where it was most perfectly and most beautifully visible; and I assure you, that with the heavy ominous mass of black clouds above and behind it— with the faint light of the "inconstant moon," now for a moment brightly visible, and now wholly hid behind a driving cloud, reflected from its columns, it was the most beautiful object of art that I ever looked at.

It was some time before we could resolve to leave it, quite sure as we were that it never could be our chance to behold it in such perfection again; and while we stayed, the storm advanced rapidly towards us, adding the distant rumbling of its angry voice to enhance the effect of the spectacle. Yet still we lingered; and were rewarded for our courage by seeing the whole of the vast edifice burst upon our sight in such a blaze of sudden brightness, that when it passed away, I thought for an instant that I was struck blind. Another flash followed—another and another. The spectacle was glorious; but the danger of being drenched to the skin became every moment more imminent, and we hastily retreated to the Boulevard. As we emerged from the gloom of the Madeleine Boulevard to the glaring gas-light from the cafés which illuminated the Italian, it seemed as if we had got into another atmosphere and another world. No rain had as yet fallen; and the crowd, thicker than ever, were still sitting and lounging about, apparently unconscious of the watery danger which threatened them. So great is the force of example, that, before we got to the end of the promenade, we seemed unconscious of it too, for we turned with the rest. But we were soon punished for our folly: the dark canopy burst asunder, and let down upon us as pelting a shower as ever drove feathers and flowers, and ribbons and gauze, to every point of the compass in search of shelter.

I have sometimes wondered at the short space of time it required to clear a crowded theatre of its guests; but the vanishing of the crowd from the Boulevard was more rapid still. What became of them all, Heaven knows; but they seemed to melt and dissolve away as the rain fell upon them. We took shelter in the Passage de l'Opéra; and after a few minutes the rain ceased, and we got safely home.

In the course of our excursion we encountered an English friend, who returned home with us; and though it was eleven o'clock, he looked neither shocked nor surprised when I ordered tea, but even consented to stay and partake of it with us. Our tea-table gossip was concerning a book that all the world—all the English world at least—had been long eagerly looking for, and which we had received two days before. Our English friend had made it his travelling-companion, and having just completed the perusal of it, could talk of nothing else. This book was Mrs. Butler's "Journal." Happily for the tranquillity of our tea-table, we were all perfectly well agreed in opinion respecting it: for, by his account, parties for and against it have been running very strong amongst you. I confess I heard this with astonishment; for it appears to me that all that can be said against the book lies so completely on the surface, that it must be equally visible to all the world, and that nobody can fail to perceive it. But these obvious defects once acknowledged—and they must be acknowledged by all, I should have thought that there was no possibility left for much difference of opinion,—I should have thought the genius of its author would then have carried all before it, leaving no one sufficiently cold-blooded and reasonable to remember that it contained any faults at all.

It is certainly possible that my familiarity with the scenes she describes may give her spirited sketches a charm and a value in my eyes that they may not have for those who know not their truth. But this is not all their merit: the glow of feeling, the warm eloquence, the poetic fervour with which she describes all that is beautiful, and gives praise to all that is good, must make its way to every heart, and inspire every imagination with power to appreciate the graphic skill of her descriptions even though they may have no power to judge of their accuracy.

I have been one among those who have deeply regretted the loss, the bankruptcy, which the stage has sustained in the tragic branch of its business by the secession of this lady: but her book, in my opinion, demonstrates such extraordinary powers of writing, that I am willing to flatter myself that we shall have gained eventually rather than lost by her having forsaken a profession too fatiguing, too exhausting to the spirits, and necessarily occupying too much time, to have permitted her doing what now we may fairly hope she will do,—namely, devote herself to literature. There are some passages of her hastily-written, and too hastily-published journal, which evidently indicate that her mind was at work upon composition. She appears to judge herself and her own efforts so severely, that, when speaking of the scenes of an unpublished tragedy, she says "they are not bad,"—which is, I think, the phrase she uses: I feel quite persuaded that they are admirable. Then again she says, "Began writing a novel...." I would that she would finish it too!—and as I hold it to be impossible that such a mind as hers can remain inactive, I comfort myself with the belief that we shall soon again receive some token of her English recollections handed to us across the Atlantic. That her next production will be less faulty than her last, none can doubt, because the blemishes are exactly of a nature to be found in the journal of a heedless young traveller, who having caught, in passing, a multitude of unseemly phrases, puts them forth in jest, unmindful—much too unmindful certainly— of the risk she ran that they might be fixed upon her as her own genuine individual style of expression. But we have only to read those passages where she certainly is not jesting—where poetry, feeling, goodness, and piety glow in every line—to know what her language is when she is in earnest. On these occasions her power of expression is worthy of the thoughts of which it is the vehicle,—and I can give it no higher praise.

LETTER LXVI.

A Pleasant Party—Discussion Between an Englishman and a Frenchman—National Peculiarities.

I told you yesterday that, notwithstanding the tremendous heat of the weather, we were going to a large party in the evening. We courageously kept the engagement; though, I assure you, I did it in trembling. But, to our equal surprise and satisfaction, the rooms of Mrs. M— proved to be deliciously cool and agreeable. Her receiving-apartment consists of three rooms. The first was surrounded and decorated in all possible ways with a profusion of the most beautiful flowers, intermixed with so many large glass vases for gold fish, that I am sure the air was much cooled by evaporation from the water they contained. This room was lighted wholly by a large lamp suspended from the ceiling, which was enclosed in a sort of gauze globe, just sufficiently thick to prevent any painful glare of light, but not enough so to injure the beautiful effect always produced by the illumination of flowers. The large croisées were thrown open, with very slight muslin curtains over them; and the whole effect of the room—its cool atmosphere, its delicious fragrance, and its subdued light—was so enchanting, that it was not without difficulty we passed on to pay our compliments to Mrs. M—, who was in a larger but much less fascinating apartment.

There were many French persons present, but the majority of the company was English. Having looked about us a little, we retreated to the fishes and the myrtles; and as there was a very handsome man singing buffa songs in one of the other rooms, with a score of very handsome women looking at and listening to him, the multitude assembled there; and we had the extreme felicity of finding fresh air and a sofa à notre disposition, with the additional satisfaction of accepting or refusing ices every time the trays paraded before us. You will believe that we were not long left without companions, in a position so every way desirable: and in truth we soon had about us a select committee of superlatively agreeable people; and there we sat till considerably past midnight, with a degree of enjoyment which rarely belongs to hours devoted to a very large party in very hot weather.

And what did we talk about?—I think it would be easier to enumerate the subjects we did not touch upon than those we did. Everybody seemed to think that it would be too fatiguing to run any theme far; and so, rather in the style of idle, pampered lap-dogs, than of spirited pointers and setters, we amused ourselves by skittishly pursuing whatever was started, just as it pleased us, and then turned round and reposed till something else darted into view. The whole circle, consisting of seven persons, were English with the exception of one; and that one was—he must excuse me, for I will not name him—that one was a most exceedingly clever and superlatively agreeable young Frenchman.

As we had snarled and snapped a little here and there in some of our gambols after the various objects which had passed before us, this young man suggested the possibility of his being de trop in the coterie. "Are you not gênés," said he, "by my being here to listen to all that you and yours may be disposed to say of us and ours?... Shall I have the amiability to depart?"

A general and decided negative was put upon this proposition; but one of the party moved an amendment. "Let us," said he, "agree to say everything respecting France and the French with as much unreserve as if you were on the top of Notre Dame; and do you, who have been for three months in England, treat us exactly in the same manner; and see what we shall make of each other. We are all much too languid to suffer our patriotism to mount up to 'spirit-boil,' and so there is no danger whatever that we should quarrel."

"I would accept the partie instantly," said the Frenchman, "were it not so unequal. But six to one! ... is not this too hard?"

"No! ... not the least in the world, if we take it in the quizzing vein," replied the other; "for it is well known that a Frenchman can out-quiz six Englishmen at any time."

"Eh bien!" ... said the complaisant Parisian with a sigh, "I will do my best. Begin, ladies, if you please."

"No! no! no!" exclaimed several female voices in a breath; "we will have nothing to do with it; fight it out between yourselves: we will be the judges, and award the honours of the field to him who hits the hardest."

"This is worse and worse," cried our laughing enemy: "if this be the arrangement of the combat, the judgment, à coup sûr, will be given against me. How can you expect such blind confidence from me?"

We protested against this attack upon our justice, promised to be as impartial as Jove, and desired the champions to enter the lists.

"So then," said the Englishman, "I am to enact the part of St. George ... and God defend the right!"

"And I, that of St. Denis," replied the Frenchman, his right hand upon his breast and his left gracefully sawing the air. "Mon bras ... non ...

'Ma langue à ma patrie,   Mon coeur à mon amie,Mourir gaiement pour la gloire et l'amour,C'est la devise d'un vaillant troubadour.'

Allons!... Now tell me, St. George, what say you in defence of the English mode of suffering ladies— the ladies of Britain—the most lovely ladies in the world, n'est-ce pas?—to rise from table, and leave the room, and the gentlemen—alone—with downcast eyes and timid step—without a single preux chevalier to offer them his protection or to bear them company on their melancholy way—banished, turned out—exiled from the banquet-board!—I protest to you that I have suffered martyrdom when this has happened, and I, for my sins, been present to witness it. Croyez-moi, I would have joyfully submitted to make my exit à quatre pattes, so I might but have followed them. Ah! you know not what it is for a Frenchman to remain still, when forced to behold such a spectacle as this!... Alas! I felt as if I had disgraced myself for life; but I was more than spell-bound—I was promise-bound; the friend who accompanied me to the party where I witnessed this horror had previously told me what I should have to endure—I did endure it—but I have not yet forgiven myself for participating in so outrageous a barbarism."

"The gentlemen only remain to drink the fair ladies' health," said our St. George very coolly; "and I doubt not all ladies would tell you, did they speak sincerely, that they were heartily glad to get rid of you for half an hour or so. You have no idea, my good fellow, what an agreeable interlude this makes for them: they drink coffee, sprinkle their fans with esprit de rose, refresh their wit, repair their smiles, and are ready to set off again upon a fresh campaign, certain of fresh conquests. But what can St. Denis say in defence of a Frenchman who makes love to three women at once—as I positively declare I saw you do last night at the Opera?"

"You mistook the matter altogether, mon cher; I did not make love—I only offered adoration: we are bound to adore the whole sex, and all the petits soins offered in public are but the ceremonies of this our national worship.... We never make love in public, my dear friend—ce n'est pas dans nos moeurs. But will you explain to me un peu, why Englishmen indulge themselves in the very extraordinary habit of taking their wives to market with that vilaine corde au cou that it is so dreadful to mention, and there sell them for the mesquine somme de trois francs?... Ah! be very sure that were there a single Frenchman present at your terrible Smithfield when this happened, he would buy them all up, and give them their liberty at once."

The St. George laughed—but then replied very gravely, that the custom was a very useful one, as it enabled an Englishman to get rid of a wife as soon as he found that she was not worth keeping. "But will you tell me," he continued, "how it is that you can be so inhuman as to take your innocent young daughters and sisters, and dispose of them as if they were Virginian slaves born on your estates, to the best bidder, without asking the charming little creatures themselves one single word concerning their sentiments on the subject?"

"We are too careful of our young daughters and sisters," replied the champion of France, "not to provide them with a suitable alliance and a proper protector before they shall have run the risk of making a less prudent selection for themselves: but, what can put it into the heads of English parents to send out whole ship-loads of young English demoiselles—si belles qu'elles sont!—to the other side of the earth, in order to provide them with husbands?"

Our knight paused for a moment before he answered, and I believe we all shook for him; but at length he replied very sententiously—

"When nations spread their conquests to the other side of the earth, and send forth their generals and their judges to take and to hold possession for them, it is fitting that their distant honours should be shared by their fair countrywomen. But will you explain to me why it is that the venerable grandmothers of France think it necessary to figure in a contre-danse—nay, even in a waltz, as long as they think that they have strength left to prevent their falling on their noses?"

"'Vive la bagatelle!' is the first lesson we learn in our nurses' arms—and Heaven forbid we should any of us live long enough to forget it!" answered the Frenchman. "But if the question be not too indiscreet, will you tell me, most glorious St. George, in what school of philosophy it was that Englishmen learned to seek satisfaction for their wounded honour in the receipt of a sum of money from the lovers of their wives?"

"Most puissant St. Denis," replied the knight of England, "I strongly recommend you not to touch upon any theme connected with the marriage state as it exists in England; because I opine that it would take you a longer time to comprehend it than you may have leisure to give. It will not take you so long perhaps to inform me how it happens that so gay a people as the French, whose first lesson, as you say, is 'Vive la bagatelle!' should make so frequent a practice as they do of inviting either a friend or a mistress to enjoy a tête-à-tête over a pan of charcoal, with doors, windows, and vent-holes of all kinds carefully sealed, to prevent the least possible chance that either should survive?"

"It has arisen," replied the Frenchman, "from our great intimacy with England—where the month of November is passed by one half of the population in hanging themselves, and by the other half in cutting them down. The charcoal system has been an attempt to improve upon your insular mode of proceeding; and I believe it is, on the whole, considered preferable. But may I ask you in what reign the law was passed which permits every Englishman to beat his wife with a stick as large as his thumb; and also whether the law has made any provision for the case of a man's having the gout in that member to such a degree as to swell it to twice its ordinary size?"

"It has been decided by a jury of physicians," said our able advocate, "that in all such cases of gout, the decrease of strength is in exact proportion to the increase of size in the pattern thumb, and therefore no especial law has passed our senate concerning its possible variation. As to the law itself, there is not a woman in England who will not tell you that it is as laudable as it is venerable."

"The women of England must be angels!" cried the champion of France, suddenly starting from his chair and clasping his hands together with energy,—"angels! and nothing else, or" (looking round him) "they could never smile as you do now, while tyranny so terrible was discussed before them!"

What the St. Denis thus politely called a smile, was in effect a very hearty laugh—which really and bonâ fide seemed to puzzle him, as to the feeling which gave rise to it. "I will tell you of what you all remind me at this moment," said he, reseating himself: "Did you ever see or read 'Le Médecin malgré Lui'?"

We answered in the affirmative.

"Eh bien! ... do you remember a certain scene in which a certain good man enters a house whence have issued the cries of a woman grievously beaten by her husband?"

We all nodded assent.

"Eh bien! ... and do you remember how it is that Martine, the beaten wife, receives the intercessor?—'Et je veux qu'il me batte, moi.' Voyez-vous, mesdames, I am that pitying individual—that kind-hearted M. Robert; and you—you are every one of you most perfect Martines."

"You are positively getting angry, Sir Champion," said one of the ladies: "and if that happens, we shall incontestably declare you vanquished."

"Nay, I am vanquished—I yield—I throw up the partie—I see clearly that I know nothing about the matter. What I conceived to be national barbarisms, you evidently cling to as national privileges. Allons! ... je me rends!"

"We have not given any judgment, however," said I. "But perhaps you are more tired than beaten?—you only want a little repose, and you will then be ready to start anew."

"Non! absolument non!—but I will willingly change sides, and tell you how greatly I admire England...."

The conversation then started off in another direction, and ceased not till the number of parties who passed us in making their exit roused us at length to the necessity of leaving our flowery retreat, and making ours also.

LETTER LXVII.

Chamber of Deputies—Punishment of Journalists—Institute for the Encouragement of Industry—Men of Genius.

Of all the ladies in the world, the English, I believe, are the most anxious to enter a representative chamber. The reason for this is sufficiently obvious,—they are the only ones who are denied this privilege in their own country; though I believe that they are in general rather disposed to consider this exclusion as a compliment, inasmuch as it evidently manifests something like a fear that their conversation might be found sufficiently attractive to draw the Solons and Lycurguses from their duty.

But however well they may be disposed to submit to the privation at home, it is a certain fact that Englishwomen dearly love to find themselves in a legislative assembly abroad. There certainly is something more than commonly exciting in the interest inspired by seeing the moral strength of a great people collected together, and in the act of exerting their judgment and their power for the well-being and safety of millions. I suspect, however, that the sublimity of the spectacle would be considerably lessened by a too great familiarity with it; and that if, instead of being occasionally hoisted outside a lantern to catch an uncertain sight and a broken sound of what was passing within the temple, we were in the constant habit of being ushered into so commodious a tribune as we occupied yesterday at the Chamber of Deputies, we might soon cease to experience the sort of reverence with which we looked down from thence upon the collected wisdom of France.

Nothing can be more agreeable than the arrangement of this chamber for spectators. The galleries command the whole of it perfectly; and the orator of the hour, if he can be heard by any one, cannot fail of being heard by those who occupy them. Another peculiar advantage for strangers is, that the position of every member is so distinctly marked, that you have the satisfaction of knowing at a glance where to find the brawling republican, the melancholy legitimatist, and the active doctrinaire. The ministers, too, are as much distinguished by their place in the Chamber as in the Red Book, (or whatever may be the distinctive symbol of that important record here,) and by giving a franc at the entrance, for a sort of map that they call a "Table figurative" of the Chamber, you know the name and constituency of every member present.

This greatly increases the interest felt by a stranger. It is very agreeable to hear a man speak with fervour and eloquence, let him be who he may; but it enhances the pleasure prodigiously to know at the same time who and what he is. If he be a minister, every word has either more or less weight according ... to circumstances; and if he be in opposition, one is also more au fait as to the positive value of his sentiments from being acquainted with the fact.

The business before the house when we were there was stirring and interesting enough. It was on the subject of the fines and imprisonment to be imposed on those journalists who had outraged law and decency by their inflammatory publications respecting the trials going on at the Luxembourg— General Bugeaud made an excellent speech upon the abuse of the freedom of the press; a subject which certainly has given birth to more "cant," properly so called, than any other I know of. To so strange an extent has this been carried, that it really requires a considerable portion of moral courage to face the question fairly and honestly, and boldly to say, that this unrestricted power, which has for years been dwelt upon as the greatest blessing which can be accorded to the people, is in truth a most fearful evil. If this unrestricted power had been advocated only by demagogues and malcontents, the difficulties respecting the question would be slight indeed, compared to what they are at present; but so many good men have pleaded for it, that it is only with the greatest caution, and the strongest conviction from the result of experience, that the law should interfere to restrain it.

Nothing, in fact, is so plausible as the sophistry with which a young enthusiast for liberty seeks to show that the unrestrained exercise of intellect must not only be the birthright of every man, but that its exercise must also of necessity be beneficial to the whole human race. How easy is it to talk of the loss which the ever-accumulating mass of human knowledge must sustain from stopping by the strong hand of power the diffusion of speculation and experience! How very easy is it to paint in odious colours the tyranny that would check the divine efforts of the immortal mind!—And yet it is as clear as the bright light of heaven, that not all the sufferings which all the tyrants who ever cursed the earth have brought on man can compare to those which the malign influence of an unchecked press is calculated to inflict upon him.

The influence of the press is unquestionably the most awful engine that Providence has permitted the hand of man to wield. If used for good, it has the power of raising us higher in the intellectual scale than Plato ever dreamed; but if employed for evil, the Prince of Darkness may throw down his arms before its unmeasured strength—he has no weapon like it.

What are the temptations—the seductions of the world which the zealous preacher deprecates, which the watchful parent dreads, compared to the corruption that may glide like an envenomed snake into the bosom of innocence from this insidious agency? Where is the retreat that can be secured from it? Where is the shelter that can baffle its assaults?—Blasphemy, treason, and debauchery are licensed by the act of the legislature to do their worst upon the morals of every people among whom an unrestricted press is established by law.

Surely, but perhaps slowly, will this truth become visible to all men: and if society still hangs together at all, our grandchildren will probably enjoy the blessing without the curse of knowledge. The head of the serpent has been bruised, and therefore we may hope for this,—but it is not yet.

The discussions in the Chamber on this important subject, not only yesterday, but on several occasions since the question of these fines has been started, have been very animated and very interesting. Never was the right and the wrong in an argument more ably brought out than by some of the speeches on this business: and, on the other hand, never did effrontery go farther than in some of the defences which have been set up for the accused gérans of the journals in question. For instance, M. Raspail expresses a very grave astonishment that the Chamber of Peers, instead of objecting to the liberties which have been taken with them, do not rather return thanks for the useful lesson they have received. He states too in this same defence, as he is pleased to call it, that the conductors of the "Réformateur" have adopted a resolution to publish without restriction or alteration every article addressed to them by the accused parties or their defenders. This resolution, then, is to be pleaded as an excuse for whatever their columns may contain! The concluding argument of this defence is put in the form of a declaration, purporting that whoever dooms a fellow-creature to the horrors of imprisonment ought to undergo the same punishment for the term of twenty years as an expiation of the crime. This is logical.

There is a tone of vulgar, insolent defiance in all that is recorded of the manner and language adopted by the partisans of these Lyons prisoners, which gives what must, I think, be considered as very satisfactory proof that the party is not one to be greatly feared. After the vote had passed the Chamber of Peers for bringing to account the persons who subscribed the protest against their proceedings, two individuals who were not included in this vote of reprobation sent in a written petition that they might be so. What was the official answer to this piece of bravado, or whether it received any, I know not; but I was told that some one present proposed that a reply should be returned as follows:—

"The court regrets that the request cannot be granted, inasmuch as the sentence has been already passed on those whom it concerned;—but that if the gentlemen wished it, they might perhaps contrive to get themselves included in the next indictment for treason."

In the evening we went to the Institute for the encouragement of Industry. The meeting was held in the Salle St. Jean, at the Hôtel de Ville. It was extremely full, and was altogether a display extremely interesting to a stranger. The speeches made by several of the members were in excellently good taste and extremely to the purpose: I heard nothing at all approaching to that popular strain of eloquence which has prevailed of late so much in England upon all similar occasions,—nothing that looked like an attempt to bamboozle the respectable citizens of the metropolis into the belief that they were considered by wise men as belonging to the first class in society.

The speeches were admirably calculated to excite ingenuity, emulation, and industry; and I really believe that there was not a single word of nonsense spoken on the occasion. Several ingenious improvements and inventions were displayed, and the meeting was considerably égayé by two or three pieces exceedingly well played on a piano-forte of an improved construction.

Many prizes were bestowed, and received with that sort of genuine pleasure which it is so agreeable to witness;—but these were all for useful improvements in some branch of practical mechanics, and not, as I saw by the newspapers had recently been the case at a similar meeting in London, for essays! One of the prize compositions was, as I perceived, "The best Essay on Education," from the pen of a young bell-hanger! Next year, perhaps, the best essay on medicine may be produced by a young tinker, or a gold medal be awarded to Betty the housemaid for a digest of the laws of the land. Our long-boasted common sense seems to have emigrated, and taken up its abode here; for, spite of their recent revolution, you hear of no such stuff on this side the water;—mechanics are mechanics still, and though they some of them make themselves exceeding busy in politics, and discuss their different kings with much energy over a bottle of small wine, I have not yet heard of any of the "operative classes" throwing aside their files and their hammers to write essays.

This queer mixture of occupations reminds me of a conversation I listened to the other day upon the best manner in which a nation could recompense and encourage her literary men. One English gentleman, with no great enthusiasm of manner or expression, quietly observed that he thought a moderate pension, sufficient to prevent the mind from being painfully driven from speculative to practical difficulties, would be the most fitting recompense that the country could offer.

"Is it possible you can really think so, my dear sir?" replied another, who is an amateur, and a connoisseur, and a bel esprit, and an antiquary, and a fiddler, and a critic, and a poet. "I own my ideas on the subject are very different. Good God! ... what a reward for a man of genius!... Why, what would you do for an old nurse?"

"I would give her a pension too," said the quiet gentleman.

"I thought so!" retorted the man of taste. "And do you really feel no repugnance in placing the immortal efforts of genius on a par with rocking a few babies to sleep?—Fie on such philosophy!"

"And what is the recompense which you would propose, sir?" inquired the advocate for the pension.

"I, sir?—I would give the first offices and the first honours of the state to our men of genius: by so doing, a country ennobles itself in the face of the whole earth."

"Yes, sir.... But the first offices of the state are attended with a good deal of troublesome business, which might, I think, interfere with the intellectual labour you wish to encourage. I should really be very sorry to see Dr. Southey made secretary-at-war,—and yet he deserves something of his country too."

"A man of genius, sir, deserves everything of his country.... It is not a paltry pension can pay him. He should be put forward in parliament ... he should be..."

"I think, sir, he should be put at his ease: depend upon it, this would suit him better than being returned knight of the shire for any county in England."

"Good Heaven, sir!"... resumed the enthusiast; but he looked up and his opponent was gone.

LETTER LXVIII.

Walk to the Marché des Innocens—Escape of a Canary Bird—A Street Orator—Burying Place of the Victims of July.

I must give you to-day an account of the adventures I have encountered in a course à pied to the Marché des Innocens. You must know that there is at one of the corners of this said Marché a shop sacred to the ladies, which débits all those unclassable articles that come under the comprehensive term of haberdashery,—a term, by the way, which was once interpreted to me by a celebrated etymologist of my acquaintance to signify "avoir d'acheter." My magasin "à la Mère de Famille" in the Marché des Innocens fully deserves this description, for there are few female wants in which it fails to "avoir d'acheter." It was to this compendium of utilities that I was notably proceeding when I saw before me, exactly on a spot that I was obliged to pass, a throng of people that at the first glance I really thought was a prodigious mob; but at the second, I confess that they shrank and dwindled considerably. Nevertheless, it looked ominous; and as I was alone, I felt a much stronger inclination to turn back than to proceed. I paused to decide which I should do; and observing, as I did so, a very respectable-looking woman at the door of a shop very near the tumult, I ventured to address an inquiry to her respecting the cause of this unwonted assembling of the people in so peaceable a part of the town; but, unfortunately, I used a phrase in the inquiry which brought upon me more evident quizzing than one often gets from the civil Parisians. My words, I think, were,— "Pourriez-vous me dire, madame, ce que signifie tout ce monde?... Est-ce qu'il y a quelque mouvement?"

This unfortunate word mouvement amused her infinitely; for it is in fact the phrase used in speaking of all the real political hubbubs that have taken place, and was certainly on this occasion as ridiculous as if some one, on seeing forty or fifty people collected together around a pick-pocket or a broken-down carriage in London, were to gravely inquire of his neighbour if the crowd he saw indicated a revolution.

"Mouvement!" she repeated with a very speaking smile: "est-ce que madame est effrayée?... Mouvement ... oui, madame, il y a beaucoup de mouvement; mais cependant c'est sans mouvement.... C'est tout bonnement le petit serin de la marchande de modes là bas qui vient de s'envoler. Je puis vous assurer la chose," she added, laughing, "car je l'ai vu partir."

"Is that all?" said I. "Is it possible that the escape of a bird can have brought all these people together?"

"Oui, madame, rien autre chose.... Mais regardez—voilà les agens de police qui s'approchent pour voir ce que c'est—ils en saisissent un, je crois.... Ah! ils ont une manière si étonnante de reconnaître leur monde!"

This last hint quite decided my return, and I thanked the obliging bonnetière for her communications.

"Bonjour, madame," she replied with a very mystifying sort of smile,—"bonjour; soyez tranquille—il n'y a pas de danger d'un mouvement."

I am quite sure she was the wife of a doctrinaire; for nothing affronts the whole party, from the highest to the lowest, so much as to breathe a hint that you think it possible any riot should arise to disturb their dear tranquillity. On this occasion, however, I really had no such matter in my thoughts, and sinned only by a blundering phrase.

I returned home to look for an escort; and having enlisted one, set forth again for the Marché des Innocens, which I reached this time without any other adventure than being splashed twice, and nearly run over thrice. Having made my purchases, I was setting my face towards home again, when my companion proposed that we should go across the market to look at the monuments raised over some half-dozen or half-score of revolutionary heroes who fell and were buried on a spot at no great distance from the fountain, on the 29th July 1830.

When we reached the little enclosure, we remarked a man, who looked, I thought, very much like a printer's devil, leaning against the rail, and haranguing a girl who stood near him with her eyes wide open as if she were watching for, as well as listening to, every word which should drop from his oracular lips. A little boy, almost equally attentive to his eloquence, occupied the space between them, and completed the group.

I felt a strong inclination to hear what he was saying, and stationed myself doucement, doucement at a short distance, looking, I believe, almost as respectfully attentive as the girl for whose particular advantage he was evidently holding forth. He perceived our approach, but appeared nowise annoyed by it; on the contrary, it seemed to me that he was pleased to have an increased audience, for he evidently threw more energy into his manner, waved his right hand with more dignity, and raised his voice higher.

I will not attempt to give you his discourse verbatim, for some of his phrases were so extraordinary, or at least so new to me, that I cannot recall them; but the general purport of it made an impression both on me and my companion, from its containing so completely the very soul and essence of the party to which he evidently belonged. The theme was the cruel treatment of the amiable, patriotic, and noble-minded prisoners at the Luxembourg. "What did we fight for?" ... said he, pointing to the tombs within the enclosure: "was it not to make France and Frenchmen free?... And do they call it freedom to be locked up in a prison ... actually locked up?... What! can a slave be worse than that? Slaves have got chains on ... qu'est-ce que cela fait?... If a man is locked up, he cannot go farther than if he was chained—c'est clair ... it is all one, and Frenchmen are again slaves.... This is what we have got by our revolution...."

The girl, who continued to stand looking at him with undeviating attention, and, as I presume, with proportionate admiration, turned every now and then a glance our way, to see what effect it produced on us. My attention, at least, was quite as much riveted on the speaker as her own; and I would willingly have remained listening to his reasons, which were quite as "plentiful as blackberries," why no Frenchman in the world, let him do what he would, (except, I suppose, when they obey their king, like the unfortunate victims of popular tyranny at Ham,) should ever be restricted in his freedom—because freedom was what they fought for—and being in prison was not being free—and so on round and round in his logical circle. But as his vehemence increased, so did his audience; and as I did not choose to be present at a second "mouvement" on the same day, or at any rate of running the risk of again seeing the police approaching a throng of which I made one, I walked off. The last words I heard from him, as he pointed piteously to the tombs, were—"V'là les restes de notre révolution de Juillet!" In truth, this fellow talked treason so glibly, that I felt very glad to get quietly away; but I was also glad to have fallen in with such an admirable display of popular eloquence, with so little trouble or inconvenience.

We lingered long enough within reach of the tombs, while listening to this man, for me to read and note the inscription on one of them. The name and description of the "victime de Juillet" who lay beneath it was, "Hapel, du département de la Sarthe, tué le 29 Juillet 1830."

Nothing can be more trumpery than the appearance of this burying-place of "the immortals," with its flags and its foppery of spears and halberds. There is another similar to it in the most eastern court of the Louvre, and, I believe, in several other places. If it be deemed advisable to leave memorials upon these unconsecrated graves, it would be in better taste to make them of such dignity as might excuse their erection in these conspicuous situations; but at present the effect is decidedly ludicrous. If the bodies of those who fell are really deposited within these fantastical enclosures, it would show much more reverence for them and their cause if they were all to receive Christian burial at Père Lachaise, with all such honours, due or undue, as might suit the feelings of the time; and over them it would be well to record, as a matter of historical interest, the time and manner of their death. This would look like the result of national feeling, and have something respectable in it; which certainly cannot be said of the faded flaunting flags and tassels which now wave over them, so much in the style of decorations in the barn of a strolling company of comedians.

As we left the spot, my attention was directed to the Rue de la Ferronnerie, which is close to the Marché des Innocens, and in which street Henri Quatre lost his life by the assassin hand of Ravaillac. It struck me as we talked of this event, and of the many others to which the streets of this beautiful but turbulent capital have been witness, that a most interesting—and, if accompanied by good architectural engravings, a most beautiful—work might be compiled on the same plan, or at least following the same idea as Mr. Leigh Hunt has taken in his work on the interesting localities of London. A history of the streets of Paris might contain a mixture of tragedy, comedy, and poetry—of history, biography, and romance, that might furnish volumes of "entertaining knowledge," which being the favourite genre amidst the swelling mass of modern literature, could hardly fail of meeting with success.

How pleasantly might an easy writer go on anecdotizing through century after century, as widely and wildly as he pleased, and yet sufficiently tied together to come legitimately under one common title; and how wide a grasp of history might one little spot sometimes contain! Where some scattered traces of the stones may still be seen that were to have been reared into a palace for the King of Rome, once stood the convent of the "Visitation de Sainte Marie," founded by Henriette the beautiful and the good, after the death of her martyred husband, our first Charles; within whose church were enshrined her heart, and those of her daughter, and of James the Second of England. Where English nuns took refuge from English protestantism, is now—most truly English still—a manufactory for spinning cotton. Where stood the most holy altar of Le Verbe Incarné, now stands a caserne. In short, it is almost impossible to take a single step in Paris without discovering, if one does but take the trouble of inquiring a little, some tradition attached to it that might contribute information to such a work.

I have often thought that a history of the convents of Paris during that year of barbarous profanation 1790, would make, if the materials were well collected, one of the most interesting books in the world. The number of nuns returned upon the world from the convents of that city alone amounted to many thousands; and when one thinks of all the varieties of feeling which this act must have occasioned, differing probably from the brightest joy for recovered hope and life, to the deepest desolation of wretched helplessness, it seems extraordinary that so little of its history has reached us.

Paris is delightful enough, as every one knows, to all who look at it, even with the superficial glance that seeks no farther than its external aspect at the present moment; but it would, I imagine, be interesting beyond all other cities of the modern world if carefully travelled through with a consummate antiquarian who had given enough learned attention to the subject to enable him to do justice to it. There is something so piquant in the contrasts offered by some localities between their present and their past conditions,—such records furnished at every corner, of the enormous greatness of the human animal, and his most chétif want of all stability—traces of such wit and such weakness, such piety and profanation, such bland and soft politeness, and such ferocious barbarism,—that I do not believe any other page of human nature could furnish the like.

I am sure, at least, that no British records could furnish pictures of native manners and native acts so dissimilar at different times from each other as may be found to have existed here. The most striking contrast that we can show is between the effects of Oliver Cromwell's rule and that of Charles the Second; but this was unity and concord compared to the changes in character which have repeatedly taken place in France. That this contrast with us was, speaking of the general mass of the population, little more than the mannerism arising from adopting the style of "the court" for the time being, is proved by the wondrously easy transition from one tone to the other which followed the restoration. This was chiefly the affair of courtiers, or of public men, who as necessarily put on the manners of their master as a domestic servant does a livery; but Englishmen were still in all essentials the same. Not so the French when they threw themselves headlong, from one extremity of the country to the other, into all the desperate religious wildness which marks the history of the Ligue; not so the French when from the worship of their monarchs they suddenly turned as at one accord and flew at their throats like bloodhounds. Were they then the same people?—did they testify any single trait of moral affinity to what the world thought to be their national character one short year before? Then again look at them under Napoleon, and look at them under Louis-Philippe. It is a great, a powerful, a magnificent people, let them put on what outward seeming they will; but I doubt if there be any nation in the world that would so completely throw out a theorist who wished to establish the doctrine of distinct races as the French.

You will think that I have made a very circuitous ramble from the Marché des Innocens; but I have only given you the results of the family speculation we fell into after returning thence, which arose, I believe, from my narrating how I had passed from the tombeaux of the victims de Juillet to the place where Henri Quatre received his death. This set us to meditate on the different political objects of the slain; and we all agreed that it was a much easier task to define those of the king than those of the subject. There is every reason in the world to believe that the royal Henri wished the happiness and prosperity of France; but the guessing with any appearance of correctness what might be the especial wish and desire of the Sieur Hapel du département de la Sarthe, is a matter infinitely more difficult to decide.

LETTER LXIX.

A Philosophical Spectator—Collection of Baron Sylvestre—Hôtel des Monnaies—Musée d'Artillerie.

We have been indebted to M. J—, the same obliging and amiable friend of whom I have before spoken, for one or two more very delightful mornings. We saw many things, and we talked of many more.

M. J— is inexhaustible in piquant and original observation, and possesses such extensive knowledge on all those subjects which are the most intimately connected with the internal history of France during the last eventful forty years, as to make every word he utters not only interesting, but really precious. When I converse with him, I feel that I have opened a rich vein of information, which if I had but time and opportunity to derive from it all it could give, would positively leave me ignorant of nothing I wish to know respecting the country.

The Memoirs of such a man as M. J— would be a work of no common value. The military history of the period is as familiar to all the world as the marches of Alexander or the conquests of Cæsar; the political history of the country during the same interval is equally well known; its literary history speaks for itself: but such Memoirs as I am sure M. J— could write, would furnish a picture that is yet wanting.

We are not without full and minute details of all the great events which have made France the principal object for all Europe to stare at for the last half-century; but these details have uniformly proceeded from individuals who have either been personally engaged in or nearly connected with these stirring events; and they are accordingly all tinctured more or less with such strong party feeling, as to give no very impartial colouring to every circumstance they recount. The inevitable consequence of this is, that, with all our extensive reading on the subject, we are still far from having a correct impression of the internal and domestic state of the country throughout this period.

We know a great deal about old nobles who have laid down their titles and become men of the people, and about new nobles who have laid down their muskets to become men of the court,—of ministers, ambassadors, and princes who have dropped out of sight, and of parvenus of all sorts who have started into it; but, meanwhile, what do we know of the mass—not of the people—of them also we know quite enough,—but of the gentlemen, who, as each successive change came round, felt called upon by no especial duty to quit their honourable and peaceable professions in order to resist or advance them? Yet of these it is certain there must be hundreds who, on the old principle that "lookers-on see most of the game," are more capable of telling us what effect these momentous changes really produced than any of those who helped to cause them.

M. J— is one of these; and I could not but remark, while listening to him, how completely the tone in which he spoke of all the public events he had witnessed was that of a philosophical spectator. He seemed disposed, beyond any Frenchman I have yet conversed with, to give to each epoch its just character, and to each individual his just value: I never before had the good fortune to hear any citizen of the Great Nation converse freely, calmly, reasonably, without prejudice or partiality, of that most marvellous individual Napoleon.

It is not necessary to attempt recalling the precise expressions used respecting him; for the general impression left on my mind is much more deeply engraven than the language which conveyed it: besides, it is possible that my inferences may have been more conclusive and distinct than I had any right to make them, and yet so sincerely the result of the casual observations scattered here and there in a conversation that was anything but suivie, that were I to attempt to repeat the words which conveyed them, I might be betrayed into involuntary and unconscious exaggeration.

The impression, then, which I received is, that he was a most magnificent tyrant. His projects seem to have been conceived with the vastness and energy of a moral giant, even when they related to the internal regulation only of the vast empire he had seized upon; but the mode in which he brought them into action was uniformly marked by barefaced, unshrinking, uncompromising tyranny. The famous Ordonnances of Charles Dix were no more to be compared, as an act of arbitrary power, to the daily deeds of Napoleon, than the action of a dainty pair of golden sugar-tongs to that of the firmest vice that ever Vulcan forged. But this enormous, this tremendous power, was never wantonly employed; and the country when under his dominion had more frequent cause to exclaim in triumph—

"'Tis excellent to have a giant's strength,"

than to add in suffering,

"But tyrannous to use it like a giant."

It was the conviction of this—the firm belief that the GLORY of France was the object of her autocrat, which consecrated and confirmed his power while she bent her proud neck to his yoke, and which has since and will for ever make his name sound in the ears of her children like a pæan to their own glory. What is there which men, and most especially Frenchmen, will not suffer and endure to hear that note? Had Napoleon been granted to them in all his splendour as their emperor for ever, they would for ever have remained his willing slaves.

When, however, he was lost to them, there is every reason to believe that France would gladly have knit together the severed thread of her ancient glory with her hopes of future greatness, had the act by which it was to be achieved been her own: but it was the hand of an enemy that did it—the hand of a triumphant enemy; and though a host of powerful, valiant, noble, and loyal-hearted Frenchmen welcomed the son of St. Louis to his lawful throne with as deep and sincere fidelity as ever warmed the heart of man, there was still a national feeling of wounded pride which gnawed the hearts of the multitude, and even in the brightest days of the Restoration prevented their rightful king from being in their eyes what he would have been had they purchased his return by the act of drawing their swords, instead of laying them down. It was a greatness that was thrust upon them—and for that reason, and I truly believe for that reason only, it was distasteful.

In days of old, if it happened by accident that a king was unpopular, it mattered very little to the general prosperity of his country, and still less to the general peace of Europe. Even if hatred went so far as to raise the hand of an assassin against him, the tranquillity of the rest of the human race was but little affected thereby. But in these times the effect is very different: disaffection has been taught to display itself in acts that may at one stroke overthrow the prosperity of millions at home, and endanger the precious blessings of peace abroad; and it becomes therefore a matter of importance to the whole of Europe that every throne established within her limits should be sustained not only by its own subjects, but by a system of mutual support that may insure peace and security to all. To do this where a king is rejected by the majority of the people, is, to say the least of it, a very difficult task; and it will probably be found that to support power firmly and legally established, will contribute more to the success of this system of mutual support for the preservation of universal tranquillity, than any crusade that could be undertaken in any part of the world for the purpose of substituting an exiled dynasty for a reigning one.

This is the doctrine to which I have now listened so long and so often, that I have ceased all attempts to refute it. I have, however, while stating it, been led to wander a little from those reminiscences respecting fair France which I found so interesting, coming forth as they did, as if by accident, from the rich storehouse of my agreeable friend's memory: but I believe it would be quite in vain were I to go back to the point at which I deviated, for I could do justice neither to the matter nor the manner of the conversations which afforded me so much pleasure;—I believe therefore that I had better spare you any more politics just at present, and tell you something of several things which we had the pleasure of seeing with him.

One of these was Baron Gros' magnificent sketch, if I must so call a very finished painting, of his fine picture of the Plague of Jaffa. A week or two before I had seen the picture itself at the Luxembourg, and felt persuaded then that it was by far the finest work of the master; but this first developement of his idea is certainly finer still. It is a beautiful composition, and there are groups in it that would not have lowered the reputation of Michael Angelo. The severe simplicity of the Emperor's figure and position is in the very purest taste.

This very admirable work was, when we saw it, in the possession of the Baron de Sylvestre, whose collection, without having the dignity of a gallery, has some beautiful things in it. Our visit to it and its owner was one of great interest to me. I have seldom seen any one with a more genuine and enthusiastic love of art. He has one cabinet,—it is, I believe, his own bed-room,—which almost from floor to ceiling is hung with little gems, so closely set together as to produce at first sight the effect of almost inextricable confusion;—portraits, landscapes, and historic sketches—pencil crayon, water-colour and oil—with frames and without frames, all blended together in utter defiance of all symmetry or order whatever. But it was a rich confusion, and many a collector would have rejoiced at receiving permission to seize upon a chance handful of the heterogeneous mass of which it was composed.

Curious, well-authenticated, original drawings of the great masters, though reduced to a mere rag, have always great interest in my eyes,—and the Baron de Sylvestre has many such: but it was his own air of comfortable domestic intimacy with every scrap, however small, on the lofty and thickly-studded walls of this room, which delighted me;—it reminded me of Denon, who many years ago showed me his large and very miscellaneous collection with equal enthusiasm. I dearly love to meet with people who are really and truly in earnest.

On the same morning that we made this agreeable acquaintance, we passed an hour or two at the Hôtel des Monnaies, which is situated on the Quai Conti, and, I believe, on the exact spot where the old Hôtel de Conti formerly stood. The building, like all the public establishments in France, is very magnificent, and we amused ourselves very agreeably with our intelligent and amiable cicisbeo in examining an immense collection of coins and medals. This collection was formerly placed at the Louvre, but transferred to this hôtel as soon as its erection was completed. The medals, as usual in all such examinations, occupied the greater part of our time and attention. It is quite a gallery of portraits, and many of them of the highest historical interest: but perhaps our amusement was as much derived from observing how many ignoble heads, who had no more business there than so many turnips, had found place nevertheless, by the outrageous vanity either of themselves or their friends, amidst kings, heroes, poets, and philosophers. It is perfectly astonishing to see how many such as these have sought a bronze or brazen immortality at the Hôtel des Monnaies: every medal struck in France has an impression preserved here, and it is probably the knowledge of this fact which has tempted these little people so preposterously to distinguish themselves.

On another occasion we went with the same agreeable escort to visit the national museum of ancient armour. This Musée d'Artillerie is not quite so splendid a spectacle as the same species of exhibition at the Tower; but there are a great many beautiful things there too. Some exquisitely-finished muskets and arquebuses of considerable antiquity, and splendid with a profusion of inlaid ivory, mother-of-pearl, and precious stones, are well arranged for exhibition, as are likewise some complete suits of armour of various dates;—among them is one worn in battle by the unfortunate Maid of Orleans.

But this is not only a curious antiquarian exhibition,—it is in truth a national institution wherein military men may study the art of war from almost its first barbarous simplicity up to its present terrible perfection. The models of all manner of slaughtering instruments are beautifully executed, and must be of great interest to all who wish to study the theory of that science which may be proved "par raison démonstrative," as Molière observes, to consist wholly "dans l'art de donner et ne pas recevoir." But I believe the object which most amused me in the exhibition, was a written notice, repeated at intervals along all the racks on which were placed the more modern and ordinary muskets, to this effect:—

"Manquant, au second rang de ce râtelier d'armes, environ quatre-vingt carabines à rouet, ornées d'incrustation d'ivoire et de nacre, dans le genre de celles du premier rang. Toutes celles qu'on voit ici ont servi dans les journées de Juillet, et ont été rendues après. Les personnes qui auraient encore celles qui manquent sont priées de les rapporter."

There is such a superlative degree of bonhomie in the belief that because all the ordinary muskets which were seized upon by the July patriots were returned, those also adorned with "incrustations d'ivoire et de nacre" would be returned too, that it was quite impossible to restrain a smile at it. Such unwearied confidence and hope deserve a better reward than, I fear, they will meet: the "incrustations d'ivoire et de nacre" are, I doubt not, in very safe keeping, and have been converted, by the patriot hands that seized them, to other purposes, as dear to the hearts they belonged to as that of firing at the Royal Guard over a barricade. Our doctrinaire friend himself confessed that he thought it was time these naïve notices should be removed.

It was, I think, in the course of this excursion that our friend gave me an anecdote which I think is curious and characteristic. Upon some occasion which led to a private interview between Charles Dix and himself, some desultory conversation followed the discussion of the business which led to the audience. The name of Malesherbes, the intrepid defender of Louis Seize, was mentioned by our friend. The monarch frowned.

"Sire!"—was uttered almost involuntarily.

"Il nous a fait beaucoup de mal," said the king in reply to the exclamation—adding with emphasis, "Mais il l'a payé par sa tête!"

Concert in the Champs Elysées—Horticultural Exhibition—Forced Flowers—Republican Hats—Carlist Hats—Juste-Milieu Hats—Popular Funeral.

The advancing season begins to render the atmosphere of the theatres insupportable, and even a crowded soirée is not so agreeable as it has been; so last night we sought our amusement in listening to the concert "en plein air" in the Champs Elysées. I hear that you too have been enjoying this new delight of al-fresco music in London. France and England are exceedingly like the interlocutors of an eclogue, where first one puts forth all his power and poetry to enchant the world, and then the other "takes up the wondrous tale," and does his utmost to exceed and excel, and so go on, each straining every nerve to outdo the other.

Thus it is with the two great rivals who perform their various feats à l'envi l'un de l'autre on the opposite sides of the Channel. No sooner does one burst out with some new and bright idea which like a newly-kindled torch makes for awhile all other lights look dim, than the other catches it, finds out some ingenious way of making it his own, and then grows as proud and as fond of it as if it had been truly the offspring of his own brain. But in this strife and this stealing neither party has any right to reproach the other, for the exchange is very nearly at par between them.

A very few years ago, half a dozen scraping fiddlers, and now and then a screaming "sirène ambulante," furnished all the music of the Champs Elysées; but now there is the prettiest "salon de concert en plein air" imaginable.

By the way, I confess that this phrase "salon de concert en plein air" has something rather paradoxical in it: nevertheless, it is perfectly correct; the concerts of the Champs Elysées are decidedly en plein air, and yet they are enclosed within what may very fairly be called a salon. The effect of this fanciful arrangement is really very pretty; and if you have managed your echo of this agreeable fantasia as skilfully, an idle London summer evening has gained much. Shall I tell you how it has been done in Paris?

In the lower part of the Champs Elysées, a round space is enclosed by a low rail. Within this, to the extent of about fifteen or twenty feet, are ranged sundry circular rows of chairs that are sheltered by a light awning. Within these, a troop of graceful nymphs, formed of white plaster, but which a spectator if he be amiably disposed may take for white marble, stand each one with a lamp upon her head, forming altogether a delicate halo, which, as daylight fades, throws a faint but sufficient degree of illumination upon the company. In the centre of the enclosure rises a stage, covered by a tent-like canopy and brilliant as lamps can make it. Here the band is stationed, which is sufficiently good and sufficiently full to produce a very delightful effect: it must indeed be very villanous music which, listened to while the cool breeze of a summer's evening refreshes the spirit, should not be agreeable. The whole space between the exterior awning and the centre pavilion appropriated to the band is filled with chairs, which, though so very literally en plein air, were all filled with company, and the effect of the whole thing was quite delightful.

The price of entrance to all this prettiness is one franc! This, by the bye, is a part of the arrangement which I suspect is not rivalled in England. Neither will you, I believe, soon learn the easy sort of unpremeditated tone in which it is resorted to. It is ten to one, I think, that no one—no ladies at least—will ever go to your al-fresco concert without arranging a party beforehand; and there will be a question of whether it shall be before tea or after tea, in a carriage or on foot, &c. &c. But here it is enjoyed in the very spirit of sans souci:—you take your evening ramble—the lamps sparkle in the distance, or the sound of the instruments reaches your ears, and this is all the preparation required. And then, as you may always be perfectly sure that everybody you know in Paris is occupied as well as yourself in seeking amusement, the chances are greatly in your favour that you will not reach the little bureau at the gate without encountering some friend or friends whom you may induce to promener their idleness the same way.

I often marvel, as I look around me in our walks and drives, where all the sorrow and suffering which we know to be the lot of man contrives to hide itself at Paris. Everywhere else you see people looking anxious and busy at least, if not quite woe-begone and utterly miserable: but here the glance of every eye is a gay one; and even though this may perhaps be only worn in the sunshine and put on just as other people put on their hats and bonnets, the effect is delightfully cheering to the spirits of a wandering stranger.

It was we, I think, who set the example of an annual public exhibition by an horticultural society. It has been followed here, but not as yet upon the same splendid scale as in London and its neighbourhood. The Orangery of the Louvre is the scene of this display, which is employed for the purpose as soon as the royal trees that pass their winters in it are taken out to the Gardens of the Tuileries. I never on any occasion remember having been exposed to so oppressive a degree of heat as on the morning that we visited this exhibition. The sun shone with intolerable splendour upon the long range of windows, and the place was so full of company, that it was with the greatest difficulty we crept on an inch at a time from one extremity of the hall to the other. Some of the African plants were very fine; but in general the show was certainly not very magnificent. I suspect that the extreme heat of the apartment had considerably destroyed the beauty of some of the more delicate flowering plants, for there were scarcely any of the frail blossoms of our hothouse treasures in perfection. The collection of geraniums was, compared to those I have seen in England, very poor, and so little either of novelty or splendour about them, that I suspect the cultivation of this lovely race, and the production of a new variety in it, is not a matter of so great interest in France as in England.

The climate of France is perhaps more congenial to delicate flowers than our own; and yet it appears to me that, with some few exceptions, such as oranges and the laurier-rose, I have seen nothing in Paris this year equal to the specimens found at the first-rate florists' round London. Even in the decoration of rooms, though flowers are often abundant here, they are certainly less choice than with us; and, excepting in one or two instances, I have observed no plants whatever forced into premature bloom to gratify the pampered taste of the town amateur. I do not, however, mention this as a defect; on the contrary, I perfectly agree in the truth of Rousseau's observation, that such impatient science by no means increases the sum of the year's enjoyment. "Ce n'est pas parer l'hiver," he says,—"c'est déparer le printemps:" and the truth of this is obvious, not only in the indifference with which those who are accustomed to receive this unnatural and precocious produce welcome the abounding treasures of that real spring-time which comes when it pleases Heaven to send it, but also in the worthless weakness of the untimely product itself. I certainly know many who appear to gaze with ecstasy on the pale hectic-looking bloom of a frail rose-tree in the month of February, who can walk unmoved in the spicy evenings of June amidst thousands of rich blossoms all opening their bright bosoms to the breeze in the sweet healthy freshness of unforced nature: yet I will not assert that this proceeds from affectation—indeed, I verily believe that fine ladies do in all sincerity think that roses at Christmas are really much prettier and sweeter things than roses in June; but, at least, I may confess that I think otherwise.

Among the numerous company assembled to look at this display of exotics, was a figure perhaps the most remarkably absurd that we have yet seen in the grotesque extremity of his republican costume. We watched him for some time with considerable interest,—and the more so, as we perceived that he was an object of curiosity to many besides ourselves. In truth, his pointed hat and enormous lapels out-Heroded Herod; and I presume the attention he excited was occasioned more by the extravagant excess than the unusual style of his costume. A gentleman who was with us at the Orangery told me an anecdote respecting a part of this sort of symbolic attire, which had become, he said, the foundation of a vaudeville, but which nevertheless was the record of a circumstance which actually occurred at Paris.

A young provincial happened to arrive in the capital just at the time that these hieroglyphic habiliments were first brought into use, and having occasion for a new hat, repaired to the magasin of a noted chapelier, where everything of the newest invention was sure to be found. The young man, alike innocent of politics and ignorant of its symbols, selected a hat as high and as pointed as that of the toughest roundhead at the court of Cromwell, and sallied forth, proud of being one of the first in a new fashion, to visit a young relative who was en pension at an establishment rather celebrated for its freely-proclaimed Carlist propensities. His young cousin, he was told, was enjoying the hour of recreation with his schoolfellows in the play-ground behind the mansion. He desired to be led to him; and was accordingly shown the way to the spot, where about fifty young legitimatists were assembled. No sooner, however, had he and his hat obtained the entrée to this enclosure, than the most violent and hideous yell was heard to issue from every part of it.

At first the simple-minded provincial smiled, from believing that this uproar, wild as it was, might be intended to express a juvenile welcome; and having descried his young kinsman on the opposite side of the enclosure, he walked boldly forward to reach him. But, before he had proceeded half a dozen steps, he was assailed on all sides by pebbles, tops, flying hoops, and well-directed handfuls of mud. Startled, astounded, and totally unable to comprehend the motives for so violent an assault, he paused for a moment, uncertain whether to advance boldly, or shelter himself by flight from an attack which seemed every moment to increase in violence. Ere he had well decided what course to pursue, his bold-hearted little relative rushed up to him, screaming, as loud as his young voice would allow,—"Sauve-toi, mon cousin! sauve-toi! Ôte ton vilain chapeau!... C'est le chapeau! le méchant chapeau!"

The young man again stopped short, in the hope of being able to comprehend the vociferations of his little friend; but the hostile missives rang about his ears with such effect, that he suddenly came to the decision at which Falstaff arrived before him, and feeling that, at least on the present occasion, discretion was the better part of valour, he turned round, and made his escape as speedily as possible, muttering, however, as he went, "Qu'est-ce que c'est donc qu'un chapeau à-la-mode pour en faire ce vacarme de diable?"

Having made good his retreat, he repaired without delay to the hatter of whom he had purchased this offensive article, described the scene he had passed through, and requested an explanation of it.

"Mais, monsieur," replied the unoffending tradesman, "c'est tout bonnement un chapeau républicain;" adding, that if he had known monsieur's principles were not in accordance with a high crown, he would most certainly have pointed out the possible inconvenience of wearing one. As he spoke, he uncovered and displayed to view one of those delicate light-coloured hats which are known at Paris to speak the loyal principles of the wearer.

"This hat," said he, gracefully presenting it, "may be safely worn by monsieur even if he chose to take his seat in the extremest corner of the côté droit."

Once more the inexperienced youth walked forth; and this time he directed his steps towards the stupendous plaster elephant on the Place de la Bastile, now and ever the favourite object of country curiosity. He had taken correct instructions for his route, and proceeded securely by the gay succession of Boulevards towards the spot he sought. For some time he pursued his pleasant walk without any adventure or interruption whatever; but as he approached the region of the Porte St. Martin sundry little sifflemens became audible, and ere he had half traversed the Boulevard du Temple he became fully convinced that whatever fate might have awaited his new, new hat at the pensionnat of his little cousin, both he and it ran great risk of being rolled in the mud which stagnated in sullen darkness near the spot where once stood the awful Temple.

No sooner did he discover that the covering of his unlucky head was again obnoxious, than he hastened once more to the treacherous hatter, as he now fully believed him to be, and in no measured tone expressed his indignation of a line of conduct which had thus twice exposed the tranquillity—nay, perhaps the life of an unoffending individual to the fury of the mob. The worthy hatter with all possible respect and civility repelled the charge, declaring that his only wish and intention was to accommodate every gentleman who did him the honour to enter his magasin with exactly that species of hat which might best accord with his taste and principles. "If, however," he added with a modest bow, "monsieur really intended to condescend so far as to ask his advice as to which species of hat it was best and safest to wear at the present time in Paris, he should beyond the slightest shadow of doubt respectfully recommend the juste milieu." The young provincial followed his advice; and the moral of the story is, that he walked in peace and quietness through the streets of Paris as long as he stayed.

On our way home this morning we met a most magnificent funeral array: I reckoned twenty carriages, but the piétons were beyond counting. I forget the name of the individual, but it was some one who had made himself very popular among the people. There was not, however, the least appearance of riot or confusion; nor were there any military to protect the procession,—a dignity which is always accorded by this thoughtful government to every person whose funeral is likely to be honoured by too great a demonstration of popular affection. Every man as it passed took off his hat; but this they would have done had no cortége accompanied the hearse, for no one ever meets a funeral in France without it.

But though everything had so peaceful an air, we still felt disposed to avoid the crowd, and to effect this, turned from the quay down a street that led to the Palais Royal. Here there was no pavement; and the improved cleanliness of Paris, which I had admitted an hour before to a native who had remarked upon it, now appeared so questionable to some of my party, that I was challenged to describe what it had been before this improvement took place. But notwithstanding this want of faith, which was perhaps natural enough in the Rue des Bons Enfans, into which we had blundered, it is nevertheless a positive fact that Paris is greatly improved in this respect; and if the next seven years do as much towards its purification as the last have done, we may reasonably hope that in process of time it will be possible to drive—nay, even walk through its crowded streets without the aid either of aromatic vinegar or eau de Cologne. Much, however, still remains to be done; and done it undoubtedly will be, from one end of the "belle ville" to the other, if no barricades arise to interfere with the purifying process. But English noses must still have a little patience.

LETTER LXXI.

Minor French Novelists.

It is not long since, in writing to you of modern French works of imagination, I avowed my great and irresistible admiration for the high talent manifested in some of the writings published under the signature of George Sand; and I remember that the observations I ventured to make respecting them swelled into such length as to prevent my then uttering the protest which all Christian souls are called upon to make against the ordinary productions of the minor French story-tellers of the day. I must therefore now make this amende to the cause of morality and truth, and declare to you with all sincerity, that I believe nothing can be more contemptible, yet at the same time more deeply dangerous to the cause of virtue, than the productions of this unprincipled class of writers.

While conversing a short time ago on the subject of these noxious ephemera with a gentleman whose professional occupations of necessity bring him into occasional contact with them, he struck off for my edification a sketch which he assured me might stand as a portrait, with wonderfully little variation, for any individual of the fraternity. It may lose something of its raciness by the processes of recollecting and translating; but I flatter myself that I shall be able to preserve enough of the likeness to justify my giving it to you.

"These authors," said their lively historian, "swarm au sixième in every quarter of Paris. For the most part, they are either idle scholars who, having taken an aversion to the vulgar drudgery of education, determine upon finding a short cut to the temple of Fame; or else they are young artisans— journeymen workers at some craft or other, which brings them in just francs enough to sustain an honest decent existence, but wholly insufficient to minister to the sublime necessities of revolutionary ambition. As perfect a sympathy appears to exist in the politics of all these gentry as in their doctrine of morals: they all hold themselves ready for rebellion at the first convenient opportunity—be it against Louis, Charles, Henri, or Philippe, it is all one; rebellion against constituted and recognised authority being, according to their high-minded code, their first duty, as well as their dearest recreation.

They must wait, however, till the fitting moment come; and, meanwhile, how may they better the condition in which the tyranny of kings and law-makers has placed them? Shall they listen to the inward whisperings which tell them, that, being utterly unfitted to do their duty in that state of life to which it has pleased God to call them, they must of necessity and by the inevitable nature of things be fitted for some other?... What may it be?... Treason and rapine, of course, if time be ripe for it—but en attendant?

To trace on an immortal page the burning thoughts that mar their handicraft ... to teach the world what fools the sages who have lived, and spoken, and gone to rest, would make of them ... to cause the voice of passion to be heard high above that of law or of gospel.... Yes ... it is thus they will at once beguile the tedious hours that must precede another revolution, and earn by the noble labours of genius the luxuries denied to grovelling industry.

This sublime occupation once decided on, it follows as a necessary result that they must begin by awakening all those tender sympathies of nature, which are to the imagination what oil is to the lamp. A favourite grisette is fixed upon, and invited to share the glory, the cabbage, the inspiration, and the garret of the exalted journeyman or truant scholar. It is said that the whole of this class of authors are supposed to place particular faith in that tinsel sentiment, so prettily and poetically untrue,—

"Love, light as air, at sight of human ties,
Spreads his bright wings, and in a moment flies;"

and the inspired young man gently insinuates his unfettered ideas on the subject to the chosen fair one, who, if her acquaintance has lain much among these "fully-developed intelligences," is not unfrequently found to be as sublime in her notions of such subjects as himself; so the interesting little ménage is monté on the immortal basis of freedom.

Then comes the literary labour, and its monstrous birth—a volume of tales, glowing with love and murder, blasphemy and treason, or downright obscenity, affecting to clothe itself in the playful drapery of wit. It is not difficult to find a publisher who knows where to meet with young customers ever ready to barter their last sous for such commodities, and the bargain is made.

At the actual sight and at the actual touch of the unhoped-for sum of three hundred francs, the flood of inspiration rises higher still. More hideous love and bloodier murders, more phrensied blasphemy and deadlier treason, follow; and thus the fair metropolis of France is furnished with intellectual food for the craving appetites of the most useful and productive part of its population.

Can we wonder that the Morgue is seldom untenanted?... or that the tender hand of affection is so often seen to pillow its loved victim where the fumes of charcoal shall soon extinguish a life too precious to be prolonged in a world where laws still exist, and where man must live, and woman too, by the sweat of their brows?

It was some time after the conversation in which I received this sketch, that I fell into company with an Englishman who enjoys the reputation of high cultivation and considerable talent, and who certainly is not without that species of power in conversation which is produced by the belief that hyperbole is the soul of eloquence, and the stout defence of a paradox the highest proof of intellectual strength.

To say I conversed with this gifted individual would hardly be correct; but I listened to him, and gained thereby additional confirmation of a fact which I had repeatedly heard insisted on in Paris, that admiration for the present French school of décousu writing is manifested by critics of a higher class in England than could be found to tolerate it in France.

"Have you read the works of the young men of France?" was the comprehensive question by which this gentleman opened the flood-gates of the eloquence which was intended to prove, that without having studied well the bold and sublime compositions which have been put forth by this class, no one had a right to form a judgment of the existing state of human intelligence.

For myself, I confess that my reading in this line, though greatly beyond what was agreeable to my taste, has never approached anything that deserved the name of study; and, indeed, I should as soon have thought of forming an estimate of the "existing state of human intelligence" from the height to which the boys of Paris made their kites mount from the top of Montmartre, as from the compositions to which he alluded: but, nevertheless, I listened to him very attentively; and I only wish that my memory would serve me, that I might repeat to you all the fine things he said in praise of a multitude of authors, of whom, however, it is more than probable you never heard, and of works that it is hardly possible you should have ever seen.

It would be difficult to give you any just idea of the energy and enthusiasm which he manifested on this subject. His eyes almost started from his head, and the blood rushed over his face and temples, when one of the party hinted that the taste in which most of these works were composed was not of the most classic elegance, nor their apparent object any very high degree of moral utility.

It is a well-known fact that people are seldom angry when they are quite in the right; and I believe it is equally rare to see such an extremity of vehemence as this individual displayed in asserting the high intellectual claims of his favourites exhibited on any question where reason and truth are on the side espoused by the speaker. I never saw the veins of the forehead swell in an attempt to prove that "Hamlet" was a fine tragedy, or that "Ivanhoe" was a fine romance; but on this occasion most of the company shrank into silence before the impassioned pleadings of this advocate for ... modern French historiettes.

In the course of the discussion many young names were cited; and when a few very palpable hits were made to tell on the literary reputations of some among them, the critic seemed suddenly determined to shake off all slighter skirmishing, and to defend the broad battle-field of the cause under the distinguished banner of M. Balzac himself. And here, I confess, he had most decidedly the advantage of me; for my acquaintance with the writings of this gentleman was exceedingly slight and superficial,—whereas he appeared to have studied every line he has ever written, with a feeling of reverence that seemed almost to bear a character of religious devotion. Among many of his works whose names he cited with enthusiasm, that entitled "La Peau de Chagrin" was the one which evidently raised his spirit to the most exalted pitch. It is difficult to imagine admiration and delight expressed more forcibly; and as I had never read a single line of this "Peau de Chagrin," my preconceived notions of the merit of M. Balzac's compositions really gave way before his enthusiasm; and I not only made a silent resolution to peruse this incomparable work with as little delay as possible, but I do assure you that I really and truly expected to find in it some very striking traits of genius, and a perfection of natural feeling and deep pathos which could not fail to give me pleasure, whatever I might think of the tone of its principles or the correctness of its moral tendency.

Early then on the following morning I sent for "La Peau de Chagrin."... I have not the slightest wish or intention of entering into a critical examination of its merits; it would be hardly possible, I think, to occupy time more unprofitably: but as every author makes use of his preface to speak in his own person, whatever one finds written there assuming the form of a literary dictum may be quoted with propriety as furnishing the best and fairest testimony of his opinions, and I will therefore take the liberty of transcribing a few short sentences from the preface of M. Balzac, for the purpose of directing your attention to the theory upon which it is his intention to raise his literary reputation.

The preface to "La Peau de Chagrin" appears to be written chiefly for the purpose of excusing the licentiousness of a former work entitled "La Physiologie du Mariage." In speaking of this work he says, frankly enough certainly, that it was written as "une tentative faite pour retourner à la littérature fine, vive, railleuse et gaie du dix-huitième siècle, où les auteurs ne se tenaient pas toujours droits et raides.... L'auteur de ce livre cherche à favoriser la réaction littéraire que préparent certains bons esprits.... Il ne comprend pas la pruderie, l'hypocrisie de nos moeurs, et refuse, du reste, aux gens blasés le droit d'être difficiles."

This is telling his readers fairly enough what they have to expect; and if after this they will persist in plunging headlong into the mud which nearly a century of constantly-increasing refinement has gone far to drag us out of ... why they must.

As another reason why his pen has done ... what it has done, M. Balzac tells us that it is absolutely necessary to have something in a genre unlike anything that the public has lately been familiar with. He says that the reading world (which is in fact all the world) "est las aujourd'hui" ... of a great many different styles of composition which he enumerates, summing up all with ... "et l'Histoire de France, Walter-Scottée.... Que nous reste-t-il donc?" he continues. "Si le public condamne les efforts des écrivains qui essaient de remettre en honneur la littérature franche de nos ancêtres...."

As another specimen of the theories of these new immortals, let me also quote the following sentence:—"Si Polyeucte n'existait pas, plus d'un poète moderne est capable de refaire Corneille."

Again, as a reason for going back to the tone of literature which he has chosen, he says,—"Les auteurs ont souvent raison dans leurs impertinences contre le tems présent. Le monde nous demande de belles peintures—où en seraient les types? Vos habits mesquins—vos révolutions manquées—vos bourgeois discoureurs—votre religion morte—vos pouvoirs éteints—vos rois en demi-solde—sont-ils donc si poétiques qu'il faille vous les transfigurer?... Nous ne pouvons aujourd'hui que nous moquer—la raillerie est toute la littérature des sociétés expirantes."

M. Balzac concludes this curious essay on modern literature thus:—"Enfin, le tems présent marche si vite—la vie intellectuelle déborde partout avec tant de force, que plusieurs idées ont vieilli pendant que l'auteur imprimait son ouvrage."

This last phrase is admirable, and gives the best and clearest idea of the notions of the school on the subject of composition that I have anywhere met with. Imagine Shakspeare and Spenser, Swift and Pope, Voltaire and Rousseau, publishing a work with a similar prefatory apology!... But M. Balzac is quite right. The ideas that are generated to-day will be old to-morrow, and dead and buried the day after. I should indeed be truly sorry to differ from him on this point; for herein lies the only consolation that the wisdom of man can suggest for the heavy calamity of witnessing the unprecedented perversion of the human understanding which marks the present hour. IT WILL NOT LAST: Common Sense will reclaim her rights, and our children will learn to laugh at these spasmodic efforts to be great and original as cordially as Cervantes did at the chronicles of knight-errantry which turned his hero's brain.

LETTER LXXII.

Breaking-up of the Paris Season—Soirée at Madame Récamier's—Recitation—Storm— Disappointment—Atonement—Farewell.

My letters from Paris, my dear friend, must now be brought to a close—and perhaps you will say that it is high time it should be so. The summer sun has in truth got so high into the heavens, that its perpendicular beams are beginning to make all the gay folks in Paris fret—or, at any rate, run away. Everybody we see is preparing to be off in some direction or other,—some to the sea, some to philosophise under the shadow of their own vines, and some, happier than all the rest, to visit the enchanting watering-places of lovely Germany.

We too have at length fixed the day for our departure, and this is positively the last letter you will receive from me dated from the beauteous capital of the Great Nation. It is lucky for our sensibilities, or for our love of pleasure, or for any other feeling that goes to make up the disagreeable emotion usually produced by saying farewell to scenes where we have been very happy, that the majority of those whose society made them delightful are going to say farewell to them likewise: leaving Paris a month ago would have been a much more dismal business to us than leaving it now.

Our last soirée has been passed at the Abbaye-aux-Bois; and often as I have taken you there already, I must describe this last evening, because the manner in which we passed it was more essentially un-English than any other.

About ten days before this our farewell visit, we met, at one of Madame Récamier's delightful reception-nights, a M. Lafond, a tragic actor of such distinguished merit, that even in the days of Talma he contrived, as I understand, to obtain a high reputation in Paris, though I do not believe his name is much known to us;—in fact, the fame of Talma so completely overshadowed every other in his own walk, that few actors of his day were remembered in England when the subject of the French drama was on the tapis.

On the evening we met this gentleman at the Abbaye-aux-Bois, he was prevailed upon by our charming hostess (to whom I suspect that nobody can be found tough enough to pronounce a refusal of anything she asks) to recite a very spirited address from the pen of Casimir Delavigne to the people of Rouen, which M. Lafond had publicly spoken in the theatre of that city when the statue of Racine, who was native to it, was erected there.

The verses are good, full of fervour, spirit and true poetical feeling, and the manner in which they were spoken by M. Lafond gave them their full effect. The whole scene was, indeed, striking and beautiful. A circle of elegant women,—among whom, by the way, was a niece of Napoleon's,— surrounded the performer: the gentlemen were stationed in groups behind them; while the inspired figure of Gérard's Corinne, strongly brought forward from the rest of the picture by a very skilful arrangement of lamps concealed from the eye of the spectator, really looked like the Genius of Poetry standing apart in her own proper atmosphere of golden light to listen to the honours rendered to one of her favourite sons.

I was greatly delighted; and Madame Récamier, who perceived the pleasure which this recitation gave me, proposed to me that I should come to her on a future evening to hear M. Lafond read a play of Racine's.

No proposition could have been more agreeable to us all. The party was immediately arranged; M. Lafond promised to be punctually there at the hour named, and we returned home well pleased to think that the last soirée we should pass in Paris would be occupied so delightfully.

Last night was the time fixed for this engagement. The morning was fair, but there was no movement in the air, and the heat was intense. As the day advanced, thick clouds came to shelter us from the sun while we set forth to make some of our last farewell calls; but they brought no coolness with them, and their gloomy shade afforded little relief from the heavy heat that oppressed us: on the contrary, the sultry weight of the atmosphere seemed to increase every moment, and we were soon driven home by the ominous blackness which appeared to rest on every object, giving very intelligible notice of a violent summer-storm.

It was not, however, till late in the evening that the full fury of this threatened deluge fell upon Paris; but about nine o'clock it really seemed as if an ocean had broken through the dark canopy above us, so violent were the torrents of rain which then fell in one vast waterspout upon her roofs.

We listened to the rushing sound with very considerable uneasiness, for our anxious thoughts were fixed upon our promised visit to the Abbaye-aux-Bois; and we immediately gave orders that the porter's scout—a sturdy little personage well known to be good at need—should be despatched without a moment's delay for a fiacre: and you never, I am sure, saw a more blank set of faces than those exhibited in our drawing-room when the tidings reached us that not a single voiture could be found!

After a moment's consultation, it was decided that the experienced porter himself should be humbly requested to run the risk of being drowned in one direction, while his attendant satellite again dared the same fate in another. This prompt and spirited decision produced at length the desired effect; and after another feverish half-hour of expectation, we had the inexpressible delight of finding ourselves safely enveloped in cloaks, which rendered it highly probable we might be able to step from the vehicle without getting wet to the skin, and deposited in the corners of one of those curiously-contrived swinging machines, whose motion is such that nothing but long practice or the most vigilant care can enable you to endure without losing your balance, and running a very dangerous tilt against the head of your opposite neighbour with your own.

I never quitted the shelter of a roof in so unmerciful a night. The rain battered the top of our vehicle as if enraged at the opposition it presented to its impetuous descent upon the earth. The thunder roared loud above the rattling and creaking of all the crazy wheels we met, as well as the ceaseless grinding of those which carried us; and the lightning flashed with such rapidity and brightness, that the very mud we dashed through seemed illuminated.

The effect of this storm as we passed the Pont Neuf was really beautiful. One instant our eyes looked out upon the thickest darkness; and the next, the old towers of Notre Dame, the pointed roofs of the Palais de Justice, and the fine bold elevation of St. Jacques, were "instant seen and instant gone." One bright blue flash fell full, as we dashed by it, on the noble figure of Henri Quatre, and the statua gentilissima, horse and all, looked as ghastly and as spectre-like as heart could wish.

At length we reached the lofty iron grille of the venerable Abbaye. The ample court was filled with carriages: we felt that we were late, and hastening up the spacious stairs, in a moment found ourselves in a region as different as possible from that we had left. Instead of darkness, we were surrounded by a flood of light; rain and the howling blast were exchanged for smiles and gentle greetings; and the growling thunder of the storm, for the sweet voice of Madame Récamier, which told us however that M. Lafond was not yet arrived.

As the party expected was a large one, it was Miss C—'s noble saloon that received us. It was already nearly full, but its stately monastic doors still continued to open from time to time for the reception of new arrivals—yet still M. Lafond came not.

At length, when disappointment was beginning to take place of expectation, a note arrived from the tragedian to Madame Récamier, stating that the deluge of rain which had fallen rendered the streets of Paris utterly impassable without a carriage, and the same cause made it absolutely impossible to procure one; ergo, we could have no M. Lafond—no Racine.

Such a contre-tems as this, however, is by no means very difficult to bear at the Abbaye-aux-Bois. But Madame Récamier appeared very sorry for it, though nobody else did; and admirable as M. Lafond's reading is known to be, I am persuaded that the idea of her being vexed by his failing to appear caused infinitely more regret to every one present than the loss of a dozen tragedies could have done. And then it was that the spirit of genuine French amabilité shone forth; and in order to chase whatever was disagreeable in this change in the destination of our evening's occupations, one of the gentlemen present most good-humouredly consented to recite some verses of his own, which, both from their own merit, and from the graceful and amiable manner in which they were given, were well calculated to remove every shadow of dissatisfaction from all who heard them.

This example was immediately followed in the same delightful spirit by another, who in like manner gave us more than one proof of his own poetic power, as well as of that charming national amenity of manner which knows so well how to round and polish every rough and jutting corner which untoward accidents may and must occasionally throw across the path of life.

One of the pieces thus recited was an extremely pretty legend, called, if I mistake not, "Les Soeurs Grises," in which there is a sweet and touching description of a female character made up of softness, goodness, and grace. As this description fell trait by trait from the lips of the poet, many an eye turned involuntarily towards Madame Récamier; and the Duchesse d'Abrantes, near whom I was sitting, making a slight movement of the hand in the same direction, said in a half whisper,—

"C'est bien elle!"

On the whole, therefore, our disappointment was but lightly felt; and when we rose to quit this delightful Abbaye-aux-Bois for the last time, all the regret of which we were conscious arose from recollecting how doubtful it was whether we should ever find ourselves within its venerable walls again.

POSTSCRIPT.

The letters which are herewith presented to the public contain nothing beyond passing notices of such objects as chiefly attracted my attention during nine very agreeable weeks passed amidst the care-killing amusements of Paris. I hardly know what they contain; for though I have certainly been desirous of giving my correspondent, as far as I was able, some idea of Paris at the present day, I have been at least equally anxious to avoid everything approaching to so presumptuous an attempt as it would have been to give a detailed history of all that was going on there during the period of our stay.

These letters, therefore, have been designedly as unconnected as possible: I have in this been décousu upon principle, and would rather have given a regular journal, after the manner of Lloyd's List, noting all the diligences which have come in and gone out of "la belle ville" during my stay there, than have attempted to analyse and define the many unintelligible incongruities which appeared to me to mark the race and mark the time.

But though I felt quite incapable of philosophically examining this copious subject, or, in fact, of going one inch beneath the surface while describing the outward aspect of all around me, I cannot but confess that the very incongruity which I dared not pretend to analyse appeared to me by far the most remarkable feature in the present state of the country.

There has, I know, always been something of this kind attributed to the French character. Splendour and poverty—grace and grimace—delicacy and filth—learning and folly—science and frivolity, have often been observed among them in a closeness of juxta-position quite unexampled elsewhere; but of late it has become infinitely more conspicuous,—or rather, perhaps, this want of consistency has seemed to embrace objects of more importance than formerly. Heretofore, though it was often suspected in graver matters, it was openly demonstrated only on points which concerned the externals of society rather than the vital interests of the country; but from the removal of that restraint which old laws, old customs, and old authority imposed upon the public acts of the people, the unsettled temper of mind which in time past showed itself only in what might, comparatively speaking, be called trifles, may in these latter days be traced without much difficulty in affairs of much greater moment.

No one of any party will now deny, I believe, that many things which by their very nature appear to be incompatible have been lately seen to exist in Paris, side by side, in a manner which certainly resembled nothing that could be found elsewhere.

As instances of this kind pressed upon me, I have sometimes felt as if I had got behind the scenes of a theatre, and that all sorts of materials, for all sorts of performances, were jumbled together around me, that they might be ready at a moment's notice if called for. Here a crown—there a cap of liberty. On this peg, a mantle embroidered with fleurs-de-lis; on that, a tri-coloured flag. In one corner, all the paraphernalia necessary to deck out the pomp and pageantry of the Catholic church; and in another, all the symbols that can be found which might enable them to show respect and honour to Jews, Turks, infidels, and heretics. In this department might be seen very noble preparations to support a grand military spectacle; and in that, all the prettiest pageants in the world, to typify eternal peace.

I saw all these things, for it was impossible not to see them; but as to the scene-shifters who were to prepare the different tableaux, I in truth knew nothing about them. Their trap-doors, wires, and other machinery were very wisely kept out of sight of such eyes as mine; for had I known anything of the matter, I should most assuredly have told it all, which would greatly tend to mar the effect of the next change of decorations.

It was with this feeling, and in this spirit of purely superficial observation, that the foregoing letters were written; but, ere I commit them to the press, I wish to add a few graver thoughts which rest upon my mind as the result of all that I saw and heard while at Paris, connected as they now are with the eventful changes which have occurred in the short interval that has elapsed since I left it.

"The country is in a state of transition," is a phrase which I have often listened to, and often been disposed to laugh at, as a sort of oracular interpretation of paradoxes which, in truth, no one could understand: but the phrase may now be used without any Delphic obscurity. France was indeed in a state of transition exactly at the period of which I have been writing; but this uncertain state is past, nearly all the puzzling anomalies which so completely defied interpretation have disappeared, and it may now be fairly permitted, to simple-minded travellers who pretend not to any conjuring skill, to guess a little what she is about.

I revisited France with that animating sensation of pleasure which arises from the hope of reviving old and agreeable impressions; but this pleasure was nevertheless dashed with such feeling of regret as an English conservative may be supposed to feel for the popular violence which had banished from her throne its legitimate sovereign.

As an abstract question of right and wrong, my opinion of this act cannot change; but the deed is done,—France has chosen to set aside the claim of the prince who by the law of hereditary succession has a right to the crown, in favour of another prince of the same royal line, whom in her policy she deems more capable of insuring the prosperity of the country. The deed is done; and the welfare of tens of millions who had, perhaps, no active share in bringing it about now hangs upon the continuance of the tranquillity which has followed the change.

However deep therefore may be the respect felt for those who, having sworn fealty to Charles the Tenth, continue steadfastly undeviating in their declaration of his right, and firm in their refusal to recognise that of any other, still a stranger and sojourner in the land may honestly acknowledge the belief that the prosperity of France at the present hour depends upon her allegiance to the king she has chosen, without being accused of advocating the cause of revolution.

To judge fairly of France as she actually exists, it is absolutely necessary to throw aside all memory of the purer course she might have pursued five years ago, by the temperate pleading of her chartered rights, to obtain redress of such evils as really existed. The popular clamour which rose and did the work of revolution, though it originated with factious demagogues and idle boys, left the new power it had set in action in the hands of men capable of redeeming the noble country they were called to govern from the state of disjointed weakness in which they found it. The task has been one of almost unequalled difficulty and peril; but every day gives greater confidence to the hope, that after forty years of blundering, blustering policy, and changes so multiplied as to render the very name of revolution ridiculous, this superb kingdom, so long our rival, and now, as we firmly trust, our most assured ally, will establish her government on a basis firm enough to strengthen the cause of social order and happiness throughout all Europe.

The days, thank Heaven! are past when Englishmen believed it patriotic to deny their Gallic neighbours every faculty except those of making a bow and of eating a frog, while they were repaid by all the weighty satire comprised in the two impressive words JOHN BULL. We now know each other better—we have had a long fight, and we shake hands across the water with all the mutual good-will and respect which is generated by a hard struggle, bravely sustained on both sides, and finally terminated by a hearty reconciliation.

The position, the prospects, the prosperity of France are become a subject of the deepest interest to the English nation; and it is therefore that the observations of any one who has been a recent looker-on there may have some value, even though they are professedly drawn from the surface only. But when did ever the surface of human affairs present an aspect so full of interest? Now that so many of the circumstances which have been alluded to above as puzzling and incongruous have been interpreted by the unexpected events which have lately crowded upon each other, I feel aware that I have indeed been looking on upon the dénouement of one of the most interesting political dramas that ever was enacted. The movements of King Philippe remind one of those by which a bold rider settles himself in the saddle, when he has made up his mind for a rough ride, and is quite determined not to be thrown. When he first mounted, indeed, he took his seat less firmly; one groom held the stirrup, another the reins: he felt doubtful how far he should be likely to go—the weather looked cloudy—he might dismount directly.... But soon the sun burst from behind the cloud that threatened him: Now for it, then! neck or nothing! He orders his girths to be tightened, his curb to be well set, and the reins fairly and horsemanly put into his hands.... Now he is off! and may his ride be prosperous!—for should he fall, it is impossible to guess how the dust which such a catastrophe might raise would settle itself.

The interest which his situation excites is sufficiently awakening, and produces a species of romantic feeling, that may be compared to what the spectators experienced in the tournaments of old, when they sat quietly by to watch the result of a combat à outrance. But greater, far greater is the interest produced by getting a near view of the wishes and hopes of the great people who have placed their destinies in his hands.

Nothing that is going on in Paris—in the Chamber of Deputies, in the Chamber of Peers, or even in the Cabinet of the King—could touch me so much, or give me half so much pleasure to listen to, as the tone in which I have heard some of the most distinguished men in France speak of the repeated changes and revolutions in her government.

It is not in one or two instances only that I have remarked this tone,—in fact, I might say that I have met it whenever I was in the society of those whose opinions especially deserved attention. I hardly know, however, how to describe it, for it cannot be done by repeating isolated phrases and observations. I should say, that it marks distinctly a consciousness that such frequent changes are not creditable to any nation—that they feel half ashamed to talk of them gravely, yet more than half vexed to speak of the land they love with anything approaching to lightness or contempt. That the men of whom I speak do love their country with a true, devoted, Romanlike attachment, I am quite sure; and I never remember to have felt the conviction that I was listening to real patriots so strongly as when I have heard them reason on the causes, deplore the effects, and deprecate the recurrence of these direful and devastating convulsions.

It is, if I mistake not, this noble feeling of wishing to preserve their country from the disgrace of any farther demonstrations of such frail inconstancy, which will tend to keep Louis-Philippe on his throne as much, or even more perhaps, than that newly-awakened energy in favour of the boutique and the bourse of which we hear so much.

It is nowise surprising that this proud but virtuous sentiment should yet exist, notwithstanding all that has happened to check and to chill it. Frenchmen have still much of which they may justly boast. After a greater continuance of external war and internal commotion than perhaps any country was ever exposed to within the same space of time, France is in no degree behind the most favoured nations of Europe in any one of the advantages which have ever been considered as among the especial blessings of peace. Tremendous as have been her efforts and her struggles, the march of science has never faltered: the fine arts have been cherished with unremitting zeal and a most constant care, even while every citizen was a soldier; and now, in this breathing-time that Heaven has granted her, she presents a spectacle of hopeful industry, active improvement, and prosperous energy, which is unequalled, I believe, in any European country except our own.

Can we wonder, then, that the nation is disposed to rally round a prince whom Fate seems to have given expressly as an anchor to keep her firm and steady through the heavy swell that the late storms have left? Can we wonder that feelings, and even principles, are found to bend before an influence so salutary and so strong?

However irregular the manner in which he ascended the throne, Louis-Philippe had himself little more to do with it than yielding to the voice of the triumphant party who called upon him to mount its troublesome pre-eminence; and at the moment he did so, he might very fairly have exclaimed—

"If chance will have me king, why chance may crown meWithout my stir."

Never certainly did any event brought on by tumult and confusion give such fair promise of producing eventually the reverse, as the accession of King Louis-Philippe to the throne of France.

The manner of this unexpected change itself, the scenes which led to it, and even the state of parties and of feelings which came afterwards, all bore a character of unsettled confusion which threatened every species of misery to the country.

When we look back upon this period, all the events which occurred during the course of it appear like the rough and ill-assorted fragments of worsted on the reverse of a piece of tapestry. No one could guess, not even the agents in them, what the final result would be. But they were at work upon a design drawn by the all-powerful and unerring hand of Providence; and strange as the medley has appeared to us during the process, the whole when completed seems likely to produce an excellent effect.

The incongruous elements, however, of which the chaos was composed from whence this new order of things was to arise, though daily and by slow degrees assuming shape and form, were still in a state of "most admired disorder" during our abode in Paris. It was impossible to guess where-unto all those things tended which were evidently in movement around us; and the signs of the times were in many instances so contrary to each other, that nothing was left for those who came to view the land, but to gaze—to wonder, and pass on, without attempting to reconcile contradictions so totally unintelligible.

But, during the few weeks that have elapsed since I left the capital of France, this obscurity has been dispersed like a mist. It was the explosion of an infernal machine that scattered it; but it is the light of heaven that now shines upon the land, making visible to the whole world on what foundation rest its hopes, and by what means they shall be brought to fruition.

Never, perhaps, did even a successful attempt upon the life of an individual produce results so important as those likely to ensue from the failure of the atrocious plot against the King of the French and his sons. It has roused the whole nation as a sleeping army is roused by the sound of a trumpet. The indifferent, the doubting—nay, even the adverse, are now bound together by one common feeling: an assassin has raised his daring arm against France, and France in an instant assumes an attitude so firm, so bold, so steady, and so powerful, that all her enemies must quail before it.

As for the wretched faction who sent forth this bloody agent to do their work, they stand now before the face of all men in the broad light of truth. High and noble natures may sometimes reason amiss, and may mistake the worse cause for the better; but however deeply this may involve them in error, it will not lead them one inch towards crime. Such men have nothing in common with the republicans of 1835.

From their earliest existence as a party, these republicans have avowed themselves the unrelenting enemies of all the powers that be: social order, and all that sustains it, is their abhorrence; and neither honour, conscience, nor humanity has force sufficient to restrain them from the most hideous crimes when its destruction is the object proposed. Honest men of all shades of political opinion must agree in considering this unbridled faction as the common enemies of the human race. In every struggle to sustain the laws which bind society together, their hand is against every man; and the inevitable consequence must and will be, that every man's hand shall be against them.

Deplorable therefore as were the consequences of the Fieschi plot in its partial murderous success, it is likely to prove in its ultimate result of the most important and lasting benefit to France. It has given union and strength to her councils, energy and boldness to her acts; and if it be the will of Heaven that anything shall stay the plague of insurrection and revolt which, with infection more fearful than that of the Asiatic pest, has tainted the air of Europe with its poisonous breath, it is from France, where the evil first arose, that the antidote to it is most likely to come.

It will be in vain that any republican clamour shall attempt to stigmatise the acts of the French legislature with the odium of an undue and tyrannical use of the power which it has been compelled to assume. The system upon which this legislature has bound itself to act is in its very nature incompatible with individual power and individual ambition: its acts may be absolute—and high time is it that they should be so,—but the absolutism will not be that of an autocrat.

The theory of the doctrinaire government is not so well, or at least so generally, understood as it will be; but every day is making it better known to Europe,—and whether the new principles on which it is founded be approved or not, its power will be seen to rest upon them, and not upon the tyrannical will of any man or body of men whatever.

It is not uncommon to hear persons declare that they understand no difference between the juste-milieu party and that of the doctrinaires; but they cannot have listened very attentively to the reasonings of either party.

The juste-milieu party, if I understand them aright, consists of politicians whose principles are in exact conformity to the expressive title they have chosen. They approve neither of a pure despotism nor of a pure democracy, but plead for a justly-balanced constitutional government with a monarch at its head.

The doctrinaires are much less definite in their specification of the form of government which they believe the circumstances of France to require. It might be thought indeed, from some of their speculations, that they were almost indifferent as to what form the government should assume, or by what name it should be known to the world, provided always that it have within itself power and efficacy sufficient to adopt and carry into vigorous effect such measures as its chiefs shall deem most beneficial to the country for the time being. A government formed on these principles can pledge itself by no guarantee to any particular line of politics, and the country must rest contented in the belief that its interests shall be cared for by those who are placed in a situation to control them.

Upon these principles, it is evident that the circumstances in which the country is placed, internally and externally, must regulate the policy of her cabinet, and not any abstract theory connected with the name assumed by her government. Thus despotism may be the offspring of a republic; and liberty, the gift of a dynasty which has reigned for ages by right divine.

M. de Carné, a political writer of much ability, in his essay on parties and "le mouvement actuel," ridicules in a spirit of keen satire the idea that any order of men in France at the present day should be supposed to interest themselves seriously for any abstract political opinion.

"Croit-on bien sérieusement encore," he says, "au mécanisme constitutionnel—à la multiplicité de ses poids et contre-poids—à l'inviolabilité sacrée de la pensée dirigeante, combinée avec la responsabilité d'argent?"...

And again he says,—"Est-il beaucoup d'esprits graves qui attachent aujourd'hui une importance de premier ordre pour le bien-être moral et matériel de la race humaine à la substitution d'une présidence américaine, à la royauté de 1830?"

It is evident from the tone sustained through the whole of this ingenious essay, that it is the object of M. Carné to convince his readers of the equal and total futility of every political creed founded on any fixed and abstract principle. Who is it, he asks, "qui a établi en France un despotisme dont on ne trouve d'exemple qu'en remontant aux monarchies de l'Asie?—Napoleon—lequel régnait comme les Césars Romains, en vertu de la souveraineté du peuple. Qui a fondé, après tant d'impuissantes tentatives, une liberté sérieuse, et l'a fait entrer dans nos moeurs au point de ne pouvoir plus lui résister?—La maison de Bourbon, qui régnait par le droit divin."

In advocating this system of intrusting the right as well as the power of governing a country to the hands of its rulers, without exacting from them a pledge that their measures shall be guided by theoretical instead of practical wisdom, M. Carné naturally refers to his own—that is to say, the doctrinaire party, and expresses himself thus:—"Cette disposition à chercher dans les circonstances et dans la morale privée la seule règle d'action politique, a donné naissance à un parti qui s'est trop hâté de se produire, mais chez lequel il y a assez d'avenir pour résister à ses propres fautes. Il serait difficile d'en formuler le programme, si vaporeux encore, autrement qu'en disant qu'il s'attache à substituer l'étude des lois de la richesse publique aux spéculations constitutionnelles, dont le principal résultat est d'équilibrer sur le papier des forces qui se déplacent inévitablement dans leur action."

It is certainly possible that this distaste for pledging themselves to any form or system of government, and the apparent readiness to accommodate their principles to the exigences of the hour, may be as much the result of weariness arising from all the restless experiments they have made, as from conviction that this loose mode of wearing a political colour, ready to drop it, or change it according to circumstances, is in reality the best condition in which a great nation can place itself.

It can hardly be doubted that the French people have become as weary of changes and experiments as their neighbours are of watching them. They have tried revolutions of every size and form till they are satiated, and their spirits are worn out and exhausted by the labour of making new projects of laws, new charters, and new kings. It is, in truth, contrary to their nature to be kept so long at work. No people in the world, perhaps, have equal energy in springing forward to answer some sudden call, whether it be to pull down a Bastile with Lafayette, to overturn a throne with Robespierre, to overrun Europe with Napoleon, or to reorganise a monarchy with Louis-Philippe. All these deeds could be done with enthusiasm, and therefore they were natural to Frenchmen. But that the mass of the people should for long years together check their gay spirits, and submit themselves, without the recompense of any striking stage effect, to prose over the thorny theories of untried governments, is quite impossible,—for such a state would be utterly hostile to the strongest propensities of the people. "Chassez le naturel, il revient au galop." It is for this reason that "la loi bourgeoise" has been proclaimed; which being interpreted, certainly means the law of being contented to remain as they are, making themselves as rich and as comfortable as they possibly can, under the shelter of a king who has the will and the power to protect them.

M. Carné truly says,—"Le plus puissant argument que puisse employer la royauté pour tenir en respect la bourgeoisie, est celui dont usait l'astrologue de Louis Onze pour avoir raison des capricieuses velléités de son maître,—'Je mourrai juste trois jours avant votre majesté.'"

This quotation, though it sound not very courtier-like, may be uttered before Louis-Philippe without offence; for it is impossible, let one's previous political bias have been what it will, not to perceive in every act of his government a firm determination to support and sustain in honour and in safety the order of things which it has established, or to perish; and the consequence of this straightforward policy is, that thousands and tens of thousands who at first acknowledged his rule only to escape from anarchy, now cling to it, not only as a present shelter, but as a powerful and sure defence against the return of the miserable vicissitudes to which they have been so long exposed.

Among many obvious advantages which the comprehensive principles of the "doctrine" offered to France under the peculiar circumstances in which she was placed at the time it was first propagated, was, that it offered a common resting-place to all who were weary of revolutions, let them be of what party they would. This is well expressed by M. Carné when he says,—"Ce parti semble appelé, par ce qu'il a de vague en lui, à devenir le sympathique lien de ces nombreuses intelligences dévoyées qui ont pénétré le vide de l'idée politique."

There cannot, I think, be a happier phrase to describe the host who have bewildered themselves in the interminable mazes of a science so little understood by the multitude, than this of "intelligences dévoyées qui ont pénétré le vide de l'idée politique." For these, it is indeed a blessing to have found one common name (vague though it be) under which they may all shelter themselves, and, without the slightest reproach to the consistency of their patriotism, join heart and hand in support of a government which has so ably contrived to "draw golden opinions from all sorts of men."

In turning over the pages of Hume's History in pursuit of a particular passage, I accidentally came upon his short and pithy sketch of the character and position of our Henry the Seventh. In many points it approaches very nearly to what might be said of Louis-Philippe.

"The personal character of the man was full of vigour, industry, and severity; deliberate in all his projects, steady in every purpose, and attended with caution, as well as good fortune, in each enterprise. He came to the throne after long and bloody civil wars. The nation was tired with discord and intestine convulsions, and willing to submit to usurpations and even injuries rather than plunge themselves anew into like miseries. The fruitless efforts made against him served always, as is usual, to confirm his authority."

Such a passage as this, and some others with which I occasionally indulge myself from the records of the days that are gone, have in them a most consoling tendency. We are apt to believe that the scenes we are painfully witnessing contain, amidst the materials of which they are formed, elements of mischief more terrible than ever before threatened the tranquillity of mankind; yet a little recollection, and a little confidence in the Providence so visible in every page of the world's history, may suffice to inspire us with better hopes for the future than some of our doubting spirits have courage to anticipate.

"The fruitless efforts made against" King Philippe "have served to confirm his authority," and have done the same good office to him that similar outrages did to our "princely Tudor" in the fourteenth century. The people were sick of "discord and intestine convulsions" in his days: so are they at the present time in France; so will they be again, at no very distant period, in England.

While congratulating the country I have so recently left, as I do most heartily, on the very essential improvements which have taken place since my departure, I feel as if I ought to apologise for some statements to be found in the preceding pages of these volumes which if made now might fairly be challenged as untrue. But during the last few months, letters from France should have been both written and read post-haste, or the news they contained would not be of much worth. We left Paris towards the end of June, and before the end of July the whole moral condition of France had received a shock, and undergone a change which, though it does not falsify any of my statements, renders it necessary at least that the tense of many of them should be altered.

Thus, when I say that an unbounded license in caricaturing prevails, and that the walls of the capital are scrawled over with grotesque representations of the sovereign, the errata should have—"for prevails, read did prevail; for are, read were;" and the like in many other instances.

The task of declaring that such statements are no longer correct is, however, infinitely more agreeable than that of making them. The daring profligacy of all kinds which was exposed to the eyes and the understanding at Paris before the establishment of the laws, which have now taken the morals of the people under their protection, was fast sinking the country into the worst and coarsest species of barbarism; and there is a sort of patriotism, not belonging to the kingdom, but to the planet that gave one birth, which must be gratified by seeing a check given to what tended to lower human nature itself.

As a matter of hope, and consolation too, under similar evils which beset us at home, there is much satisfaction to be derived from perceiving that, however inveterate the taint may appear which unchecked licentiousness has brought upon a land, there is power enough in the hands of a vigorous and efficient magistracy to stay its progress and wipe out the stain. A "Te Deum" for this cleansing law should be performed in every church in Christendom.

There is something assuredly of more than common political interest in the present position of France, interesting to all Europe, but most especially interesting to us. The wildest democracy has been advocated by her press, and even in her senate. The highest court of justice in the kingdom has not been held sufficiently sacred to prevent the utterance of opinions within it which, if acted upon, would have taken the sceptre from the hands of the king and placed it in those of the mob. Her journals have poured forth the most unbridled abuse, the most unmitigated execrations against the acts of the government, and almost against the persons of its agents. And what has been the result of all this? Steadily, tranquilly, firmly, and without a shadow of vacillation, has that government proceeded in performing the duties intrusted to it by the country. It has done nothing hastily, nothing rashly, nothing weakly. On first receiving the perilous deposit of a nation's welfare,—at a moment too when a thousand dangers from within and without were threatening,—the most cautious and consummate wisdom was manifested, not only in what it did, but in what it did not do. Like a skilful general standing on the defensive, it remained still a while, till the first headlong rush which was intended to dislodge it from its new position had passed by; and when this was over, it contemplated well the ground, the force, and the resources placed under its command, before it stirred one step towards improving them.

When I recollect all the nonsense I listened to in Paris previous to the trial of the Lyons prisoners; the prophecies that the king would not DARE to persevere in it; the assurances from some that the populace would rise to rescue them,—from others, that the peers would refuse to sit in judgment,— and from more still, that if nothing of all this occurred in Paris, a counter-revolution would assuredly break out in the South;—when I remember all this, and compare it to the steady march of daily-increasing power which has marked every act of this singularly vigorous government from that period to the present, I feel it difficult to lament that, at this eventful epoch of the world's history, power should have fallen into hands so capable of using it wisely.

Yet, with all this courage and boldness of decision, there has been nothing reckless, nothing like indifference to public opinion, in the acts of the French government. The ministers have uniformly appeared willing to hear and to render reason respecting all the measures they have pursued; and the king himself has never ceased to manifest the same temper of mind which, through all the vicissitudes of his remarkable life, have rendered him so universally popular. But it is quite clear that, whatever were the circumstances which led to his being placed on the throne of France, Louis-Philippe can never become the tool of a faction: I can well conceive him replying, to any accusation brought against him, in the gentle but dignified words of Athalie—

"Ce que j'ai fait, Abner, j'ai cru le devoir faire—Je ne prends point pour juge un peuple téméraire."

And who is there, of all those whom nature, fortune, and education have placed, as it were, in inevitable opposition to him, but must be forced to acknowledge that he is right? None, I truly believe,—save only that unfortunate, bewildered, puzzle-headed set of politicians, the republicans, who seem still to hang together chiefly because no other party will have anything to say to them, and because they alone, of all the host of would-be lawgivers, dare not to seek for standing-room under the ample shelter of the doctrine, inasmuch as its motto is "Public Order," and the well-known gathering word of their tribe is "Confusion and Misrule."

There are still many persons, I believe, who, though nowise desirous themselves of seeing any farther change in the government of France, yet still anticipate that change must come, because they consider it impossible that this restless party can long remain quiet. I have heard several who wish heartily well to the government of Louis-Philippe express very gloomy forebodings on this subject. They say, that however beneficial the present order of things has been found for France, it is vain to hope it should long endure, contrary to the wish and will of so numerous a faction; especially as the present government is formed on the doctrine, that the protection of arts and industry, and the fostering of all the objects connected with that wealth and prosperity to which the restoration of peace has led, should be its first object: whereas the republicans are ever ready to be up and doing in any cause that promises change and tumult, and will therefore be found, whenever a struggle shall arise, infinitely better prepared to fight it out than the peaceable and well-contented majority, of whom they are the declared enemies.

I think, however, that such reasoners are altogether wrong: they leave out of their consideration one broad and palpable fact, which is, however, infinitely more important than any other,—namely, that a republic is a form of government completely at variance with the spirit of the French people. That it has been already tried and found to fail, is only one among many proofs that might easily be brought forward to show this. That love of glory which all the world seems to agree in attributing to France as one of her most remarkable national characteristics, must ever prevent her placing the care of her dignity and her renown in the hands of a mob. It was in a moment of "drunken enthusiasm" that her first degrading revolution was brought about; and deep as was the disgrace of it, no one can fairly say that the nation should be judged by the wild acts then perpetrated. Everything that has since followed goes to establish the conviction, that France cannot exist as a republic.

There is a love of public splendour in their nature that seems as much born with them as their black eyes; and they must have, as a centre to that splendour, a king and a court, round which they may move, and to which they may do homage in the face of Europe without fearing that their honour or their dignity can be compromised thereby. It has been said (by an Englishman) that the present is the government of the bourgeoisie, and that Louis-Philippe is "un roi bourgeois." His Bourbon blood, however, saves him from this jest; and if by "the government of the bourgeoisie" is meant a cabinet composed of and sustained by the wealth of the country, as well as its talent and its nobility, there is nothing in the statement to shock either patrician pride or regal dignity.

The splendid military pageant in which the French people followed the imperial knight-errant who led them as conquerors over half Europe, might well have sufficient charm to make so warlike a nation forget for a while all the blessings of peace, as well as the more enduring glory which advancing science and well-instructed industry might bring. But even had Napoleon not fallen, the delirium of this military fever could not have been much longer mistaken for national prosperity by such a country as France; and, happily for her, it was not permitted to go on long enough to exhaust her strength so entirely as to prevent her repairing its effects, and starting with fresh vigour in a far nobler course.

But even now, with objects and ambition so new and so widely different before their eyes, what is the period to which the memory of the people turns with the greatest complacency?... Is it to the Convention, or to the Directory?—Is it to their mimicry of Roman Consulships? Alas! for the classic young-headed republicans of France!... they may not hope that their cherished vision can ever endure within the realm of St. Louis long enough to have its lictors' and its tribunes' robes definitively decided on.

No! it is not to this sort of schoolboy mummery that Gallic fancies best love to return,—but to that portentous interval when the bright blaze of a magnificent meteor shone upon their iron chains, and made them look like gold. If this be true—if it cannot be denied that the affections of the French people cling with more gratitude to the splendid despotism of Napoleon than to any other period of their history, is it to be greatly feared that they should turn from the substantial power and fame that now

"Flames in the forehead of the morning sky"

before their eyes, accompanied as they are by the brightest promise of individual prosperity and well-being, in order to plunge themselves again into the mingled "blood and mire" with which their republic begrimed its altars?

Were there even no other assurance against such a deplorable effort at national self-destruction than that which is furnished by the cutting ridicule so freely and so generally bestowed upon it, this alone, in a country where a laugh is so omnipotent, might suffice to reassure the spirits of the timid and the doubting. It has been said sturdily by a French interpreter of French feelings, that "si le diable sortait de l'enfer pour se battre, il se présenterait un Français pour accepter le défi." I dare say this may be very true, provided said diable does not come to the combat equipped from the armoury of Ridicule,—in which case the French champion would, I think, be as likely to run away as not: and for this reason, if for no other, I truly believe it to be impossible that any support should now be given in France to a party which has not only made itself supremely detestable by its atrocities, but supremely ridiculous by its absurdities.

It is needless to recapitulate here observations already made. They have been recorded lightly, however, and their effect upon the reader may not be so serious as that produced upon my own mind by the circumstances which drew them forth; but it is certain that had not the terrible and most ferocious plot against the King's life given a character of horror to the acts of the republican party in France, I should be tempted to conclude my statement of all I have seen and heard of them by saying, that they had mixed too much of weakness and of folly in their literature, in their political acts, and in their general bearing and demeanour, to be ever again considered as a formidable enemy by the government.

I was amused the other day by reading in an English newspaper, or rather in an extract from an Irish one, (The Dublin Journal,) a passage in a speech of Mr. Daniel O'Connell's to the "Dublin Trades' Union," the logic of which, allowing perhaps a little for the well-known peculiarities in the eloquence of the "Emerald Isle," reminded me strongly of some of the republican reasonings to which I have lately listened in Paris.

"The House of Commons," says Mr. Daniel O'Connell, "will always be a pure and independent body, BECAUSE we are under the lash of our masters, and we will be kicked out if we do not perform the duties imposed on us by the people."

Trifling as are the foregoing pages, and little as they may seem obnoxious to any very grave criticism, I am quite aware that they expose me to the reproach of having permitted myself to be wrought upon by the "wind of doctrine." I will not deny the charge; but I will say in defence of this "shadow of turning," (for it is in truth no more,) that I return with the same steadfast belief which I carried forth, in the necessity of a government for every country which should possess power and courage to resist at all times the voice of a wavering populace, while its cares were steadily directed to the promotion of the general welfare.

As well might every voice on board a seventy-four be lifted to advise the captain how to manage her, as the judgment of all the working classes in a state be offered on questions concerning her government.

A self-regulating populace is a chimera, and a dire one. The French have discovered this already; the Americans are beginning, as I hear, to feel some glimmerings of this important truth breaking in upon them; and for our England, spite of all the trash upon this point that she has been pleased to speak and to hear, she is not a country likely to submit, if the struggle should come, to be torn to pieces by her own mob.

Admirably, however, as this jury-mast of "the doctrine" appears to answer in France, where the whirlwind and the storm had nearly made the brave vessel a wreck, it would be a heavy day for England were she to find herself compelled to have recourse to the same experiment for safety—for the need of it can never arise without being accompanied by a necessity for such increased severity of discipline as would be very distasteful to her. It is true, indeed, that her spars do creak and crack rather ominously just at present: nevertheless, it will require a tougher gale than any she has yet had to encounter, before she will be tempted to throw overboard such a noble piece of heart of oak as her constitution, which does in truth tower above every other, and, "like the tall mast of some proud admiral," looks down upon those around, whether old or new, well-seasoned and durable, or only skilfully erected for the nonce, with a feeling of conscious superiority that she would be very sorry to give up.

But whatever the actual position of England may be, it must be advantageous to her, as well as to every other country in Europe, that France should assume the attitude she has now taken. The cause of social order is a common cause throughout the civilised world, and whatever tends to promote it is a common blessing. Obvious as is this truth, its importance is not yet fully understood; but the time must come when it will be,—and then all the nations of the earth will be heard to proclaim in chorus, that

"Le pire des états, c'est l'état populaire."

Frances Milton Trollope – A Short Biography

Frances Milton Trollope was born on March 10th, 1779 at Stapleton in Bristol.

She was the third daughter of the Reverend William Milton and Mary, née Gresley. Her mother died after the birth of a son, and her father was now left with three children to raise. It was a difficult and traumatic time.

As a young girl Frances was widely read and was able to read English, French, and Italian literature.

In 1803, her brother Henry Milton was employed in the War Office and moved to Bloomsbury in London.
Her father remarried to Sarah Partington, who Frances didn't like and so, together with her sister Mary, moved in with her brother Henry.

She married, at age 30, Thomas A Trollope, a barrister, at Heckfield in Hampshire on May 23rd, 1809. Frances had seven children but the marriage was to prove difficult due to Thomas' financial misfortunes, and, it was said, to his ill temper.

In 1827 Frances decided that a new life should be found and the family travelled to Fanny Wright's Utopian Community, the Nashoba Commune, in the United States. Unfortunately, the community was not much more than a malaria infested swamp near the Mississippi. The venture quickly failed and she was soon in Cincinnati, Ohio looking for ways to support them all.

This too was to end in failure and necessitated a return to England.

It was now that Frances decided that writing would provide the income and career to move the family on to a more stable footing, an ambition that to her seemed realistic despite nearing fifty years of age.

It was, of course, the beginnings of not only her own prolific and respected career, but also a literary dynasty. Her sons Anthony and Thomas Adolphus, together with his second wife, Frances, would become much lauded as writers.

Her first book, in 1832, Domestic Manners of the Americans, gained her immediate notice. Although it was a one sided view of the failings of Americans, as was a common prejudice among the English elite at the time, it was also witty and acerbic. A good piece of writing that now established her with a willing audience to whom she could now address further works.

More of the same, in all respects came with The Refugee in America and with, The Abbess, in 1833, she moved her view on social standing to social justice and anti-Catholicism, which was also the theme of Father Eustace in 1847.

Together with her son, Thomas Adolphus, she wrote works on travel, such as Belgium and Western Germany in 1833, Paris and the Parisians in 1835, and Vienna and the Austrians, this last one published in 1838.

But much of the attention she received was for her strong novels of social protest. Jonathan Jefferson Whitlaw, published in 1836, was the first anti-slavery novel, and was a great influence on the American writer Harriet Beecher Stowe and her more famous Uncle Tom's Cabin in 1852. Michael Armstrong: Factory Boy began publication in 1840 and was the first industrial novel to be published in Britain.

These were followed by three volumes of The Vicar of Wrexhill, which examined the corruption in the Church of England and evangelical circles.

However her greatest work is more often considered to be the Widow Barnaby trilogy (published between 1839–1843). This set a pattern of sequels which her son Anthony Trollope also used in his career.

In later years Frances Milton Trollope continued to write novels and books on wide, varied and miscellaneous subjects, writing in all in excess of a quite incredible 100 volumes.

In her time she was considered to have great powers of observation, together with a sharp and caustic wit. Her large output though somewhat diminished the impact of much of her work as did a more modern style of writing that was gaining traction and with it a more public criticism of books and arts by the rising mass of critics. Frances was unfairly scorned by some of them with the patronizing moniker of 'Fanny' Trollope.

Her novels were to rouse public conscience and incite social reforms that could help protect the various downtrodden groups, usually women and children and were influential in shaping subsequent women's writing.

In the modern age few of her works receive the readership they deserve. Gradually others are coming to the realization that she was an important author who wrote well, wrote much and brought many social causes to public attention.

Frances Milton Trollope died on October 6th, 1863.

She is buried nearby to four other members of the Trollope household in the English Cemetery of Florence.

Frances Milton Trollope – A Concise Bibliography

Major Works

Domestic Manners of the Americans (1832)
The Refugee in America (1832)
The Abbess (1833)
Belgium and Western Germany in 1833 (1834)
Paris and the Parisians in 1835 (1836)
The Life and Adventures of Jonathan Jefferson Whitlaw; or Scenes on the Mississippi (1836)
The Vicar of Wrexhill (1837)
Frances Trollope (1838),
Vienna and the Austrians (1838)
The Widow Barnaby (1839)
The Widow Married; A Sequel to the Widow Barnaby (1840)
Michael Armstrong: Factory Boy (published in 1840)
The Widow Wedded; or The Adventures of the Barnabys in America (1843)
Jessie Phillips: A Tale of the Present Day (1844)
Father Eustace (1847)
The Lottery of Marriage (1849)